EX LIBRIS

Romance Treasury

THE ROMANCE TREASURY ASSOCIATION

TORONTO · NEW YORK · LOS ANGELES · LONDON
AMSTERDAM · PARIS · SYDNEY · HAMBURG
STOCKHOLM · ATHENS · TOKYO · MILAN

These stories were originally published as follows:

THE SHIFTING SANDS
Copyright © 1975 by Kay Thorpe
First published by Mills & Boon Limited in 1975

PORTRAIT OF JAIME
Copyright © 1977 by Margaret Way
First published by Mills & Boon Limited in 1977

TOUCHED BY FIRE
Copyright © 1977 by Jane Donnelly
First published by Mills & Boon Limited in 1977

ROMANCE TREASURY is published by
The Romance Treasury Association, Stratford, Ontario, Canada.

Editorial Board: A.W. Boon, Judith Burgess, Ruth Palmour, Alice E. Johnson and Ilene Burgess.

Dust Jacket Art by Emile LaLiberté
Story Illustrations by Emile LaLiberté
Book Design by Charles Kadin
Printed and bound by R.R. Donnelley & Sons Co.

ISBN 0-373-04092-X

Printed in U.S.A.   AO 92

CONTENTS

THE SHIFTING SANDS

The
Shifting Sands
Kay Thorpe

When the father she'd come to Algiers to find suddenly died, Ruth Gillen was left alone in the world. Young and inexperienced, she contemplated her future with alarm.

Andre DuBois, the handsome enigmatic man who had taken her to see her father, had a solution. Marry him. His assurance that it would be a marriage in name only pursuaded her to accept.

It was only afterward that Ruth began to wonder about the role of the glamorous Simone Chantal in Andre's life—and then to wonder why she should care. Surely she wasn't falling in love with her husband!

CHAPTER ONE

IT WAS BLESSEDLY cool in the dimness of the room. Cool and quiet. Through the fretted screen covering the window embrasure, Ruth looked out on to the sun-dappled inner courtyard of the villa with its wreathed columns and sculptured doors, her nostrils filled with the heady scent of jasmine. It was still difficult to believe that she was actually here in Algiers—Ruth Gillen who had never been more than a few miles from home on her own before. Not that she had given much thought to that aspect at the time of deciding to come to North Africa. The discovery she had made had been too momentous for rational thought at all. All she had been aware of was the need to reach this place. What happened after that was something she had not even allowed herself to consider.

Behind her the door opened softly, and she turned to see a man framed in the opening. He was in his early thirties, she judged, tall and leanly built in a superbly tailored silver-grey suit. Even in the dimness she was conscious of the penetrating quality of his gaze.

"I'm sorry to have kept you waiting," he said in excellent though slightly accented English. "I'm André Dubois. I understand that you're looking for Leo Gillen?"

"Yes," Ruth answered in as steady a tone as she could manage. "Is—is he here?"

He didn't reply immediately. As he came further into the room and closed the door she saw his features clearly for the first time—the strong jut of his nose above a well-cut mouth, the taut stretch of tanned skin over high cheekbones, the faint waviness in the dark hair which grew forward in a widow's peak over his forehead. A handsome face, yet with a hint of ruthlessness in its lines.

"Please take a seat," he invited, indicating one of the heavily carved chairs facing the huge ornate desk to which he had moved.

Ruth did so, feeling him studying her as she in turn came into the direct stream of light from the window. It took an effort to meet that dark blue gaze equably. There was something about this man which made her feel on edge, although she could not have explained why.

"You haven't answered my question," she pointed out with a coolness she was a long way from feeling. "This is the address I was given, but perhaps—"

"How old are you?" he asked unexpectedly.

She looked back at him in momentary confusion, unable to see what her age should have to do with anything. Nevertheless, she found herself answering, "Eighteen."

He leaned against a corner of the desk, one hand thrust casually into his trouser pocket, the other curved over the edge of the wood at his side, long and strong and brown with a gleam of gold on the little finger.

"Might I be permitted to ask what a young woman of your age could want with a man of fifty?"

Green eyes sparked briefly. "I'm Ruth Gillen," she said. "Leo Gillen is my father."

For a brief fleeting moment there was incredulity in his eyes, then without warning he leaned forward and put a hand under her chin to tilt her face further into the light, once more assessing the quality of the small fine features beneath the long straight fall of auburn hair.

"I see little resemblance."

"I take after my mother." She moved her head away from his hand, her skin tingling to his touch. "I can prove my identity—when I see my father."

Subtly his expression altered. "He isn't here, I'm afraid."

"Oh." Disappointment cut through her like a knife. She had been counting on seeing her father today, had built herself up for it. And now she was going to have to wait even longer. She tried not to let her feelings show too much as she asked, "When are you expecting him back?"

"He won't be back. For the last few months he's been living out in the desert at a place called El Bakra." There was a sudden odd note in his voice. "He has no wish to leave it."

Ruth gazed at him for a long moment, her brows drawing together a little. His attitude seemed strange, almost as if he were reluctant to pass on information regarding her father's whereabouts. Her own mouth firmed. "How far away is this El Bakra?"

"A few hours' journey by plane." He gave her a narrow glance. "You're not thinking of going there?"

"Why not?" she demanded. "I've come this far—why should a few miles make any difference? Is there a regular flight, do you know, *monsieur*?"

"There is no scheduled flight at all," he said. "El Bakra is too small and insignificant a place to merit a call by the airlines. I was speaking of the time it takes me to fly down there myself." He paused. "This proof of identity you speak of?"

Ruth sighed and gave in. It was quite apparent that she was going to get precisely nowhere with this man until he had all the details sorted out. "I have my birth certificate here," she said, opening her handbag. "And papers to—"

"The papers I will see later." The interruption was abrupt. "For the present I want to hear your story from your own lips. I knew that Leo had a wife and child back in England, but he hasn't been back there for almost seventeen years. Why, after all this time, have you decided to seek him out?"

Ruth looked down at her hands clasped tightly in her lap. "It's rather a long story. You see, I'd always understood that my father had died when I was a baby. It was only after my—" her voice quivered slightly despite all her efforts to stop it—"after my mother's death a few weeks ago that I learned the truth. Apparently she had been receiving money from him all these years— money she invested for my future. When she knew she was going to die she instructed her solicitors to pass on his last known address to me afterwards. There was more than enough money to bring me out here and keep me for a while—and I still have the house in Oxford." Her head lifted. "I don't intend becoming a liability to my father, if that's what you're thinking, Monsieur Dubois."

He ignored the last. "Would it not have been fairer on your mother's part to have told you the truth from the beginning? Or was she so afraid of losing you?"

"I'd never have left her," Ruth said. "And whatever her reasons for allowing me to think he was dead I'm sure she really believed that it was for the best. After all, he left her alone with a young baby. You can hardly blame her for wanting to forget him."

"But you have no bitterness yourself?"

She hesitated. "A little, I think, when I first found out about him. But not now. All I want is to see him and get to know him. Surely that's understandable?"

He lifted broad shoulders. "He's a stranger to you, and you to him. Why not leave it that way after so long."

"Because he's my father!" Trembling a little, she came abruptly to her feet. "I can see you're not willing to give me any further help, so I'll leave. I can find my own way to El Bakra if I have to."

"Sit down." It was said quietly, but with an emphasis which brought her up short. She looked at him uncertainly, assessed the set of the strong mouth and found herself subsiding back into the chair she had just vacated without a murmur, her eyes coming to rest on the gold ring with a sense of resentment. This André Dubois was no ordinary man; he was used to commanding, used to being obeyed, but that gave him no right to assume that same authority with her. Yet if she wanted to see her father the quickest way was obviously through him.

"I didn't say I wouldn't help you," he continued in the same controlled tones. "But there are certain matters you should be made aware of before you decide further. Had you arrived out here a year ago I would have said that it was the best thing that could have happened for Leo. Now—" his hesitation was brief but obvious—"now he is a changed man. When he first came to work for my father he was a heavy drinker, but he could control it. It was only after my father's death five years ago that I discovered the reasons for his drinking, and there was no way in which I could help him. Since then—" He broke off with a slight shrug. "You must understand what long years of loneliness and regret can do to a man before you judge him."

Ruth sat very still, her throat tight and dry. "You mean that he's an alcoholic?" she said at last.

"I mean that he chooses to drown his memories rather than live with them." He was watching her face, his own impassive. "Do you still want to see him?"

"Yes." There was no hesitation in her reply. "Did you think I'd be so easily put off?"

For the first time a smile touched his lips. "I think it would probably take a great deal to do that. You have spirit for one so young—though perhaps you should learn to temper it with caution. Didn't it occur to you to write to your father first before making the journey?"

"I was afraid he might tell me not to come," she admitted frankly. "You see, he's all I have left now that my mother is gone. I don't care what he did in the past, or what he is now. I just want to be with him."

"Even if Leo wanted that too it might not be quite so simple," he said. "Bakra is little more than a village in the Sahara. The only Europeans who go there are tourists on their way south to Tamanrasset and Djanet, and they only stay the one night in the rest camp. There's no entertainment of any kind, just a few rough houses and such gathered along the *wadi*, and the garage which Leo manages for me."

"That won't bother me. I'm used to a quiet life. I prefer it that way."

Cynicism hardened the line of his mouth again. "How can you know if you've never had the opportunity to compare? At your age you should be enjoying all that life has to offer, not planning to bury yourself in isolation with a man you don't even know."

"He's my father," she said again flatly. "There's plenty of time to think about the future."

"Yes." His tone was thoughtful. "A lot of time." He straightened abruptly away from the desk, moving across to the window to stand gazing out to the courtyard much as she had done herself earlier. "I was, as a matter of fact, already planning to fly down to Bakra myself tomorrow," he said. "I'll tell Leo that you're here in Algiers and leave it to him to decide what he wants to do about it."

"No!" She was on her feet again, face pale but determined. "I can't just sit around and wait like that. I won't! If he doesn't want me he'll have to tell me so himself."

The dark head was turned towards her, brows lifted sardonically. "And how do you propose to reach him?"

"There must be other private planes, other pilots. I'm not *begging* for help, *monsieur*. I can afford to pay for my passage!"

His eyes narrowed suddenly and coldly. "I'm not interested in your payment, and I won't be spoken to in that manner even by the daughter of an old friend. You'll apologise for your insinuation."

Trembling but controlling her voice, she said, "I owe you no apology. And I don't intend to stay in Algiers any longer than it takes me to find another way of getting to El Bakra. You can refuse to take me yourself, but you can't stop me from seeing him!"

She was halfway to the door before he reached her. Mouth a taut line, he took her arm and propelled her forcefully back to her chair, putting her into it and standing over her with an expression that dared her to move again.

"Spirit I can admire," he said. "Insolence I refuse to tolerate! Before we go any further with this matter you *will* apologise!"

Ruth bit her lip, aware that he had some justification for being angry. If the truth were known, she had surprised herself by the strength of her reactions to his manner. She had never in her life come up against a man like this one before, and didn't care if she never did again. He made her feel totally inadequate.

"All right," she said in low tones, "I'm sorry. Now may I go?"

"No." He moved away, but only to the desk, looking down at her with his jaw still set. "Why shouldn't Leo have the right to decide his own life after all these years?"

"He does." She tried to keep her voice level. "But so do I have rights. I've come a long way to see my father and try to get to know him. I can hardly do that if he's in one place and I'm in another."

"Only for a matter of days."

"Not necessarily. What if he says he doesn't want to see me? What if he believes, as you obviously believe, that I couldn't accept his way of life? Without meeting me first he can't know what kind of person I am!"

The dark eyes were enigmatic. "Are you sure *you* know what kind of person you are? The desert is no holiday camp. Life there is hard and uncompromising Leo has already paid dearly for his mistakes. I don't intend that he should suffer any further. In any case—" He paused, his expression altering as if he had been going to say something he had not intended. "It isn't possible to take you with me tomorrow," he finished flatly.

"Why?" She pounced on the hesitation, some instinct prompting a sudden feeling of apprehension. "Is there something wrong in El Bakra?"

There was a pause before he answered. "I don't know," he admitted at last with some reluctance. "I've been unable to contact Leo by radio for almost a week. It could be a simple matter of a breakdown, or—"

"Or he could be ill." She was sitting on the extreme edge of her seat, hands gripping the armrests so tightly that her knuckles showed white. "And if he is he's going to need someone to stay with him. Can *you* do that, Monsieur Dubois?"

"Not for long," he acknowledged. "But neither would I be willing to leave a young girl alone in Bakra with a sick man." He paused again, thoughtfully appraising her, and added with deliberation, "If I take you with me it must be on the strict understanding that you do exactly as I say. Is that clearly understood?"

"Yes." Ruth had no intention of arguing the terms at the present time. What happened when they got to El Bakra would depend largely on the circumstances they found. If her father was indeed ill then wild horses wouldn't drag her away from his side, but there was no need to tell André Dubois that as yet.

"Very well." He straightened. "You are staying where?"

Ruth told him, and watched him stride across to the door. There was a murmured consultation with someone out in the corridor, then he was coming back into the room.

"Your luggage will be fetched," he said. "You will, of course, stay here tonight."

"Oh, but that isn't at all necessary!" she began to protest, and felt her voice peter out before the look in his eyes.

"You'll be well chaperoned," he said. "Apart from Maria, my housekeeper, there are several others living here in the villa."

Ruth flushed. "That wasn't what I meant. It's very kind of you to ask me to stay, *monsieur*."

"Your father calls me André. You had better do the same. No doubt you'll be ready to rest. I'll have you shown to your room and some refreshment brought to you. Perhaps you'd like to join myself and some friends for dinner. If you come down to the salon about eight."

Ruth opened her mouth to plead that she would far rather stay in her room for the evening, then closed it again abruptly. She wasn't being given a choice, and this wasn't the time to antagonise him afresh. She had a strong feeling that it would be some time before he forgave her for persuading him to change his mind about taking her with him tomorrow at all, but that was immaterial. She *was* going with him, and that was all she cared about.

The elderly woman in the plain black dress who had received her into the villa earlier showed her up an imposing staircase to a closely shuttered bedroom coolly tiled underfoot. The furnishings were rich and dark and heavy, the bed draped in silk damask and intimidatingly large. Ruth thanked the housekeeper in French, and received a smile in response.

"It is said downstairs that Mademoiselle is the daughter of Monsieur Gillen," she said diffidently. "Does this mean that the *monsieur* will be returning to Algiers?"

"I'm not sure," Ruth returned slowly, feeling for the words she had had no cause to use since her schooldays. "He may prefer to stay in El Bakra, in which case I shall be staying with him there."

"In the desert?" The elder woman looked astonished. "That is no place for any woman, *mademoiselle*, much less one of your years. You cannot seriously intend to spend any time there! The master will not allow it!"

"I suppose I shall have to see what happens when we get there," Ruth answered lightly. "Perhaps he will want to come back after all." She paused, eyeing Maria with speculation. "You know my father?"

"He was often here when he was in Algiers," nodded the other. "He is a good man, *mademoiselle*, despite his weaknesses in the way of—" She stopped, her expression changing to one of dismay at the realisation of what she had said.

"It's all right," Ruth said softly. "I do know about it. And thank you for saying what you did before, Maria—about him being a good man."

"It is the truth," came the reply. "You have everything you need for the moment, *mademoiselle*? A tray will be brought in a few moments."

Left alone, Ruth went across and opened the shutters over the window, stepping out on to the arched balcony overlooking the courtyard. Flowers spilled everywhere below, trailing from tall urns and earthenware containers set at random about the mosaic floor, growing thickly in the bed surrounding the central fountain—roses, jasmine, smilax, and many others she didn't even recognise. The vines winding about the lower columns had tendrils reaching over the stone parapet where she stood, green and succulent despite the climate in which they grew.

The afternoon was passing into evening now, the heat diminishing little by little as the sun's rays lost their strength. The light was opaque, the sky faintly misted. In a short while it would be dark. Her first night in a strange land.

Ruth shivered suddenly in spite of the warmth. Things were not turning out quite as she had anticipated. Had she been right to come in search of her father, or would it really have been better to have left things as they were? She didn't know the answer. She wouldn't know it until she finally came face to face with the man who had walked out on her and her mother all those years ago.

Standing there, she recalled her childhood, the first time that she had realised she was not like other children in that they had two parents while she only had the one. All her life she had envied those of her friends who had fathers to turn to in times of stress. Her mother had done her best to play both roles, but it hadn't been enough. And later, when she started to be ill, Ruth had had to take over those roles herself, to become the comforter, the decision-maker, the leaning post in her turn. For eighteen months her whole life had been bound by the four walls of the house, her only excursions the daily walk to the local shopping centre and a weekly visit to town.

Not that she had resented the necessity of leaving school early in order to look after her mother properly. There just hadn't been enough money to pay for anyone to come in on a regular basis—and of course she hadn't known then of the investments made over the years. She only wished she knew more of her father's reasons for leaving them as he had. Loneliness and regret had turned him to drink, André Dubois had said. He probably knew the whole story, though she doubted that he would be willing to pass it on to her.

Of André himself she knew absolutely nothing, she realised, and yet here she was a guest in his house. In so many ways he made her feel terribly young, although he couldn't be very much more than thirty-one or two. He had such an air of self-assurance about him, of authority. She didn't like him, would even go so far as to say that she disliked him intensely, and yet he was a man who had stuck by her father despite all his failings.

A man to be trusted? Ruth could only hope so. She was placing herself entirely in his hands tomorrow.

CHAPTER TWO

RUTH'S SUITCASE was delivered to her room at six-thirty. She didn't bother to unpack more than her nightdress and the one dress she had brought with her which might suffice for the evening. It was a floor-length cotton guipure which she had bought purely on impulse the previous day in London. It appeared now that this might very well be the only chance she would have to wear it anyway.

A young maidservant was sent to conduct her to the long, Moorish-inspired salon at the appointed hour. André was already there with his other guests. Ruth had just time to register the thick luxury of the Persian carpet beneath her feet and the silken sheen of the bronze curtains covering the long windows before André drew her forward to introduce her to his friends.

Louis and Eloise Villet were a somewhat older couple who immediately made her feel at ease, a relaxation of tension quickly vanquished by the deliberate and disparaging appraisal afforded her by the second of the two women. Simone Chantal obviously had little interest in members of her own sex, reserving her undoubted charm for the man at whose side she

stood. She was beautiful, with that expensive glossy
finish exclusive to the French, her pale blonde hair
swept up and back from a face which reminded Ruth of
a Leonardo da Vinci painting, except that her mouth
spoiled the image a little with its rather too narrow
lines. Ruth judged her to be about twenty-six or seven,
and envied the cool poise and confidence which ex-
uded from her. At this particular time she could have
done with more of it herself.

"So you are Leo's daughter," observed Eloise with
interest as André moved away to get Ruth a drink.
"This is quite a distance to travel alone. Didn't you
have anyone who could have accompanied you?"

Ruth shook her head, grateful that the other had
spoken in English. "But everyone has been very helpful," she hastened to add. "And I'm extremely grateful to Monsieur Dubois for allowing me to accompany
him to El Bakra tomorrow."

"I told you to call me André." He was at her side,
holding out a glass, the dark eyes enigmatic as they
rested on her face. In the white dinner jacket with a
black cummerbund at his waist he looked both devas-
tatingly handsome and supremely male. Ruth felt a
sudden tensing of nerve and muscle as her fingers
touched his in taking the glass from him.

"I'm sorry," she murmured. "I forgot."

"How long will you be gone, André?" queried Simone in French on a softly persuasive note. "I was
counting on you being in Algiers for the weekend."

"I'll be back within two days," he assured her with a
smile. "That I promise."

"It was lucky for our young friend that you were already planning to fly down to Bakra," put in Louis Villet. "Otherwise she may well have been stuck here in Algiers for days before other transport could be arranged." He smiled at Ruth. "On the other hand, it would at least have given you some time in which to see the place. You'll find conditions in the desert very different from this, I'm afraid. I have never visited El Bakra myself, but one village is much the same as another. Hardly an ideal place for visiting, but no doubt Leo will be prepared to return to Algiers with you."

"I hope so." Momentarily Ruth's glance flashed to André as she wondered how much he had told these people about her before she had joined them. She resented anyone else knowing the details, yet she supposed that the truth was the only explanation of her sudden appearance that he could have given.

Dinner was served in the room adjoining the salon, where a long, highly polished table gleamed with silver and glassware. To Ruth, tired after a day's travelling, the meal seemed to go on for ever, although she found the food itself highly enjoyable. In particular she liked the *dolma*, which consisted of a variety of vegetables stuffed with meat and spices and cooked in butter. A bit different from the kind of meal she was used to at home, she thought with a pang of nostalgia. Plain and wholesome had always been her mother's maxim.

Back in the salon for coffee and liqueurs, she found it difficult to concentrate on the conversation flowing around her. Her eyelids felt so heavy she had to fight to keep them open at all. She wondered how long the eve-

ning would last, and whether it would be regarded as
rudeness on her part if she asked to be excused. She
didn't see why it should. In fact, it might be something
of a relief to the others in the party as it would relieve
them of the obligation to include her in the conversation.

As it happened it was André himself who made the
suggestion that she should retire.

"You've been travelling most of the day," he said,
"and tomorrow we must make an early start. I'm certain that no one will mind if you wish to leave us."

"Of course not," said Eloise quickly for them all. "I
hope you find Leo well. Perhaps we might see the two
of you here together in a few days."

"Perhaps," agreed Ruth politely, not sure what else
she could say when she didn't even know her own
plans for certain.

André accompanied her out to the hallway with its
intricately patterned wall hangings, pausing at the foot
of the staircase with one hand resting lightly on the
carved wood of the lower post. In the dim glow from
the bronze and copper lantern overhead he looked
alien and aloof.

"I've arranged for you to be called," he said. "We
should be in Bakra by early afternoon. Can you find
your way to your room again, or shall I send someone
to show you?"

"I know the way, thank you," she said quickly, and
then paused, hardly knowing how to take her leave of
him. "I'm very grateful for all that you're doing for
me," she got out.

His mouth was sardonic. "Shall we say that I prefer to have you where I can control your actions. Go to bed, child. Tomorrow there will be time to talk."

DESPITE HER WEARINESS Ruth had not expected to sleep very well in a strange bed, but before she knew where she was she was opening her eyes to daylight and the face of the young maid who had fetched her down to the salon the night before.

"The master will be waiting for you downstairs when you are ready, *mademoiselle,*" said the latter as she placed a tray within easy reach. "You will take coffee?"

"Please. But nothing to eat," returned Ruth, unable to face the thought of food of any kind with her stomach churning over as it was. Today was the day she was to meet her father, the man she had come thousands of miles to find. But supposing he didn't want her? Supposing he told her to go back to where she had come from? Suddenly and desperately she wished she were back in Oxford among the old and familiar. This whole thing was crazy. Seventeen years was too long a time to bridge. But it was too late now to back out, especially after having fought so hard to get André Dubois to agree to take her with him. She was committed to continuing this journey begun in such high hopes.

André was waiting at the foot of the stairs when Ruth went down. He was dressed in practical denim slacks and jacket with a thin cotton sweater beneath, and looked disconcertingly different from the suave stranger of the previous day. He greeted her briefly, expressing approval of her own choice of slacks and shirt before leading the way out to the Citroën parked in the forecourt.

It was still early as they left the villa, but already the streets were teeming with life and colour, the air heavy with heat and strange spicy scents. Ruth looked at it all and saw very little, her mind too occupied with other matters. She was vibrantly aware of the man at her side, of the lean strength in the hands holding the wheel. Everything about him breathed masculinity in a way she had never experienced before, tying her tongue in knots. She couldn't think of a single intelligent remark to make.

André himself did not seem disposed towards conversation during the half an hour it took them to drive out to the airport. He seemed preoccupied with his own thoughts, almost as if he had forgotten she was there. Ruth wondered if he was thinking about Simone, perhaps regretting the necessity of spending two days without her company. She had gathered last night that the two of them had known one another for some time, and there had been a certain proprietorial air in Simone's request for him to be back in Algiers for the weekend. Perhaps a more permanent relationship was in the offing.

For some reason that latter thought left her feeling even more depressed.

It took them twenty minutes to complete the necessary formalities at the airport. The plane in which they were to spend the coming hours was a single-engined four-seater which looked terrifyingly small and frail to Ruth's inexperienced eyes. Yet once seated beside

André as they taxied out to the runway she found her nerves settling before the quiet confidence in his handling of the controls. There was a brief wait for clearance, and then they were off, lofting into the brilliant blue sky and coming round in a steep turn to the south.

Ruth must have released her pent-up breath in a faint sigh when they finally levelled out, for André glanced at her.

"Flying makes you nervous?"

"A bit," she admitted. "Yesterday was my first time ever."

"And now you find yourself in a machine which looks as if the slightest puff of wind could blow it out of the sky," he remarked with an understanding that surprised her. "Will you believe me if I assure you that there is nothing to fear?"

"I'll try," she said, and drew the first real smile of the day from him.

"That's all I ask."

Time slipped by swiftly at first. There was some turbulence over the Atlas mountains, but once beyond they settled to a steady droning course over great stretches of shimmering apricot desert. At irregular intervals splurges of green betokened oases ranging from a huddle of date palms around a waterhole to some approaching a small town in size. Once there was a camel train, strung out along the rim of a dune, each long-legged animal standing out in detail against the sand. Nomads, André said. The wanderers of the desert, never staying in one place longer than a few days or weeks at a time.

Around midday they landed to refuel at one of the oases, which turned out to be little more than an airstrip with a few rough buildings among the palms. They ate a packed lunch here, and within half an hour were on their way again, this time to pass over the great oilfields of Hassi Messaoud. Ruth was only too glad to exchange the acres of pylons and derricks and columns of black smoke for the rippling sea of canary yellow dunes which formed the Grand Erg Occidental. This was the Sahara of a thousand films, the romantically beautiful, shifting sands of P. C. Wren. Even seen from a height there was something about the rolling emptiness which caught at her throat—a strange drawing power she could not have explained.

"It's said that no one ever comes away from the desert unchanged," commented André at one point, as if sensing her thoughts. "Some, having seen it once, can never bring themselves to leave it again, while others who do go away find themselves forced to return. Down there is an atmosphere such as can be found nowhere else on earth. I suppose one could call it a kind of peace."

"Is that what my father found in El Bakra?" she asked huskily, and felt his eyes flicker towards her.

"Leo makes his own kind of peace. For him the desert is one place where he can live out his life the way he wants to with no one to hound him."

"He still works for you," she pointed out after a moment. "Surely that makes him answerable in one way."

His shrug was eloquent. "The job is merely supervisory. He has his solitude and I have my figurehead. The arrangement suits us both." He paused, his tone changing. "Perhaps now is as good a time as any to tell you that I have no intention of leaving you alone with Leo in Bakra, no matter what happens. I brought you with me because I could see no other way of preventing you from doing as you threatened yesterday, but that doesn't mean that I'm ready to change my mind about the rest."

Ruth looked at him swiftly, her heart thudding into her throat. "I don't think you can legally prevent me from staying with my father," she said with careful control. "I'm fully of age, and even if I weren't *he* would be the one to say whether I go or stay!"

"Legally there are a lot of things I possibly can't do," came the even reply. "But we'll leave that aspect until later." He waited a moment before adding slowly, "And supposing your father does tell you to go?"

Her chest felt tight. "Then I'll go, of course."

A silence fell between them. Ruth gazed unseeingly at the panel of instruments for several minutes before finally nerving herself to ask the question which had been uppermost in her mind since the previous evening. "André," she said, "do you know the reason why he left my mother?"

There was another pause before he answered. "Are you sure *you* want to know?"

She swallowed dryly. "Yes."

"Very well." His tone was quite unemotional. "He formed an attachment for another woman who he mistakenly imagined could give him more than he already had. By the time he discovered his mistake it was too late. Your mother refused to take him back."

"I see." Ruth tried to keep her own voice as level. "That's more or less what I imagined, I suppose—except that I hadn't thought of him wanting to come back. You—you can't really blame my mother for feeling the way she did. Look what he'd done to her—to all of us!"

"He'd made a mistake and quickly regretted it. Few men can go through life without a slip, and any woman who really loved a man could surely find enough understanding to forgive him the one."

She said thickly, "So in your estimation my mother was entirely to blame."

"That wasn't what I said. But in any case it isn't important what I think. It was all a long time ago, and nothing can alter the fact that you were deprived of a father. My concern now is that you don't make the mistake of believing that you can cancel out the last seventeen years. Leo Gillen today is nothing like the man he once was."

So it seemed that her waking instincts might have been right after all, she thought. It was too late. And yet she had had to try. She could not have lived through the rest of her life with this question always hanging over her.

It must have been another half an hour or so before she began to realise that something was wrong. André hadn't said anything, but he seemed to be scanning the terrain ahead with increasing intensity, a line deepening between his brows. Ruth followed his eyes and saw nothing but the sweeping dunes stretching to infinity on all sides. Perhaps it was that very same emptiness which had planted the doubt that had made her sensitive to the change in André's demeanour. When she glanced at her watch she saw that it was already gone two o'clock.

"Shouldn't we be nearly there by now?" she asked with diffidence after another moment or two, and saw his mouth take on a firmer line.

"We should have been there more than fifteen minutes ago," he said. "I'm going to put down and take a bearing."

"But surely the compass tells you whether we're on course?" she questioned with a leap of alarm. "Perhaps we've simply taken longer than you usually do."

"No," he said, "I'm afraid not. And compasses have been known to slip. There's nothing to worry about. I carry a sextant and chronometer, and once I've worked out our true position I can allow for any variation. Within a short time we'll be on our way again." He was peering out of the side window as he spoke. "What we need is a place suitable for a landing. Some valley between the dunes long enough to allow us room to take off again."

"Down there?" asked Ruth, pointing off to her own side of the aircraft and trying to conceal her feelings. "Is that large enough?"

André leaned across her to look. "It will do," he said briefly.

He swung the machine round in a wide S-turn which brought him into the wind as he lined up on the narrow gap between two dunes beyond which lay the defile.

Ruth clenched perspiring palms as they lost height. They seemed to be going in so fast, the sand rushing up to meet them. The valley itself looked far narrower than it had from the air—only just wide enough to take the full span of the wings.

Suddenly the left wing seemed to jerk as though struck by some unseen force from below, and the whole aircraft lurched sideways. To Ruth it was as if the world had turned turtle, the horizon tilting crazily before her eyes before exploding into a million coloured lights.

WHEN SHE recovered consciousness she was lying some distance away from the wrecked aircraft with André bending over her. His face was dark and tense, and there was a smear of blood on one cheek. Relief sprang in his eyes as she stirred her limbs. He slid an arm beneath her shoulders and raised her a little, supporting her against his bent knee.

"You must stay still for a while," he said. "You've had a bump on the head. There's no fracture, so far as I can tell, but there may be concussion."

Ruth lifted a heavy hand and gingerly touched the tender area towards the base of her skull where a lump was already forming beneath the skin, wincing as she did so. "What happened?" she murmured. "Did we hit something?"

"We were caught by a current of hot air rising from the sand," he said. "The wing tip touched a dune and almost turned us over before it snapped. We're fortunate to be without serious injury."

From where she lay, Ruth could see the stricken machine lying against the slope of the dune, one wing sticking forlornly into the air and the other shattered under it. It needed no mechanical bent to realise that it would never fly again. Oddly enough she felt no particular alarm at the realisation that they were stranded out here in the desert. The crash had been a nasty experience, but as André had said, they were lucky to have come out of it alive and relatively unharmed. Once he had calculated exactly where they were he could put out a call for help on the plane's radio. Meanwhile, they would have to make the best of the situation.

The heat down here among the dunes was intense, the sand itself searing to the touch. Wherever she looked there was sand, rising in great sweeping curves to razor-sharp crests etched against an indigo sky. But it was the silence which struck her the most forcibly. Nothing stirred out there. It was like another world—and an alien one at that. Ruth ran the tip of her tongue over dry lips and made an effort to think rationally.

"Is there anything to drink?" she asked. "I've got an awful thirst."

A flash of some unreadable expression passed through his eyes. "There is a water tank in the rear of the cabin," he said. "If I can right the plane it will provide some shelter from the sun. Can you stand, or shall I carry you again?"

"I'll be all right," Ruth claimed quickly. She accepted his help in getting to her feet, freezing a grimace of pain as her head throbbed anew at the movement. "I suppose the sand saved our lives."

"It helped," he agreed. "Are you sure you feel capable of walking?"

"I've felt worse than this after a go on the big wheel at the fair," she returned with a weak attempt at humour, and drew a faint smile.

"You English constantly amaze me," he said. "I can think of no other race who could joke in such a situation."

"Well, the worst is over, isn't it?" she returned practically. "All but the waiting. How long will it take a rescue plane to get here once you've radioed our position, do you think?"

The pause was so long that she looked round at him in puzzlement, to see an expression on his face which gave rise to a new flutter of alarm. "You *can* radio for help, can't you?"

He shook his head wryly. "I'm afraid not. The radio was on the side which bore the worst damage."

Even then the full implications failed to sink in. Radio or no radio, she supposed that the alarm would be raised when they failed to arrive in El Bakra, though if André was right about the compass they could be some miles off their scheduled course. But a search would surely be made, and the plane must be visible for miles in this sparklingly clear air. All it meant was that rescue might take a little longer than she had anticipated, that was all.

"Well," she said in as steady a tone as she could manage, "I suppose we'll just have to sit it out till they come looking for us." She turned towards the plane. "At least we have something to drink—providing the tank hasn't sprung a leak."

It took André only a matter of minutes to swing the uptilted wing down so that he could wedge the crimpled side of the fuselage against the dune, but by the time he had finished the cotton sweater was soaked through with perspiration. He took it off and slung it over a strut to dry before helping Ruth up into the battered cabin.

The water tank was intact, much to her relief. André drew off about half a pint into a plastic cup, but took none for himself, denying any need of liquid as yet.

There was a box of instruments in a locker under the rear seats. She watched him extract a small hand compass and lean forward to compare it with the fixed one up front, envying him the freedom to strip off as he had. He looked supremely fit, his arms strong and muscular, his chest broad beneath the thick mat of curling black hair where a silver medallion hung on a thin chain. For the first time it occurred to her that she was alone out here in the desert with a man who was still an unknown quantity, a man she hadn't even known existed twenty-four hours ago. And for how long would they be here? Already it was three o'clock in the afternoon. Even if a search had already been put in hand there was very little chance of help arriving before darkness fell.

Perhaps some subtle tension in the atmosphere communicated itself to him, for suddenly he looked up from what he was doing directly into her eyes. For a long moment neither of them moved, then Ruth averted her gaze out of the side window, feeling the warmth flood her skin.

"It's so hot!" she exclaimed. "If only it weren't so hot!"

"Ruth." He said her name quietly but with emphasis. "Whatever ideas are going through your mind, you can forget them. You have nothing to fear from me."

She was glad of the long hair falling forward over her cheek. "I don't know what you're talking about," she said. "It never occurred to me that—"

"Oh, yes, it did. The moment that you realised we might have to spend the night alone together. Well, you can stop worrying. Even if I were in the habit of ravishing little girls, I've got more to think about right now."

An odd sensation swept over and through her. "I am *not* a little girl!" she snapped back. "Don't patronise me!"

"Isn't that better than the fate you imagined for yourself a moment ago?" came the dry retort. He thrust his body out through the doorway. "Stay where you are until I get back."

He stopped to put on his sweater again before setting off to climb the side of the dune, carrying the box of instruments with him. From where she sat Ruth soon lost sight of him, but she made no attempt to alter her position. She felt small and scared, and her head ached. She was also thirsty again, but she forced herself to ignore that. What water they had must be conserved until they knew how they stood.

André seemed to be gone a long time. When he did return his expression gave nothing away. Ruth made herself meet his gaze as he climbed back into the cabin with a sheet map in his hand, the unspoken question plain in her eyes.

"As I thought," he said. "The compass is out several degrees. I can only think that it must have slipped when we met that air turbulence over Hassi Messaoud." He was spreading the map out as he spoke, studying its detail. "I calculate that we're now about here"—stabbing a finger at a pencilled-in mark some small distance above and to the left of the isolated black circle which represented El Bakra. "That puts us some sixty miles north-west."

Sixty miles. It didn't sound so very much considering. Ruth said so, and drew a grim smile.

"It will take us three, perhaps four days to cover that distance on foot."

"On foot!" She stared at him. "But surely it would be safer to just stay here and wait for them to find us? They must have realised that something is wrong in El Bakra by now. Surely they'll organise a search?"

He shook his head. "You forget what I told you yesterday. I've been unable to contact Leo for days, and there is no other radio in the village. If there had been I'd hardly have been making this journey in the first place."

Ruth felt suddenly sick. She had completely forgotten about the radio, and had been taking for granted that someone knew they were supposed to be on their way. Her heart jerked. But someone did, of course!

"What about Simone?" she burst out. "Won't she suspect anything when you don't get back tomorrow?"

"She may do. Enough, anyway, to report it to the authorities. But even then it may be a further twenty-four hours before a search is instigated." He paused with some deliberation. "We have sufficient emergency rations to last us out, but only enough water for two days at the most." Once again his finger tapped the map. "There's a waterhole shown here that we can reach if we start at once. It means a detour to the south, but it's the only way. With water the second stage will be relatively easy."

It was all so unreal, thought Ruth dazedly. How many times had she seen this very scene enacted on film? But this was no film set with cameras whirring on the sidelines. This was the stuff of nightmares! She fought the panic rising thick and fast inside her. Hysteria would help nothing. She had to believe André when he said they could make it. She had to believe him!

She drew a slow, deep breath. "I suppose we'd better get going, then. What do you want me to do?"

A gleam of admiration sprang in his eyes. "You have a lot of courage, little one," he said softly. "How does your head feel now?"

In these last few emotive moments Ruth hadn't given a thought to her head injury. "Not too bad," she said. "Providing I don't bang it again I think it will stay on."

His laugh was a reassuring sound in itself, creating a brief illusion of normality. "Come," he said, "we must sort out what we'll need for the journey."

CHAPTER THREE

THEY WERE READY to move inside half an hour, equipped with what André considered the bare necessities for survival. He had been ruthless in sorting out priorities. Each extra pound of unessential weight meant that much more energy dissipated to no purpose. The water had been transferred into canteens covered in goatskin which had been stored in the seat locker along with other items of emergency equipment. From these latter, André selected a Very pistol and several flares which went into a small rucksack along with the food and their personal papers. Into this also went the map, together with a ruler, dividers and a protractor. Ruth was allowed the one sweater she had in her suitcase, plus a tube of moisturised face cream, and that was all.

Just before they left, André made one final, seemingly incongruous choice in the shape of the large, gaily patterned rug that had been spread across the rear seats.

"You'll see," he said briefly in answer to Ruth's sidelong glance at the folded bulk strapped to the rucksack.

She was still in the grip of unreality when they began the obliquely angled climb to the rim of the dune, but by the time they had gone a dozen steps in the softly shifting sand she was completely and shatteringly aware of what lay ahead. The sun was much lower in the sky, yet even so its heat was still fierce, beating down on the crown of her head like a tangible weight. She was infinitely glad of the doubled thickness of silk scarf which André had insisted she should knot over her hair—although its effectiveness was probably as much mental as physical.

They were almost at the rim of the dune before she looked back. The plane was almost hidden from this point, only the tip of the wing still in view. Beyond and to either hand rose the dunes, sparkling in the afternoon light, their silence infinte and complete.

"I've noted the position," said André, pausing with her. "Later our possessions can be recovered. It's unlikely that they'll have been removed—unless stumbled on by accident."

Possessions were the last thing on Ruth's mind at that moment, but she refrained from comment. Things were going to be difficult enough as it was without giving voice to the doubts and fears crowding in on her. She turned when he turned, setting her face to the journey before them.

Night comes early in the desert. By five-thirty the dunes were deeply shadowed, the colour changing from yellow to ochre and then to purple as the sun sank into the horizon.

At six, after two hours on the move, André called a halt, choosing a spot in the lee of the large dune they had just descended. Ruth sank gratefully on to the sand, already feeling the effects of the swiftly lowering temperature and glad to draw on the sweater she had carried so reluctantly through the heat of the afternoon. The coolness, however, brought little respite from her burning thirst. She felt she could have drained her canteen dry, but André made certain that she took only the bare half pint.

"Little and reasonably often is the best way," he said. "We still have many miles to cover, although if we can keep up the same pace we should have no difficulty. We must have covered more than four miles since we left the plane."

Four miles! Ruth felt like crying. It had seemed like twenty-four! And they had missed the worst heat of the day. At noon the sand would be like burning coals, the sun a white-hot torture. It didn't bear thinking about.

She felt even more like crying when André shared out the food which must last them until morning.

"Dates!" she exclaimed in dismay, staring at the compressed wad in her hand. "Is that all?"

"I'm afraid so," he returned. "But we won't starve. The date contains all that's needed to feed the human body over a period. Actually, some of the native population live almost entirely on them for half the year."

"But I don't even like dates!" Her voice was plaintive in the still air.

"Then you'll have to learn to like them," was the unmoved reply. "You have to eat to keep up your strength. Try them. Perhaps you've never tasted ones like these before."

Ruth hadn't, but she still didn't care for them, finding them too sweet for her taste. She was still nibbling
reluctantly at them when André began scraping away
in the sand nearby to form a shallow hollow about six
feet long.

"The sand retains some dregee of heat for a while,"
he explained. "With the rug to cover us we should gen-
erate enough of our own to see us through the night
without too much discomfort." He caught the swift
change in her expression and smiled grimly. "There's
no other way. The closer we lie the warmer we'll be.
You'll have to try and think of me in the same way you
would regard a hot-water bottle."

The sun had vanished completely now, turning the
dunes grey. Ruth shivered in the steadily increasing
cold. She had known André for little more than
twenty-four hours, but she had already learned that it
was useless to try arguing with him—and in any case,
what he said made sense. She only wished that she
could formulate the same objective attitude with which
he obviously regarded the whole situation, but that was
beyond her as yet.

She was glad of the darkness when she lay down in
the hollow and felt André slide down beside her. He
had tucked the rug around the two of them so that it
formed a kind of cocoon, leaving just enough of an
opening to breathe through. Now he slid an arm over
her waist and drew her more firmly against him, sigh-
ing impatiently as he felt the tension in her.

"I'm not going to bite," he said in her ear. "If it will
set your mind at rest I'm far too tired and chilled

through to even consider the physical differences between us, so you can forget your girlish scruples and let me hold you more comfortably."

Ruth forced herself to relax as he settled her into a better position with her head on his shoulder, feeling the warmth of his body chasing out the chill. This was by no means the first time he had lain with a woman in his arms, she realised. Only on other occasions she doubted that he would have had to overcome resistance.

Lying there with her face turned into his shoulder, she listened to the sound of his breathing and wondered what it would be like to be loved by such a man as André Dubois, to know the emotions she had so far only read about and seen depicted on film. At eighteen she had only twice in her life been kissed, and neither time had been very exciting—perhaps because on both occasions it had been boys of her own age who had kissed her. André was a man, mature and experienced. When he kissed someone there would be no awkwardness, no uncertainty. He would be strong and sure and in command.

She caught herself up there with a sense of shock at her own thoughts. The last thing she wanted was for André to make any kind of love to her. Not that there was much danger of it—he had made it quite clear that he regarded her as little more than a child. She tried to turn her thoughts to her father sixty miles away in Bakra, but he had become too shadowy a figure. This was the only reality, the here and now. And André was the only other person in it.

It was a long night of cramped muscles and fitful dozing. Dawn was a relief, the first warming rays of the sun a God-given restorative. But not for long. By nine o'clock the heat was so intense that the sand itself writhed in its murderous grip, burning through the soles of Ruth's light canvas shoes until she felt as if she were walking on fire.

Stumbling in André's wake throughout the terrible day, she lost all track of time, living only for the blessed moments of respite when she could put her lips to the neck of her canteen and feel the life-giving liquid trickling down her parched and aching throat. Even the dates became objects of desire, their juice a nectar such as she had never in her life tasted before. There was little conversation between the two of them while they moved. The effort of forming words was too great. In that kind of heat the very mind congealed, thoughts slipping in and out to no recognisable pattern, sanity itself hinging only on the necessity of putting one foot in front of the other.

This time she knew no reserve when darkness came and André once more dug out their bed in the sand, thankful for the warmth and strength of his arms in the teeth-chattering cold of the night. Towards dawn a wind sprang to life, rushing through the dunes with a noise like an express train. Huddled against André's chest, Ruth found her mouth and nostrils suddenly filled with sand as it rose in choking clouds about them, her eyes stinging with tears of irritation as he dragged her to her feet.

They spent the next hour until sunrise sitting with

their backs to the wind and the rug over their heads in
the lee of the dune, the cold a misery which had to be
endured if they were not to be buried alive in the sand.
Breathing became a matter of filtering air through a
section of the rug held over the mouth, and even then
the sand got through, clogging the throat and coating
the lips, sticking like grit to the teeth.

It was gone eight before the storm abated enough for
them to consider moving out. The sand was still lifting
into the air but no longer whipping in frenzied spirals
about their heads. Despite the growing heat of the
sun's rays the wind was cold enough to cut into exposed flesh like a lance, so that one burned and
shivered both at the same time. The effort of moving
forward into that cutting force brought racking gasps
from Ruth's lips, although André did his best to
shield her by insisting on walking in front. When they
stopped to check she had to hold the map down for him
in the sand while he busied himself with protractor and
dividers, kneeling on one flapping corner with her
hands spread to the others and her hair tearing loose
from its covering scarf to whip painfully across her
cheeks.

"If my calculations are correct we should reach the
waterhole by mid-afternoon," he said briefly as he finally wrestled the map back into its folds again.

And if they weren't? Ruth dared not dwell on what
that would inevitably mean. So far they still had hope,
but without water to replenish the now almost emptied
canteens there was nothing left to hope for.

When the wind finally dropped it went with the same

swiftness with which it had arisen, leaving the dunes to settle back into canary-yellow silence under the mercilessly empty violet sky. Once they trudged past the skeleton of some long-gone animal, the bones dried white in the sun. Ruth turned her face away from the grim reminder of what could happen to travellers in the desert, refusing to allow fear to claim her mind. She even managed a cracked smile for André when he glanced round at her, blanking her mind to the pull of her burned skin, the ceaseless throbbing in her head. His eyes were rimmed in red from the bite of the sand earlier in the day, his jaw black with stubble, his lips puffed and blistered. She knew she must look as bad, if not worse, and could not conjure up the strength to care. When he stretched out his hand to aid her in the last few steps up to the rim of this present dune she took it gladly, grateful for the contact.

She had so longed for a touch of green in the arid landscape that at first she thought the small circle of palms to the right was the product of her own imagination—or at best a mirage. It was only when André murmured a brief word of relief that she realised the truth. They had won through! Down there was water, their lifeline back to civilisation. There would be enough to pour down tight throats and over blistered faces, enough to fill their canteens and take them to safety.

From somewhere she found a reserve of energy she had not known she possessed, running down the slope at André's side, laughing out loud as the sand slid from beneath her feet. The waterhole lay towards the rear of the little oasis in a slight defile. Ruth felt the laughter fade from her lips as her eyes registered what her mind did not want to believe.

How long the two of them just stood there gazing at the dried-up bed she had afterwards no clear idea. André was the first to move, kneeling in the sand to scrape at a patch which seemed darker than the rest. There was water there still, but so thick with sand that it had consistency, oozing with frightening slowness into the hole André had made.

"Give me your water bottle," he said urgently.

Ruth did so, and watched with a total lack of emotion as he reached into the rucksack to take out the map and tear off a section from one corner. This latter he swiftly formed into a cone shape which he inserted into the neck of the water bottle. Then he stripped off his cotton sweater and held it out to her.

"Hold this over the funnel. And hold it tightly!"

She wound her fingers into the material as he scooped handfuls of the wet sand and flung them into the makeshift strainer, willing the precious liquid to drain through and give them a fighting chance of life.

The process was slow, but it worked. An hour later they had about a pint, but by then the moisture had also dried to an extent where it would no longer even ooze any more.

"It will start welling again later," André said, finally desisting in his efforts and sitting back on his heels to wipe his face with the back of his hand. "Meanwhile we have enough, with care, to take us through the rest of the day."

"And that means that we have to stay here," said Ruth flatly.

"It would appear so. Bakra is still two days' march away." He got to his feet again and brushed the sand from his hands and slacks, carefully avoiding her eyes. "It may not be a bad thing. This place is marked on the map, which means that it must be visited fairly regularly by caravans. All we have to do is sit and wait for the next one to turn up."

When would that be? she wondered. Tomorrow? Next week? Next month? Whenever it was it would more than likely be too late. But if André wanted to pretend that everything was going to be all right she could do no less than go along with him. She owed him that much for having got them this far.

At least the trees provided shade. They sat in the sand beneath them with nothing to do but try to think of something other than the heat and the raging thirst. Ruth's head ached with a steady, pulsating throb which was slowly eating into her reserves of courage. When she tried to lick her dry lips there wasn't even enough moisture left in her mouth to make any difference. Her tongue felt like leather and her throat was on fire. The utter hopelessness of their situation crept over her inexorably, fingers of fear biting into her mind. She fought it with desperation, jaw clenched against the desire to fling herself sobbing into André's arms. Tears were a luxury she could not afford.

His hand appeared suddenly in her line of vision, holding out the canteen with its top already off. "One good mouthful," he said. "We must make this last until nightfall."

Ruth seized on the bottle and tilted it to her lips, rinsing the liquid round her mouth and down her throat a few drops at a time, feeling the pressure valve lift a little. The water was gritty with sand but marvellous. It took every ounce of control she possessed to stop herself from taking more than the allotted amount and hand the bottle back to André with a murmured word of thanks.

"You don't have anything to thank me for," he returned on a harsh note. "I blame myself that you're here at all. I should never have brought you with me."

"You couldn't have known what was going to happen," she pointed out. "And I did make it rather difficult for you to do anything else."

His lips twisted. "I could have followed my first inclinations and put you under guard until I got back from seeing your father."

Her father. It was the first time Ruth had thought of him since that first night, the first time she had thought of anything beyond their immediate situation. She wondered if a search was already under way, and if so what chance they had of being found. In the two days since they had left the plane they had covered about thirty miles, but not in a logical direction owing to the necessity of finding this waterhole. And the sandstorm would have covered any tracks they had left. It was useless hoping for help to arrive from that direction, she decided. Their only chance lay in the camel trains André had spoken of. She only wished that she could bring herself to believe in that possibility.

She stole a glance at the man at her side, to find him leaning back against the bole of the palm with his eyes closed. The light filtering through the fronds above gave a green cast to his features, gauntly highlighting the strong bones. There was sand in the dark hair above his closed eyes, and coating the lines from nose to jaw and clinging in a fine film to his bare shoulders. The silver chain had tarnished against the damp heat of his skin, but the medallion it supported still gleamed brightly among the black hair on his chest. For the first time she was able to see that it was a St. Christopher medal; the patron saint of travellers. Her lips curved without mirth at the irony even as she wondered who had given the medal to him in the first place. His mother, perhaps? It was the kind of thing a mother would do.

Looking at him now it was difficult to believe that this was the same man who had received her at the villa in Algiers just four days ago. She had started out distrusting him, resenting his assumption of authority over her movements. Yet without him now she would be lost. It was only his strength and purpose that had kept her from going to pieces way back there in the storm, only his presence here with her at this moment which gave her the incentive to keep on fighting the hopelessness threatening to overtake her. She leaned her own head back against the bole beside his and composed herself to wait out the endless minutes until it was time for the next drink.

Darkness brought some measure of respite. André had a lighter in his pocket, and for the first time there was something to burn. Warmed as they were by the fire, there was no need for the pit he had dug the previous two nights, although the rug was still a boon. Comforted a little by the flickering glow of the flames, Ruth eventually drifted into an exhausted sleep, her last conscious memory the weight of André's arm across her waist.

When she awoke she was alone, the rug tucked neatly about her. The fire had been replenished, but of André there was no sign. Her head swam dizzily when she sat up, and she was conscious of nausea which came and went in waves. Beyond the huddle of palms the dunes gleamed silver in the moonlight, eerie and unreal. Nothing moved out there. No figure broke the undulating skyline.

The fear which she had kept in check for two long days and nights rose up suddenly and uncontrollably, thick and choking in her throat, leaving no room for rationalisation, no room for anything but the blind terror of having been left. With no recollection of having got to her feet she found herself running, shouting André's name as she stumbled up the sides of the nearest dune. The sand slid away from beneath her feet, pulling her down into its clinging softness, holding her back.

Sobbing, she fought it, struggling desperately to reach the distant rim outlined against the night sky. When hands caught her from behind, turning her about, she fought those too, striking out with both fists at the dark shape looming over her, too far gone to register the identity of this new barrier.

And then she was down in the sand and André was kneeling over her, pinning both her hands above her head in a grip of steel. "Ruth, stop it! It's all right! Do you hear me? It's all right!"

Sanity returned at last, snapping her back to reality and recognition. She gave a small strangled cry and relaxed the tautness of her body, her hands unclenching in his. "I thought you'd gone," she whispered painfully. "I thought you'd gone!"

"I know." He was lifting her gently, holding her close against him, his breath warm against her hair. "I went to see if there was any more water coming in."

It was only then that she realised he was minus his shirt again, his chest bare beneath the denim jacket. She put out a trembling hand to touch the medal, tracing the figuring on it with the tip of a finger. "Are we going to die?" she said.

"No." His voice was steady, without undue emphasis. "The water is seeping back faster than before. By morning we should be able to get enough to take us out of here."

Ruth heard the words, but felt no reaction. She had been too close to the brink in these last few hours to register any further emotion regarding their possible escape. For the moment she was conscious only of the security in the arms about her, of the warm, hard reality of the flesh beneath her slowly moving hand as she slid it up under the jacket to his shoulder, wanting she knew not what. She felt his arms tighten, hurting her yet not hurting her, saw his eyes take on a new expression in the moonlight. Then without warning his features blurred and the nausea returned worse than before, accompanied by shivering she could not control.

She sensed the change in him, the sudden difference in tension.

"You're ill," he said. "I must get you back to the fire."

Ruth clung to him as he lifted her, the world spinning about her. Her head felt as though it didn't belong to her any more, while her limbs ached with a dull intensity. When he laid her down next to the flames and held the water bottle to her mouth she found the effort of swallowing almost too much for her, although she craved the moisture. André's face kept receding, wavering in front of her eyes.

She closed them, whispered faintly, "Don't leave me again."

"I won't," he said.

Time ran together in a series of impressions after that. She imagined she was back home in Oxford, walking down by the river with the cool water lapping at her feet and birds singing in the trees overhead. Someone kept calling her, but she couldn't see who it was. It got hot, so hot she felt herself burning up. There seemed to be a great deal of noise and confusion, figures moving about clad in long robes which veiled their faces. Then there was movement, jolting movement that hurt her head and made her cry out. Faintly and far far away she heard André's voice saying something she couldn't understand, then that too faded and there was nothing but darkness.

CHAPTER FOUR

IT WAS BROAD DAYLIGHT when Ruth opened her eyes, although the brightness was dimmed a little by the cheap cotton blind drawn part way over the narrow window opposite to where she lay. For the space of a few seconds she couldn't think who, never mind where she was, then memory returned in a rush, drawing a faint exclamation to her lips.

Somewhere in the austere little room something moved. A face came into view—a strongly carved face, deeply sunburned. "Hello," said André softly. "Are you back for good this time?"

"I think so." She tried to lift her head, and was surprised by her own weakness. Relaxing back into the pillows, she looked up at the man with whom she had spent a lifetime in the desert and tried to bring her thoughts into some kind of order. There was a great deal that she wanted to know, but the most important thing of all needed no telling. They had been saved from the fate which had threatened to overtake them out there in the sand. "How—how long have I been like this?" she whispered.

"Almost four days." He sat down on the edge of the narrow bed, taking her wrist between finger and thumb to feel her pulse, expression unrevealing. "You've been very ill, but we'll soon have you up and fit again. Are you hungry?"

Ruth moved her head in negative reply, her eyes travelling over the room again with its whitewashed bare brick walls and few poor sticks of furniture. "What is this place?"

"The mission at Bakra." There was something almost evasive in the way he said it. "We were brought here by the Touaregs who found us by the waterhole. Don't you remember any of it?"

"Very little." Her brow puckered with the effort of concentration. "It's all misty, like something that happened in a dream. Four days, did you say?" The green eyes took on a sudden new expression. "Have you seen my father?"

André kept his gaze steady on her face, his hand covering hers as it lay on the cover between them. "Leo died of kidney failure on the day that we left Algiers," he said. "I'm sorry, child."

Numbly she closed her eyes. So it had all been for nothing. She would never know her father now. Strangely enough she felt no pain, just a kind of resigned acceptance. The die was cast. She was on her own. The only place to go from here was back to Oxford and the lonely house she had once called home.

"Ruth." André's voice was unusually gentle. She opened her eyes and looked at him, taking in the new lines etched in the taut-skinned features, realising the extent of his own ordeal out there in the desert. She had known him such a little time, and yet so long.

"I'm all right," she said emotionlessly. "In a way, I suppose I always knew that it was too late. I'm only sorry that all this had to happen because of me."

"It would have happened in any case," he returned. "I had already planned the flight. What we have to be thankful for is our lives."

Ruth inclined her head in mute acceptance of that statement. "I suppose you've managed to inform someone by now?" she got out.

"Yes. A valve had burned out in the radio, and no one but Leo knew enough about it to effect a repair."

"Was he—was he ill for very long?"

"A few days only." He released her hand and got up from the bed. "You must rest. Try and get some sleep. I'll stay here with you if you'd like me to."

"Please." Her voice was husky. "I don't want to be alone. Not—not just yet."

"You won't be left." He moved away for a moment, coming back to the bedside with some cloudy liquid in a glass. "Drink this. It will help you to sleep."

She felt his arm slide under her shoulders, lifting her from the pillows a little way as he held the glass to her lips. The draught tasted slightly bitter, but she managed to get it down. When he let her sink gently back again she had to fight against the overwhelming desire to beg him to go on holding her. Only in his arms did she feel secure.

She had no recollection of going to sleep, but when she woke again it was evening and the light was fading fast. This time she felt much stronger physically, although the returning memories allowed no peace of mind. Another man had taken André's place in the room, an older man, oddly familiar, clad in a faded brown *burnous* about five or six inches too short, revealing a pair of thick woollen socks. He got up from the chair when he saw that she was awake and came over to the bed, his worn features creasing into a smile.

"You are feeling better now?" he inquired in heavily accented English.

"Much better, thanks." This could only be the missionary himself, Ruth realised. He looked like a man dedicated to the good of others. "Is this your bed I've taken?" she asked hesitantly.

He shook his head. "On rare occasions we have visitors even here in Bakra. There are two other rooms such as this in the mission. Only one of them is normally in use at a time, but the other ones are always prepared. Sometimes, too, they are used as a hospital, as now. You would perhaps like some food?"

She managed a smile herself. "I think I would, please—providing it isn't dates."

The door opened and André entered the room, bringing with him an oil lamp already lit.

"I think we might turn to something a bit better than that," he said, catching her last words. He put the lamp down on the bare wooden table which with the chair and bed constituted the whole of the furnishings, and came across to look down at her appraisingly. "Do you feel strong enough to sit up a little more?

Ruth said that she did, and warmed to the touch of his hands as he propped up the two pillows at her back. For the first time she became aware of the garment she was wearing, like a long, shapeless shirt in unbleached cotton with a single drawstring fastening at the neck. Beneath it she was naked. Her eyes lifted suddenly to meet André's and she felt the colour stain her cheeks. There were apparently no women here at the mission, so who had taken her own clothing from here and substituted this while she lay in delirium?

"Your own things are quite safe," he said with a touch of irony. "You have our friend to thank for your present attire."

The missionary had left, presumably to fetch the promised food. Ruth decided that the whole question of who had taken care of her was probably best left forgotten. It was a little late now to start worrying about the affront to her modesty—a little too late and somewhat ridiculous under the circumstances. From the way her ribs seemed to be sticking out she had lost quite a lot of weight during these past few days. In fact she seemed to be nothing but skin and bone. Suddenly the thought of food became a real need.

"When will we be able to get away?" she asked.

"I've radioed through for a plane to be here tomorrow," he said. "Perhaps a little soon, but you will have better care in Algiers. You won't be afraid to fly again?"

"I don't think so." She attempted a joke. "They say that lightning never strikes twice in the same place."

He came to sit on the edge of the bed as he had earlier, lean and powerful in the white cotton sweater which still showed faint marks from the use to which it had been put, despite the wash it had obviously been given. It had also shrunk, fitting him so closely now that she could see the shape of the medallion against his chest. The memory of those moments of terror rose up sharp and clear in her mind, and a tremor ran through her. She was unaware that her hands had gone out appealingly towards him until she felt his arms come round her, holding her close as he had done on that other night, not saying anything, just sitting there like the rock she needed.

Realisation of her own actions brought a flush of embarrassment to her cheeks. She pressed herself away from him abruptly, unable to bring herself to meet his eyes. What must he be thinking of her clinging to him like that!

"I'm sorry," she said in low tones. "I'm just being silly. It's all over now. There's nothing at all to be afraid of."

"But the nightmares still keep returning." He said it without emotion. "Don't despise yourself for a natural reaction. What you've been through this past week is enough to undermine even the greatest courage." There was a brief pause while he studied her features, a strange expression in his eyes. When he spoke again his voice sounded different. "We have to talk about your future," he said. "You have no other relatives living in England?"

Ruth shook her head. "But I'll be perfectly all right," she said staunchly. "I have some friends in Oxford—and I can easily get a job."

"Yes?" He looked sceptical. "As what, may I ask?"

"I'm not sure. I'm not trained for anything, but

there must be plenty of jobs I could do without particular qualifications."

"I don't think so. Without qualifications the jobs you could obtain would not earn you enough to keep you comfortably."

"I can always sell the house and use the money to give me an extra income." Ruth listened to her own words with a sense of indifference. None of this seemed to matter at the moment. Nothing very much seemed to matter at all. England, Oxford—it was all so far away. There was nothing there for her any more, nothing to draw her back. "There doesn't appear to be any alternative," she added, speaking her thoughts aloud.

"There is one," he said. "You can stay here in Algeria."

Her head lifted. "I don't really see how that—"

"It's quite simple," he interrupted in the same level tone. "You can marry me."

The silence stretched for seconds before Ruth could find her voice. "What did you say?" she asked faintly.

He smiled a little. "Is the idea so abhorrent to you? It seems the obvious solution. Leo was my friend, and my father's friend before that. What better way could there be of taking care of his daughter?"

"But—marriage!" She still couldn't take it in. Her eyes searched his face, looking for she knew not what. "André—"

"You didn't answer my question," he said. "Would marriage to me be so very unbearable?"

Would it? Ruth forced herself to consider the idea rationally. As André's wife she would have security for the rest of her life, someone to lean on and trust in. André would take care of her, relieve her of the necessity of looking out for herself, provide her with a home. But there was more to marriage than just those things. She had also to think about his needs. Would she be capable of making *him* happy too? She knew so little about men, and André was no inexperienced boy. Out there on that first night she had been stirred by the thought of his kissing her, but certainly no more than that. She hardly felt ready for more than that, and yet he would certainly expect, and be entitled to expect, more from the woman he made his wife.

"No," she said slowly at last, "I don't think it would be unbearable. Only—" Her voice petered out and she bit her lip, trying to think of some way to say what she felt. "We—hardly know one another," she finally got out.

His expression was difficult to read. "There'll be plenty of time to do that. I'd ask for no more than you were prepared to give. For the present our relationship could be like that of brother and sister, if that's what you'd prefer. Marriage simply removes the barriers against you staying permanently in Algeria."

Ruth gazed at him for a long moment, aware of the magnitude of what he was offering her. "Why should you do all this for me?" she whispered.

The strong mouth twisted. "You're very young, little one, and too modest. There are many qualities you possess that a man might look for in a wife. As to your feelings for me—" He paused, expression suddenly quizzical. "Am I wrong in believing that you're not entirely unaware of me in the physical sense?"

Her pulse quickened and her eyes slid away from his. "No," she acknowledged in a small voice.

"Then we have a basis to build on. Our missionary friend is licensed to perform marriages right here in Bakra. It can take place in the morning before the plane arrives to take us back to Algiers. The minor details can be seen to later."

Ruth's eyes had widened afresh. "Wouldn't it be better to wait until we do get back?" she asked hesitantly.

"No." His tone was decisive. "I prefer it this way." He turned his head as the door opened again. "This is your supper, I think."

Ruth leaned back dazedly as he got to his feet to go and take the rough wooden tray from their benefactor. It was all settled. She was to marry André in the morning. It didn't seem possible, and yet she had to believe it. Suddenly she felt herself relax inside. Why question what was happening to her? André wanted to take care of her, to share his life and home with her, and wanted those things badly enough to contemplate the kind of arrangement he had spoken of. A man like that would surely not be difficult to love?

THEY ARRIVED in Algiers at four in the afternoon of the following day. Ruth was tired after the flight, and weak enough still to make no protests when André insisted on carrying her across to the car where Louis Villet waited to greet them.

She was dismayed when a small crowd of photographers and pressmen descended upon them halfway there, turning her face into André's shoulder as flashbulbs popped and notebooks were waved under their noses. There was a babble of French, most of it too fast for her to understand properly. André answered the questions shot at him with clipped brevity as he put Ruth into the rear seat of the car with Louis's help. Then he was behind the wheel, with Louis in the passenger seat, and they were moving away.

"I had hoped to spare you that," Louis said ruefully. "I left Eloise at the villa in the hope that I would be able to slip out unnoticed. You were headline news for two days after we discovered that you had never arrived in Bakra. Your chances of survival were thought to be very small." He paused. "They found the plane easily enough after you radioed the bearings, but they say that in the pattern they were searching it would have been days before they covered that area—and even then they doubt that they could have seen the plane from the air. Apparently it was almost completely covered during a sandstorm the day after you crashed." He turned his head to look back at Ruth with a smile. "You are a very lucky young woman to be alive at all."

"Yes," she agreed softly, "I know. If it hadn't been for André—"

"If it hadn't been for André you wouldn't have been there at all," he put in from the driving seat. "Don't waste your strength in talking. You have some time to go before you regain all that you've lost these last days." He addressed himself to Louis. "Everything is prepared?"

"Yes. Maria has seen to everything that you asked for in your message last night." An element of constraint entered the other man's manner. "I'm sorry, I should have offered my congratulations before this. I suppose I haven't really taken it in yet that the two of you are married. It was rather—sudden."

"Yes." André's tone was short. "Who gave it to the Press?"

Louis lifted his shoulders. "How do the Press ever get to know these things?" His glance slid sideways. "Was there any particular reason why it should not be made public?"

"None at all." Through the driving mirror blue eyes found green briefly. "It is a fact."

Lying stretched out on the wide back seat covered lightly with a rug, Ruth closed her eyes, recalling the austere little ceremony which had made her and André man and wife that morning, the sense of unreality as she made the necessary responses from the narrow truckle bed. Little more than a week ago she had traversed this very road as Ruth Gillen, fresh out from England and full of hopes for the future. Now she was Madame Dubois, and her heart was heavy with doubt. A brother-and-sister relationship to begin with, André had said last night, but could any marriage really hope to work on such a footing? She owed him so much. He surely deserved a wife who would make every effort to bring him happiness.

The villa was as imposing as she remembered it, set

behind high white walls over which grew jasmine and honeysuckle in colourful profusion, its many windows covered in fretted iron grilles. Mosaic glowed golden in the afternoon sunlight. The heavy, nail-studded door stood open in welcome.

Eloise appeared in the doorway as André helped Ruth from the car, a smile lighting the thin, aristocratic features.

"It is wonderful to have you back safely," she said. "I cannot tell you how we all felt when it became known that something had happened to you both." There was speculation mingled with the concern in her swift appraisal of Ruth's appearance. "You look exhausted, *ma petite!* Should she not be taken to the hospital, André?"

He answered levelly. "There is nothing wrong that rest and care will not put right, and that she can have right here at home." He bent and slid an arm beneath Ruth's knees, swinging her effortlessly up into his arms to carry her indoors. "I'll take her straight upstairs. Perhaps you would ask Maria to come up in a moment or two, Eloise."

"Yes, of course." The Villets followed the two of them inside, pausing in the hallway as André continued on towards the staircase.

The room to which he took her was larger and more richly furnished than the one Ruth had occupied before. The inevitable shutters were closed over the windows, letting in mere slats of light. André put her down on the bed and went to partially open one pair, turning back to look at her as she sat there on the silk spread.

"Maria will help you into bed," he said. "Your suitcase was recovered from the plane two days ago, so by now your own things will have been made for use again. These"—with a disparaging wave of his hand—"are fit only for cleaning rags, along with my own. Maria will take them away."

Ruth looked down at the garments she was wearing, clean but unironed, the colour bleached out unevenly by the sun. For the first time that day it occurred to her to wonder what she looked like. There had been no mirrors in the mission, and in any case her looks hadn't seemed important compared with everything else that had happened. She ran a hand over her hair, feeling its roughness, and became aware that André was watching her with a slight smile on his lips.

"A sign that you're well on your way to normality," he said. "Don't worry, you're young enough to have little need of artificial aids to beauty." He moved towards another door in the opposite wall. "My room is through here. I'll return when Maria has finished with you."

Ruth sat very still for a long moment after the door had closed behind him, then she slowly pressed herself to her feet. Her legs felt wobbly and her head seemed to be filled with cotton wool, but she forced herself across the room to stand in front of the heavily framed mirror set over a chest of drawers. The face that looked back at her had lost all trace of its former girlish roundness, the cheekbones standing out under a skin several shades darker than it had ever been before. She could see the points of her collarbone at the open neckline of her shirt, and already knew that the waistline of her slacks was almost two inches too large. Her eyes were dark and lacklustre.

She looked dreadful, she thought in dismay. Like some waif brought in from the streets! With sudden painful clarity there rose in her mind a picture of Simone as she had last seen her, the classically lovely face crowned by the smooth chignon of blonde hair. What could André see in her, Ruth, compared with that vision of beauty? And yet he had chosen her for his wife. There came that same stirring of emotion she had felt earlier in the car. A little soon yet to call it love, but what she was beginning to feel for the man she had married was surely not too far from it. Time was all she needed. Time and knowledge. There had been no real opportunity as yet to discuss details of the Dubois family background. She wasn't even sure what André did for a living. But all that could come later. For now it was enough to know that she belonged somewhere again.

A tap on the door heralded Maria's arrival. She looked concerned to see Ruth on her feet, and set to with ruthless efficiency to carry out her employer's instructions. Twenty minutes later, Ruth was bathed and in bed, wearing one of her own nightdresses and feeling pleasantly drowsy.

When André came back into the room she was not far from sleep, but alert enough to note that he had changed his denims for a suit of pale cream linen worn with a shirt in tan silk. Everything about him had that stamp of expensive good taste. Until that moment she

had not paused to consider that she was married to a
man to whom money was obviously no problem. In a
way that awareness made her feel less at ease with him,
although she could not have explained why.

"First rest, and then feed," he said from the foot of
the bed. "We must concentrate on regaining your
strength. Fortunately you have the resilience of youth
to hasten the process."

"When will I be able to get up?" she asked diffidently.

"Perhaps tomorrow for a little time, after the doctor
has examined you. We'll see what he has to say about
your condition in the morning." He came forward to
lay a hand lightly against her forehead, his touch sending a tremor through her. "You have no fever, at any
rate. Are you quite comfortable?"

"Very, thank you." They sounded more like doctor
and patient than husband and wife, she thought. "Are
you—will I see you again tonight?"

"If you want to." He smiled suddenly. "I'll bring
you your supper and make sure that you eat all of it. Go
to sleep now, child."

I'm not a child, she wanted to protest, but it was too
much of an effort. By the time the door had closed she
was asleep.

CHAPTER FIVE

IT WAS FIVE DAYS before Ruth could say with truth that
she was feeling anything like her old self again. Five days
during which she progressed from bedroom to salon,
with brief periods sitting out in the courtyard soaking in a
comparatively gentle sunshine. There were no visitors
during those first days, for which she was thankful. She
did not yet feel up to meeting new people.

André spent as much time with her as he could
spare from his business commitments, but as these appeared particularly pressing at the time it was often late
afternoon before she saw anything of him. Very gradually she learned a little more about the man she had
married. His mother had been Scottish, she discovered,
a certain Margaret Powell who had come out to Algiers
as governess to the then British ambassador and married André's father within two months. It had been
basically a very good marriage, Ruth gathered from the
details André imparted, but with an element of sadness in that Margaret had never stopped pining for the
country she had left. Ruth could sympathise with her in
that. There were times when she would have given
anything herself for the feel of soft English rain on her
face.

With regard to André's business affairs she was still very hazy. There seemed to be so many of them. She knew that he owned a great deal of property in the city, and was on the boards of two major companies, but as well as this he apparently owned a tourist company taking the more adventurous visitors overland to Tamanrasset and Djanet and all points south. That, of course, explained the garage her father had managed for him in such an out-of-the-way place as Bakra. Ruth wondered nervously what would be expected of the wife of a man of such obvious standing in the community, but hesitated to ask. There would be time enough to face up to the demands of her new role when she had to do so.

She was staying down to dinner in the evenings now, but André still insisted on her retiring to her room almost immediately afterwards, coming in to say goodnight after she was in bed.

"I'm not ill any longer," she protested one evening. "Isn't it time I was beginning to lead a normal life again?"

"You had four days of high fever during which we feared for your life," he returned. "The body takes time to recover from that kind of stress. Perhaps by the weekend you can begin staying up longer."

"But that's three days away yet, and I feel fine!"

"The weekend," he repeated firmly. "But tomorrow Eloise is to take you into town on a shopping expedition. Buy whatever you wish."

"There's nothing I need," she said, and saw him smile.

"I didn't say what you needed, I said what you wanted. You wouldn't be female if you didn't like new clothes. Eloise will help you in your choice. She has excellent taste."

Which she herself could not be trusted to have, Ruth supposed, and was immediately ashamed of the thought. André was trying to please her. It wasn't his fault that he was only succeeding in making her feel like a child who had to be indulged. In many ways they seemed to be even further apart than they had in the beginning. Not that he was to blame for that either. His manner with her was always easy and natural. It was her own doubts which created any tension between them.

After he had left her she lay for some time trying to sort out her emotions. For better or for worse she was married to André, and that was something she had to start accepting as fact. The main trouble was that she didn't feel married in any way, nor could she bring herself to think of the villa as home. Sometimes André himself seemed more like a thoughtful host than a husband. The remedy to that, she supposed, lay in her own hands. If she wanted a real husband then she must be prepared to act like a real wife. Only she wasn't ready for that step yet. Not while he was still to all intents and purposes a stranger to her.

ELOISE ARRIVED driving her own car the following morning. Going to greet her at the door, Ruth was surprised at her rush of pleasure on seeing the older woman again.

"I would have come over sooner than this," Eloise remarked when they were in the car and turning out of the gates. "But André thought that you needed to be quiet for a few days. I think perhaps he was right. You certainly look a different person from the girl he had to carry indoors that first day."

"I feel different," Ruth acknowledged. "But I would have welcomed your company, Eloise."

The other smiled. "One does not defy your husband lightly. I have yet to see him really angry, but he has a demoralising manner with those who manage to cross him—or have you not yet discovered that side of him?"

Ruth could have said that she had discovered it on their very first time of meeting, but she refrained. Instead she made some suitable light reply and turned her attention to the windows, wondering if Eloise guessed how little she did really know about the man she had married.

It was the first time in almost a week that she had been outside the villa grounds, and within a moment or two all thought of André was pushed temporarily to the back of her mind as she gazed out eagerly at the passing scenery. She was dazzled by the sparkling whiteness of the buildings, the brilliant colours of the flowers spilling everywhere, the magnificent sweep of the bay. Algiers was built like an amphitheatre, rising in tiers to the hills at its back, affording breathtaking glimpses at every street corner. Her spirits lifted progressively. In the bright light of day no problem was insurmountable.

The commercial centre of Algiers seemed to be concentrated into two main streets. Eloise chose the stores to visit, and steered Ruth through the various departments, conjuring up eager assistance with a flick of her finger and picking out the best from the garments brought out for inspection with a practised eye.

"André said you were to have a complete new wardrobe," she said at one point when Ruth demurred over the acquisition of a pair of slender-heeled sandals which cost the earth. "He will hardly expect you to economise on it. We'll take these," she added in French to the hovering assistant. "And the other two pairs, too. They are to go on Monsieur Dubois' account."

André appeared to have accounts everywhere, and his name brought immediate recognition. Long before the expedition was over, Ruth gave up arguing and let Eloise have her way, unable to deny the pleasure in spending money without having to worry about it for the first time in her life. In one place, Eloise insisted that she keep on a particularly lovely little suit in pale cream shantung which brought out the highlights in her hair, matching it with handbag and shoes in tan leather. Her own blue dress was left to be sent on with other items, although Ruth had the feeling that Eloise privately considered it hardly worth the bother.

"We will have to do something about your hair," said the latter when they were outside again. "It's a lovely colour but sadly neglected. There is a salon on the rue Larbi Ben M'Hidi which might fit you in without an appointment." She paused, eyeing the young face before her with a sudden wry expression. "I hope you have no objection to my making such a suggestion? I thought simply to add a little final polish to your appearance."

Ruth's answering smile was deliberately bright. "Of course I don't mind. Do you really think they will put me in?"

Eloise laughed. "For Madame Dubois many things are more than possible!"

Accompanying her, Ruth tried not to let her thoughts dwell too much on what all this expediture really meant. She was being groomed for the role she had taken on, made to look a little more like the wife of one of the city's most prominent business men should look—as far as it was possible. It hurt to realise that André was not happy with the way she looked now, but if it was to please him she would go along with anything Eloise suggested. That was all she wanted, to please him.

The salon was able to fit her in at once on the mention of the Dubois name. Eloise left her in the care of an assistant, saying she would be back in an hour. Ruth was taken to a thickly carpeted cubicle where a dapper, middle-aged Frenchman came and looked at her hair with much shaking of his head and pursing of his lips. In the following twenty minutes she was styled and shampooed, had her hair set on rollers and found herself under a dryer with a cup of coffee at her elbow and a magazine in her hands.

It was perhaps some ten minutes or so later when one of the roller clips began to give trouble, sticking painfully into her scalp. She thought of summoning the assistant, but decided that it was too minor a matter to bother her with when all she needed to do was to ease the clip round a bit.

She pushed the dryer upwards away from her head without bothering to switch it off, looking in the mirror as she carefully adjusted the roller to a more comfortable position. At first the voices coming from the far side of the partition made no particular impression. It was only when she caught the name of Gillen that the conversation itself began to register.

"I met him several times," came one woman's smooth tones. "Apparently he left his family many years ago and never returned to England. It was only after the mother died that the daughter attempted to seek him out, and turned up here in Algiers. The girl is very young, I believe, and quite alone in the world. André obviously felt that the responsibility for her future had to be his." A pause, and a change of tone. "It must have been a great shock for Simone when he returned to Algiers with a wife. After all, she expected to be Madame Dubois herself before the year was out."

It seemed an age before Ruth could force her nerveless hand to reach up and pull the dryer back down about her ears again, shutting out the voices which had brought her such pain. Was it true? Had André really sacrificed his own future plans in order to fulfil a sense of duty? She didn't want to believe it, but every aspect of their relationship seemed to point to its being the truth. He treated her like a child because that was how he regarded her still—a child to be taken care of. He had even said as much that night in Bakra when he had

first suggested marriage to her. Suggested? Her lower
lip quivered faintly. Decided would be a better word.
And once made, that decision had allowed neither of
them any time for reflection.

She closed her eyes to shut out the sight of her pale
face gazing back at her from the mirror, recalling the
words he had used that night. A basis to build on, he
had said, and she had believed it because she wanted to
believe it, because she yearned for the security he was
offering her together with the promise of better things
to come. But this was no basis on which to build any
kind of relationship. Surely he must have seen that?
Surely he could have found some other way of satisfying his sense of responsibility. In those few moments
Ruth left girlhood behind her for ever.

She was outwardly composed when Eloise came back
to the salon to pick her up, a poised, well-groomed
young woman wearing a fixed smile that went nowhere
near her eyes. Eloise expressed glowing approval of her
appearance, and suggested that they adjourned to a
nearby restaurant for a belated lunch before returning
to the villa. Ruth was only too willing to put off the
moment of return. Right then she felt that she wanted
to see neither André nor his home ever again.

They had to go back some time, of course. They
reached the villa a little after four o'clock to find
André's car in the courtyard. Ruth accompanied Eloise
reluctantly indoors, her heart jerking painfully when he
came out from the salon.

"So there you are at last," he said. "I was beginning
to think I should have to come and look for the two of

you." His eyes went over Ruth, and his smile widened. "You look delightful!"

She moved abruptly, unable to stand there any longer under his scrutiny without giving away something of her inner feelings. "Eloise must take the credit," she said. "I—I think I'll go straight upstairs, if you don't mind. I'm feeling rather tired."

In her room she took off the jacket of the cream suit and hung it carefully away in the wardrobe, then sat down in front of the mirror to survey her new image with dispassionate eyes. The auburn hair had been trimmed to just above shoulder level, the ends clubbed to turn under thickly. Beneath the side-swept fringe her face had a newly nourished glow, with the light but expertly applied make-up making the most of its contours. Her lipstick exactly matched the varnish on her nails. She knew she had never looked better, and it meant nothing.

A hard lump came into her throat; she swallowed on it roughly. It was difficult to know how to even begin to tackle a situation like this one. Legally she was André's wife, but nothing else tied them together. She wondered if it were possible to get an annulment here in Algiers— only she couldn't imagine André agreeing to that, anyway. Having made a decision to such importance he would stick by it through thick and thin. That was one thing she *had* learnt about him.

One solution was to go away, she supposed. But where would she go? André had been in touch with her mother's solicitors and arranged for the house in Oxford to be put in the hands of a reputable estate agent, severing her last real tie with her former life. If she went back to England she would be entirely alone and homeless, with very little, as André himself had pointed out, in the way of qualifications for a job. In any case, he would find her and bring her back. No matter how much he might regret the step he had felt himself bound to take he would never allow her to just walk out on him.

Which left one other alternative. Despite the fact that he had not married her for love, André appeared to have every intention of trying to make this marriage work. If she— was going to be adult about things she owed it to him to make the same effort. A tremor ran through her and she looked away from the green eyes reflected in the mirror. Easy enough to say, not so easy to put into practice. Perhaps men regarded these things differently, but she was going to need more than just a sense of duty to contemplate the kind of relationship André would eventually expect.

The brief tap on the door made her heart thud. When André came into the room she made no move, watching him through the mirror as he paused by the bed to study her.

"Are you all right?" he asked. "Eloise was worried that she might have kept you out too long."

"I'm just tired, that's all." Ruth managed to keep her voice level. "An hour's rest and I'll be fine. It—it isn't Eloise's fault. I should have asked to come back instead of staying in town for lunch."

"Ah well, no harm done. All the same, I think it

might be a good idea if you stayed in bed for the rest of the day and made sure of no ill-effects."

"No!" The retort came out sharper than she had intended. She made an attempt to modify it. "I've spent enough time here in bed, André. All I need is a lie-down. I'm perfectly well now."

There was a moment when she thought he was going to argue about it, then he smiled and lifted his shoulders. "Very well. You know best how you feel." He came over to stand behind her, studying her through the mirror. "I must admit that you certainly don't look in any danger of a relapse." One hand came out to smooth the line of her hair. "You enjoyed your shopping excursion?"

"Yes." His closeness was sending quivers down her spine. "I'm afraid we—I spent far too much. I don't really need all those things."

"Since when did a woman *need* all the clothes she buys?" He sounded amused. "There is no need to feel guilty because you did as I said. I can afford to indulge your tastes." His hand had come to rest on her shoulder at the base of her neck, his fingers lightly tracing the bone through the thin material of her blouse. "You are very deceptive," he remarked. "Who would guess that such a slight frame could house the kind of strength you displayed in the desert?"

He must have sensed the tension in her, for suddenly his hand fell away. There was an ironic line to his mouth. "I'm forgetting your tiredness," he said. "I will see you later." In the act of turning away, he added, "Incidentally, your purchases have begun arriving.

I'll have them brought up in an hour or so. Was there anything you wanted in the meantime?"

Ruth shook her head numbly. "I don't think so."

"Then I'll leave you to get on with your rest," he said, and went swiftly from the room.

RUTH'S HEALTH picked up slowly but surely as the days passed. By the end of her second week of marriage she was back to her original eight stone again, and fit enough to convince André that she would not suffer from an extension of activities. Apart from the Villets she had met none of his acquaintances as yet. His suggestion that they should give a small dinner party for the closer ones the following week brought a certain apprehension, but she was sensible enough to realise that she had to face them sooner or later and might as well get it over with.

As the evening approached she found herself even beginning to look forward to the break. Perhaps people were what she needed to take her out of herself—people other than the few she saw every day. With so many new things from which to choose, she found herself with a difficulty in deciding what to wear for the occasion. She supposed she could have asked André what would be the most suitable, but something in her shrank from any gesture which reminded her of his place in her life.

Eventually, she plumped for a long-sleeved dress of Italian silk jersey in a shade of turquoise which did wonders for her hair and skin. It was the most expensive garment she had ever owned. Viewing her reflection on the evening of the dinner before going down to meet their guests, Ruth hoped that she did it justice. It certainly fitted her perfectly, tight from the modest neckline down to the narrow waist, then swirling out softly over her hips. She had been down to Constantines during the afternoon and had her hair shampooed and set again. It gleamed like beaten copper in the glow of the lamps, so well styled that it fell naturally into place no matter how she moved her head.

Money certainly made a difference, she acknowledged with a wry little smile. The people she had known in Oxford would hardly recognise her now. In three weeks she had become another person—on the surface, at any rate.

The original suggestion for a small, intimate party had stretched somewhat over the weekend to include a dozen people all told. Ruth was grateful that the Villets were the first arrivals, feeling a little more confident with Eloise close to hand to help her through the difficult first moments. She was coming to depend on Eloise in a lot of ways, she realised. Although she was only in her mid-thirties, there was a mature serenity about the older woman that she found oddly comforting.

It was when the final couple of guests arrived that her reserves were taxed to the limits, however. Somehow it had never occurred to her that André would have asked Simone. But she was here, and looking as beautiful as Ruth remembered her in a long, silkily clinging dress of oyster silk. A small, expectant silence seemed to settle over the assembly as the two of them

came face to face, but there was no trace of anything
other than cool appraisal in Simone's amber eyes.

"I have brought along one of your own countrymen
as my small contribution to the evening," she said,
drawing forward the young man with the thick red-
brown hair who had accompanied her. "Paul is an engineer with an oil company working out on the border,
but he has four weeks' leave to spend right here in Algiers. Is that not correct, Paul?"

"Almost," he agreed with an engaging smile at
Ruth. "I've got three weeks and two days still to go.
Whereabouts in England do you hail from yourself?"

She told him, and saw his eyes widen in pleased surprise. "Well, I'll be blowed!" he exclaimed. "I'm from
Abingdon myself. How about that for a coincidence?"

"A small world indeed." André's tone was dry, his
regard slightly narrowed as it rested a moment on Simone. "I am sure my wife will appreciate the opportunity to exchange reminiscences of scenes and places
you will both know, but perhaps later on. What will you
have to drink?"

Dinner was not quite the ordeal Ruth had anticipated
as she had Louis on one side of her, but as always it
seemed to go on for ever. Paul Brent had been placed
about halfway down the long table. It wasn't until they
were having coffee in the salon that he made his way
over to Ruth's side again.

"Simone was telling me about your desert adventure
before we got here," he said. "That must have been a
rotten experience."

"It wasn't very pleasant," Ruth agreed with some

understatement. She smiled back at him. "It's nice to meet someone else from England. My French isn't all that good yet, I'm afraid."

"Nor mine. Never was much good at languages, and where I am you need a smattering of the local lingo too."

"Where is that?"

"Out near Gad Ames. We're running a pipeline up to the coast." He pushed back the comma of hair which kept falling over his forehead and pulled a face. "We'll be at it for donkey's years yet, worse luck. What a country! It's as hot as hell out there, land twice as nasty. Give me Europe any day!"

"I suppose having to work in it doesn't help," she said with sympathy. "The tourists seem to enjoy the Sahara better than anyone."

"Better than you must have done, certainly." He hesitated, his boyishly attractive features expressing a certain curiosity. "Maybe I shouldn't have mentioned that again. I don't suppose you want reminding."

"No," Ruth admitted. "I'd rather forget about it." She changed the subject quickly. "How long have you known Simone?"

"Just a couple of days or so. One of the lads back at camp is her cousin or something. Anyway, he gave me her address before I came away on leave and said she'd introduce me to some people. She has too. It's quite a hectic social whirl you have in the European community, isn't it?"

Ruth laughed and shook her head. "I wouldn't know. I'm only a beginner myself. Tonight must seem

pretty dull to you if you've been going the rounds with
Simone."

"No, it doesn't. Not a bit." There was a sudden
meaningful note in his voice. "I'm enjoying every minute of it—especially being able to talk English without
getting the guilty feeling that I ought to be making the
effort to merge in with the majority. Of course, I know
that practically everybody in the darned town speaks
better English than I speak French, but—well, you
know what I mean. It's a matter of common courtesy."

"Yes, I do know. I feel the same." Ruth looked at him
for a moment, thinking what an unexpected mixture he
was, one minute a bit brash and overbearing, the next
coming out with the kind of remark he had just made.
She placed him at around twenty-five or six, which made
him a lot closer to her own age than anyone else here
tonight—except Simone herself, of course.

She glanced round for the other girl, and found her
over by the curtained window alcove talking with
André. The two of them made a striking couple, she
acknowledged, and felt a swift constriction in her chest.

"Your husband is a lot older than you, isn't he?"
said Paul, following her eyes.

"It depends what you call a lot," she answered after
a moment. "André is only thirty-one."

"And you're what—twenty?"

Promotion, she reflected on an edge of satire. She
supposed she should feel flattered considering. "About
that," she said. "But I'm ageing fast."

He laughed, patting her hand with mock— solicita-
tion. "It doesn't show." There was a slight pause be-

fore he added lightly, "How does a French husband feel about his wife having lunch with a fellow countryman?"

Ruth looked at him swiftly and away again. "I'm not sure."

"If he didn't mind, would you come?"

She hesitated, not certain whether he meant it or was just testing her reactions. Either way she decided to play along for the moment. "I might. Why don't you ask him?"

"All right," he said. "I will."

He wouldn't. Ruth was fairly certain of that. He was just talking, putting on an act for her benefit. "How is it that you're spending your leave in Algiers?" she queried. "I'd have thought a month was plenty of time to get to and from England in."

"Nobody in particular to go back to," he said with a shrug. "Only an old aunt who wouldn't thank me for landing myself on her. That's why I came out in the first place. The money's good, and I thought if I could stick it till I'm thirty I'd have a good start."

"Is that when you plan to get married?"

"That was the idea. Get a nest egg together, then find a nice girl and settle down." He said it on an oddly wry note. "Trouble is the best ones are already gone."

A romance gone wrong somewhere in the past? Ruth wondered. He had sounded so down for a moment. She gave him an encouraging smile. "I'm sure you'll manage when the time comes."

Eloise joined them. "I have decided that Louis and I shall hold a *mechou* next week," she announced with a flourish of her brandy glass. "It is quite a time since we last ate out of doors." She caught Ruth's enquiring look and laughed. "You will enjoy it. At a *mechou* we roast a whole sheep on a spit and eat it with the fingers. It is the best way of all to eat meat. A very casual affair, you understand?"

"It sounds fun," Ruth acknowledged, and hesitated. "Have you mentioned it to André yet, Eloise?"

"But of course. Now that you have regained your health and strength there is no reason why the two of you should not resume a full social life. There are many people eager to meet the bride of one of our foremost citizens—especially those who were convinced that André would never succumb to marriage." Her smile was totally without malice. "You have something that a dozen other female hearts will envy you for—the name of Dubois."

But that was all she had, the name. Ruth wondered what Eloise would say if she knew the truth of their marriage.

It was when they were leaving that Paul took her completely by surprise in carrying out his promise.

"Would you have any objection if I took your wife out to lunch one day while I'm still in Algiers?" he asked as he shook hands with André. "I'd very much appreciate the pleasure of her company."

André took a second or two to answer. Ruth hardly dared look at him.

"I'm afraid," he said with icy politeness, "that my wife's time is fully reserved. Perhaps we shall meet again before you leave."

"I hope so." Paul sounded rueful, aware that he had blundered. "Goodnight then, and thanks once again."

"A very forward young man, even by British standards," observed Louis on a light note as the outer doors closed behind Simone and her escort. "Still, I suppose he meant no harm."

André's eyes found Ruth's with an expression which made her pulses quicken. "We shall understand if you want to go straight up," he said. "You have had a long day."

There was little else she could do then but obey the unspoken command. Ruth murmured goodnight to the Villets and went on up the stairs to her room, knowing the three of them would most probably go back to the salon for a nightcap before the French couple left. It was like being demoted to childhood yet again, and she bitterly resented it. Now, however, was hardly the time or place to state her feelings. André was angry enough as it was. Darn Paul, she thought vexedly. Who would have thought for a moment that he would actually take her at her word!

She was undressed and sitting at the dressing table in a blue silk wrap when the anticipated tap came on the door. André came in and closed the door again with a firm click, then regarded her grimly across the width of the room.

"Never put me in that position again," he said.

"I'm sorry." Her voice sounded a little breathless. "It never occurred to me that he really would ask. I thought—"

"Thought what?" he prompted as she paused uncertainly. "That your coquettish little games would not be taken seriously? Do you think I was unaware of the way you were smiling and laughing with Brent, of the way he took hold of your hand? Everyone noted it!" He drew in a controlling breath. "I'll not tolerate that kind of humiliation!"

Ruth's chin lifted, the colour coming faintly under her skin. "I did *not* humiliate you," she stated with some spirit. "At least, not intentionally. And I can't see what was so terribly wrong with what Paul did. After all, he at least asked. Some men wouldn't have bothered."

"You know so much about men?" His tone was sardonic. "Perhaps in England you had the freedom to accept any invitation you chose, but you weren't married then. As my wife you'll pay me the compliment of behaving in a manner which can't be misinterpreted should we meet up with this man again before he leaves Algiers. Is that understood?"

Ruth bit her lip. "Perfectly. But I think you're being totally unfair."

"To you or to Paul?" The question was abrupt.

"To both of us." She swung round on the stool to face him, forcing herself to remain as calm as possible about this. "André, I have no interest in Paul Brent, nor he in me, apart from the fact that we both happen to be English in a country that's still strange to us. If we did give the wrong impression tonight then I'm sorry. I just didn't think."

His features relaxed slightly as he looked at her. "I believe you," he said. "But don't attempt to excuse

Brent's behaviour along the same lines. He's old enough to know better."

"And I'm not?" She lowered her eyes to the brush she still held in her hand, running her fingertip over the bristles. "It might help if you stopped thinking of me as one step up from a schoolgirl," she tagged on huskily.

"You are just one step up from a schoolgirl." His tone was harsh again. "That's the problem."

She was very still, avoiding his gaze. "Perhaps you should never have married me."

It seemed an age before he replied, and when he did his voice was hard and uncompromising. "Mistake or not, it's a fact we're both of us going to have to live with to the best of our ability. Marriages aren't always made in heaven—they have to be worked at. Some more than others. Having you shrink away from me every time I come anywhere near you isn't exactly helping matters. How can our relationship progress when you won't even let me touch you?" He paused. "Perhaps that's a large part of the trouble, that I don't press the issue more. Perhaps things would be better between us if I ignored the promise I made you and took steps to put our marriage on a proper footing."

Ruth's head came up sharply, her eyes widening a little. "André—"

He made a small, weary gesture. "Don't look like that. I didn't mean here and now. But you have to realise that this state of affairs can't go on indefinitely. I want a wife, not a ward."

Ruth sat looking at the door for a long time after he

had gone, an aching dryness in her throat. André was right, of course. As marriages went theirs was a mess, but it was up to the two of them to at least try to make something of it. He was still the same man she had relied on so completely in the desert, the man to whom she owed her life. Did she not also owe him her trust?

CHAPTER SIX

NORMALLY ANDRE had already left the villa by the time Ruth got down to breakfast, but on the following morning he was still seated at the table set out on the patio, lean and vital in pale slacks and a dark brown shirt casually laced at the throat. He greeted her pleasantly, and pushed across the basket of rolls.

"These are still warm," he said. "But we can send for fresh, if you prefer."

"No, these will do perfectly," she assured him hurriedly. She took one and split it, spreading both halves with preserve. She wasn't hungry, and would have been satisfied with the coffee alone, but felt the necessity to put on a show of having an appetite of sorts.

At this hour the heat was not too intense. Usually she enjoyed just sitting here with her coffee in a mood of relaxation, but with André across from her she could not conjure up that ease of mind. She wished desperately that she were older, more capable of meeting him on an equal basis—only if she had been older she would hardly have been in this position to start with.

"Are you going out later?" she asked at last for something to say.

"We both are," he returned. "I thought it was time I took a day off and showed you something of our surroundings now that you're back to normal health again. Do you have any preference as to how we spend it, or will you leave it to me?"

"I'll leave it to you." She hesitated, searching the unreadable dark features, aware that the motives behind this idea must stem from what had passed between them the previous night. "It's very thoughtful of you," she added.

His lips twisted. "And kind? You said that once before." He pressed himself to his feet with an abrupt movement. "There are some matters I must attend to before we set out. Be ready in half an hour. And bring a scarf—it may be breezy along the coast road."

Ruth watched him go with mixed feelings. A whole day with André. Was she going to be able to cope with it? She supposed that was almost laughable considering the fact that she had been far more alone with him during the days they had spent in the desert. Only that had been different. Circumstances had drawn them together, given them a common bond. Here there were so many other influences at work, not least among them the memory of how he and Simone had looked together last night.

She sighed, and got up to go and prepare for the day which lay ahead.

They drove west out of Algiers along the coast road, winding through bays and round promontories which jutted out into a halcyon sea. It was hot in the car, but with both windows down the breeze created by their speed was enough to keep the temperature at a bearable level. Ruth leaned an elbow on the sill and gave herself over to enjoyment of the scenery, absorbed enough to forget who was doing the driving for minutes on end.

André himself seemed content to let the miles flow by in near silence, only occasionally breaking it with some casual remark. Out here, away from the constricting surroundings of the villa, he seemed more like the man she had known before. Gradually she found herself beginning to open up, with him, to proffer observations herself instead of waiting for him to speak first, at one point breaking into laughter with him at her own pronunciation of place names like Ain Benian and Djemila.

They reached the Roman ruins at Tipasa just before noon, and spent some time looking round the impressive amphitheatre and temple. They were not alone in this pursuit, tourists being fairly well scattered over the site. Coming back to where they had left the car, they found a coach just drawn in beside it to start disgorging a British party. Listening to the babble of voices, Ruth failed to notice that André was holding open the door for her until she felt his hand come under her arm, propelling her forward and into the seat.

His mouth was set a little harder when he came round the bonnet to slide in beside her, but he made no comment until he had turned the car and was heading back along the coast.

"Could you try to make your preference for English company not quite so apparent?" he asked on a harsh note. "You were looking at those people as if you would willingly have changed places with any one of them."

"As a matter of fact," Ruth answered almost truthfully, "I was thinking that tourists abroad seem to have a set vocabulary. All they talk about is the heat and the food."

The pause was lengthy, his smile reluctant. "Are you trying to tell me that I imagined the homesickness?"

It was Ruth's turn to pause. "No," she was forced to admit at length. "That's something I can't help. But I'm also aware that it could never be the same even if I did go back."

"No," he agreed. "This is your country now. Perhaps one day we'll pay a visit to England together, but not until we have resolved the difficulties between us." He glanced at her. "At least you seem to be trying to find some liking for me again today."

"I've never disliked you," she denied, then paused and went faintly pink. "Only a little, perhaps, when we first met, but that seems a long time ago now."

"Just four weeks ago today, to be exact." There was an odd note in his voice. "It only seems a long time because such a lot has happened to you during it. What was it you disliked about me that first day?"

"Your attitude," she said after a moment. "You were so determined that I wasn't going to see my father—and I'd come such a long way." She laughed. "I seem to remember that I was rather rude to you."

"Yes," on a dry note. "You were very much Leo's daughter at that moment, despite the lack of physical resemblance—two jampots high and full of fight! I'm glad to find that you can talk about him quite freely. You haven't mentioned him since we returned to Algiers."

There had been too many other matters to occupy her attention, Ruth reflected. "I suppose the most regrettable part is that he never even knew I was looking for him," she said.

"Possibly." André swung the wheel, accelerating out of the bend. "On the other hand, it could possibly have made matters worse for him. At the most he only had a few months to live—he was told that some time ago. I tried to persuade him to spend what time he had left to him here in Algiers with his friends, but he preferred the solitude he'd found in Bakra."

Ruth turned her head to view the lean profile. "So that's why you were so reluctant to take me to him?"

"For both your sakes. It was too late. It's far easier to forget an image carried only in the mind than a real flesh and blood person."

Ruth thought she knew what he meant, but wasn't sure that she agreed with him on that score. Not that it made any difference. Leo was gone, and no amount of wishing could bring him back. What she had to concentrate on now was the future—hers and André's. And maybe in time he would come to love her as she wanted to be loved.

They stopped for the late Algerian lunch at one of the little villages with which the coastline abounded, and feasted on freshly caught seafoods in a tiny restaurant overlooking the picturesque harbour. There were a couple of fishing boats gently riding the flooding tide, while a small group of roughly clad men lounged idly at the far end of the curving stone wall.

"The tourists rarely stop here," André said when Ruth commented on the tranquillity of the place. "There isn't enough to draw them at the present time, and not enough room for exploitation." He touched the bottle standing between them on the table. "You would like some more wine?"

She shook her head. "It makes me dizzy." She waited a moment before adding almost shyly, "I've enjoyed today, André."

His eyes were enigmatic. "It isn't over yet. Tonight you can put on another of those delightful new dresses and we'll go out. You like to dance?"

Her smile was uncertain. "I haven't done very much. A few local hops with some old school friends, that's all. I won't be up to your standard."

"I wasn't thinking of entering for any competitive work." He studied her a moment, finger and thumb curving the stem of his glass. "You have a lot of catching up to do on your playtime," he said. "Responsibility came too early for you—robbed you of your girlhood. I intend to make up for that lack."

"André—" she hesitated, chewing her lip—"you don't have to make up for anything. I mean, you don't have to go out of your way to provide the things you think I want. As a matter of fact, I'd be quite happy to have a quiet dinner at—at home tonight."

His brows lifted with a hint of satire. "That took quite an effort!"

She flushed. "Don't mock me. I know I'm young and inexperienced, but I'm trying to be adult about things now. I've thought a lot about what you said last night and—"

"There is more to being adult than the matters I spoke of last night." The interruption was brusque. "Teaching you the basic facts of life would only be a start. Do you imagine that the physical side of our marriage is the only one I am interested in?"

"No." There was a tremor in her voice she could not quite control. "I think having taken it on you'll do everything you can towards making it as good as it possibly can be." She stopped, met his eyes and felt her heart contract painfully. On impulse she put a hand on his sleeve. "André, I realise how bitter you must feel about the way things are, but—"

"Do you?" His voice was soft, with an underlying note she could not define. There was a brief pause while they looked at one another, then he smiled faintly and inclined his head. "So from now on I treat you like a woman and you respond to me on the same level. As simple as that?"

Ruth gave a little sigh. "I don't suppose so. But at least I'll be learning as we go along. Only—" she looked away from him, running a finger around the rim of her glass—"you won't expect too much too soon, will you, André? I mean—"

"I know what you mean. You don't have to underline it any further." He drained his glass, putting it back on the table with a hand which looked ready to crack the slender stem. "We'll see how it goes, shall we?"

Ruth didn't have to ask what *he* meant by that. He might be prepared to afford her a more equal status generally speaking, but so far as their personal relationship was concerned he would set the pace. Male pride, she thought, and was aware that lesson number one on how to handle this man she had married had already been learned.

There was a message waiting for André when they reached the villa about four o'clock. He read it swiftly, glancing her way with a regretful shrug. "I'm afraid I have to go out again."

"Business?" she asked.

"Yes." He was turning away towards the staircase as he spoke. "I must change."

Apparently she was not to be told what the business was. Ruth went through to the salon with a sense of deflation, smiling her agreement when Maria appeared to ask if she would like some tea prepared. The staff here were nothing if not helpful. It wasn't their fault that she still felt like a visitor rather than the mistress of the place.

She was sitting there sipping the fragrant, lemon-flavoured brew when André came in. He had changed his slacks and shirt for a tropical worsted in pale blue, and had obviously found time for a quick shower, for his hair was still damp at the ends, curling into the nape of his neck in a way which gave her an odd sensation in the pit of her stomach.

"I may be gone some time," he said. "Unfortunate, but necessary." He eyed her for a moment across the few yards of carpet separating them, his glance running over her slender bare legs under the short yellow skirt. A smile touched his lips. "The heat seems to have little effect on you. You look as fresh as when we left this morning."

Ruth didn't feel it, but the wilting was more inside than out. Why she should feel like this just because André had to go out again so soon, she couldn't imagine. Not so very long ago she would have been only too relieved to be left on her own for a while.

"Will you be back for dinner?" she asked.

"I will be back in time to take you out to dinner," he replied. "What I said earlier still applies." The smile acquired a slight edge of cynicism. "I might even show you how to gamble. You're just old enough to take into a casino." He lifted a casual hand in farewell. "Enjoy your tea."

So he wasn't prepared to endure the boredom of an evening alone with her, Ruth surmised dully. Not that she could blame him. She hadn't exactly proved herself the most scintillating company during the hours they had so far spent alone together. She supposed she should feel grateful that he had at least made an effort to cater for her less sophisticated tastes that day. She doubted that it would have occurred to him to take anyone else to a restaurant such as the one they had visited for lunch. By anyone else meaning Simone, of course. For her it would have to be the best and only the best. Like the Casino, for instance.

Ruth hoped that André hadn't been serious about that. She simply wasn't cut out for that kind of atmosphere.

The hours crawled slowly by while he was gone. She spent a couple of them lying on her bed with a few magazines, but her French was barely good enough yet to make reading an enjoyable pastime. She would have to ask André if there were any English books in the villa. There would certainly have been some when his mother was alive.

He had not said what time to be ready for, but it seemed a good idea to make it reasonably early. She had just come out of the bathroom when a tap came on the communicating door. Ruth pulled the belt of her long white bathrobe more tightly about her before inviting her husband to enter.

To her surprise André was already changed into a tuxedo. Either he had come up to his room so quietly that she hadn't heard him earlier, or he had been very quick. He had an oblong box in his hand—a jeweller's box, she realised with a sudden fluttering of her nerves.

"You look like a wood nymph with your hair done up like that," he commented lightly. "I thought you would be ready."

"I'm sorry," she said. "I didn't realise—"

He made a small sound of impatience. "Don't take everything I say as a criticism. We don't have to hurry anywhere." He paused, his gaze flicking over her again. "What are you going to wear?"

Ruth turned towards the long ornate doors of the wardrobe. "I wasn't sure what would be the right kind of thing," she said. "I thought perhaps this—" taking out a lemon voile with narrow shoulder straps.

"Pretty," he said, "but not quite good enough for the Malhabi Casino." He riffled through the rows of garments and selected a figured white silk with butterfly sleeves cut out across the shoulders. "This is better."

Ruth took the dress from him without a word and went to lay it across the bed ready to put on. When she turned back he was watching her with a quizzical expression.

"You resent my interference in such matters?"

"Not resent," she murmured with careful candour, "more deplore the need."

"I fail to see why you should feel ashamed because you needed advice on what to wear to a place you've never before visited. In any case, my main reason for suggesting the change was because of this—" holding out the case. "I collected it on my way back just now."

Back from where? she wondered irrelevantly, and could not bring herself to ask the obvious question.

"I'll wait until you're dressed," he said after a brief moment, and went back into his own room, leaving her with the defeated knowledge that she had managed to irritate him afresh.

The deceptively simple cut of the white dress somehow contrived to make her look subtly older than her years. Ruth wondered fleetingly if that was why André had chosen it. She was applying lipstick when he returned. She put the tube down with a hand that trembled a little and stood there waiting for the verdict.

"Perfect," he said. "Eloise has a sure eye." He put the long case down on the dressing table and took out its contents, moving behind her to slide the necklace about her throat. She quivered to the touch of his fingers on her skin, vitally conscious of his lean strength. Then the necklace was fastened and he was turning her round to the mirror to see it, standing behind her with his hands still resting on her shoulders. "There," he said. "Now do you see what I meant about the dress?"

Ruth did indeed. The circlet of sapphires with its single drop needed the starkness of the white to offset its brilliance. She put up a hand to touch the stones, her eyes meeting his in the mirror. "They're beautiful," she managed. "But they must be worth a fortune."

He did not deny it. "They belonged to my mother," he said. "I had them re-set because the original design would have been too heavy for you. Later I will have Anton look at the rubies." His mouth was sardonic. "You look almost a woman tonight, *ma petite*—except that most women would find some pleasure in a present. Do you dislike the sapphire?"

Ruth shook her head numbly, unable to explain that she would have been delighted with the cheapest string of beads had it been chosen for her personally. He hadn't needed to tell her that these were family jewels — it was only too obvious. She was a Dubois now, and must look the part. "It's just that I shall be terrified of losing them," she got out.

"They are insured. And they belong next to the skin, not in a bank vault." His hands tightened slightly, turning her towards him. With some deliberation he tilted her chin. "Is it too much to hope for some voluntary gesture by way of return?"

Heart beating fast, she reached up and put her lips shyly to his for a brief moment, the contact sending an electric impulse down her spine. "Thank you," she murmured.

His movement away from her was abrupt. "It's time we were going."

Well, what had she expected? Ruth asked herself as he picked up the long coat which matched the dress and held it out for her to slip her arms into the sleeves. One fleeting, self-conscious kiss was hardly likely to start the flame of passion burning within him. All the same, he could surely have found some small response—just enough to give her confidence in herself.

The Casino belonged to one of the town's newest hotels, a plush, opulent place, dimly lit except for the pools of brighter light over each of the gaming tables. Moving at André's side through the expensively dressed throng, Ruth was aware of the glances directed their way, of the whispered comments. André acknowledged several people, but made no attempt to stop and introduce her to anyone, for which she was thankful. Her spoken French was improving daily, but still left her feeling inadequate to any involved conversational demands.

They watched for a while at one of the roulette tables, until a seat came spare and André bade her take it. Despite herself, Ruth felt a small thrill of anticipation as he provided her with some chips and showed her how to place her bets.

She lost on the first spin, and again on the second, but on the third had the satisfaction of seeing a small pile of chips pushed across the table towards her. André smiled tolerantly at her obvious pleasure and placed some bets of his own, working to some system Ruth could not follow. She wasn't even sure whether or not he had won until the croupier slid across a stack of black chips plus a solitary white one. Interest began to build up around the table as he casually placed the lot on twenty-seven red, swelling to an excited murmuring when he came up again. Almost imperceptibly the crowd thickened, eyes avariciously calculating the value of the winnings so far. André picked up one of the new white plaques and added it to the original stake still standing on number twenty-seven—watched it go down without emotion. A sigh ran through the spectators, half of disappointment, half of relief. For some the only thing worse than losing oneself was to watch someone else win.

André put another of the white plaques into Ruth's hand. "You try."

"Oh no, I couldn't!" She was uncertain of the actual face value of the plaque but aware that each one must represent a fairly large amount to have drawn such attention on a gathering like this. "What if I lose?"

She had spoken in English, attracting the attention of those nearest to them. André answered in French. "Then you lose."

"Place your bets, *mesdames, messieurs*," intoned the croupier, and Ruth took a deep breath before leaning forward to place the plaque squarely on the red seven.

The wheel seemed to be revolving for a year, the colours merging into one continuous streak. Then it was slowing, and there was the breath-restricting clatter of the tumbling ball, the craning necks. "Black twenty-four," said the croupier without expression.

Ruth pressed herself to her feet with a wry shake of her head when André suggested another go. The loss might not bother him; it certainly bothered her. One thing was certain, she could never become a gambler—not in any serious fashion. The strain was too much for her.

"A bad evening for you, André," said a familiar husky voice behind her. "You are not usually so unlucky at the tables."

"There are other times," he returned equably as Simone came into view on the arm of a heavily built, dark-skinned man some twenty years her senior. His own hand rested under Ruth's elbow as he acknowledged the other man. "But the house is the only real winner, eh, Youssef?"

"But of course." The other's voice was cultured, his manner expansive. "Will you not introduce me to your so charming wife, André?"

The hand under her elbow tightened fractionally. "Ruth, this is Youssef Malhabi, the owner of this place."

The Algerian took the hand Ruth shyly proffered and bowed low over it. "Enchanted!"

She murmured the appropriate response, self-conscious beneath Simone's critical gaze. Once again she found herself wishing for just a little of the other's unfailing poise and assurance, her familiarity with this kind of life. As André's wife *she* would have been entirely in her element. He had known that she would be here at the casino, of course. That had been his whole reason for suggesting an evening he must have realised was hardly her own environment. Anything just to see the woman he should have married.

Ruth willed steel into her body and a smile to her lips as she met the amber eyes. It wasn't Simone's fault that things had turned out the way they had. If anyone at all was to blame for the mess it was herself for creating the situation in the first place. André would never love her. Not as she wanted him to love her. At the best their marriage could only be a pale shadow of the real thing. In that moment something which had been slowly opening within her abruptly closed again.

CHAPTER SEVEN

"Perhaps you will do me the honour of joining Simone and myself for dinner?" asked Youssef formally. "It has been many weeks since we last talked together, André."

"Yes," the other agreed on a dry note. "Is this invitation in aid of business or pleasure, Youssef?"

"Something of both," returned the Algerian equably. "I have a proposition in view on which I would appreciate your advice."

André inclined his head. "You were never one to waste opportunity." He glanced down at Ruth, expression inscrutable. "You would like to stay?"

Did she have a choice? she wondered with a flash of anger quickly subdued. "Of course," she said carefully. "Thank you, Monsieur Malhabi."

"You must call me Youssef," he said. "André and I are old acquaintances. Let us go to my apartments for a drink before we eat—unless you would prefer to dine in the hotel restaurant?"

"Not at all." Ruth wished she had had the courage to plead tiredness or something when she had the chance— although at barely gone eight-thirty in the evening she supposed that might have sounded a bit unconvincing.

The owner's private apartment was on the top floor of the hotel in what would have been called the penthouse suite in any English-speaking country. It had the air of luxury to which Ruth was becoming accustomed, thickly carpeted throughout, and liberally sprinkled in the lounging areas with soft upholstered chairs and deep leather couches. The soft lighting came from lamps of intricately worked metal crowned with shades in glowing silks, while on one low table was ranged a collection of jade figurines. Beyond sliding glass doors a long balcony looked out over the bay and the sparkling panorama of light which was the city by night.

"May I offer you a sherry?" asked Youssef as Ruth turned from her contemplation of the view. "Or perhaps a cocktail?"

"A sherry, I think, please," she said. "Just a small one." Nervousness impelled her to add unnecessarily, "I don't drink very much."

"I wish I could say the same," he returned on a light note as he handed over the crystal glass half filled with amber liquid. "However, a man must indulge the vices. It is the way he is made."

"The way *you* are made," put in Simone with mocking intonation. "There is no other man quite like you, Youssef."

"I trust not," he returned. "I would hate to think that I was not an original." He raised his own glass in Ruth's direction, his eyes resting with unconcealed pleasure on her face. "To unspoiled youth and beauty. André, you are a fortunate man!"

"Thank you." The other man's voice was dry. "I'm not unaware of it."

Sudden resentment swept through Ruth, lifting her chin and sparkling her eyes. Young she might be, but not too young to recognise irony when she heard it. He didn't need to underline the shortcomings of this marriage of theirs; they were only too obvious. She looked across at him standing there at Simone's side and felt her heart contract at the memory of her earlier cautious hopes. No matter how hard she tried she could never be the kind of wife he should have had. That was inescapable fact. So where was the point in trying at all? What was needed was an annulment, if only André could be made to see things straight.

Ruth could not have said afterwards what they ate for dinner that evening. All she did remember was that it all tasted like sawdust. Youssef paid her a flattering attention throughout, asking her about her former life in England and exclaiming in wonder at the realisation that this was the very first time she had been outside her own country. She had a feeling that André disliked all this emphasis on her background, yet saw no way of forestalling Youssef's questions without appearing rude. In any case, she was sure that his interest was genuine and not just the product of curiosity.

It was over coffee that André reminded Youssef a trifle brusquely of his request for advice. Youssef took up the offer right away, asking the two girls to excuse them for a few minutes while he and André talked in the privacy of his study.

As the double doors closed behind the two men, Simone leaned back in her chair and subjected Ruth to a look which made the latter stir uneasily in her seat.

"So you are now in possession of the sapphires," she said softly. "Was it your own idea to have them reset?"

"No." Involuntarily Ruth's hand went up to finger the stones. "As a matter of fact, they were a complete surprise."

"A surprise?" The other's beautifully shaped brows arched. "Are you trying to say that you knew nothing of the Dubois family jewels before André presented you with these? I suppose next you will be telling me that you were unaware he was a wealthy man at all before you came here to Algiers in the way you did."

"It happens to be the truth." Ruth kept a hold on her swiftly rising temper with an effort. She had not expected such an immediate attack; what she *had* expected she wasn't quite sure. "I didn't even know that André existed until I got here. All I had was an address."

"Really?" Simone's tone was frankly sceptical. "So you came thousands of miles just on the chance of finding a man you had never even seen, and for no other reason? You will forgive me if I find that rather difficult to believe."

"All right." Ruth was too angry now to feel any reticence about showing it. "What would *your* version be?"

Simone smiled coldly. "The obvious one. You knew about Leo's association with the Dubois family and saw your chance of sharing in it. His death at that particular moment in time was fortuitous, was it not? All you had to do was to play upon André's sympathies for your predicament, on his regard for your father and natural wish to do what was right." The amber eyes were glittering with an odd light. "You know it is the truth. You know that André does not love you."

The anger washed out of Ruth suddenly, leaving her trembling and cold. "How can you be so sure?" she said thickly, and heard the husky laugh.

"Is that not also obvious? A man cannot be in love with two women at the same time. You may bear his name, but I—" She broke off with deliberation, a glint of satisfaction in her eyes as she regarded Ruth's pale face. "Did you really believe you could ever hope to make a man like André happy? He married you out of charity, and now he finds himself trapped by responsibility." There was a slight pause before she added on a softer, insinuating note, "If you were to do the right thing yourself you would take steps to ensure that he has his freedom returned to him."

"He—would never agree." The words were torn from Ruth's lips without volition. She sat huddled into a corner of the huge couch, her face small and pinched. The only way Simone could know so much about the way things were between her and André was from André himself, and the thought of having been the subject of discussion between the two of them was almost more than she could bear. In that moment she wanted to hurt André as he had hurt her—only how did she hurt a man who had no feelings for her beyond pity? Not that it should have come as such a shock to her it put into words again. It was she who had been foolish in closing her mind and her memory to the knowledge she had gained that day in the hairdressers.

"It would depend on how you went about it," came the reply in the same soft tone. "If you gave him adequate reason—"

"I don't know what you mean." She shouldn't even be listening to this, thought Ruth numbly, but she couldn't *not* listen. It was impossible to ignore the fact that Simone was probably right in what she said. She herself was the only one who could do anything to change the situation. "What—kind of reason?"

"Quite simple." Simone examined her nails with meticulous attention. "You must make him believe that you are in love with another man. It should not be difficult. Paul Brent, for instance, is of your own nationality and already an acknowledged admirer. From what he said last night after we left the villa he would be only too ready to see you again, even at the risk of incurring André's displeasure." Her swift glance held an element of speculation. "Whatever it was that the two of you were talking about after dinner you certainly seem to have left a vivid impression on our English friend. He spent the whole of the journey back to my home bemoaning the fact that fate could be so cruel as to forbid him contact with a girl who was everything he had ever looked for."

"Please!" Ruth's voice quivered. "I don't want to know about the way Paul Brent feels—even if you are telling the truth about it." She made an effort to gain control of herself, to stop this whole horrible discussion. "I'm not going to pretend anything. If André wants to be free of me then he will have to tell me so himself."

"You know he will not do that. He has too much integrity. But if you were the one who wanted your freedom then it would be another matter." The soft tones took on an edge. "Of course, if you think so little of the man who saved your life that you would deliberately continue to ruin his then there is nothing more I can say. Perhaps the material comforts of your present situation more than compensate for the knowledge that you are not even wanted as a woman by your husband, much less loved."

Ruth drew in a tautly painful little breath. "He said—that?"

"He has no need to say it. I know from the way you are with him that he does not make love to you. No woman who had ever experienced André's love-making could fail to be changed by it. He is a man who understands the subtleties of the female mind, the needs locked deep within her. Of course, should you stay married to him you will eventually know the physical delights to be found in his arms. But what will it mean to you to be aware that he performs the functions of a husband only as a duty? How would you feel if you one day bore a child conceived without love?"

"Stop it!" Ruth was no longer huddled into the corner of the couch. She was sitting on the extreme edge, her knuckles white on the hand which gripped the armrest. "I won't talk about this any further with you!"

"Because you cannot bear to hear the truth?" Simone shook her head, her mouth contemptuous. "Then continue to hide from it!" Her tone changed abruptly as the door opened again to re-admit the two men, her eyes losing their angry brilliance, her features assuming the familiar social mask. "So soon back? Your business did not take long."

"No." Youssef looked faintly put out. "Our friend is a man of few words."

"I'm sorry I could not tell you what you wanted to hear." André's eyes were on Ruth. "You look pale. Do you not feel well?"

She took a hold on herself, pride lending a hand. Not for anything was she going to let Simone see her break down. "I feel fine, but I think I could do with a breath of air." She conjured a smile for Youssef. "Could we look at the view from the balcony?"

"With pleasure," he returned with alacrity. "I shall be very delighted to show you the sights of this town of ours by the light of the stars."

There was actually more movement of air inside than out, Ruth discovered, but she didn't care. For the moment she needed to be away from André, needed time to let this dreadful ache pass a little. She wanted, desperately, to be alone, but that was impossible just yet. She was here with Youssef, her host, and she had to make an attempt to be sociable.

"It's very lovely," she said. "So many millions of lights!"

"And behind them people, all living their separate lives," he responded, "and yet all doing the same things. Sometimes I think that life itself is futile. One acquires wealth and power in order to acquire more wealth and power, but to what aim?" He was silent for a moment, then he shook his head and turned to look at her with a faint smile. "Forgive me, I was becoming introspective, and that is no compliment to a beautiful woman. Let me feast my eyes upon you instead and envy André the constant privilege." The smile grew as he noted her response. "You must become accustomed to admiration from men. It is a natural reaction. There will be many who will look at you and want you, and even try to steal you away from André. And one day, though you cannot see it now, you will realise what a weapon you hold in your hands and learn to use it as all women do."

It was a little time before Ruth could find an answer. "I think," she said at length, "that you must have known only one kind of woman."

"Perhaps." He sounded sceptical. "Time will prove me right or wrong. In five years from now I would like to remind you of this moment and see then how you feel."

Five years from now. Where would she be then? *Who* would she be then? Ruth shivered suddenly despite the heat. "Shall we go back indoors?" she said stiffly.

Youssef made a small, semi-apologetic gesture with his hands. "I have upset you with such talk. Perhaps you may prove me wrong. I hope that you do prove me wrong. I would much like to have some of my illusions restored to me." His glance went briefly beyond her to where Simone and André sat together on the couch in conversation. "You are of a different type from the women one usually finds in our community, but then you are young, and the young are impressionable. May I offer you some small advice?" He took her silence for agreement. "Do not allow others to influence you. Stay true to yourself." His voice briskened. "And now we will return indoors."

André got to his feet as they entered the room again. "We should be going," he said. "It is getting late."

"So soon?" Youssef looked from him to Simone still sitting on the couch and seemed to read something in the glinting amber eyes. "Ah well, if you must you must. We should do this again before too long."

There was no prolonged leavetakings. That was not André's way. But Ruth was aware of his last long glance at Simone before the doors closed between them. Outside the car was waiting for them. She got into her seat, her pulses leaping to the touch of his fingers as he tucked the skirt of her dress in around her legs so that it would not get caught in the door. He was always so thoughtful, so solicitous of her comfort. Yet he would be that way with any woman. It was in his nature and meant nothing.

Tension lay thickly between them as the vehicle began to move. Glancing at the sharply etched profile, Ruth felt a dryness come into her throat. There was a look about his mouth that she did not like, a certain cruelty of line she had not seen there before. She thought she understood the emotions behind that look.

Tonight he had been in close proximity to the woman he loved, the woman he wanted above all others. And he could not have her—at least, not openly. And because of that he wanted to hurt someone. She couldn't really blame him for feeling that way, but she could and did fear his reactions. In this mood he was capable of anything.

When he spoke he made her jump. "What did you have to say to Youssef out there on the balcony?"

So he was making Youssef his excuse. Ruth brought her hands together loosely in her lap and tried to answer evenly. "Nothing very much. He offered me some advice."

"I am sure he did." His voice was dangerously soft. "I hope you'll find it of use to you."

"André—" Her throat hurt. "I know how you feel, believe me, but you—"

"You have no concept of my feelings, now or at any other time." The same note was there, an implacability she could not fail to recognise. "Nor I of yours, apparently. So we must begin again, must we not? Only this time there will be no promises, no rules. This time you'll learn to accept things the way they are."

"No, I won't!" Pride lent her voice strength. "You're the one who must learn to accept that it's no use. You've done your best—we've both done our best, but we made a mistake. If you want to begin again we could do it with an annulment. There's nothing to stop us from doing that. Without—love we have nothing anyway."

"Love?" The word came out with clipped ferocity. "What would you know about love, infant? You who never even kissed a man before you kissed me this evening!"

Her skin was hot. "That's hardly my fault!"

"So little is your fault. I suppose it was no doing of yours which began this whole sorry affair!" He paused, gaze flicking sideways to her rigidly set lips with no softening of expression. "Well, you did begin it, however unwittingly, and you're going to have to reconcile yourself to it. There will be no annulment because there will be no grounds for an annulment. As of tonight we share the same room."

Ruth made no answer because she couldn't trust herself to answer. André meant what he said. In spite of everything he would not go back on that decision taken in Bakra. Yet what he intended now was no solution either. This afternoon, when she had almost begun to believe in the possibility of them growing closer, it had been different, but now, knowing what she did know, the very thought was abhorrent to her.

It was only a little after eleven-thirty when they reached the villa, but all was in darkness. Apparently the servants had taken the opportunity for an early night themselves, obviously not expecting them back before the early hours. Maria, however, obviously believed in covering all eventualities, for she had left a flask of coffee on a tray in the outer hall where they could not miss it. Ruth shook her head without speaking when André asked her if she wanted any.

They mounted the stairs together, their footsteps loud in the silence of the house. Expecting it though she had been, she could not suppress a quivering in her limbs when André followed her into her room, but she said nothing, walking across to hang away the long silk coat before turning slowly to look at him.

It was then, faced with the husband who was more of a stranger to her than ever, that her emotions underwent a sudden and dramatic change, the numbness giving way to an upsurge of feeling closely akin to hatred. So why should he be the only one to feel bitter? What about her? She hadn't asked him to marry her; it had been entirely his own idea. If anyone had any right to regrets it was herself!

"André," she said, "if you stay here tonight I shall despise you. I promise you that!"

His expression did not change. "Then despise me," he said, and came purposefully towards her.

THE VILLETS' home lay some two miles away by road. Alighting from the car, Ruth viewed the lantern-lit courtyard and thought that apart from a few minor differences the villa could well have been the same one they had left some minutes previously. Impossible still to think of it as home, she acknowledged with a twist of her lips. In spite of everything she felt no more a Dubois now than when she had first arrived in Algiers.

André took her arm as they entered the door, his touch light and impersonal—a gesture made only in the interests of preserving some outward semblance of marital harmony, Ruth told herself with a cynicism developing daily. She summoned a smile for Eloise, con-

scious that the other woman's swift scrutiny had not
missed the shadows beneath her eyes despite the careful application of cream and powder.

"I've been looking forward to this *mechou* of yours,"
she announced brightly. "It sounded fun."

"They usually are." Eloise took her hand, leaving
André to follow on behind with Louis. "Come and
see for yourself."

Behind the villa three terraces dropped away in steps
to yet another courtyard enclosed by the inevitable high
stone walls. Part of the top level had been roped off to
accommodate a four-piece combo which was just swinging into a medley of modern hit tunes for the benefit of
the dancers already taking the floor, while below another
group of guests were gathered about the slowly turning
spit on which the sheep's carcass crackled and spluttered. There were lanterns strung along the walls, highlighting the laughing, animated faces and gaily informal
colours of dresses and shirts. Voices and music created a
blanket of sound which drowned out even the incessant
shrilling of the cicadas.

"Noisy, is it not?" commented Eloise with a laugh.
"On these occasions we all feel able to let ourselves go.
Some of us you already know from last week, of
course, but the rest you will find equally friendly. Louis
will get you some wine and introduce you to one or two
people, and then it will be time for him to don his white
hat and join our chefs for the ceremony of cutting the
first portions."

A glass in one hand, Ruth found herself suddenly a
part of the chattering throng and even beginning to en-

joy herself in a superficial kind of way. Out of the corner of her eye she caught a glimpse of André following a smiling Simone on to the dance-floor, but she refused to allow even that to dampen her spirits. For tonight she was going to concentrate on having a good time and be damned to everything else. Let André do what he liked! She didn't care. He had killed what spark of feeling she had known for him five nights ago when he had used her to satisfy his longing for another woman. Since then he had made no attempt to touch her again, nor had he kept his threat to make her share a room with him. In a way, that made things even worse, because it proved that he had not really wanted *her* at all. She wished she could hate him, but there was nothing left inside her to hate with. She felt scoured of all emotion.

"You're looking very pensive all of a sudden," said a familiar English voice at her elbow, and she turned her head to see Paul Brent standing there looking at her with a faintly hesitant expression in his brown eyes. "Am I allowed to talk to you?" he added. "Or is your husband still sore at me over the other night?"

Ruth found a smile and a light shrug. "It's a party, and my husband is otherwise occupied at the moment. Still enjoying your leave, Paul?"

"Let's say I'm going through all the motions." The pause was brief. "Look, I don't want to harp on it, but I hope I didn't cause you any bother that night. I was an idiot to ask in the first place. It was just that I thought he might not mind, with our both being British."

"Forget it," Ruth advised on an edge of impatience,

wondering why some people found it so necessary to
rake up matters best put out of mind. "It really doesn't
matter. Who did you come with tonight?"

"Simone," he said. "Although I've hardly seen her
since we arrived."

Ruth didn't know why she had bothered to ask. Of
course Simone would have brought him. She wasn't
the type to give up easily when it came down to something *she* wanted. She stole a glance towards the dance-
floor where the two of them were still together. André
was facing this way, but it was too dark to see his expression, although he appeared to be finding great interest in whatever it was that Simone was saying to
him. They moved together with the ease of long cus-
tom, she acknowledged—a handsome couple, well
matched by any standards. If they had already been
married when she came in search of her father none of
this mess would have happened. She would have been
alone, it was true, but free. Whereas now—

She gave herself a mental shake and looked back at
Paul. "Are you going to ask me to dance?"

"With pleasure," he said. "I was working up to it."

André glanced their way as they took to the floor, his
mouth visibly tautening. Dog-in-the-manger, thought
Ruth, and studiously ignored him. Paul danced well,
easy to follow. It was a relief to be with a man who had no
hidden depths. Listening to his lighthearted, inconse-
quential chat she could relax and be herself again for the
first time in weeks—or at least, as close to herself as she
was likely to get. She felt a pang of nostalgia for the innocent days of her girlhood. Things had been so simple

then, although she had failed to appreciate the fact at the time. Growing up was such a complex affair. One had to learn to be so many different people. Like now, for instance, putting on a bright party face when inside she felt more like curling up in a corner somewhere.

"Sorry," she said, realising suddenly that Paul was waiting expectantly. "What did you say?"

He looked wry. "I thought you weren't quite with me. I said they've started dishing out the food. Would you like to eat?"

"Why not?" A sense of recklessness swept over her. "Eat, drink and be merry, etcetera. Let's get some more wine too."

Louis was wielding the tools of his temporary trade when they reached the front of the throng gathered about the spit, slicing rough cuts of meat on to waiting plates. There were no knives and forks. One simply took hold of the mutton in a napkin and bit straight into it, tearing off strips with the teeth. On a long side table set to one side of the courtyard there were great dishes of salad and assorted pickles; long crusty loaves ready cut into thick wedges; cheeses of every imaginable type. Ruth wondered what would happen to all the food which would inevitably be left over. There was enough here to feed a hundred people, never mind forty or fifty!

"Fun, this!" said Paul, wiping the mutton fat from his chin for the umpteenth time. "These folk certainly know how to live it up! I'm going to have some of the lads back at base green with envy when I tell them how I spent my leave. In fact, I'd say that cousin of Simone's is going to be a very popular guy!"

"Simone might not take kindly to a constant stream of lonely oilmen turning up at her door," Ruth observed over the rim of her glass. "Cousin or no cousin, I can't see her keeping open house."

"Oh, I don't know. She certainly made me feel welcome enough."

With good reason, she thought. Paul must have seemed like the answer to a prayer. He might even have been the answer to hers under other circumstances. Good-looking, fun to be with, a good job—he was everything a girl was supposed to want in a man. Certainly very different from the one she had finished up with. Her throat contracted suddenly. She held out the empty glass to Paul. "Would you like to get me a refill?"

"I think," said André quietly at her back, "that you have had quite enough for the moment."

Ruth did not turn. "Who's counting?"

"I am," he said. His hand came over her shoulder and took the glass from her and placed it on the nearby table. "We will dance."

Ruth smiled with deliberation at Paul, who was looking distinctly ill at ease. "Do excuse us."

"Sure," he said hastily. "Of course."

André waited until they were on the floor before stating his mind. "I thought we had agreed that you were not to encourage Paul Brent again. Is this how you keep your word?"

"I could hardly ignore him," she pointed out stiffly.

"I wouldn't have expected you to ignore him. But neither do I see any adequate reason for spending the last hour with him alone. Are there not enough people here to suit your tastes in variety?''

"I'll tell you what," she said on the same surge of recklessness. "I'll circulate if you will."

The contraction of his fingers into the small of her back was painful enough to bring an exclamation to her lips. "Don't make conditions with me," he clipped. "Do you wish me to take you home?"

Something inside her twisted sharply. "Like last time?" she murmured with deliberation, and had the satisfaction of feeling him tense.

"No," he answered at last very quietly. "You need have no fears on that score."

Over his shoulder Ruth saw one of the women to whom she had been introduced earlier nodding and smiling and found herself automatically returning the gesture. She had a strong feeling that André himself would be wearing a falsely pleasant expression for the benefit of those who happened to be looking. No one must know that all was not perfect between them. The pride of the Dubois name rested upon it. Her own pride came to her rescue. "I suppose I should be grateful for that."

He said harshly, "Gratitude is the last thing I want from you!" He waited a moment, then added on a more controlled note, "Perhaps a period apart might be of some help to us both. I have a cousin in Kabylia who would be glad to have you visit her for a few days. How would that suit?"

Simone was on the lower terrace leaning gracefully against a stone urn as she looked into the eyes of the man with her. Ruth wondered if she already knew of André's plans to send her away, or if he planned to surprise her. Either way, the Frenchwoman would not be the loser. Her type never was. Well, let them have one another. She couldn't care less. Maybe Simone could even persuade André to give her her freedom.

"Fine," she said without a tremor. "How soon can we go?"

His hands were hard. "I'll take you this coming Sunday, if you can wait that long."

Sunday. And today was Friday. André, it seemed was the one who couldn't wait to have her out of the way. Ruth closed her mind and her heart to all but the fiercely reiterated wish that Sunday was already here.

CHAPTER EIGHT

KABYLIA LAY some hundred or so kilometres from Algiers, a region rich in olives and figs rising to the Djurdjura mountains in the south. Up here the air was clean and pure, the sunlight sharper, unobscured by the faint haze of the coastal plains. Time and progress had touched but not spoiled the wild beauty of the landscape with its thickly forested hills and towering backcloth. Here, in the villages crowning every crest, the old traditions still held sway over the new, and perhaps always would.

The fig plantation owned and run by Claudine Dubois was situated some little way outside a small but lively market town. From the standard of living which Claudine obviously enjoyed, Ruth surmised that the plantation was a prosperous business in its own right, although she was certain that even if it had not been so no one bearing the Dubois name would be allowed to live in any other fashion.

Claudine herself was about ten or eleven years older than André, and unmarried, a thin wiry woman with cropped dark hair and sharp, intelligent features. She greeted André with brisk affection, swept a shrewdly observant glance over Ruth's slight frame and reached some apparent conclusion of her own before taking them both indoors to the cool simplicity of her terrazzo-floored living room.

"It must be six months since you were last here, André," she said when they had been provided with drinks. "How long can you stay?"

"Only until this evening, I'm afraid," he answered, reclining easily into the rattan chair. "But I'd like to leave Ruth here with you for a few days. She finds the heat in Algiers too much for her at present."

"That is hardly surprising at this time of the year. I would no doubt find it so myself." The dark eyes turned towards Ruth again. "André should have brought you here to recuperate after your illness. The town is no place in which to regain one's health and vitality. You look even younger than I had imagined, but perhaps that is because you are so *petite*." A smile flashed briskly and kindly. "We shall have to fatten you up a little on our country fare."

"But not too much. It wouldn't suit her." André sounded abrupt. "How do you find that new manager of yours? Is he still living up to expectations?"

"But of course. He would not still be here if he were not." Claudine accepted the change of topic without demur. "If profits are down on last season it will be the fault of market fluctuations, not the standard of the crop. Henri has done more than his share."

"Really?" Her cousin's regard was quizzical. "You apparently knew what you were doing when you offered him the job."

"The Dubois always know what they are doing—and

why." A faint smile passed across Claudine's thin features. "You will meet him again tonight before you leave. He is calling in after dinner."

"A business call?"

"Of course." She turned her attention once more to Ruth. "You are very quiet. The journey tired you?"

"A little. It was very hot in the car." Ruth hesitated, needing to be on her own for a while yet not knowing quite how to effect it. "Would you think me impolite if I lay down for half an hour?" she asked at length.

"But not at all. It is a most sensible thing to do." Claudine got to her feet. "I will show you your room. Kala can prepare it for your stay with us later."

Ruth studiously avoided André's eyes as she followed the older woman through the sliding doors on to a wide veranda which ran round three sides of the villa. Her bedroom faced the mountains; a double room, she was quick to note. The pale green walls and white paintwork looked cool and refreshing. On the bed lay a white crochet coverlet which brought a pang. It was very much like the one she had used on her own bed back in Oxford.

"Some friends sent it out from England," Claudine explained, following her gaze. "Would you like me to have tea brought to you here in about an hour, or will you be joining us again for refreshment?"

"I'll come out to you," Ruth rejoined, squashing the impulse to plump for the former offer. André would be furious if she made a point of keeping out of his way all afternoon. "It's very kind of you to go to all this trouble, Claudine."

"No trouble at all. I wanted André to bring you out to see me before this, but he has been too busy. He works too hard and too long. Now that he has a wife he must take more time off. Could you not have persuaded him to stay at least overnight?"

Ruth shook her head, forcing a smile. "As you say, he's too occupied with other matters right now. He—he only suggested this for my sake."

"Yes." Claudine looked as if she wanted to say more, but refrained. "So he indicated. I can only hope that you won't find it too quiet alone with me. I live the life of a semi-recluse these days."

"I don't think so." Ruth speculated briefly on the possibility of some special reason for Claudine's retirement to country life, but her own problems were too pressing to allow for any deep interest on someone else's behalf. "I'm looking forward to seeing the plantation, for one thing."

"I shall get Henri to take you round," Claudine promised.

Left alone in the quietness of the room, Ruth kicked off her shoes and turned back the white cover before lying down on the bed. There was an electric fan set into the ceiling which revolved with a slow rhythmic motion that was hypnotic. Through the shuttered doorway came the repetitive cry of some bird, a plaintive sound which seemed to mock her. She wondered if André would discuss her with Claudine at all, and came to the conclusion that it was unlikely. He had brought her here because he could trust his cousin to keep an eye on her, but that did not mean that he would be willing to share the full depth of his problems. Only Simone was allowed to know the real truth of their relationship, and even she might not know quite all of it. Not now.

She must have slept, for when next she looked at her watch the hour was almost up. Feeling outwardly if not inwardly refreshed, she tidied her hair and smoothed down her dress, then applied a touch of lipstick in an attempt to bring some sparkle to her face.

André was coming along the veranda when she left her room. He stopped when he saw her, and waited for her to reach him, hands thrust casually into the pockets of his immaculate white slacks.

"I was coming to check on you," he said. "Claudine has ordered tea specially for you. Have you quite recovered from the strain of the journey?"

She stiffened at the irony but answered levelly, "More or less. This is a restful place."

"Yes," he agreed, "it is. Perhaps because it offers so few distractions."

No Paul Brents, for instance. Ruth knew then that he did not intend her to have the opportunity of seeing the young Englishman again. By the time she returned to Algiers he would have made sure that Paul was gone. That meant that she would have to be here at the plantation for at least two weeks, not the few days he had spoken of. Well, that was fine by her. She had no wish to go back.

The afternoon dropped swiftly into night. Because of André's coming drive back to the capital, dinner was served early, but Ruth could not eat a great deal. Despite the comparative coolness of the night there was something oppressive in the atmosphere around the table. She was relieved when the meal was over at last and they could separate across the width of the living room with their coffee.

It was gone eight-thirty when the plantation manager put in his promised appearance. He was a big, heavy man in his mid-forties with broad, honest features and a slow deliberate way of speaking as if he liked to weigh each word before putting it down. His manner towards Caludine was respectful but by no means servile. From the easy way in which he accepted her offer of a cognac and took a seat it was apparent that this was by no means his first semi-social visit to the villa.

He remained just as calm and unruffled during the following twenty minutes or so of André's business-like questioning. Once or twice Ruth stole a glance in Claudine's direction during the catechism, to find her listening to the conversation with no visible sign of resentment at this taking over of her role by a man ten years her junior. She supposed that a lifetime of acknowledging the males of the family as the automatic leaders had to bring about a lasting effect. It was probably a part of her own problem that she could not bring herself to take that secondary role as easily.

André eventually left at ten. For the look of the thing, Ruth went out with him to the car, although she would have preferred to say her goodbyes in the company of the others. The night air was delightfully cool on her skin, and thick with sound. Down through the trees she could see the twinkling lights of the little town and catch the distant sound of music mingling with the shrilling of the crickets. Perhaps some kind of fiesta was in progress. These people seemed to need so little excuse for celebrating.

"I'll come again next weekend," said André after a moment or two during which he appeared to be waiting for her to say something. His face was austere in the moonlight.

"To take me back?" she asked softly, and saw a muscle twitch in the side of his jaw.

"That depends a great deal on you," he returned. "Until you can bring yourself to accept the fact that marriage is not a garment which can be cast off if found not to your taste, we're better apart. When I do take you back to Algiers I shall want a wife who is prepared to make some real effort towards effecting a proper relationship, not a child who weeps into her pillow because her romantic dreams weren't fulfilled. Think hard on that."

He opened the car door. Ruth watched him get into his seat and start the engine and knew a sudden desperate urge to beg him to stay. Only the memory of what he was returning to kept her still and silent as he put the car into motion away from her. He had already made his choice in bringing her here at all. Let him go to Simone!

The following two days passed with grinding slowness. Ruth ate and slept, chatted in somewhat desultory fashion with Claudine from time to time, and explored the immediate surroundings to the villa. On the second morning Henri drove her round the plantation. She listened attentively to everything he had to tell her about the growing and harvesting of the fig, and managed enough of a show of intelligent comprehension to apparently satisfy him, but could not have repeated one word of what she had learned had she been asked. She felt as though she were living in some kind of limbo waiting for the weekend to come round again. What was going to happen then she didn't even try to consider just yet.

She was out on the veranda on the Wednesday when Kala came out to tell her that she had a visitor. The sight of Paul Brent standing in the arched entrance hall was enough of a surprise to jerk her momentarily out of the apathy of the last few days. He was the last person she had expected to see.

"Simone gave me your address," he proffered without waiting for her to ask the obvious question. "There's a flap on back at the base and I'm flying back out there tomorrow." He hesitated, obviously not quite as sure of himself as he was trying to make out. "I wanted to see you again before I left. I thought perhaps we might have a run down into that town I came through on the way here and have lunch. You haven't eaten yet?"

Ruth shook her head, uncertain as to how to reply. What on earth was Paul thinking of coming here like this? What would André do when he heard of it? André. The thought of him hardened her heart again. Why should she worry about his reactions? What right did he have to object anyway, considering the way he was no doubt spending *his* free time this week.

"I hardly think—" she began, and stopped abruptly

as Claudine appeared in the archway leading through to the living room.

"Kala told me we had a visitor," said the newcomer, giving Paul a comprehensive scrutiny. Her smile was cool. "A friend of yours, Ruth?"

"Yes." It was Paul who answered on a faint note of belligerence. "We come from the same part of the country back home. I'm Paul Brent. I was just asking Ruth if I might take her out to lunch. I have to leave Algiers tomorrow, you see, and—"

Claudine's thin eyebrows had lifted just a fraction. "I hardly think that would be suitable," she interrupted smoothly. "However, you are welcome to stay and eat with us." Her glance came round to Ruth. "Take Mr. Brent through to the veranda. He must be thirsty after his journey. I will tell Kala to lay another place."

Ruth led the way in silence, hating the position in which Paul had put her. Claudine could hardly be blamed for her attitude. So far as she was concerned the situation was improper, to say the least. She would go along with it up to a point, but that did not include allowing her cousin's wife out of her sight with a man she did not know. That she was going to require some explanation later on was very apparent.

"You shouldn't have come," she said when they were outside. "You know you shouldn't, Paul. What made you do it?"

"I told you—I had to see you before I went back." There was an urgency in his voice. "Look, we're obviously not going to get much time to talk on our own, so I'm going to have to make it quick." He drew a breath,

his eyes on her face. "Ruth, is it true that you and
André are breaking up?"

Her body and mind went rigid for a long, horrible
moment. "Who—told you that?" she got out after
what seemed an age.

"Simone." He hesitated. "She wouldn't have told
me if she hadn't known how I feel about you, Ruth."

"How you feel about me?" She stared at him, eyes
dark. "Paul, we've met just twice. How can you possibly know *what* you feel about a person after such a
short time?"

"I knew the very first moment I saw you," he said.
"Honestly, Ruth, it happens like that sometimes." He
moved towards her pausing when he saw her slight
withdrawal. "All right, I won't touch you, I promise.
Only you have to believe me." He was speaking in low
tones but with a note of pleading. "I know it's far too
soon to be saying all this, but I wanted you to know
before I went back that I'll be there if you want me.
Annulments don't take as long as divorce, and I expect
a man of André's importance can get it through even
quicker than most. I realise you don't feel the same
way about me yet, but we get on so well and have so
much in common that I think you possibly could some
day. Anyway, you're going to need somebody—although I don't suppose André will leave you without
an arrangement of some kind. Not that that has anything to do with my being here," he tagged on hastily.
"I wouldn't give a damn if he left you without a penny.
All I'm trying to say is—"

"Don't!" She was shaking. "Please, Paul, don't say

any more. You've said too much already. I can't discuss this with you, and Simone had no right to."

"She did it for my sake." He looked at her for a long searching moment and an element of defeat came into his expression. "She seemed to believe that you had some kind of feeling for me too, but it appears she was wrong, doesn't it?"

"Yes, she was," Ruth said it quietly and with dignity. "I'm sorry, Paul, but I could never feel the way you want me to, no matter—" her voice faltered just a little— "no matter what happens. Simone has used you for her own ends, I'm afraid." She turned away from him, unable to bear the look in his eyes. "I think it would be better if you just went away again."

"Ruth." Again the note of appeal. "This is my fault, not Simone's. I know I've done it all wrong. I didn't have time to think properly. All right, I'll go, but only if you'll say that I can keep in touch with you. I'll be getting the rest of my leave as soon as this trouble is over, and by then—"

"No!" She could stand no more. "I told you, it's no good. I don't want to see or hear from you ever again. After this it would be impossible. Now, please go away!"

"I think that leaves little room for misinterpretation, Mr. Brent." Claudine spoke very quietly but with an air of finality as she stepped into view from behind the curve of the rattan screen which broke up this section of the veranda from the rest. "Would you prefer me to accompany you to the door, or can you find your own way out?"

Paul looked from her to Ruth's averted face and shook his head. "I'll take myself off, thanks. As you say, there's obviously nothing to stay for." He paused biting his lips. "I'm sorry, Ruth, I got it all wrong. I won't bother you again. I hope things turn out right for you."

There was a long silence after he had gone. Ruth listened to the sound of the car engine fading into the distance and tried to find the necessary courage to turn round and face Claudine. How much the other had overheard she wasn't sure, but it had obviously been enough. She wondered if she had deliberately listened, and decided that it hardly mattered. Sooner or later she would have had to know the facts of her cousin's marriage, and from what Simone had apparently told Paul it would be out in the open soon enough. The only point she did not appear to be aware of was that an annulment was no longer possible, but no doubt that wouldn't worry her too much. She had won.

"Well?" It was Claudine who spoke first, her voice calm and reasonable. "Do you have nothing at all to say to me?"

Ruth had to turn then. "I'm not sure what you want me to say," she managed. "You probably realised that things weren't quite right between André and me when he brought me here."

"Of course. I am not a fool. A man does not deposit his bride of a few weeks with a relative without good cause." She paused, her gaze softening as it rested on Ruth's drawn features. "Would you like to talk about it? Perhaps a woman might be of help where a man fails to understand."

A faint warmth tinged Ruth's cheeks. "There's nothing really to talk about. André made a mistake in marrying me and now he realises it. It's Simone Chantal he wants. It always has been Simone. He only married me because he felt responsible for me."

"You mean because of your father?" Claudine looked thoughtful. "I wouldn't have imagined that an adequate reason for André to have taken such a step." She went on in a different tone, "I met Simone Chantal on two occasions the last time I was in Algiers. She is very beautiful, but not the kind of woman I would have wanted André to marry—not the kind I would have *expected* him to marry. What makes you so certain that she is the cause of the trouble between you and André?"

"I didn't say she was the cause," replied Ruth wearily. "She just happens to be *one* of the reasons why our marriage was never likely to work out, but it was doomed to failure even without her."

"Why?" The question was gentle.

"Because I'm not equipped to live with a man who doesn't love me." It was painful to say, but it had to be said. "I know men regard these things differently, only I can't. Especially knowing that he and Simone—" She broke off.

"You think Simone is his mistress?" Claudine spoke matter-of-factly. "Perhaps you are right at that. If a man is denied the favours of his wife he will find solace

elsewhere. That is a fact of life. As to love"—she
shrugged—"you are hardly giving that emotion a
chance to develop by keeping him at a distance from
you. Men are not romantics by nature; their emotions
are basically far more physical than ours. They can
learn to regard one woman as necessary to their happiness in a way that others are not, but only if she is
capable of loving as much with her body as she does
with her heart."

Ruth's head was down, her mouth vulnerable. "That's
assuming that I do love him."

"And you do not?" Claudine's tone was sardonic.
"You must think me blind if you expect me to believe
that. If you have no love for André why have you
looked the way you did these last few days, as if all the
life had gone out of you? And why did you appear so
stricken just now when your young friend spoke of an
annulment? If you didn't love André you would have
been glad to hear that he was planning your freedom."

It was true, and Ruth knew it—the knowledge she
had been fighting to conceal from herself since Sunday
night when she had watched André drive away from
her. Only it was too late. He had given in, decided to
rectify his mistake. Sending Paul out here had simply
been a gesture of triumph on Simone's part.

"I don't want to talk about it any more," she said in
a tight little voice. "I'm sorry, Claudine, but you don't
understand. I won't fight Simone for him."

"Then you deserve to lose him. If the man you love
is not worth fighting for then who is? You could do
worse than to learn from Simone herself. She lets noth-

ing stand in the way of what *she* wants. But of course she is French, and a Frenchwoman does not sit back and wait for a man to fall in love with her. She *makes* him love her!''

"You can't shame me into it." Ruth turned abruptly away. "If André wants her then he can have her. I'll tell him so myself when he comes at the weekend."

Claudine sighed, and shrugged. "Have it your own way. We had better go and eat."

It was a long, dragging afternoon, Ruth spent it on her bed with the veranda doors closed against the light and a dull void inside her. At five she got up and took a shower, put on a crisp white cotton and went along the veranda to have the tea and sandwiches Kala had prepared. Claudine greeted her pleasantly, and talked about the plantation and some planned extensions to the villa, suggested a drive over to her nearest neighbours the following morning and a trip into the town for lunch. She didn't mention André at all. Ruth assumed that she had decided there was nothing to be gained from discussing the situation any further, and agreed with her. From now until Saturday it would remain a closed subject.

They were almost through dinner when they heard the car coming up the incline from the town. Very little traffic used that road, especially after dark, and Henri lived on the other side of the plantation, so it couldn't be him.

"It won't be coming here," said Claudine, glancing at the time. "It is too late for visitors in these parts, unless by invitation."

She was proved wrong when the vehicle turned in at the villa entrance gates and came to a stop on the forecourt. Ruth caught a glimpse of her reflection in one of the mirrors lining the end wall, face tautly drawn. She made no move when André came in through the arch from the living-room, just sat there looking at him.

He made no attempt to offer a greeting to his cousin, concentrating all his attention on his wife. There was a leashed violence in his manner.

"I have one question to ask you," he clipped. "Did you receive Paul Brent out here today?"

Claudine rose unhastily to her feet. "I will see about the coffee," she said. "You will have some too, André?"

He looked at her then, a long look which seemed to read some unspoken message in the dark eyes so like his own. "Thank you," he said, "but later, perhaps. I wish to speak with Ruth alone." His glance returned to her. "We will go outside."

She rose without a word and accompanied him, her head held high. Out on the veranda he brusquely invited her to a seat but did not take one himself, moving to stand with his back to the rail so that his face was in shadow.

"What arrangements have you made with Brent?" he demanded. "You will tell me, if we are here all night."

"None." Her voice was low and tremulous. "Paul is leaving Algiers tomorrow. What arrangements could I have made?"

"To have him come for you here and take you with

him. Do you think I have no recollection of the first time we met him? He was not due to return from his leave for another week or more—if he ever intends to return." The last on a savage note. "If I had been able to find him tonight he would have no stomach for a journey of any kind for a long time to come. And after tonight neither will you. No matter how much you might hate the thought, you're my wife and you're staying my wife. Attempt to run away from me, with Brent or anyone else, and I'll come after you and fetch you back, so you may as well reconcile yourself to your position. There's no escape, Ruth. The vows we took in that mission chapel were for better or for worse, and I have no intention of going back on them. Furthermore"—his tone was inexorable—"I've no intention of putting up with the present state of affairs between us. You can despise me if you wish, but this time tears won't move me. Perhaps the sooner you're provided with a family the sooner you'll settle down." He paused, added harshly, "Now go and pack your things. I'm taking you back with me."

A child conceived without love—Simone's words like poison in her mind. So the Frenchwoman had not, after all, got all that she had wanted. Sending Paul out here had been a last desperate attempt which had not worked out. But she still had too much.

"I won't come with you willingly, André," she said without emotion.

"Very well," Jaw set, he reached out and jerked her to her feet. "We'll leave your things until another time."

Claudine had the coffee all ready for them. She looked from one to the other of them with changing expression, taking in the hand still firmly holding Ruth's arm.

"André, you can't go this way," she said. "You are in no fit state of mind to drive all the way back to Algiers tonight."

"I drove all the way out without mishap," he returned. "I'm sorry, Claudine, but I must ask you to stay out of this. You can have no concept of my state of mind without knowing all the details of the situation." He met her eyes and broke off, a bitter comprehension in his own. The hand holding Ruth tightened its grasp cruelly. "I see. Apparently my wife can discuss her problems with everyone except me!"

"*I* am not everyone," returned his cousin mildly. "Neither did I need to be told most of it. Look to your own faults, André. You may not have made it easy."

"If I haven't," came the brittle reply, "then the matter is about to be rectified. I'll telephone you when we are safely arrived."

Claudine made no further attempt to dissuade him. She came out with them to the car, kissing Ruth on both cheeks before she got into her seat. "It will be all right," she murmured. "You will see."

Ruth waited until they were through the town and heading towards the coast before she spoke at all. "Who else am I supposed to have talked to apart from Claudine?" she asked into the taut silence.

André glanced at her with no softening of his features. "Who else indeed? If you could be so frank with someone you like as little as Simone what, I wonder, have you imparted to Eloise and Paul Brent? There are few things I consider worse than having one's private affairs made the subject of open discussion. Have you no pride at all, that you parade our difficulties for the entertainment of all?"

"Pride?" The word came out thickly. "What pride am I supposed to have left after what *you've* said and done! I didn't tell Simone anything; she already knew it all from you. And what she didn't know she could guess. Frenchwomen are very perceptive that way, or hadn't you noticed?"

"From me?" He swung the car suddenly and sharply into the side of the road and brought it to a halt, turning to look at her with an expression she found bewildering. "Simone learned nothing from me. She would be the last person I would take into my confidence."

Ruth gazed at him, eyes wide and dark. "But you're in love with her," she whispered. "You were going to marry her."

"Was I indeed?" He sounded shaken himself. "In that case, why did I marry you?"

"Because you felt you owed it to my father to look after me." She was trembling with the effort of keeping her hopes from running away with her, of trying not to believe too soon the message her senses were beginning to convey. "Because you felt responsible for me. That—that's what everyone else thought."

"Everyone else! Who is everyone else?" He was suddenly and furiously angry. "Who the devil filled you up with that kind of rubbish? Simone?"

"Not initially. I—I heard some talk in the hairdressers when Eloise took me into town that day."

"You heard some talk in the hairdressers," he repeated blankly. "You hear some stupid, speculating gossip and from that manage to deduce *my* feelings!" His hands gripped hard on the wheel, curving over the rim as if to stop himself from reaching out and shaking her. "Did it never occur to you that there were other ways of securing your future?"

"Yes. And I wished then that you had found one." She didn't know whether she wanted to laugh or to cry. "Is it so surprising that I accepted that deduction at its face value? You actually mentioned those self-same reasons when you first suggested marriage."

"I also mentioned a lot of other things." The anger was fading. "If I missed anything out it was only because you were so young and unworldly that I was afraid of rushing you. Had circumstances been different I would have waited until we had time to get to know one another a little better before attempting to show my feelings, but it was best to have our relationship made official as soon as possible." He looked into her stunned green eyes and smiled faintly. "I realise that you may never learn to love me the way I want you to, but the fact that you feel enough to have been jealous of Simone is a good start. If it helps, there was never any possibility of my marrying her at any time. The only times I've seen her since you came into my life are those when we've met her together. The last time was the night we had dinner with her and Youssef." Momentarily his mouth hardened again. "The night she taunted me over details of our marriage I thought she could only have learned from you."

"I suppose she did learn them from me," Ruth admitted, remembering. "As I said before, she is very good at guessing."

"And at manoeuvring, apparently. It was Simone who rang me late this afternoon to tell me that Paul had been out here to see you."

"She sent him here, in the hope that I might take advantage of a suggestion she once made. She was convinced that you would let me go if you thought I was in love with another man."

"Was she?" He said it softly, dangerously. "It appears that I've underestimated her all the way along."

By how much he would never know, Ruth decided. It no longer mattered. Simone had lost after all. André loved her. He loved *her*! Nothing mattered but that.

He was watching her, trying to assess the play of expression across her face. "What about Paul Brent?" he asked. "*Did* you intend using him to get away from me?"

"No. Not at any time." She looked back at him with eyes gone misty. "And especially not now. I don't want to get away from you, André—ever. Maybe I don't know very much about loving yet, but I'm learning by the minute."

He searched her features almost unbelievingly for a long moment before reaching out to take her into his arms. She met his kiss halfway, turning up her mouth with all the loving warmth in her heart, knowing the security in being loved in return.

"When did you start loving me?" she murmured some time later with her cheek pressed against his, and felt him smile.

"The moment I saw you, I think. You were so small and valiant—a lovely young innocent come halfway across the world in search of a dream. I wanted to keep you that way, to protect you from disillusionment. Instead I took you into the desert and put you through an ordeal few women could have withstood."

"And saved both our lives." She put her lips to the line of his jaw, savouring her new-found confidence. "I want to go back to the desert with you, André. I want to sleep under the stars again. Will you take me?"

"Yes," he said. "Only this time we won't get ourselves lost."

PORTRAIT OF JAIME

Portrait of Jaime
Margaret Way

Jaime's joy in getting to know her grandfather was marred by his illness and the hostility plainly shown by the rest of the family — her uncles, aunts and cousins.

In a way she could understand it. Her grandfather, Sir Rolf Hunter, saw in Jaime the return of his daughter, Jaime's mother, who had died when Jaime was born. And they were all afraid of Sir Rolf's attachment to her.

There was only Quinn Sterling — a vital handsome man — to back her up. And Jaime wasn't at all sure whether his interest in her was real or whether he was using her as a pawn against her grandfather....

CHAPTER ONE

JAIME DIDN'T KNOW her father had a visitor. She came up from the beach, her hair a slick wet rope over one shoulder, her face and her slender body tanned to an even gold lightly glistening with sea water. There was something about this visit she didn't know about, and the first pang of apprehension struck her. No one, except Tavia came to the beach house without an invitation. The gallery handled her father's work and most of his clients. She glanced at the Mercedes parked in the driveway and made a wry face to herself, stopping abruptly to slip her beach coat over her brief swimsuit. It was well after four and the beach was deserted, incredibly beautiful in the late afternoon sunlight. She turned at the top of the stairs and looked back at it.

Her life had been an endless procession of hide-aways: the silent inland, the bush and the mountains. She hadn't always liked them, but because she loved her father she had always kept silent. Here she loved best of all. The eternal summer of Queensland, the blue and the gold. It was a picture that would never be erased from her mind. Here, too, her father seemed happiest and painted best of all. He might never make the national galleries, but he was more than just a competent

professional artist. He had very real style and a lyrical
quality that helped him escape mediocrity. His land-
scapes and seascapes, the occasional portrait and still
life, found a ready market among collectors who demanded decorative professionalism at moderate prices.
In any event, his painting and pottery had been his sole
source of income for ten years now. If there was no
money for luxuries, they lived comfortably enough in
an arrangement Derry Gilmore fondly imagined suited
both of them, with Jaime as his dedicated unpaid
housekeeper and assistant, herself with an artistic potential he consciously avoided. Jaime was the only
person on earth Derrick Gilmore, a charming, deeply
self-centered man, had ever been known to make the
slightest sacrifices for. His wit and his talent and his
attractive appearance adequately saved him from obliv-
ion and unnecessary hardships. There had been plenty
of women in his life, but only one wife, and she had
died too easily and without protest when Jaime was
born.

Somehow with the help of several faithful and unre-
warded inamoratas, Jaime had been reared, though
from that day forward Derrick Gilmore made no mention of his wife or of his wife's family, whom Jaime
came to suspect he detested. If was almost like being an
orphan, but her father in his own way adored her. By
the time she was nineteen, she had almost forgotten
she had a mother and somehwere perhaps, a ready-
made family. Now she stood in the scented shade of
the massed oleanders, listening to the sound of voices.
Her father's charming, light drawl filled with obvious

bonhomie, and that of another in no sense gay, but dark and resonant, with a subtle glint of steel through the velvet. A voice that partly filled her with dread, because what he was saying was audible and he was talking about her.

All at once Jaime moved, running up the stairs, sliding back the glass door and entering the one large room in the house, the living-dining room. If it was attractively and imaginatively furnished, all due to her own efforts, she didn't notice as she whipped the sunglasses off the bridge of her nose.

"Jaime, love!" her father cried delightedly, a satisfied smile at her beauty, "we didn't hear you!"

"I heard you!" she said abruptly, her glance locked with that of the stranger who had come to his feet, appraising her so absolutely. "But I didn't understand the lines!"

Her father laughed again. "My daughter is a wonderful girl, Mr. Sterling, and clever too, though I expect you didn't miss that!"

"Among other things!" the stranger rejoined smoothly, responding to Derrick Gilmore's introductions and moving towards Jaime's instinctively outstretched hand. His marked attention was odd and rather frightening, but it was real and it almost defeated her. There was no hint of the immediate and often unwelcome admiration she had already become used to, but a glittering silent scrutiny she endured as long as possible. She might well have been a questionable collector's item, not a living girl, so dehumanising was that searching gaze.

She couldn't keep the tremble out of her hand and

she had to look up a good way to him. "How do you do, Mr. Sterling."

"Jaime." He held her hand for an instant only, then released it. He was a man of an added dimension. The kind of man who drew recognition, a man who belonged to a world of power and position—an unfamiliar world. He was very tall and superbly lean, with hair as black as her own and brilliant black eyes to match. A ruthless adversary if you like, with those silver points of light at the centre of his eyes, the dark, high-bred features rather remote until he favoured her at long last with a smile. It ridded his sombre dark face of its formidable quality, revealing an exact and easy command of a brand of charm her father could never hope to aspire to for all his careful study and application of that very asset. Jaime felt almost crushed into insignificance beside him with her bare feet and her wet swimsuit and her damp trail of hair. The excuse to escape was a godsend.

"I'll go and change, she said hurriedly, "I seem to be dripping sea water all over the place."

"No hurry, darling!" her father said brightly. "Mr. Sterling is staying on for a while. You'll share a meal with us, surely?" He turned to the younger man.

"If you're sure it's no bother," Quinn Sterling answered conventionally but with no trace of diffidence in his disturbing voice.

"No bother at all, my dear fellow! Jaime is an excellent cook, aren't you, darling?"

"I'll allow Mr. Sterling to discover that, as he's staying." Distrust and hostility were in her voice and

Quinn Sterling turned his dark head swiftly to acknowledge it. "I'll be glad to give an opinion, Jaime,"
he said with light mockery.

"Now what about a drink?" Derry Gilmore suggested in a tone full of lustre, but Jaime waited to hear
no more. She flew along the passageway to her room,
her skin crawling with a frightful awareness. She was
unable to even consider what lay beyond this visit.
What she had overheard and its significance alarmed
her. She only knew her own world, yet Quinn Sterling
was here to remove her from it, and all apparently with
her father's approval when he had refused her plea to
continue her art studies in the city and come home at
the weekends. It didn't make sense, nor his bogus affability. She wasn't such a child that she couldn't detect
acting on both sides.

A sick little feeling began to press down on her. She
closed her door and locked it for God knows what reason, then stepped out of her things. The small room
reflected the golden warmth of the afternoon, drying
her body. She shook out her long hair and went to the
built-in wardrobe, selecting, inexplicably, her prettiest
after-sundown dress, one she had designed and made
herself, hand-painting the ankle-length hemline with
flowers and birds. It was easy to imagine she had paid
quite a price for it, so professional was the concept and
finish, but what to wear would never be too much of a
problem to her, for she was unusually gifted at handling fabric, the design, cut-out and assembly. Irresist-
ibly her mind was drawn back to Lucy, the nicest and

kindest of all her father's women friends. Lucy, with her own small dressmaking business, had taught the young Jaime to sew, in turn delighted and surprised at her pupil's aptitude. At one time, Jaime had hoped her father would make an honest woman out of Lucy until he had told her quite plainly that Lucy under the same roof would drive him insane. That had been nearly nine years ago, but Jaime had never forgotten Lucy, nor her many kindnesses and interest in Jaime for her own sake. The rest of them had only been interested in her father. One day she would repay Lucy, but obviously not now when she was only a penniless nineteen-year-old with a few hidden talents. Well, not so hidden. A few people had provided her with a few sincere, straightforward compliments.

She had to use the hand dryer to finish off her hair, then she parted it in the centre and drew it back into a smooth shining chignon at her nape, leaving a few softening side and nape tendrils. Her mirrored face, wearing a little make-up, looked unfamiliar. She usually didn't bother except for a lip gloss to protect her mouth and no one could find fault with her skin. She mightn't look expensive, but she looked perfectly presentable. She wasn't out to impress anyone anyway.

When she went back to the living room her father gave her a sly, conspiratorial grin as if she had spent her time attempting to do just that. Quinn Sterling came to his feet and she waved him down again.

"Please don't let me disturb you. I've been eavesdropping all my life. Here, let me get you something to go with that drink!"

"Then come and join us, darling!" her father said. "Mr. Sterling has something to tell you."

"I can always listen from here. Just who are you, Mr. Sterling?"

"Better wait until you're sitting down," Derrick Gilmore suggested dryly, enjoying himself in some awful way.

Jaime shrugged again, aware that Quinn Sterling was watching her. She tipped olives into a bowl, found crackers and pretzels and cheese and got them all together in a beautiful polished wood platter with separate compartments. The men were drinking icy cold beer, so she poured herself a glass of red wine and walked down the two steps from the raised kitchen area into the living-dining room.

Quinn Sterling got up to take the platter from her and set it down on the long low occasional table her father had made with its beaten copper top. Jaime sank into the armchair opposite him, admiring the way he wore his clothes despite herself, the beautiful casual jacket and slacks, the body shirt he teamed with it. She would always have this eye for cut and line and she had to admit Quinn Sterling had a lot of things going for him. She tipped her head to one side, studying him.

"Well?"

He raised his eyes to her and she found herself flushing without even knowing why. "I don't know how much you overheard, Jaime, but I've been sent here by your grandfather."

Jaime reached out for her glass and took a sip because her mouth had gone so dry. "My *mother's* father?"

"Your mother's father!" Derrick Gilmore confirmed, his hazel eyes crinkling against the spurt of cigarette smoke he sent up.

"Glory to God!" said Jaime, in evidence of her four years at a convent school. "I suppose you realise, Mr. Sterling, I didn't even know I had a grandfather."

"Oh, you have one, darling," Derrick Gilmore said, undeniably malicious.

"The one you never told me about," Jaime shot at him, irritated and full of suspense.

"The same one," her father smiled unpleasantly. "Look here, Sterling, why don't I let you tell your own story? I haven't a decent wine to offer you for dinner. I'll just slip down to the pub while you're talking."

"There's the dry red you had no objection to last night," Jaime pointed out, frowning.

"I think our guest deserves something much better than that, my darling. You're no judge as yet. Besides, he's come a long way."

And I don't give a damn about that! Jaime thought, her eyes flashing.

"Please yourself," Quinn Sterling said dryly, not taking either of them too seriously.

Derrick Gilmore got up immediately, a slight, very attractive man, still disgustingly boyish-looking in middle age with his bleached blond hair and smooth, deeply-tanned skin. "I won't be more than ten minutes," he said, beginning the usual hunt for the car keys.

"They're in the pottery bowl, Derry," Jaime said with faint outrage. "The same place I always leave them."

"Very methodical, my daughter. She doesn't take after her dear father in that respect. Right now!" he flourished the keys before them. "Tell her the important news, Sterling. It might take a few minutes to penetrate, even allowing for the fact she's intelligent. I've kept her pretty much in the dark regarding the Borgias."

"It's very kind of you to allow me," Quinn Sterling said suavely.

"Think nothing of it!" Derrick went out quickly and after a few minutes they heard the car start up and pull away from the front of the house.

Jaime was not unduly upset at losing her father's support. He had been doing the same kind of thing for years and it had made her more than usually self-reliant. Anyway, she loved him and wasn't torn to change him. Quinn Sterling had settled back in his chair, his brilliant dark eyes taking in every aspect of Jaime's appearance, but whether he was pleased or not it was impossible to tell.

"The young Rowena," he finally offered with perceptible irony.

"Oh yes, my mother! I've only one photograph of her. It isn't very good."

"You have a mirror, haven't you?"

"So you knew my mother?" she asked eagerly.

"I saw her many times when I was a boy. Never after she married your father."

"Derry wasn't good enough, I suppose?"

"Actually, Jaime," he said rather impatiently, "your mother was engaged to my Uncle Nigel. She left him

quite literally at the altar where most of us would die of
stupid pride. He was there. The church was packed. She
wasn't—she'd run off to marry your father. Nigel
never forgave her for that. Very few men would if they
were given to high drama. Nigel was, and died poeti-
cally about six months after. But that's in the past."

Jaime couldn't take it calmly. "I'm sorry," she said,
gripping her glass. "It seems unbelievable!"

"I assure you it's quite true. I can see that it has
affected you, but it's exactly the way it happened.
You've heard of Hunter Sterling, I suppose?"

"The consulting engineers, freeways, bridges, all
that sort of thing?"

"Rolf Hunter is your grandfather. Sir Rolf Hunter.
He was knighted a few years back."

"Not for his humanity, I'm sure!" she snapped.

"Hard to take, Jaime?" he asked rather curtly.
"Your mother was Rowena Hunter." Up until now the
most beautiful woman I've ever seen, he thought dispassionately, but didn't consider mentioning it. Rowena Hunter had had that same true, rare shade of black
hair, the same exquisite Oriental blue eyes, the same
arching black brows, and neat, elegant bones, all of
which was making him angry, yet Jaime, the daughter,
had a vibrant, challenging quality that Rowena Hunter's painted face at least had lacked. Very likely, she
would inspire the same sort of spineless passion. Putting a woman on a pedestal had definite disadvantages.
In a way it was priceless, poor old Nigel's romance; the
old horror story in the family. He longed all of a sudden
to hurt this child, then immediately was irritated most

of all by himself. The whole thing was fantastic, yet he was here to take her captive. The Old Man would stop at nothing to have his granddaughter returned to him. She had her held tilted back for a moment, her eyes closed, the lovely line of her throat and chin unconsciously provocative. She couldn't help it, this pure sensuality, it clung to her like a second skin.

"So I resemble my mother," she was saying in a hushed voice.

"Almost exactly. The colouring certainly, the bone structure. Hers was an unusual beauty far more dangerous than prettiness. Your grandfather adored her. She was his only daughter. He was fond of my Uncle Nigel as well, in fact he promoted the match—one of his few mistakes. Sir Rolf and my grandfather founded the Hunter Sterling Corporation—nearly all of us in both families have gone into the firm. You have uncles and cousins you've never even heard about."

"I've no room in my heart to love them," she pointed out dryly. "They mean nothing to me. I might have been nuts about them had they dandled me on their knees. But why should my grandfather send you to me Mr. Sterling? Why should he suddenly bother now? I mean, I've never meant a thing to him for nearly twenty years."

"You can believe that, but it's not true. Anyway, I won't attempt to explain that part of it to you. I think the whole thing is a mistake. Your mother had everything, wealth, beauty, position, a fiancé who became too unhappy and morose to live without her. She threw it all up for your father. Had she lived, who knows, your grandfather might have been moved to heal the great rift in the family, but she died when you were born—tragedy all round. In fairness to Sir Rolf your father did his level best to outrage and wound everyone at the funeral. Apparently he did it to perfection, further isolating the old man."

"Surely his grief allowed him a few hasty words? I asked you before and you didn't answer me, why *now*?"

Quinn Sterling shrugged. "Human nature, perhaps. He's old now and the things that once were important to him no longer seem to matter. He wants to see you, make amends. You're not his only granddaughter. Your mother had two brothers and they have daughters a few years older than you are, but it's you he wants to see."

"The outsider?"

His autocratic dark face suggested he agreed with her. "Something like that, Jaime, and you never knew your grandfather's identity?"

"Would I say I didn't if I did?"

"Please tell me."

"I've told you, Mr. Sterling. My father has never breathed a word either about my mother or her entire family. I might have come out of a cabbage. I've heard of Hunter Sterling, of course, who hasn't? But why send you? You're not a member of my family. Why not one of my uncles or my cousins? I might have had something in common with them."

"I could have been your cousin, Jaime, perish the thought. As it happens your grandfather trusts me to handle a lot of his affairs quite outside Corporation matters. I had to come to Queensland on business in any case. It's been a little difficult to track you down. You've lived in so many places."

"Dragged up, why don't you say it?" she flared.

"Possibly because I never thought it," he said tersely, looking as though he'd like to turn her over his knee.

She stared back at him unrepentant, her dark blue eyes hazed with violet. "I suppose I should be overcome and burst into floods of grateful tears, but the fact is I don't want to. I might have needed my grandfather once, but I don't any more."

"Must I underline the fact that he hasn't long to live?"

"How old is he anyway? Late sixties, early seventies?"

"He's seventy-two and he survived a massive heart attack last year. He won't again. Aren't you curious, Jaime, even if you're determined not to be compassionate?"

Her heart seemed to twist and she hated him for his consummate ability to place her in the wrong. "You come to me, a stranger," she said a little wildly, "talking about either?"

"I'm not a stranger at all," he pointed out. "I've been used to your face since I was a small boy. There's a portrait of your mother in the drawing room at Falconer, your grandfather's home."

"I'm surprised it wasn't removed!" she flashed at him.

"It was for some years."

"I wish I had it, I would treasure it," she said impulsively.

Through the black glimmering lashes he saw the startling blue eyes ablaze with sudden tears. Her eyes were remarkable, Ming blue into mauve, the same beautiful underglaze blue he had seen in Imperial Chinese porcelain. She was an exotic young creature and once her grandfather had her, he would guard her fiercely. It was his intention anyway, that much Quinn knew.

Only the fact that his own taste didn't include young girls permitted him to sit back and study her so dispassionately. Her dress was a soft yet dense blue several shades lighter than her eyes, and it had to be a prized possession, for it was beautifully cut and designed, hand-painted in the Oriental fashion with birds and flowering sprays of blossom in pinks and jade and bluish purple. Despite her youth, she wore it with considerable panache, her flawless young skin gleaming against the duller sheen of the fabric.

Instead of being the forlorn orphan, she would hopelessly outshine her cousins, not that they weren't angry enough and shocked into bewilderment by the Old Man's decision to invite Rowena's daughter to Falconer. Only she was so beautiful and in complete contrast to what he had expected; he would have felt sorry for her, but she was a fighter, a confident young creature, not lost and lovely. There was a delicate determination and strength to those precisely cut features, shown to great advantage with her hair swept severely back to her nape. He hadn't the slightest doubt she would stir up a lot of feeling with her flame-like quality. No one, not even Rolf, would crush her if his assessment of her temperament was accurate. Perhaps she had a lot of the Old Man in her.

Something about his expression, a dark brooding, made the colour burn in her cheeks. "What are you thinking about?" she demanded.

"If I told you, Jaime, I'd regret it."

"I can't imagine my uncles and cousins would be pleased to see me," she said.

"Only your Uncle Gerard lives at Falconer with his father. His wife's name is Georgina and they have a son and a daughter, Simon and Sue-Ellen, both of them several years older than you are."

A faint tension was on him, showing itself in the set of his midnight-dark head, the hard, charming smile.

"How did your uncle die?" she asked him.

"By design," he said in a voice that completely stopped her, and she blurted:

"I can't see you suffering on a woman's account."

"You're dead right!"

"You don't like me, do you?"

"If I'm bound to answer you, I don't have to like you, Jaime, nor you me. It's not important. The thing for you to do is consider your grandfather's invitation."

"Have no fear, I will. What *is* it exactly?"

He leaned forward, not taking his eyes off her. "Come to Falconer for an indefinite period. As long as you like. An extended holiday if you like."

"And what am I supposed to do all day?"

"I'm sure that'll be no problem."

"What do my cousins do?"

"Simon has a degree in law. He's part of the firm, the Hunter Sterling Land Corporation. Sue-Ellen keeps busy pulling out all the pleasure stops."

"That's all very well, but I have to earn my living."

"What do you do now?" he asked.

"Look after my father."

"Surely he can look after himself?" He lifted one eyebrow.

"I mean I assist him with his work, the painting and the pottery—the donkey work, of course, but I have ability of my own. I wanted to do a fine arts course, but I couldn't talk him into it."

"Couldn't you do it yourself?"

"Courses have to be paid for, Mr. Sterling."

He gave her a mocking, speculative look. "Then I think you should be pretty happy to accept your grandfather's invitation. Now that I've seen you, I think he'll give you anything you want in this world."

"He can't give me my mother back or all the lost years."

"Were they lonely?"

His brilliant black eyes seemed to be raying right through her and she averted her head, her heart beating rapidly. "Of course they were. What a question! I don't think you're trying to persuade me overmuch."

"True. I think you'll make up your own mind."

She turned her head back quickly to meet those veiled dark eyes. "Or you have a very subtle way of manipulating people, Mr. Sterling. What's your position in the scheme of things?"

"Aide to the General," he said; his eyes gleaming.

"What about my uncles and cousins?"

"They're around."

"It's strange, nevertheless, that you were chosen. What were you looking for, the supreme opportunist?"

"I was looking for Rowena's daughter."

"A rare honour due to my grandfather's advanced age and mellowness. Well, your trip didn't work out as well as you thought, because I don't feel like visiting Falconer at this late stage, and I don't feel like meeting the lions."

"You ought to. You aren't the one to curl up quietly in a corner."

"I mean to shine in my own way, Mr. Sterling," she retorted.

"Can't you make it Quinn? After all, I've been calling you Jaime."

"And I didn't say you could!"

"You're not serious!" His glance travelled over her.

"Perhaps you thought you were jollying along a schoolgirl?"

'I know exactly how old you are, Jaime. I even know your birthday."

"Go on, what else?"

"That you're stubborn."

"Moderately. Surely you didn't expect me to act the dutiful, loving granddaughter—let bygones be bygones?"

"As a matter of fact I do. Your grandfather is a very rich man. I think he wants to put his affairs in order. Not the business, that's all taken care of, but family matters. You may think it extremely odd, but he adored your mother, and he's notably anxious to transfer that adoration to you."

"How charming!" She flickered him a burningly blue glance. "There's no denying a miracle has occurred to soften his old heart."

"They do happen."

"I suppose I should be generous," she pondered.

"Don't imagine him a suffering silver-haired old gentleman," he said. "Your grandfather's formidability is enormous."

"Do you like him?" she asked with concentrated attention.

"I admire him in many ways. He's brilliant and shrewd and ruthless and his business faculty is little short of genius."

"In other words, someone like you."

"Do I seem that way to you, Jaime?"

"Yes, or you're planning to be!"

"Will you come?" he asked.

He had a fascinating voice that could shrivel a woman under different circumstances, she thought. "I wonder if my mother would want me to? Did you hate my mother, by the way, for what she did to your uncle?"

"I was only a boy," he said looking at her through hooded lids.

"Children feel and erupt. I think you're fairly volcanic under that patrician remoteness."

"If you were a woman you might find out, but you're only an impudent child."

"Oh no, I'm not!" she said softly, knowing he was not to be trusted, but against her will liking the sound and the sight of him. "Anyway," she said, pretending a casualness she did not feel, "I'll have to speak to Derry."

"He's all for it!"

"I gathered as much, but what I don't know is *why*?"

Something flickered in his night-black eyes, an intolerable cynicism. "Perhaps your father has decided your mother's portion is due to you and you'd better go along and collect it."

"One powerful reason not to go at all!" she said passionately.

"Do you fear a family reaction—jealousy?"

"In a word, *no*! I don't fear one of those Christian souls. Not only did my grandfather desert me but my uncles as well. They're all pretty short on charity. What about the Sterlings? They must have known my mother well?"

"I believe they treated her like a daughter, but their love and trust was shattered when she eloped with your father. Nigel's habitual stupor, then untimely demise, eventually and understandably hardened their hearts."

"Why did she do it?" she murmured, staring at him with her glowing blue eyes.

"That's a strange question from you, Jaime. Obviously she was quite mad about your father. He's taken good care of you, hasn't he?"

"I've no complaints!" And forget the bad times, she thought.

He was silent for a minute, his dark gaze holding her still. "Family ties bind us all. Come to Falconer and meet your grandfather."

"And leave in an hour if I decide to?" she insisted.

"I'll drive you to the airport myself."

"I might keep you to that, Mr. Sterling."

"That sounds as if you're coming."

"I might take an instant dislike to him."

"As you've taken to me?"

She caught the mockery on his face and the brilliance of his gaze dazzled her. "I don't dislike you, Mr. Sterling," she said with mock gentleness, "I just don't trust you, that's all. Neither should my grandfather."

"Now why on earth should you say that?"

"There's a lot goes on behind your black eyes."

He smiled and leaned forward, catching her hand in his lean strong fingers. "I'll try not to keep anything from *you*, Jaime, if you come. And please do call me Quinn."

"I might, but deep inside me I'll think of you as a Sterling, maybe even the enemy."

"The reverse is true," he said, pinning her trembling wrist. "I'll never hurt you."

"You've wanted to at least once since we've met."

"Do you really think so?"

He released her and her hand fell away. "Men like you sometimes do feel like that."

"You'd better tell me what you mean, Jaime. You look very sheltered to me for all your bravado."

"I don't mean anyone *has* ever hurt me, I mean I can recognise male hostility."

"I could appreciate it better if you'd only sensed interest," he rejoined.

"That too."

"Well, you should be a meek little girl with sandy hair instead of a challenging beauty."

"That doesn't mean you can't be kind to me," she said.

"Does it matter anyway, Jaime?"

"No, but having you on my side would be a help rather than a hindrance."

"You're so right!"

She got up and turned on a light and it splashed down on her shining jet black hair. She was a lovely, destructive young thing, perhaps already set on her mother's path, promising all the lure of the Garden of Eden and delivering nothing. Rowena the witch had made a battlefield of his family, and made a few people desperately unhappy. What was he doing here helping her daughter to put some other poor fool in bondage? Her beauty at that moment was almost an affront and it was unstressed, unpolished and still heart-stopping. She might start off an epidemic of self-executions. Quinn nearly groaned aloud as so many memories passed before his eyes in a pitiless kaleidoscope. His white teeth clamped together and he looked towards the paintings on the wall, deliberately seeking out a safe topic.

"Do you paint yourself?"

"A little," she said, aware of the menace in him.

"Do you get paid for it?"

"No."

"What would you like to do?" he asked rather

curtly. Besides go to a man's head, he thought to himself ironically.

There was about him a palpable aura of sexual antagonism against which Jaime had to protect herself. He might say he didn't resent her, but he did. Perhaps he didn't see her as herself at all but a girl in a portrait. He realised she hadn't answered him and he turned his head to her.

"I said what would you like to do?"

"I heard you." Her blue-violet eyes met his directly and quite fearlessly. "Something creative, I think. I have potential."

"That you have, but in what field were you thinking of?"

"Women's fashions perhaps. I think I'd like to start my own business—design, cut-out assembly. I can handle the lot."

"Did you make that dress you have on?"

"I did," she said with not a flicker of self-consciousness.

"Then you obviously know what you're about, but it takes a lot more than that."

"I'm aware of it, and I'm not about to ask my grandfather to pitch in and help."

"Let it lie for a moment, Jaime. Who taught you to sew?"

"A good friend a long time ago," she said almost aggressively, "a few years at school. It's a natural flair and easy enough. I learnt it all in a quarter of the time, though the nuns were very good teachers. The only mistakes they made was in thinking all girls sew well naturally. They don't."

"I believe it. Your cousins Sue-Ellen and Leigh have never plied a needle in their lives."

"How do you know?"

"I know them quite well. In any case I've never seen them look better than you do in that dress."

"There's nothing wrong with your flattery," she said definitely.

"Why pretend?" He lifted his head and stared at her. "You know how you look."

She sighed at the hardness of his expression. "Which mightn't make my cousins so fond of me."

"Perhaps not. We'll exclude Simon and Brett."

Jaime frowned. "It's difficult to keep track of all the names. I don't really think it would work. I can see by your face you can't assure me of a warm welcome."

"That's overdoing it!" he said as though he meant it. "I thought you told me you were moderate."

"I'm not really."

"I know that. One good reason why I think you'll come."

"Do you always know how people will react?" she asked.

"I've had considerable experience. Isn't it true you like to hurdle difficulties?"

"I usually shove myself over them. If you're going to stay and have dinner with us, I'd better prepare it."

"Why don't I take you out to a restaurant? Your father won't mind."

"Well, that's a suggestion," she said, looking at him in surprise. "I sometimes feel sorry for myself."

"You're not honour bound to cook for your father

all the time. He's still a young man and he did mention
a particular friend. Tavia, isn't it?''

"He'll never marry her," Jaime said briefly.

"Why not?"

"I'm sure of it," she said rather tautly. "The flesh is
weak but the head is strong."

He laughed under his breath, a dark attractive sound.
"There's always the woman to upset a man's plans."

"I didn't ask you, are you married?"

For the first time she looked little more than a child,
an honest question in her dark blue eyes. "Don't look
so earnest, Jaime," he taunted her. "I'm not a bad
man asking you out to dinner and then a stroll on a
moonlit beach. I'm a determined bachelor."

"I can almost hear the Thank God!"

"Don't tell me!" His black eyes mocked her.

"To my certain knowledge you thought it."

"So I did. I might have known with your black hair
and your blue eyes you'd be a witch. That's what poor
old Nigel used to call your mother. Rowena, the
witch!"

"Who brought him to grief."

"She didn't fare so well herself."

"God knows that's true."

"Now what?" he asked rather tersely.

"Don't confuse me with my mother."

"It's difficult not to. I know every line of your face,
the shape of your eyes and the tilt of your brows, even
the curve of your cheek. Only the expression is different. You'll see what I mean when you get to Falconer."

Jaime shook her head a little as though he was trying

to put her into a trance. "I don't need to bother with anyone else's face, not even my mother's. Anyway, Derry painted my portrait not so long ago. Would you like to see it? It might rid you of the vision of the other one—the one you don't like."

"You're determined to read my mind, Jaime."

"I would say I'm not too far off now. Do you want to see the portrait?"

"I can't think of anything I'd like better at the moment."

"I'd get it, but it's too heavy to move and I'd have to stand on a chair. You'll have to come to it. It's in my room."

Her heart was racing and she stood up, determined to hold fast on the giddy feeling that had befallen her since she met this man.

"You lead and I'll follow," he said with a faint smile. "What's the matter, Jaime, you did invite me."

"There's nothing the matter," she said abruptly, "and I wouldn't admit it even if there were!"

"Good girl! I couldn't have taught you better myself."

"I thought that myself," she admitted. "It's best to size up the other side should our lives get linked up."

Something flickered in his black eyes. "You're going to make your mark, Jaime!"

"I have a few projects in mind. Most of my father's women friends have been women on their own— women who've had to turn their hands to something to support themselves and their children of broken marriages. No man is going to have me at his mercy. Whatever assets I've got I'm going to use them to their fullest extent. I'm always going to be ready."

"You might make some men nervous, Jaime."

"Not you, I'm sure!"

"I was brought up in a hard school myself. Incidentally, it was all to the good, though I often wanted to alter it at the time."

"You look unassailable now," she commented.

"Is that a compliment, Jaime? It doesn't sound like it."

"It's a compliment in its way, coupled with something else I'll leave you to find out."

"That's guaranteed to keep me on a knife edge." He moved a little closer to her and the room seemed to spin. It was a strange feeling and she was a stranger to it. He was looking at her intently, his head tipped to one side. Probably it was the difference in their ages. She was nineteen, almost twenty. He had to be thirty-four or five, a successful, sophisticated man with a frightening attraction for her beneath the unvarnished distrust. She moved quickly and a little jerkily as if she were in a cage. "Let's see if my portrait holds up, shall we?"

He followed her out of the room and along the passageway, looking idly around him, liking what he saw. The bedroom door was open and Jaime switched on the light and walked to the centre of the room with Quinn Sterling coming to stand close behind her shoulder. The portrait, oil on canvas, about four feet by three, hung directly above the old Victorian brass bed with its tailored spread in a bright modern print. So naturally was Jaime posed against a blue sky, so exact her image, that one could hardly take one's eyes off her in case she came down from the plain gilded frame. It was unquestionably Derrick Gilmore's best work and he was the first to admit it. It was indisputably Jaime, the character and the strength and the purpose alongside the beauty and delicate sensitivity. The raven hair gleamed and the beautiful violet eyes were clear and smiling.

"What do you think?" Jaime asked lightly, feeling quite differently about her painted image.

"She makes me feel slightly uncomfortable," he said, his head back and his eyes narrowed.

"Why?" Jaime asked in surprise.

"Perhaps I feel I know her too well and I don't know her at all."

"Do you like her?"

"Liking is irrelevant. It's extremely good. It has to be your father's best work."

"Surely you haven't seen enough to judge?"

"On the contrary, I've seen quite a bit," he muttered, lowering his head to glance at her. "I visited the gallery before I came here."

"Typical, I suppose."

"It's just a question of researching a job." He frowned and looked back at the portrait. "Your grandfather would like this."

"It's not for sale," she said instantly.

"I'm not suggesting you sell it, Jaime, but *give* it."

"A nice gesture, but I'm not considering making it."

"Then I won't press it, but it would rate instant approval."

She was uneasy and on edge, struck into incredulity by the antagonism and attraction this man stirred up. It was strange and it made her angry, but she was always honest with herself. This tenseness and excitement she was feeling all stemmed from Quinn Sterling, and his presence so close beside her offered no respite. She moved away from him towards the door, her dark blue eyes startling against her golden tan. "Approval is pleasant," she remarked crisply, "but buying it isn't my style. It's not necessary for the Hunters or Sterlings to like me. I can only think of you as 'those people' anyway."

Quinn took one last look at the painting, his chiselled mouth faintly ironic. "You'll remind them all a great deal of your mother."

"Of whom they haven't had a recent thought for the past twenty years."

"Don't be bitter, Jaime. Considering they all toe your grandfather's line that's not surprising."

"Do you?" she asked, her violet eyes gleaming with speculation.

"We're all one big, happy family!" He joined her at the door, looking down at her, almost holding her immobile.

She shook her head and freed herself. "Nice work if you can make them believe it. I think you have your own private axe to grind."

"Surely you're a witch, Jaime!" His black eyes

mocked her, but there was a glimmer of surprise some-where there as well.

"I wouldn't care to cross you myself," she replied.

"I'm glad!" he said silkily, "because you'll be seeing quite a lot of me."

"Tell me about the business," she asked.

"It's big and it's complex. It would take a long time."

"I shouldn't be in ignorance of it."

"I think, Jaime, you've changed your mind," he teased.

"Maybe I'm like you, Mr. Sterling, with my own axe to grind."

"You'll make yourself unhappy doing it!" Unexpect-edly he caught her shoulder and turned her towards him. "Listen to me, Jaime, you're beautiful and you're clever, but you wouldn't last the first round with them because you couldn't fight their way."

She stared up at him fixedly. "What is Hunter Ster-ling, a battlefield?"

"All big business is intrigue, Jaime."

"I'm not interested in the business and I've learned how to defend myself."

"Then I fail to understand why you're trembling under my hands."

"That doesn't mean all that much."

"As it happens it might, only I don't care to have a young girl at my mercy."

"Then you've got the wrong impression. To begin with, I don't *like* you."

"I damn well don't believe it!" He released her with his rare, very attractive smile.

Her glance flicked back over him and she was talking fast. "You're at liberty to doubt it. I don't know why or how, but my opinion is formed!"

"You're not very careful with your insults, Jaime."

"It's you who's asking the favour of me."

He held up his hand. "*Please!* I think it's a mistake your coming to Falconer. It's your grandfather who wants you."

"Presumably you haven't suffered by making this visit. I mean, aren't all your expenses paid?"

"It would be a very unpleasant surprise to discover they haven't. That includes the dinner."

"Thank you for telling me. Suddenly I don't feel hungry."

"You will!" he promised.

She shrugged her delicate shoulders. "I don't really need any little pats on the head."

"No, what you really need is a few hard slaps some place else."

She felt suddenly like laughing and did. "What did I tell you? Already we're running short on civility." She stepped back and looked out through the window. "Mercifully Derry's coming back, and there's someone with him. Oh God, it's Tavia."

"Then let's go out."

She turned her head back to stare at him, so fantastically sure of himself. "I've tried and tried to like Tavia—she works in the gallery."

"I know."

"Do you know everything?" she asked.

"All the important information. Make up your mind, Jaime, I'll rescue you if you want me to."

"I've no alternative now Tavia's arrived."

"Your father's a big boy."

"Is he?" she asked, making no attempt to smile. "I promised myself I would look after him for as long as I could."

"Then now's the time to get out."

"I daresay it would suit your plans—oh, forgive me, my *grandfather's* plans."

"I'm only the errand boy," he said, his brilliant eyes gleaming.

She watched him across the room. "Oh no, you're not," she said softly, "you're a real Machiavelli!"

"I'm no threat to little girls."

"Hush, they're coming."

Quinn smiled. "What are we, Jaime, unwilling conspirators?"

"It looks like it, doesn't it? You've got me, finally. We'll go out."

With the length of the room separating them, their eyes met and held. He found himself becoming more and more involved with this vital young creature. She couldn't have offered a more complete contrast to her cousins; for all her perceptible integrity and courage a babe in the woods beside either of them, Sue-Ellen or Leigh. They heard the car engine cut, then a moment later Derrick Gilmore let himself in the front door accompanied by a rather voluptuous-looking redhead in her late thirties.

"Hello there!" Derrick said with a challenging smile. "Sorry I was so long, but I ran into Tavvy, here."

"Nice to see you again, Mr. Sterling," Tavia said in her fruity contralto. "Hi there, Jaime. That's a terrific outfit as usual. I wish you'd make something for me. I have to pay the earth."

"When I come to it I might charge the earth!" Jaime answered rather shortly. "There's been a change in plans, Derry. Mr. Sterling is taking me out to dinner."

"What a good idea!" said Tavia, obviously taken with Quinn Sterling. "Can't we all go? The Plantation is fabulous and it's new."

"It seems to me you weren't invited!" Jaime burst out, irritated by the way Tavia had transferred her whole attention to Quinn Sterling.

"I perfectly agree," said her father. "We'll have a nice dinner at home, Tavvy, and polish off this bottle of wine."

"Why?" Tavia turned her almond amber eyes on him.

"Because we do most of the time."

"I'll certainly grant you that!" Tavia said, looking at Jaime with veiled dislike. "Naturally it's none of my business, but have you decided to visit your grandfather?"

"From which I gather Derry has been gossiping again?"

"Why not?" asked Tavia, her eyes sliding back to Quinn Sterling's tall, lean figure. He was assuredly the sexiest man she had ever seen. Derry at his best couldn't come remotely close, though he was far more attractive than any other man in her circle. This man was something else again, with his lean rather imperious face and his coal-black eyes. Behind the charm, and he had it far more dangerously than Derry, there was a high degree of ruthlessness. No woman could afford to underestimate him for a second. A pity to waste him on a fledgling like Jaime.

"I'll let you know early," Jaime assured her.

"It seems to me we're holding you up," Derry said affably, the expression in his hazel eyes not matching up. "Enjoy yourselves. I'll still be up by the time you get home."

"Which reminds me," Quinn Sterling looked back at the older man, "your portrait of Jaime is excellent."

"Not too bad at all!" Derrick agreed contentedly. "She's the kind of model most artists dream about."

"There's a portrait of Rowena at Falconer."

"I never saw it. Is it surrounded by flowers and candles like a shrine?"

Jaime shuddered. "Don't speak like that, Derry!"

"I was amusing myself. I hope that old swine has suffered and suffered!"

"He has no less than you have!" Quinn Sterling said in his black velvet voice with the steel in it.

"You couldn't *like* him!" Derry maintained, an odd whiteness about his mouth and nostrils. "He's a past master of every dirty trick in the business. Didn't he practically force your father to resign?"

"He's not that good that we haven't always been able to come up with a counter-move."

"From the look of you, you know how to survive!"

Derry said grimly. "Do you wonder I have no sort of ambition? I'd never have held Rowena, had she lived. She was used to a high level of living. A frightening old eagle for a father."

"Yet you're willing to allow your daughter to visit him," Quinn countered with no trace of pity or compassion on his dark face.

"Oh well!" Derry said, brightening, a puckish smile on his face, "I'm sending her for her own sake. The old devil is a multi-millionaire. I think he should extend a few hundred thousand in Jaime's direction!"

"That's good! In your direction, you mean!" Tavia laughed cruelly.

"Take care, Tavvy, or you can walk home," Derry warned.

"That would well-nigh kill me, I'm right out of condition."

"A real Rubens!" Derry grinned, restored to good humour by the thought of her.

Jaime realised she was trembling. She had never really known her father; she only knew she had never felt carefree.

"Are you ready, Jaime?" Quinn asked, his eyes on her still face.

"Yes. I'll just get a stole, the breeze off the ocean is very cooling. I won't be a moment." She hurried out of the room hearing Tavia beginning to question Quinn on his intended movements within the next few days. Probably if she could she would track him down. Tavia was a lady vulture, but a least Derry would never be her victim. Derry, she was now coming to suspect, didn't really need anyone beyond someone to attend to his creature comforts. Tavia might stay around him a long time, but he would never marry her. Derry totally rejected commitment, though in fairness had never forsaken his only child.

Whatever he was, Jaimed loved him, though she thought of him as only a few years older than she was, so many scrapes had she got him out of. Tavia was lucky he wouldn't marry her. Damned lucky. Had he loved her mother when he had run away with her, or had he deliberately set out to spite and outrage an establishment that had refused to accept him? It sounded like Derry. He pitchforked himself into trouble. With a kind of nervous horror Jaime considered that he might be burning for vengeance, using her as once he had used her mother. No, it couldn't be so. He had loved Rowena and he had proved his love by never deserting Rowena's child. She couldn't allow these mysterious, repelling thoughts to race around in her head. Derry wouldn't use her as a form of blackmail over her grandfather. It was just a fantastic thought.

CHAPTER TWO

A LITTLE SILENCE had fallen between them, and Quinn studied the young downbent face opposite him. Her skin in the soft rosy lighting had a wonderful sensuous quality, her dark blue eyes blurred with violet, yet suddenly she looked like a spent child.

"I think you're right, Jaime," he offered with grave amusement. "You have lost your appetite."

"I've nothing to celebrate," she said, twirling her wine glass, "but please finish your lobster. This place is becoming famous for its seafood."

"A deserved reputation, but you've hardly touched anything."

"I feel rootless all of a sudden," she looked up swiftly and directly into his night-dark eyes.

"How's that?"

"Oh, Derry seems anxious to get rid of me for one reason or the other."

"Not get rid of you, Jaime. He feels quite rightly that your grandfather should acknowledge you at least and further provide for you in his will."

"May he live on for ever!" she said fervently, and took a sip of her wine. 'I don't give a tinker's curse for his money."

"Then you're the only member of his family who doesn't."

"But don't you see," she said earnestly, "I'm not a member of the family. I'm Orphan Annie."

"Anyone less like Orphan Annie I've yet to see," he said dryly, reaching forward and filling up her wine glass.

"Tell me then, what is this marvellous gift he's offering me? The chance to bask in his reflected glory and get financially rewarded at the same time. With just a little help, I can make it on my own."

"I wish you'd stop talking like a gallant child, and I'm beginning to think that's all you are. If you don't come you'll end up getting nothing at all."

Jaime lowered her face, immeasurably disenchanted. "The one thing that would have redeemed my grandfather in my eyes would have been for him to remember me without even having laid eyes on me. There are strings attached to his benevolence."

"Without a doubt," he agreed.

"He wants me to console him in his old age, absolve him from his share of the blame or whatever."

"He genuinely wants to love you."

"What a beautiful thought!" she said, gazing straight at him. "The first he's extended to me in all my young life."

Despite himself he laughed, and the light fell across his dark profile. There was a glitter of sardonic amusement in his unfathomable eyes and the words seemed to bubble up in Jaime's throat. "Just one thing Quinn. You're not attempting at all to be reassuring."

"You want me to tell you the truth, don't you?" he countered.

"I'm not so blind I can't see it for myself. My grandfather wants me to provide him with his salvation. Having been an enormous success in this life he naturally wants to make an unforgettable mark in the next."

"I think he will," he said suavely.

Her eyes were fastened to him with barely concealed apprehension. "There's too much about you to fathom. I think you want to take over where my grandfather leaves off."

"The idea appeals to me, Jaime."

"What would you do with all my uncles and cousins?"

"Step over them."

"How intolerable!"

"For them, yes," he said blandly.

"I suppose they're blissfully unaware of your plans."

"They'd demolish me if they could. Are you going to join them?"

"Not now. Not ever!" she said with quiet emphasis.

"Why not?"

"You'd make a dangerous enemy."

"I'm harmless to my friends. Life has hardened me, Jaime. My grandfather was a brilliant but very trusting man, so was my father, but I have a few accounts to settle. Both of them were used, but I don't intend that anyone will use me." A kind of lighning flashed out of his eyes and Jaime shivered, clasped her hands together and held them beneath her chin.

"You hate them, don't you?"

He smiled and the humour came back into his face. "I don't have to, Jaime. My family holds forty-eight per cent of company stock. It didn't happen overnight and they didn't like it, but it happened. My family had the engineering brains, your grandfather was the financial genius. The Hunter Sterling Oil Exploration Company was my father's brainchild. It's only fair that we should now own fifty-one per cent of the stock in that company. I was able to persuade a few of our major shareholders to sell out to us; it set us right back for a time, but we're making up for that. Both my mother and father died within a few years of each other. My grandmother is head of the family."

"Nigel's mother?"

He looked at her with brilliant, harsh alertness. "Yes."

"Then I could only cause her painful memories."

"Infinitely painful, Jaime."

"You're cruel," she said softly, feeling tears threatening.

"And you, of course, can't be blamed for your astonishing resemblance to your mother. We'll have to keep remembering that. Your face will repay itself when your grandfather sees you."

"I don't think I can take it all in! This morning none of this seemed imminent. That somewhere I had a grandfather, an important and powerful man. I remember reading once in the newspaper that some politician called him a megalomaniac."

"With some reason, but that's the way giants are."

"And he trusts you?"

"He knows I won't stoop to anything too low. That's the Sterling in me. A lot of people meeting me for the first time assume I'm a Hunter."

"Well, is that bad?"

"Being a Sterling is a lot better," he smiled.

"I guess I'll know when I meet them."

"Both Simon and Brett will try to rush you into an early marriage," he warned her.

"They're my cousins!"

"Cousins marry. Different mothers helps, if you want to look at it that way."

Jaime shook her head. "I'm like you—what I've seen of marriage, or rather broken marriages, worries me. I like men, I can't pretend not to, but I think they're very selfish, the best of them."

"Keep going. You won't embarrass me."

"All right! If you won't take any notice of my conversation, let's dance!" She stopped and looked at him, then retracted. "No, on second thoughts we won't."

"What angle are you working on now?"

"I've never met a man with such a suspicious mind. I've just reconsidered, that's all."

"And what influenced you?"

"Your enormous charisma. This way I'll keep my feet on the ground."

"Jaime?" He stood up and came round to her, slipping her chair back.

"It sounds as if you've made up *your* mind."

"You're a grown woman, or almost, you don't have to dither. I don't like indecision."

"That lets me off the hook, Mr. Sterling. I'm very decisive, just wary about you."

He smiled at her and led her out on to the dance floor where several other couples were involved with doing their own thing and came together only briefly; the rest in conventional positions enjoyed themselves just as much, but occupied the perimeter of the floor.

From the minute Quinn's arms closed around her Jaime knew she had shown wisdom in not underestimating him or his effect on her, but it was a matter of principle to look up at him and smile. She would make sure she never found herself in this position again.

"Stop frowning!" he said, and she was half mesmerised by the sound of his voice.

"Am I?"

"Yes. *And* thinking out loud. I'm the big bad wolf, that's plain, and it's quite undeserved. I've told you before, little girls don't awaken my interest."

"I sincerely hope not."

"Relax Jaime!"

"I'd have to force myself to. The whole thing's crazy!"

"Surely it's better than staying home?"

"In a word, yes. Tavia doesn't value my company, or any woman's for that matter. She was even beginning to look at you."

"Really? Then why aren't you smiling?"

"Not that it would have thrown Derry," she pursued, "he always bounces right back. It's Derry who's the bad bet, not Tavia. She would marry him tomorrow, impoverished artist and all."

"Don't take it so seriously, Jaime. Your father can handle his own life."

"What you mean is, I should start leading a life of my own."

"It's quite possible you'll make quite a success of it."

"Don't patronise me, Quinn Sterling!"

He nodded. "All right. Anything else?"

"Tell me about my cousins."

"I might as well. You might have reason to be grateful to me."

Her glance lifted and she studied his dark face. "If they're as bad as that, I'd better stay away."

"You wanted my honest opinion," he said lightly.

"Unbiased, I hope?"

"I can only try, Jaime. Your cousins, like your uncles and their wives, are controlled by your grandfather."

"That's all?"

"Isn't that enough?"

"Who controls you?" she came back.

"Some say the devil!"

Smiling like that he was an extremely handsome man, the sombreness gone from his brilliant black eyes and mouth. Jaime sighed a little, then started to laugh, a soft little laugh gurgled in her throat. He looked down at her blue-sheened head and his arm tightened, gathering her in closer to his lean frame. "Isn't it obvious?" he asked abruptly, catching her eyes. She continued to look at at him but remained silent, her body drawn and curving towards him. Some invisible current was linking them whether they want it or not. Her breath almost caught at the way his eyes were travelling over her face.

"Keep talking," she said in an agitated little voice.

"Perhaps you're right. Where was I?"

"The cousins."

"Ah well, your cousins Sue-Ellen and Leigh are both very fetching, smart as paint, and they'd both do anything for the family's sake, even marry me. Neither of them work at anything but that."

"How boring!"

"You might think so, Jaime, they don't. In any case, they fill up their time pretty completely. Simon and Brett are with the firm—company law. They have a lot of assets, so I'm told. Good looks, a big name, no known enemies beyond this room. They would never think of leading a revolt against your grandfather."

She trembled a little, hopelessly out of her depth, and he glanced at her half amused, half impatient. "It's best to know this sort of thing, Jaime. You said so yourself."

"And I'm grateful. You dance beautifully, Quinn. No doubt it's the practice with Sue-Ellen and Leigh."

"Yes, they'd have me giddy if they could. I thought you were starting to relax. In fact, I thought you were going off to sleep."

"I'm moving, aren't I?" she protested.

"Not close enough," he said deliberately, his black eyes gleaming with mockery.

"My aunts?" she prompted.

"Rapacious."

"Fascinating! It gets worse and worse."

"I'm only speaking for myself, of course. Many another would tell you they're very stylish ladies, which they are, and they do a lot of good works about which they're fairly voluble. That's how it is, violet eyes. I can feel your heart pounding."

"I've come to the conclusion I've been living in a little haven of peace," she remarked.

His jeering taunt touched her cheek. "Jaime, Jaime, our families have made economy expand enormously. Think on that and be proud."

"It's not something to be ashamed of, is it?" she looked up at him directly, her melodious young voice quite crisp with a shadow of his own mockery. He returned her gaze, his own narrowed.

"Not entirely, thank God! You're too bright, Jaime. It might go against you."

"You don't scorn brightness, do you?"

"Only in females."

"What man doesn't!" she said sourly.

"Don't be a little shrew!"

"Am I really, how interesting!"

"And a miracle of beauty, femininity, all that sort of thing that bogs a man down."

"As in quicksand?"

"That's it!" He broke into a laugh that had the true ring of amusement. "In the entrance hall of Falconer is a pair of seventeenth-century Chinese porcelains, vases about twenty or so inches high. The blue violet of the decoration is the exact colour of your eyes."

"I simply can't wait to see them!" she said, seeing her reflection in the depths of his eyes.

"Aren't I allowed to express my reverence for beauty?"

"Not at close range!"

"I'm surprised it's affecting you, Jaime."

"Don't you mean you're delighted? I think you like to make women react."

"A harmless pursuit, surely?"

"Only if one knows the score."

"Point taken. Naturally I wouldn't think of adding you to my list of—what shall we call them?—victims!"

"It wouldn't work in any case!" she said with great conviction, staring up at him intently.

"Gently, Jaime, gently. There's no need for such a strenuous protest."

"There's nothing I would dislike more than losing my head," she whispered with soft violence.

"I'd say you'd better get used to heads toppling all round. A pattern for the future with that face!"

"I'm more than a face. I'm a mind!"

"That's even more dangerous! I can see you're terribly clever," he teased her.

"And I've noticed you're a hard, mocking devil!"

He nodded his dark head agreeably. "I'm immune to insults, Jaime. I wasn't the first time, and for years after, but I am now."

"I don't like it when your eyes flash. I didn't know black eyes could have so much life in them,"

"I could easily reassure you," he said in his vibrant dark voice.

"That would be equally bad," she retorted.

"Then you'd better stop flinging down challenges. It's been part of my training to pick them up."

"But it's all in your mind!" she said sweetly. "I don't mean anything at all. You're too quick off the mark."

"I am. It doesn't pay to fumble along."

The music had stopped and she was standing in the circle of his arms looking up at him. "Why do you look at me so intently?"

"How do you want me to look?"

"Not so that you make my head swim."

"That's the wine."

"I've only had a glass and I'm quite used to it. Derry and I always have a bottle of wine with dinner."

"Well then, you're only an infant and infants do have these little problems in adjustment."

"You mean they've no head for adult games. Shouldn't we be getting back to the table? I'd like some strong black coffee."

"And you needn't drink alone. As it happens I'm ready for it myself, then I suppose I should be getting you home."

"Yes, it's dark outside."

He steered her gently but effectively back to the table, his hands on her shoulders. "What makes you say the things you do?"

"Cause and effect," she said lightly. "Some people make one vivacious."

"Particularly at nineteen."

"You obviously didn't take it seriously, what I said about patronising me."

"I'm sorry, Jaime." He held the chair for her. "I just can't help it."

"You took the words right out of my mouth. Meeting you has been a very *meaningful* experience, as Peter Ustinov would say."

"There's an hour of the evening left," he observed.

"No climaxes, please!" she begged him across the table, her eyes just faintly alarmed.

"I can't promise anything, Jaime, particularly when you look at me like that."

"If that's true, I could take a cab home."

"Don't think of it! I don't tip little day-old chicks out of the nest."

"I'm glad. For a moment you filled me with dread."

"Then don't present two faces—woman and child."

A curious excitement began to gnaw at her. There was danger in this man: danger in the way he looked, danger in the way he talked, his black eyes highly charged with vivid life. Waiters were gliding around their table and dissolving again into the swirling room with its soft lights and its flowers and women in their prettiest after-dark dresses.

"I have the strangest feeling I've been here before," she said.

"With me?"

"Yes. Isn't it weird?"

"Do you often feel like that?"

"Don't joke!"

He held up a hand. "All right then. It's just as unsettling to find I know your face exactly."

"Ghosts!" she said. "Only we're here in the present."

"Little changes, Jaime. I know damned well you could hold a man in thrall just as easily as Rowena did."

"Ah, you've got your knife out again."

"I'm not aware of it."

"Oh yes, you are! You wanted to hurt me. Not a knife, a sword that lies between us." She could feel the tension in him, his winged black brows coming together.

"For every step forward, we go back two."

"Actually I think you're trying to push me into my grandfather's arms."

"Drink your coffee, Jaime. I ordered a liqueur."

"Did you, what is it?"

"See if you like it," he told her.

"What I like might be sharply irrelevant with you." She drank the liqueur quickly.

"That was stupid. Too fast."

"You'll just have to wait and see whether I pass out or not."

"You haven't had nearly enough."

"Exactly. I'm just that little bit afraid of you."

"You don't look like a coward to me, Jaime. You're positive and aware and I can scarcely take my eyes off you, which won't do at all. Drink the rest of that coffee and we'll go."

"Aye, aye, sir!"

He paused. "Is that how you see me?"

"Forget it, I was only being flippant." She glanced at him briefly and felt a swift onrush of excitement. The thought of her own appalling inexperience suddenly struck her and she bent her small exquisite face over the coffee cup and drank religiously as though it was a potion protecting her against any transgression on his part.

For an instant her expression was transparent and Quinn found himself speaking with a tenderness that was unusual in him except in the presence of his grandmother. "Jaime, the brave and the beautiful and the anxious little girl darting violet glances at me. You're safe, for God's sake, though I shall probably regret it in the morning."

"Would you mind explaining what you mean?"

"I'd say you've more than enough imagination. Come along, you've dithered long enough."

"Anyone would dither with you!" she defended herself.

"You've got that off pat."

"What is it, your sense of power? Do you like moulding people into shape?"

"I feel you could do with a little control," he returned.

"Well!" she said, but he didn't answer her, only escorted her very firmly out of the restaurant into the beautiful star-spangled night. "I want to walk along the beach," she announced.

"You should be tired."

"Does that mean the beach is out of limits?"

"Nothing is and never has been. All right, Jaime, you suggested it, the beach."

"We'll take the car down to the esplanade."

"Just as you say."

"You sound as though I'm being unreasonable."

"No, you're getting better by the minute!"

"That's cheering! You try to like me, I know, but forgetfulness is impossible."

Quinn unlocked the car door and Jaime slid into the seat and waited for him to come round to the other side. It wasn't pleasant what she was feeling, it was almost painful, and she didn't know whether she would be able to carry it off. Neither of them could be cut off from the past. In the car beside her she recognised it in the set of his head, the little air of relentlessness about him. His profile was good as perfect, but once again it was darkly remote. He turned to her, his eyes gleaming in the light from the dashboard.

"And what momentous thoughts are occupying you now?"

"Just old pictures flitting through my mind. You have an excellent profile, Quinn. Ascetic, until you turn your head full on."

"And then?"

"It's a very contradictory face."

"And yours isn't!" he said a little tersely.

"Try to remember I'm not up to your weight."

"I've been remembering it all evening."

"Well then, take the first on your right," she said helpfully.

"Bossy little thing!"

"This mightn't work out as well as I thought."

"I feel somewhat like that myself, Jaime," he confessed.

"All right, take me home. We can go this way just as easily."

His glance pierced the gloom, raying over her face. "If you're going to force a beach walk on me, the least you can do is go along with it."

"Yes, Quinn."

"It seems to me that was *too* meek!" Suddenly he smiled at her, his maddening first hostility gone. For how long Jaime didn't know, being on a see-saw herself.

Out in the night the stars were blazing, thickly clustered over the ocean, a steady stream of fresh air like balm falling all over them and lingering on their skin and their clothes. Pools of light from the street lights spilled on to the white sand, making little radiant oases at the base of the promenade. Jaime slipped out of her sandals and carried them, feeling the cool firm sand underfoot, dry and crunchy. At this hour of the night the beach was deserted, but it was just as beautiful as under the sun. Maybe more beautiful, more mysterious and elusive.

"I've been happier here than any place else!" she said almost to herself.

Quinn picked up a shell, gave it all his attention, then slipped it in his pocket. "Yes, it's beautiful any hour of the day, perhaps more urgent at night. I'm glad to escape the deadly rat race if only for a while."

"Is it so bad?" she asked, stopping to look at him.

"Murderous! Harassing, frenetic, the build-up in tension sometimes is enormous. I wouldn't invite you to join my world, only the toughest survive."

"Yet you're an ambitious man," she said.

"Yes, but I can't say it hasn't been a fight to the top. A dirty fight a lot of the time."

"Does that give you that cold-blooded look?"

"You'll pay for that, Jaime," he said softly, but she somehow knew he meant it exactly.

"I didn't mean cold-blooded," she said truthfully, "more a terrible aloofness."

"And that's better? If I were you I'd leave it alone."

She stretched out her arms without looking at him, embracing the night. "Take a deep breath. Isn't that heavenly?"

The clean beauty of the ocean was rushing for them, the waves breaking and tumbling on to the sand but never quite making Jaime's bare feet. She felt exalted and indescribably sad, with the soft pounding of the sea filling her ears with its own kind of music. Her eyes had become accustomed to the night and she could see the sandcastles the children had made that afternoon. They wouldn't be there in the morning, like dreams, for the tide would come right up to the rock wall.

"Isn't that better," she cried rapturously, "the world of surf and stars and salt on the wind?"

"It's real *now*," he said with a mixture of worldiness and amusement. "Tomorrow it will be insubstantial. I have too much work to do."

"You're a madman in a madman's world!" The sea breeze was catching at her hair and she swept it out of its heavy coil.

"There's truth in that!" he said, tempted to catch her up and make love to her but keeping a brake on the sensations her vibrant young beauty was arousing. Her dress in the starlight was a silver blur, her face as pale as a flower, fringed by the inky blackness of her hair. An improbably beautiful girl-into-witch and vaguely exasperating with her young taunts. She was still speaking, fighting a losing but enjoyable battle with the wind in her hair.

"What you're telling me hasn't made things any easier. I've been living all these years in a separate world from yours."

"In a lost world, you mean," he said very deliberately.

Jaime glanced over her shoulder and back at him. "Are you trying to tell me only a man who makes money is important?"

"I assure you a lot of people think it's important."

"Then they should get out into the fresh air. Recover a sense of proportion."

"That's what's wrong with them, Jaime, they can't!"

"You talk the same language, don't you?"

"Definitely, but only up to a point. Remember that carefully."

He sounded a little formidable, but there was a cool sensuality in his voice she couldn't fail to notice. "When would you expect me to leave?" she asked quietly.

"I'm due back in Sydney in three days."

"Do you think I could handle them?" She appeared to be addressing the timeless ocean.

"You don't *belong* with them Jaime," he responded.

"Yet you expect me to go and live with them for old times' sake—Rowena's daughter come home."

"That's not overstating it. Only you're not Rowena. There are small differences."

"There are *big* differences," she said emphatically, "and one day you'll all see them."

"I think we can expect that," he said, his eyes never leaving her.

"So you see you weren't sent to recover a lost child at all."

"What then?"

She had been speaking with soft animation, not looking at him but out towards the first foaming line of the breakers, so that his presence right behind her came as a shock. She wanted to turn and say something, *anything*, but simultaneously his arm closed about her, her head brought back against his shoulder. Pure instinct precipitated a bid for freedom. She brought up her two hands, pushing down on his arm in a vain attempt to break his hold, her self-possession shattered like a falling star.

"You're twenty in three months, Jaime," he said with smooth mockery. "A grown woman."

"Don't tell that to me now!"

"Turn round," he ordered.

"No, I won't! What you're after is some sort of symbolic act, a surrender."

"What I'm after, Jaime, is the touch of your mouth. It talks a lot of sense—sometimes."

"Well, when you put it like that..."

"Don't misunderstand me. I'm through talking!" He spun her with just a little force right into his arms, cupping her face and turning it up to him with all the skill of a sorcerer.

"If you're going to kiss me, *kiss* me!" she said in defiance, staring up at him with wide, shining eyes.

"You don't want it?"

"I don't want it... yes, I want it!"

"That's what I thought you said."

She heard his soft laugh and was glad of it, thinking in her inexperience that a kiss would be only a gesture from this strange, complex man, but the first touch of his mouth started an intolerable showering of sparks, an actual physical ache. There was a droning sound in her ears, a muffled droning, like a frail swimmer predictably and about to be doomed. She no longer cared a hoot what he thought of her, her slender body blazing like bushfire under his hands. It couldn't be that she was out of control. It couldn't be that she was ingenuous or precariously stupid. She was vulnerable to this man, and she had recklessly shown it from the very first minute. If she couldn't understand her reaction either, he was proving very conclusively that the mind and the body led different lives.

"Stop kissing me," she whispered. "Just *stop*."

His hands shifted to her shoulders, just barely hurting her. "The hell with that!"

"This isn't part of the plan, Quinn, is it?"

"What you're asking is, did I set out to kiss you. No, I didn't, but I do get my flesh and blood moments."

"Then it's for the *cold-blooded*?"

"Do you still think I am?" he asked laconically.

"No."

"Neither are you. I could make love to you until I'm too old to succumb to temptation, but all it would do is hurt both of us."

"How?" she asked, throwing discretion to the winds.

"I deal in hard facts."

"You're stunning!" she said in a near whisper. Her skin was so sensitised that she could still feel his touch when he had half turned away from her. She might still have been clinging to him, her heart striking into his as if it were her preordained destiny. A little frantically now she shook back her hair so that it flowed about her face in silky turbulence. "It's been a very nice evening, Mr. Sterling, but do you mind if we go home now?"

"It's where you belong for tonight!"

Her words seemed to have brought him back from an immense distance. She looked around for her sandals, that one of them or both had thrown down on the sand. She couldn't for the life of her remember which one. "Don't even think of my coming to Falconer!" she said with pleasurable, renewed hostility, on course again.

"You will!" he said briefly, leaning down and retrieving the small, strappy sandals.

"You're a very strange man. You alarm me," she said, not even thanking him. She almost ran across the sand, her dress fluttering, and hesitated at the foot of the stairs to slip on her shoes. In another minute she had almost reached the car.

"Stop it, Jaime," he caught up with her and locked her wrist, flaring excitement at will. "Come with me and you'll learn a lot in the process."

"I've learned a lot already!"

"You don't know a damn thing!"

"I know what you've taught me."

"We won't mention it," he smiled at her, "until I kiss you again."

"Now that's something that won't happen!" she said with almost comical panic.

"How would you set about stopping me?" He sounded as if he was genuinely interested.

"I've a few tricks of my own," she assured him.

"You don't need any tricks at all. All *you* have to be is exactly you!"

"Thank you," she murmured with a kind of impotent rage beating at her temples.

"Don't be silly, Jaime, you've no reason to be annoyed with me. I'm not your enemy."

"You could seriously reverse my fortunes!"

He looked down at her passionate face, an odd smile in his eyes. "You're fascinating, Jaime, do you know that? I wouldn't have missed out on this trip for the world. In a lot of ways it's been a fantastic surprise."

"Don't congratulate yourself yet!" she said to him with a certain imperiousness.

Quinn smiled and smoothed back the black silky sweep of her hair. "Don't ever lose that fighting spirit. It's a precious commodity."

"I'm glad I have it, if there are men like you around."

"There you go again, and it's fatal!"

"I'll tell you what," she said purposefully, "we could strike a bargain. Get in the car and I'll tell you about it."

"Splendid!" he said, staring into her face. "You're

rather a breathless character, Jaime. A man would have
to look high and low for your like!"

He unlocked the car with barely concealed impatience for her to continue, even going so far as to turn
on the interior light, his arm sliding along the back of
the seat as he trained on her a brilliant black scrutiny.
"Please go on. I keep feeling a shift in our positions.
You're a born boss."

"If I come to Falconer, Quinn," she said earnestly,
"could you back me in a business venture?"

"Great God, what is this, blackmail?"

"Don't mention that word, it isn't in my vocabulary.
I'm not shy and retiring, you can see that; I don't have
to be stupidly modest like a Victorian relic, I have real
ability. I just know I could be a good designer. You told
me yourself you liked this dress."

"I love it!" he said with black, amused malice. "But
not one half as much as the girl in it."

"Men are unduly preoccupied with that sort of thing.
Please be serious, Quinn."

"Do you mean to tell me we're going to sit here and
discuss *business*?"

"Why not?"

"Why not, indeed! All right, Jaime, fire away.
You've got exactly five minutes. But first tell me, why
me?"

Jaime's blue eyes were startlingly beautiful, ablaze
with enthusiasm. "It could never be my grandfather,
for obvious reasons. That megalomaniac bit has always
stuck in my head and I never even knew who he was. I
know perfectly well you're too hard-headed to come

into anything foolish, but with a little help I could build up a successful business in time. I have a natural flair and I can do everything. The lot! Others have done it, Pru Acton and Jane Cattlin, why not Jaime Gilmore? The ideas just flow out, but precisely nowhere. I have to have help, then I'll work my fingers to the bone to prove myself."

"I'm indeed glad you mentioned that," he said dryly. "One thing you might have overlooked, your grandfather won't allow a moment of your time to be diverted from him."

"Don't you think I can guess that?" She leaned forward and grasped his sleeve, staring up into his dominant dark face. "Does my idea make sense to you?"

"Go easy, Jaime! My head's spinning, and not only with your proposal. I mean, I have to mix business with pleasure, but you?" He imprisoned the golden-skinned hand on his sleeve, turning it this way and that as though he could read her future in her palm. "Beautiful hands, Jaime, neat and elegant like the rest of you. I hate to think of them emaciated through overwork."

"I've got sketchbooks galore to show you," she hurried on, "I make all my own clothes, I've done so for years. I've made clothes for my friends, for nothing of course, they bought the material and I just liked doing it. I've even made a wedding dress and it was absolutely super, everybody said so."

"My God, and to think I wasn't warned!"

"Take me seriously, Quinn. Please. This really matters to me."

"A leaf out of the Old Man's book?" he enquired.

"What did you expect, another Sue-Ellen or Leigh?"

"No, I get very tired of them."

"This is business we're discussing," she said urgently as the palm of her hand began to tingle.

"Of course, Miss Gilmore. Does your father know of this burning ambition?"

"I've tried discussing it with him many times, but..."

"All right, I know the score. Ideas are all very well, Jaime, so is creative ability, but there's so much more to it, and I'd have to see a lot more of your work."

"You will, I promise you, and once you do I'm sure you'll decide in my favour."

"Jaime, you're irrestible!" he said, carrying her hand to his mouth. "The soft sell!"

She frowned. "Don't spell it out like that! I want nothing but a little strictly legitimate help and encouragement. Everyone needs a patron. Look at Michelangelo and the Pope!"

"Please don't bring them into it, Jaime. I tell you, it's unnecessary."

"I'm not asking you to back a failure, Quinn. I know I can make it. I just *know*!"

Quinn looked thoughtful. "It's given to some of us to *know*, Jaime, I can't deny that. That's how we find the strength to get to the top. Let's say for the time being you have me interested, but I promise nothing. You're on trial about a lot of things."

"So are *you*!" she said, feeling closer to him than any other human being on earth, which was extremely odd. "I didn't say I approve of you entirely."

"Well, you'd better keep quiet about it, or you won't get a penny. Perhaps you could talk it over with my grandmother. She's an extremely clever woman and her taste in all things is superb."

"She might hate me."

"She'd never hate you, Jaime, she's above that sort of thing. *Quite uncivilised*, I can hear her saying it. She might, however, stop short at the sight of your face, but I suppose she'll have to get used to it."

"But for heaven's sake, why shouldn't she bury the hatchet?" she demanded.

"Now you sound nineteen! An ignorant little girl who hasn't seen life."

"I *am* nineteen, Quinn," she said in a quick flood of words, her blue-violet eyes shimmering. "I can't be an all-suffering, sophisticated woman of the world yet."

"I don't want you to ever be," he rejoined.

"I expect it will have to happen!"

"Particularly if you're going to set the fashion world on fire'" he grinned.

"Sister Monica always used to say she could teach me anything and I let her, but actually I knew far more about sewing and handling material *then*, than she'll ever know!"

"Poor dear Sister Monica, God help her! Perhaps she should have had a patron."

"I knew you'd be extremely interested in my proposition," she said, scarcely hearing him.

"You're convincing, that's for sure! Now, not another word if you don't mind. I'm not all that keen on career women."

"Let's shake hands on it," she said, almost feeling the wine of success in her veins.

"I've a better idea." His hand wound her black hair like a silk rope, drawing her to him. "I'm not sure you're not unique. You even manage to delight my mind!" Relentlessly he lowered his head with no ordinary gift for making love to a woman, ousting every other thought from Jaime's mind. It was a brief caress, controlled, but it impressed itself deeply on Jaime's consciousness. She didn't attempt to evade him, just turned up her mouth, her lids falling. She was trembling when he released her, staring at him with an almost childlike wonder.

He spoke casually, as though she were a secretary across a desk. "I'll ring you the day after tomorrow."

"I never discuss business on the phone. Besides, this is between the two of us."

"What a good idea, and I'm not even excessively surprised. Now let me get you back to your father."

CHAPTER THREE

FALCONER was a piece of old England, a beautiful manor house built on the foreshores of Sydney Harbour. Turreted, towered with romantic Gothic windows in jewel colours, its rosy sandstone walls were almost covered with ivy and scented creepers, its terraced gardens sweeping down to the blue harbour, sheltered and enclosed on all sides by magnificent native and exotic trees that soared to such a height that the house was guaranteed a splendid isolation. Built in the 1840s by an important Colonial official, Sir Edward Wyndham, the original brilliant estate had been drastically reduced in size to the present extremely valuable but relatively small block of land, and had passed out of the hands of Sir Edward's descendants and into the vastly enriched hands of Sir Rolf Hunter some thirty years before.

It was without question the most beautiful and romantic house Jaime had ever seen or even dreamed of entering, set like some architectural jewel looking out on to the blue sparkling harbour. Only Quinn's hand beneath her elbow kept Jaime steadily walking towards it. When she had first glanced up after getting out of the car, she had glimpsed a figure at one of the upstairs

windows. She was certain it had been a woman, perhaps
her Aunt Georgia. Quinn, in turn, glancing down at
Jaime noted the fact that she was extremely nervous
and had lost colour; apart from that she couldn't have
looked better, polished but casual in one of the incredibly chic and inventive three-piece outfits she had made
herself. This one was the colour of young claret, with a
beautiful contrasting blouse in a patterned silk which
accented the golden tan of her skin and intensified the
blue-violet of her eyes until they glazed in her small
face. She had an intuitive, highly artistic sense of style,
very likely inherited from her father, and she'd be too
much for Georgia and Sue-Ellen who loathed competition above all things.

"Steady," he said, bending his dark head nearer her.
"You look super, to use one of your own words."

"I feel a complete stranger to myself," she confessed. "What am I doing here?"

"Sticking to our bargain, I hope. By the way, don't
breathe a word of it, including the fact you're a knock-
out with the scissors and the sewing machine."

"I think I'll have my hair cut now I'm in Sydney.
They have superb stylists here."

He smiled and looked down at her. "Can't you hold
on to that black mane? It's very sensuous, to say the
least."

"You'll like what I have in mind," she assured him.

"I'm sure I will. You're destined to go a long way,
Jaime."

"It's not going to be easy," she said, with a sudden

premonition that touched him as well, for he briefly agreed:

"No." He looked up towards the house again and his face changed, becoming guarded and faintly saturnine. A woman in a deep sea green caftan was gliding towards them, the sunlight streaming over her beautifully blonded hair.

It was easy to classify her—the wife of a very rich man, all subtle arrogance, her narrow green eyes smiling as they moved swifter than light over Jaime. In a few seconds she was upon them, giving Quinn an intimate smile, pressing a white jewelled hand to his cheek, and greeted Jaime with a high concentrate of attention, then took the girl's hands and kissed her cheek.

"My dear child, you're the the image of your mother!" she said as though that covered everything.

"Aunt Georgia!" Jaime responded, trying to fight out of the fumes of a very expensive and adventurous perfume.

"Welcome to Falconer, my dear," Georgia offered belatedly, a constriction somewhere under her breastbone. She turned to Quinn almost with relief and linked her hands around his jacketed arm. "How lovely to have you back again. We've *missed* you," she said as though he had been to the moon and was back again to a terrestrial paradise. Her green eyes found Jaime's. "You've no idea how fortunate you were to have Quinn. He's nobody's guide as a rule."

"He was a lot of fun, actually," Jaime said in a fit of

devilment, which made Georgia's smile chip at the corners.

"Don't let my Sue hear you say that!" Georgia warned playfully. "She would throw her life away for this man."

"How wasteful! May I see my grandfather, Aunt Georgia? I'm looking forward to meeting Sue and the rest of the family."

"As they're anxious to meet you, dear," Georgia maintained, substituting *avid* for *anxious* in her own mind.

The girl was a shock; Rowena all over again, more poised and well turned out than Georgia could credit with the insignificant background her appalling father had provided for her. Her outfit had everything; cut, line, a wonderful colour with that enviable Queensland tan, and she wore it like a professional model with considerable élan. Rowena's exotic hyacinth gaze mocked her, dominating the young face with its Indian black hair. Georgia was horrified and alarmed. In fact she earnestly wished the child had died with the mother. Rowena had always caused trouble, and her daughter struck the same chord. Georgia turned and led the way with Quinn and Jaime a few measured steps away from her.

Immediately Jaime entered the large entrance hall, her eyes feel on the tall Oriental vases that stood on either side of an eighteenth-century lacquered chest exquisitely decorated in gold and turquoise on a black background. Long blossoming branches grew out of them, reflected in the Chinese Chippendale mirror that hung above the cabinet. Against the opposite wall were a pair of Chinese armchairs inlaid with mother-of-pearl. They were clearly not intended for comfort, but they were wondrously beautiful. A great bronze doré chandelier hung directly above Jaime's head, the floor was parqueted and covered with a fine Imperial Chinese rug and the magnificent cantilevered stairway, with its elaborate carving and Gothic balusters, marked the beginning of a remarkable art collection that Jaime was to find covered every available wall in the house, and even the specially-lit corners. Reception rooms opened off either side of the hall, but Jaime was not to see them then, for a young woman suddenly winged down the stairway crying a name:

"Quinn, *darling!*"

Jaime stood resolutely, feeling extremely unwanted. With the gift of all females she had defined Georgia's true feelings instantly. Georgia's daughter Sue-Ellen was a sleek and cosmeticised twenty-four-year-old version of her mother. They had similar coloured hair and eyes and similar expressions, though Sue-Ellen's youth saved her. She was flinging herself headlong at Quinn, who took hold of her arms before she latched them round his neck, her fair-skinned face full of a delicious excitement. "Darling, darling!" she continued breathlessly, not in the least put out by a certain resistance in him.

"Sue, where are your manners?" Georgia chided her fondly. "Turn around this minute and say hello to your cousin Jaime."

"Hello, Cousin Jaime!" Sue said without turning her head.

"A welcome, I'm sure, that makes Jaime's heart glad," Quinn said smoothly.

"Dear me, dear me!" Sue-Ellen gathered herself and spun round and advanced on Jaime with her hand out. "Welcome to the bosom of the family. You've been an outsider for so long."

"And looking forward to returning," Jaime said pleasantly. "How are you, Sue?"

"Oh, terrific! Maybe the reverse. You're the living image of your mother."

"So I've been told."

"Grandfather is going to be very taken with you," Sue-Ellen said.

"Not odd in a grandparent," Quinn observed dryly, then shot back the cuff of his shirt and glanced down at his wrist watch. "I'll take Jaime up to him if I may, Georgia. There are a few things he'll want to know, then I'll be on my way."

"Surely you're staying for a while. What about dinner?" Sue-Ellen wailed.

"Not this evening," Quinn expressed his regret with his rare charming smile that hovered for a second only. "My grandmother is expecting me to dine with her."

"What happens if you rang up and said you were dining here?" Georgia suggested, a little in awe of Margo Sterling.

"I wouldn't think of disappointing her, Georgia. If you're ready to meet your grandfather, Jaime, it's this way."

"I am," Jaime said quietly, pulsating with nerves and acutely aware of the cynical thoughts that nourished mother and daughter.

"Hurry back, will you, Quinn?" Sue-Ellen begged, "I'll wait for you here. You're the last man in the world to act nursemaid—surely Jaime can go up by herself. It's the fourth door on the right as you go along the gallery."

"I think Jaime can have her hand held this once," Quinn said, his black eyes brilliant and sharp as needles.

"Just charming! How do you do it, Jaime, those big blue eyes?"

"I thought Quinn was just being considerate."

"Why, Sue, how you talk!" Georgia remonstrated with her daughter. "I don't know what Jaime will think of you."

"She'll know soon enough," Sue said a little viciously, her green eyes narrowed to slits. "By the way, Uncle Viv and the family have been invited for dinner. A little get-together in Jaime's honour. Sure you won't change your mind, Quinn? Leigh will be *so* disappointed. It's a sort of contest between us." Her green gaze, transferred to Jaime, was as instructive as a stop light.

"Shall we go up now, Jaime?" Quinn grasped Jaime's arm, quite unconcerned by all the female interest so fervently avowed.

"Yes, *please*," she said in a soft undertone, honestly considering leaving within the hour.

The gallery was long and beautifully proportioned, hung with paintings and chairs set at intervals, a lovely stained-glass window set at one end through which the sun poured on to the polished floor and the Persian runner. Jaime was beset with a strange nostalgia, a

wave of emotion that was making her eyes shimmer.
There was nothing for her here in this beautiful house.
It would have been better for her never to have
come. She tugged on Quinn's arm and he looked down
at her, an unaccustomed compassion on his dark, handsome face.

"Where's that refreshing fighting spirit?" he demanded.

"Can't you tell they don't like me? They don't want
me here."

"Did you expect anything else?"

He scrutinised her for a long minute and something
in his expression made her put her shoulders back.
"All right, we've come this far!"

"And we'll go all the rest." His strong arm descended and tightened around her delicate shoulders.
"This is going to be a new kind of life, Jaime, one
unknown to you, so that sometimes you'll feel like a
different person, but I'm convinced you'd survive any
upheaval."

"Can you tell me why?" she demanded.

"Because basically you're a very stong person."

"You don't know me."

"Because it's been only a few days?"

"Quinn?" She looked up at him, for that moment
entirely at his mercy, a young girl still, blue glints in her
hair, her young face intent, absorbed by the tragic past.

"It's all right, Jaime."

"Have you been hearing a word I've been saying?"

"God help me, I remember every one of them. Your
grandfather is waiting for you with a full heart and

that's the truth. Compassion has been nearly driven out of this family, but you have it. Keep it undimmed until you're an old, old lady with children and grand-children and great-grandchildren who adore you."

"I don't think I'm ever going to be able to thank you for this," she said. "Probably I'll forget it sometimes."

"You will, with your volatile temper. Turn your face up, beauty like yours is hard to come by and your grandfather will want to see it the very first minute."

Jaime drew a deep breath, since that was all she could do, and saw Quinn pause outside a solid cedar door that gave on to her grandfather's suite of rooms. He paused for a moment, looking back at her, then he tapped on the lustrous panelling. A woman's voice answered, calling a: "Come in," and after a few sec-onds a pleasant-faced competent-looking woman in an impeccable white nurse's uniform came to the open doorway.

"How are you, Mr. Sterling? Miss Gilmore!" She smiled at Jaime, her brown eyes searching. "Sir Rolf is expecting you." She didn't wait for an introduction but went swiftly out of the door and shut it softly behind her.

Jaime could see her grandfather quite clearly, stand-ing against the windows staring at her as though he found her face a thing of more profound beauty than any in history.

"Jaime!"

"Grandfather!"

He shook his silver head, and a terrible sadness covered his face.

It was too much for the tender-hearted Jaime. She covered the space that divided them like a gazelle, flinging out her arms for all her preconceived notions, driven by some force quite outside her, to comfort this old man who was her grandfather. Somehow her own face was pressed to his heart, his hand shaking but inexpressibly tender, shaping the back of her head. "Little Jaime, and to think I've never known you."

"Hush, Grandfather!"

"I'll die easily now."

"You won't die at all. I've only just arrived."

"So precious, so precious, my granddaughter I've never known. Can you ever forgive me for failing you?"

"I've been happy," she told him, "I love my father."

"Yes, some women are made for devotion. Look up at me, Jaime! Quinn, my dear boy, how can I ever thank you? Mission accomplished as usual."

"You could let me go ahead with Dinsmore & Donovan. How are you, Sir Rolf, you look a new man!"

"I feel it. You can talk to me later about D&D. Believe it or not, I agree with you. Can't you come to dinner, my dear boy? Bring Margo, of course, though she's never approved of me. We must welcome our youngest member of the family. Isn't she beautiful, the image of Rowena!"

"There are differences if you look for them."

"Over Nigel, isn't she—Margo?"

"As you're over your daughter. Thank you for the invitation, Sir Rolf. Naturally I'll allow my grandmother to decide. She was expecting me to dine with her."

"You'd like him to come, wouldn't you, Jaime? After all, he brought you back to me. Great powers of persuasion has Quinn!"

"He must please himself, Grandfather, and consult his grandmother. But yes, I'd like them both to come."

"Thank you, Jaime." There was no edge of mockery in that dark, sardonic voice. "I have a report here I'd like you to look at, sir. No filling in, just the facts."

Sir Rolf nodded. "Let's hope you're right."

"I am right."

"You're a ruthless young devil, Quinn. All the Sterlings rolled into one."

There was a hard flicker of anger in Quinn's dark eyes. "You could never had applied that word to any one of them. I'm the man I am because that's the way I have to be!"

Sir Rolf looked away from him, frowning. "I'd rather one of my own was that! Don't imagine I don't know what I've got in you, Quinn, a trouble shooter."

"There's no question of owning me, Sir Rolf."

"I guess I like to own everybody. You're as arrogant as that fallen angel, you know that? You're the man I pick for all the difficult assignments, but I don't know you, do I?"

Across Jaime's head Rolf Hunter studied his most brilliant executive. No one could touch him in the technical department either. He knew the business from top to bottom; plant, productivity, the latest technology. He was an expert in management. The men all chatted away to him cheerfully when they had never been known to approach his own sons. He could handle the unions as well as government officials and he was liked and respected by every member of the Board outside his own family. The boys—well, it was reasonable for them to hate him. Quinn was clever and strong and so positive when they only knew the language and went through the motions efficiently. It wasn't enough. He should be worried himself by young Quinn Sterling and he would have been even a few years back; now nothing seemed to matter. Making money was no longer important. He had more than enough of it and he would have let it all go to have Rowena's daughter come home again. Only one mistake he had ever made in his life and it had been colossal. Now he had been given the chance to make reparation.

He smiled at Quinn with ironic appreciation, proud of him in spite of the fact that Quinn was almost as big a fox as he was himself. What happened from now on he couldn't prevent. After his death, somehow Quinn Sterling would gain control, despite all the weapons his sons would bring in and use against him. Besides, there was too much he liked about Quinn himself, though occasionally he caught glimpses of Philip Sterling, his first partner, and was startled by the resemblance.

Philip with his impeccable ideals, Philip the intellectual, the brilliant engineer, with a family who found the young Rolf Hunter just that bit their social inferior though he had been a go-getter then. It had been he who put Hunter Sterling on the map, not Philip with his masterly conceptions. In a lot of ways Quinn was a radical departure from his father and grandfather, but now and again Rolf caught the same aristocratic aloofness in those brilliant black eyes. These days it amused him, though it frightened the boys, Gerald and Viv, out of their wits. His grandsons, so far, were non-events. Magnates were born, one couldn't cultivate them. Quinn Sterling would bring the wheel of fortune full circle.

What Rolf had done to Quinn's father, though provoked, had been damnable. Nothing daunted him in those days. Margo Sterling, a charming and very cultivated woman to this day, stared right at and through him, yet she had loved Rowena. Well, Rowena on whom she had lavished such affection repaid her cruelly. Margo had a son, Nigel. Life was hard. Families made one suffer. Was it any wonder he turned to business? He had made it everything up to now.

Jaime, the silent observer, looked from her grandfather to Quinn. Both of them were very striking men, much of a height, which meant over six feet, her grandfather with a full, pure silver head of hair and flaming black eyebrows, dark grey eyes like a piece of steel; Quinn with the sparkling arrogance of achievement and a look of breeding, contemptuous of hypocrisy, his black eyes flashing with complete directness, as relentless in his fashion as Rolf Hunter was in his. Both of them had tremendous charisma, and a genius for seeing right through to essentials, shutting out everything else. Both of them with an air of power, stronger now in the younger man and for a number of reasons. Rolf Hunter was coming quickly to the end of his life and he had almost forsaken the business empire he had built up.

"Grandfather?" Jaime, feeling suddenly protective of him, put out her hand to this lion of an old man and he took it and held it tightly, his wonder and peace increasing every minute he gazed at her face. "We've so much to talk about. When I get changed, can we walk in the garden? It looks incredibly beautiful, and the harbour!"

"It's nothing...*nothing*, compared to your face!" For an instant Sir Rolf looked transfixed, his mind in the past. "I always knew you'd come back, Rowena."

Jaime couldn't move or speak, taken utterly by surprise. Quinn moved suddenly, taking a manilla folder crammed with typed pages out of his briefcase and slapping it down on the writing desk near the window. "I'd like you to read this, Sir Rolf. We'll lose money if you don't!"

"Money, money!" Sir Rolf cried affably. "All right, my boy. I'll do just as you say and thank you once again."

"No thanks needed at all," Quinn said briefly. "It was a pleasure. Now if I have to get to the city and then back to Rosemount I'd better hurry. I'll see you again, Jaime."

Jaime lifted her small head high, bewildered by some razor-sharp note in his voice. "Tonight, I hope," she looked up at him gravely, her blue eyes magnetic in her golden face, but she didn't move away from her grandfather.

"I'll convey your invitation to my grandmother," he

said with exquisite courtesy, studying both their faces with a kind of sombre intensity as though marking them for ever. She had thought he despised all her family, and maybe this would be true of her as well. She was at a loss with him, uncertain, back to square one. If she wanted to go with him, and she did, she gave no sign of it, locked to her grandfather's side, appearing extremely young and graceful beside him.

Quinn moved to the door, turned quickly to salute them, then he was gone. His strength and authority, the mingled protectiveness and antagonism, whatever it was he felt for her, seemed to go with him. She was on her own and she would have to know how to cope.

WHEN QUINN ARRIVED at Rosemount, he found his grandmother waiting for him with singular, distressed curiosity. With his arm around her shoulders, he led her into the drawing room, exclaiming over the beauty of her hair which she had had specially shampooed and set that day to mark his homecoming. She listened to his compliments solemnly but with great pleasure, for she went to a great deal of trouble with her appearance when her arthritis these days often had her in indescribable pain. Enthroned in her favourite wingbacked chair, she waved her grandson into the chair opposite, searching his lean handsome face with pride and an insatiable need to hear about this girl, Jaime. Such an odd name for a girl, but that would have been her father's contribution.

Quinn took her hand, his eyes wandering over Margo's infintely dear face. A beauty in her youth, the

signs were still there in plenty—the indestructible bone
structure, the breeding, the spirit and the intelligence.
Once her eyes had been an overwhelming blue, not the
exquisite lapis lazuli of Jaime's, but the blue of the sea;
now they were faded, soft and cool like the sky seen
through rain. She had great courage. She had known
tragedy, losing her husband and two of her children,
but she had survived and her will was like iron.

"Tell me," Margo said abruptly, in her rather deep
voice. "Is she as lovely, as enchanting as Rowena?"

"I almost yearn to tell you she's as plain as a wall-
flower, but she's everything Rowena was and more."

"I find that highly painful. Do you think I'm awful,
darling?"

"No, I don't. They want us to join them for dinner,
by the way. A celebration."

"Oh no!"

"There's no need to go."

"I'll come right out with it, I can't stand them. Why
should that man be rewarded, that wicked old man?"

"I think he's repenting," Quinn soothed.

"Life is full of surprises. What he did to your father,
not Philip so much, but your dear father, I'll never forgive him!"

"I can attend to that little problem," Quinn said aus-
terely.

"I'm not sure if I approve of that either."

"Then you'll have to get used to it, darling. I'm the
tycoon, not you!"

"Oh, Quinn!" she said, and touched his cheek.
"The old stories, they're tragic, are they not?"

"They've never made me laugh. Jaime, too, has had a struggle. It hasn't been easy for her. Her father is talented, but not serious about anything except maybe revenge. He's never forgiven Rowena, either!"

Margo nodded. "Poor Rowena, I wonder if she lies easily in her grave. She was still so young when she died. From the minute she married him things went badly."

"It's impossible to dislike him. He has a lot of charm and I'm quite sure he could have been a much bigger success with just a little drive!"

"Not everyone enjoys success, my darling boy. Success carries difficulties and responsibilities, bigger and bigger worries."

"Well, I'm not going to stop here," Quinn said, swiftly and completely.

"That's no news!" Margo Sterling smiled at her grandson, studying him for that instant quite objectively. "I know your grandfather would think some of the things you've been doing lately were dangerously unsuitable!"

"Grandfather completely lacked my business judgment."

"I know that! Poor Philip, he found the world of intrigue and counter-intrigue quite impossible."

"That's why we lost out progressively to Hunter. For years he got away with the lot, but not now. It's all over!" He was staring into the past, his handsome dark face grim, his lean strong hands moving as though he comtemplated wringing someone's neck. "I even have to steel myself to accept the rest of them as vastly overpaid executives."

"Look here, Quinn," his grandmother said sternly, "they're entitled to their share of the multi-million-dollar business their father and grandfather built up."

"Not the lion's share!" Quinn said pleasantly, his black eyes brilliant. "They've had that for too long."

"Don't think they're not aware of their position. They'd hurt you if they could. Everyone knows you're running Hunter Sterling these days. It's extraordinary how that man has lost all interest in what once was his whole life."

"The change is Jaime," Quinn said bluntly. "If you could have seen his face! Fascinating. The first and only time I've seen him reach out towards another human being and mean it."

"Then you don't really remember Rowena, how could you? He adored her, so much so that her brothers could scarcely endure her. It was no secret that he paid little attention at all to the boys when they were small. They've never forgotten it, or their jealousy of their sister. One can feel some pity for them—in a way it's affected their whole lives. Their mother was so gentle, such a defenceless, beautiful creature, she just gave up and died. She never understood her husband. Never for a moment. I know, because she told me. She asked me also, to look after her daughter!" Margo Sterling sighed deeply and her frail crippled hands moved restlessly in her lap. "Perhaps I can do her daughter a service. But not now. It's cruel, but I don't think I can lay eyes on the child. I'm too old, you see. I might weep."

"I've never seen you weep," Quinn said calmly, an

expression on his face few but his grandmother had seen. "What was it Father used to say? There's no one more capable of meeting any situation than my mother!"

"That was years ago, darling, I could very easily blemish my record these days. I'm an old woman and I mean *old*!"

"And you're terribly tough! Where do you think I got it from? Quick, make the decision and I'll abide by it. I just don't know myself."

His grandmother stared at him. "That's a first for you! What is she, this Jaime?"

"A witch with long black hair and unnaturally beautiful eyes."

"You're talking about Rowena," his grandmother said strangely,

"No, Jaime. She won't go the same way as her tragic mother. She has enormous reserves and she's only a young girl. She's even made it clear to me that she expects me to back her in a business of her own."

"Why, how peculiar!" Margo Sterling had some difficulty keeping a slight hostility out of her voice. "That's the Hunter business instinct. It's skipped a couple of generations to Jaime."

Quinn looked back at her steadily. "Why on earth shouldn't it? Jaime has big plans. She wants to be another Pru Acton."

"That's a tall order."

"The raw material is there, if you'll forgive the pun. I'd like you to speak to her. She's too high voltage at the moment, but she'll learn. Her sense of style is innate and enviable. She's very chic, very modern but elegant, and she makes all her own clothes. She expects to have to work very hard and she requires listening to. She has the talent, plus the drive.''

"And she wants you to do the rest! What about her grandfather? He has a tremendous amount of money.''

"That would be involving herself in a real dilemma, and she's shrewd enough to know it.''

"It doesn't really affect me, Quinn,'' Margo Sterling said, almost pathetically desperate.

Quinn smiled. "Don't opt out, darling. I know what I'm asking of you. Perhaps not tonight, but spare her a little time. She hasn't had a fortunate life up to now, though she's very loyal to her father.''

"You would seem to have become very loyal to her in a very short time,'' the old lady observed.

"She's a child!'' Quinn said rather wearily. "I'm not going to fling her headfirst into the maelstrom. Georgia and Sue hated her on sight.''

"Then we'll go,'' Margo Stirling said, equally forceful. "You said the very thing to attract my sympathy. But then you know that, you cunning devil!''

"Anyway, you ought to take that new hairstyle out. I can honestly say that fellow you go to is an artist.''

"And I don't begrudge him a farthing of his turnover, though some people get quite annoyed.''

"Like Aunt Lucille?''

"That's right. Now, my boy, help me up. If we must go out on this errand of mercy I'll need time to prepare. At times you remind me altogether of my own father.

He was always getting us to do unimaginable things without putting himself out one bit!"

"I suppose you enjoyed it," Quinn said, smiling, but his grandmother only rested against him for a moment and patted his cheek. It would take all her calm and indomitable will to meet Rowena's daughter: Rowena, whose actions had robbed her of a son. Of course Nigel had become morbidly sensitive, but he had been young without the balance of maturity, and Rowena had been such an exceptional girl, an exact blend of the witch Nigel had always called her and a woman to set the nerves pulsing. It would be like resurrecting the old tragedy to meet her daughter, yet it had for Margo a compulsive fascination. She went up to her room on Quinn's arm only wishing to get it all over. It was so very tedious to be old.

CHAPTER FOUR

BY THE TIME dinner was over, Jaime felt a little better. It had been something of an ordeal, not only for her, but for the suffering, regal old lady who sat opposite her, her beautifully dressed head high, her misty blue eyes full of pain. It was so unfair, in its way, this resemblance she had to Rowena, for the mother Jaime had never known had made many people unhappy. At times, under the clamorous, glittering eyes of her relatives, she had felt herself akin to the fox with the whole frenzied pack after her. Her uncles Gerard and Vivian, sharp-eyed and handsome, their expensive-looking wives, her cousins Sue-Ellen and Leigh, with their vaulting ambitions, could be dangerous to her, deeply involved as they were in holding and maintaining their positions in Sir Rolf's life and when that life flickered out, in his will.

Her male cousins, smooth-faced versions of their fathers, were making it blatantly obvious they were prepared to consider her as a matrimonial prize the winning of which would be an enormous feather in their caps, both socially and financially, for Sir Rolf was making no secret of his tremendous pride and joy in his newly-found granddaughter. No one was left in any doubt that a new heiress had just been created. It was like having a beautiful dream blown up in their faces.

Only Quinn and his grandmother held themselves aloof, making suave and witty conversation, coming to Jaime's assistance whenever she needed it, and she found she did to combat the family's rapacity. For this she silently thanked them in her heart, not knowing that her beautiful eyes were conveying to Margo Sterling, at least, her sensitivity, compassion and deep gratitude.

It was these qualities, so easily recognised in Jaime, that enabled Margo to get through the evening, for Jaime was so like her mother that it had been like a physical blow, knocking her off balance and sweeping her back in time. A sudden impulse had seized Margo at the first moment of meeting and caused her to put her arms around the girl and kiss her cheek tenderly, a gesture Jaime was destined never to forget, for she had been shocked at the concealed misery in those softly blue faded eyes. Quinn had looked at her with mingled mockery and congratulation, for even he had wondered how his grandmother would react. She had been known to freeze people at a glance, but only if she considered they deserved it. Jaime obviously did not deserve to suffer for the havoc her mother had caused, if only in Margo Sterling's eyes. Jaime was too well hemmed in by her relatives and their burning, hidden fears and antagonisms. They who had so much, yet wanted more. Jaime, who had lived precariously for so many years, would be denied even the smallest legacy from her grandfather if the family had anything to do with it.

The assessment, though harsh, was quite accurate. Sir Rolf's heirs were in complete agreement about Jaime. She was enormously unwanted, though they were scrupulously polite to her in clear view and earshot of Sir Rolf. Many furious words had been said in the privacy of their own homes. It was considered not inconceivable that the Old Man, in an excess of stupid reparation for old wrongs, could *over*-compensate the girl, and it was their unpleasant duty to see that this didn't happen. Old people nearing the end of their lives invariably became maudlin about such things. The girl was an outsider, for all Rowena had been her mother. Rowena had surrendered her claim and that of her daughter, choosing her own way, and the family were markedly disinclined to accept Jaime much less take her to their hearts. The sight of Sir Rolf making such a fool of himself further repulsed them. One would have thought he didn't have two other beautiful granddaughters to dote on, and he had never been known to do that, not even when they had been the most adorably cute toddlers in their exquisite little hand-made dresses.

It was unthinkable. They hadn't really believed it until they saw it with their own eyes, but Jaime was emerging as a colossal threat to all of them. Perhaps even on a grander scale than Quinn Sterling with his frightening rise to the seat of power. Sabotage on two levels—small wonder they were so upset and worried. The only ray of light, or the only possible way about the whole bad business, was to marry the girl off to one of the boys. Simon or Brett, it didn't really matter which.

They were interchangeable and their dedication to family interests was the only remarkable thing about them.

Margo Sterling, watching all of them with her wise old eyes, was hopelessly disgusted. Only one thing saved her from total despair; there was an added strength and humour to Jaime's features beside the purity of Rowena's. She hadn't noticed it immediately, so overcome had she been, but now, hours later, she began to appreciate the subtle differences between Jaime and her memories of the young Rowena. The very best of Rowena plus something very individual. One could never have seen Rowena, for instance, ever contemplating setting up her own business. Rowena had been reared a princess. Jaime had come up the hard way and it hadn't hurt her. The end product was a very striking creature indeed, with courage and ambition, and the others were green with jealousy, the women busy deploring her beautiful face and figure, not realising that they had to give Jaime credit for the chaste little evening dress she had on, sheer as blue smoke, totally demure and inexpressibly stylish, sheening as it did her beautiful young body.

Now Margo realised with a flutter of relief that it might be a good thing to back Jaime in a business enterprise, and the pleasure and intensity of her emotion astonished her. She would talk to the girl, but for tonight she was experiencing too much remembered pain. She would have to arrange with Quinn to bring Jaime to Rosemount. Tonight her ghosts were haunting her, practically sitting beside her. Nigel, as beloved and familiar to her as Quinn was now; Rowena, so beautiful and enchanting that she could do no wrong. Then as now Rowena was Rolf Hunter's only blind spot, and Rowena lived on in her daughter. The situation was potentially dangerous, for even a man as brilliant as Rolf Hunter could still be as big a fool as any other man on earth. He had the power to make Jaime one of the richest young women in the country and in so doing throw a giant scare into his family, and he was a man without pity. Jaime would bear the brunt of his measures, a bigger and bigger rival every minute she stayed on at Falconer.

An hour later, Margo signalled to her grandson that she was ready to go. She had never enjoyed the Hunters' bitter world, as luxurious as were their surroundings, the glittering possessions, the literal fortune in paintings that hung on every wall. Very few people would ever bother to remember that Rolf Hunter had once been a struggling young university student with numerous paying sidelines to support himself and his widowed mother. A man could be a mixture of things, good and bad. It was only when he entered the jungle of big business that Rolf Hunter embarked on the course of ruthless slashing and parrying and back-stabbing that took him right to the top. He was clever. He was extraordinary. He was even a very handsome old man, but Margo Sterling had decided as always that she couldn't stand another minute of his company.

She was conscious of Jaime's presence by her side and inexplicably it now gave her a deep sense of ease. The family had all formed into a group to say goodbye, the girls Sue-Ellen and Leigh, enough alike to be sisters, vying as usual for a minute of Quinn's time. He preferred Leigh of the two, a softer, more amiable version of Sue-Ellen and very attractive tonight in a cool, halter-necked dress the same fresh green as her eyes, her hair like her cousin's with a deep fringe and swinging in casual blonde perfection just clear of her shoulders. Margo much preferred Leigh as well. Given a different background Leigh could relax and be herself, not the member of a clan whose purposes and way of life dominated her.

Leigh more and more, was coming under the influence of her younger but more cunning and selfish cousin, Sue-Ellen. Both girls were affronted by Jaime's beauty and obvious self-confidence. It put them in a rage. The family had pointed out that the girl had almost been dragged up by a failure of a father; it was therefore demoralising to be confronted by a poised and elegant young woman who regarded them all gravely and with a faint element of—*pity*? It was easily seen that their grandfather, who had never loved them and rarely smiled at them, had found again the one person in the world he could love. They all found it frightening and disquieting, though they did their best to be agreeable, with a lifetime's practice at playing it smart.

In their hearts they knew there was no question of getting used to the situation but reversing it. They would never surrender their position, Jaime would have to be the one to go. In a family used to high strategy, dominated by a fierce pride to emerge victorious, one young girl on her own should present no real problem. Rowena had run out on her father and all that she had known. Her daughter could be made to do the same.

AFTER A MONTH of her relations, Jaime felt as though she was drowning in poison. It was such a wild idea to have thought they might accept her. They never would—jealousy brought out the worst in people. The women put this across with force and clarity, smiles on their narrow arrogant mouths. Her uncles Gerard and Vivian kept her constantly under surveillance, their eyes loaded with speculation as though beating their combined brains out to devise some way of rendering her permanently harmless. Her cousins, Simon and Brett, figured largely in their plans, for had Jaime accepted all their numerous invitations to go sailing, swimming, partying and what-not, she would have been as dizzy as a child on a merry-go-round. They were all so alike in their objectives that they might have been one.

There seemed no time whatever to think of her own plans, for her grandfather rarely let her out of his sight. Blood, she had cause to know, was thicker than water, because she found herself indulging him, caught into the desire to please him, or more accurately give him peace, for his health after such a serious heart attack had markedly declined. It was always sacrifice, she thought to herself. Men seemed to demand it. First her father, now her grandfather and her woman's compassion kept her enslaved. Nevertheless it would have to stop.

Quinn, whom she saw fairly often, had been almost

formidably abrupt at their last meeting, contenting himself with hurling at her one question: "When do you intend breaking out of your prison?"

She hadn't answered him then, upset by the cold brilliance of his eyes, but she proposed to do so now. Directly after breakfast, she intended to take a taxi into the city and waylay him in his office. It was true Uncle Gerard and Simon would be leaving in the car shortly before then, but she had no wish to ask either of them for a lift even though the chances were she would run into them at the Corporation Building.

Neither Georgia nor Sue-Ellen ever came down for breakfast, her grandfather had a tray in his room, so Jaime usually endured breakfast with her uncle and cousin. It seemed incredible to her that her Uncle Gerard could have no feeling for her. They shared a family resemblance, but that meant nothing. It wasn't as though his behaviour was uncivilised, quite the reverse; he was extremely convivial, especially in front of his father, but the Judas light shone in his eyes.

It was devastating but true, and small wonder her mother had left home. After a month Jaime had come to realise that her relatives expected her to join them or they would destroy her. It was brutal, but apparently it was their way of life. If she consented in time to marry either of her cousins they would consider her in another light. For then her inheritance, and it was now certain she would receive one, could be kept in the family. Not a one of them had a guilty conscience, for family alliances kept empires alive and they were already under attack from the Sterlings.

Jaime was given to understand that she had better choose her side, and only a fool would run to the Sterlings. She would never be allowed to use any future financial power against her own family. Even now Quinn Sterling was dictating policy and ran Hunter Sterling, when their father had built the firm up into the great business enterprise it was today. Too many had already assigned their holdings to Sterling, and if Jaime inherited a very large block of shares and for whatever reason assigned them to Sterling, then the family would lose out on the majority shareholding. It was not to be borne.

When Jaime came down that morning, she found the breakfast-room occupied, the sun streaming through the great plate glass window; a modern touch, affording the most beautiful views of the garden and the blue harbour beyond. Gerard Hunter looked up with a smile, laying down his paper and greeted her most genially. Simon jumped to his feet, pulled out a chair, saw Jaime seated, and offered to serve her from any one of the silver chafing dishes that lined the sideboard. Both men, she had discovered, ate a very hearty breakfast—fruit juice, cereal, a hot dish, eggs and bacon, sausages, grilled tomatoes, enormous quantities of toast and marmalade, excellent black coffee reduced by cream. It almost hurt her to watch them, for she found breakfast the least inviting meal of the day.

Jaime returned their greeting, smiling at Simon, who was looking at her with quite unfeigned admiration. She requested black coffee with toast and heard Uncle Grerard launch into the daily and quite serious lecture on the importance of a good breakfast, involving blood levels and sugar, or blood sugar levels; she never did listen, and felt like pointing out kindly that she was in perfect health notwithstanding. Uncle Gerard suffered from severe migraine and an incipient ulcer, but to comment on that would have pleased no one, so she simply tuned out.

"And what's on the agenda today?" Simon was asking, placing her coffee cup near her right hand, having rung for fresh toast.

"I'm going into the city today!" Jaime said, inadvertently disclosing her intentions, rattled as she was by Simon's heavy breathing. Now he would be sure to offer to drive her there, which he did.

"I'll take you," he said promptly, giving her his usual embarrassing amount of attention. "Where is it you want to go?"

"I want to see Quinn," she said, something of a trouble-shooter herself.

"*Sterling?*"

Both men almost shouted her down. Uncle Gerard glared at her and came right out into the open, so severe was his shock.

"Yes, I want to talk to him!" Jaime explained artlessly.

Simon stared at her for a full ten seconds. "He'll be busy, dear," he said spitefully. "Don't you know he's a very important man? One has to make an appointment weeks in advance to see Quinn. I should know, I spend practically all of my life trying to arrange a meeting."

His father's anger was real and so obvious. "What on earth would you want to see Sterling about?"

"Surely that's my affair, Uncle Gerard."

The remark only served to further enrage him. "Look here, young lady," he cried pompously, in an achingly loud voice, "it's time you and I had a talk! I consider Quinn Sterling our enemy!"

"I thought he was a partner in the firm."

"You know nothing whatever about the true situation. Nothing whatever about big business."

"It must be an inherited trait," Jaime said calmly. "I want to speak to Quinn about my own business."

"Then kindly take my word for it," he uncle shouted, still misunderstanding her, "and I'm not going to spell it out again, Quinn Sterling is out to do us all harm."

At that very moment the housekeeper came in with the fresh toast and there was a necessary little pause, simply burning with frustration. Jaime smiled at the woman and thanked her, and they all waited until she could reasonably be expected to be out of earshot. Gerard Hunter started out again, becoming more and more angry, giving his accumulated anxieties of the past month and more, full rein.

"I expect you, Jaime," he said forcefully, "to tell me exactly what you intend to discuss with Sterling. We know, of course, of your visits to Rosemount."

"I've made no secret of them. May I remind you, Uncle Gerard, I'm a free agent, not some unfortunate employee, and I'm a guest in my grandfather's home."

Gerard Hunter held up his hand and tried belatedly to gain control of himself. Why, the insolent little chit sounded exactly like the old man! "If you're determined to misunderstand me, Jaime—"

"Oh, really, Dad, give the poor girl a go," Simon

protested, alarmed at the way things were going. "You see, Jaime, there are aspects of this you couldn't possibly know about. It should suffice for Dad to tell you Quinn Sterling is no good. He intends to take over Hunter Sterling, and that we'll never allow."

"We're talking at cross purposes," Jaime said quietly. "I wish to speak to Quinn about setting up my own business."

Gerard Hunter's heavy handsome face flushed a dark red. "Your *own* business?" he asked with ludicrous disbelief.

Simon leaned forward, laughing. "Tell us?" he begged with mock urgency.

"I intend to become a dress designer."

"A dressmaker?" her uncle wailed incredulously. "Why, my dear girl, you'll make a holy show of us!"

"A dressmaker, how freaky!" Simon crowed.

"Yes, a dressmaker, like Pru Acton and Norma Tullo. Mary Quant and Zandra Rhodes, Schiaparelli and Coco Chanel!"

"Don't draw on those names!" Simon said waspishly, looking very much like his sister.

"Why not? I have ability. I'm prepared to work just as hard."

"No woman of our family need work!" her uncle proclaimed disdainfully. "If you must do something, your aunt heads a dozen different committees. I'm sure she could find something to keep you out of mischief!"

"Mischief isn't my scene, Uncle Gerard. Work is necessary for me. I could never be content to live out the easy life. I want to have a goal in life."

"Have you had any training?" he asked coldly.

"I know what I'm about," she rejoined. "I've always known, just like some people know they're going to be singers, or concert pianists or doctors."

"How marvellous!" Simon cooed, staring intently into her blue-violet eyes. "But pray tell us, how does Sterling fit into all this? He's an unlikely partner for a dressmaker."

"He's the best brain I know," Jaime said flatly. "I can't bother Grandfather with business matters. He's not nearly well enough."

"Thank you for nothing, dear!" Simon said sweetly. "How very generous of you."

"You did ask me," she pointed out.

"I also think you'll regret it," her uncle intervened. "*You* may have forgotten it, young woman, but Sterling hasn't. You're a Hunter!"

"Correction. My name is Gilmore," Jaime said.

"It could so easily have been Sterling!" Simon mocked her. "You've heard about poor old Nigel, haven't you? That old boring tale?"

"Maybe my idea of boring doesn't match yours. I respect Quinn's judgment. I'm very fond of his grandmother. She's been very kind to me."

"Don't let the reason for that pass you by!" Gerard Hunter said sneeringly. "You're pitifully naive!"

"An ulcer is too high a price to pay for wisdom."

"How dare you!" her uncle burst out volcanically.

Jaime stared at him. "Make no mistake, Uncle Gerard, I'm aware of your hostility."

This, and the reminiscent set of her head, set a warning thrill through him. He fought to resume his mask of spurious affability and discretion. "How could you, my dear! You're my niece, my own sister's child. It appalls me to hear you say such a thing. We've done everything, *everything* we could to make you welcome. The girls have introduced you to their friends. The boys have taken you everywhere. At the end of the month we're throwing a big party to introduce you to the best people!"

"I can meet a lot of nice people on the bus or the ferry. Anyway, that was my grandfather's idea and I'm only going along with it to please him."

"You're trying very hard to do that, aren't you, pet?"

"I don't have to try at all!" Jaime said bluntly.

A sudden passion of callous jealousy stared out of Gerard Hunter's eyes. "Don't be too confident, my dear."

Jaime looked away from him out on to the beautiful garden with its magnificent shade trees and blossoming shrubs. "The close family relationship seems to have cracked wide open," she said with sad irony, "fallen apart. In a way it's a relief!"

Simon reached for her hand and pressed it affectionately. "Listen, pet, this is so undignified. We simply don't know what you mean. We're only trying to protect you, to warn you about Sterling, and this is the way you thank us! You must apologise to Dad. You've offended him. Don't waste your life on your silly, girlish ambitions. I've no doubt you made nice little dresses for your dolls. In any case, I've already made up my mind about you."

"Really, in what way?" she enquired.

"Lunch with me today and I'll tell you. I won't listen to any excuses!" Simon turned back to his father, his voice rallying. "How could you bark at the poor girl, Dad? She's lost all her colour under that gorgeous tan."

"I say, I *am* sorry," Gerard Hunter maintained. "You have gone pale. Forgive me, my dear." He tried a frank smile. "It's only that we know what's best for you. I can understand your desire to do a job of work, but there's absolutely no need to embark on a business career. Why, you'll be married in less than a year."

"Why wait as long as that?" Simon said gaily, his eyes sparkling and hugely intrigued. "Now I'm going to pour you another cup of coffee, Jaime, that's gone cold. I'll be set to leave in another twenty minutes."

"I won't be ready then."

"I'll wait longer if it will make things easier for you."

"Thank you, Simon, but it's not necessary. Perhaps I'd better ring through and make an appointment to see Quinn. Thank you for the suggestion."

"You're going to persist with this?" her uncle demanded, glancing bitterly at his son.

"Undoubtedly. I intend to succeed in life, Uncle Gerard."

"Unlike your mother and father."

"My father enjoys every day of his life. Do you?"

"Don't speak to Dad like that," Simon said heatedly. "He's not used to it."

"Put it down to my pathetic naivety," returned Jaime.

"It would be interesting to see what you make of yourself at that!" Simon said, staring at her in his febrile fashion.

"Come, Simon, we'll be late!" His father rose with dignity, folding his napkin neatly beside his plate. "Don't imagine, young lady, that you'll be striking out on your own. Quinn Sterling is a highly skilled manipulator of people. He isn't to be trusted, and this time he's gone too far. Do you really think my father would want you to bypass him for Quinn Sterling?"

"I'm sure Grandfather, like you, would prefer me to lead a life of leisure, surrounded by luxury. It sounds great, but in actual fact it doesn't seem to work out. There's beauty in hard work. Salvation. I believe it's necessary if only to keep us on course."

"How quaint!" Simon said as though he had given a great deal of thought to the matter. "I find it enormously boring!"

"Your aunt will be horrified," Gerard Hunter intoned.

"Whatever for?" Jaime looked up at him.

"You know perfectly well what I mean. This idea of yours is extraordinary. I mean, a tatty dressmaker!"

"Would you call this suit I have on tatty? The dress I had on last night? It inspired my cousins to stare at me all evening. Leigh wouldn't rest until I told her where I bought it."

"You mean you made it yourself?" Simon said incredulously. "You're not such a fool as I took you for."

"*I'm* not the fool, Simon!" She looked back at him levelly.

"This is lovely, a dressmaker in the family! Wait until I tell Mother. Tell me, are you going to use Falconer as your premises?"

"I won't tell you anything at all," Jaime returned crisply. "I didn't really expect you to be interested, much less wish me luck!"

"Have you spoken to my father?" Gerard Hunter looked down his fine, straight nose at her, bitterly shocked.

"Not as yet, but I will in my own good time."

"I'll speak to him," he retaliated with cold ferocity.

"I'm sure you will, Uncle Gerard, but have a care. It will do you no good at all to criticise me."

"Ah!" he released a long choking breath. "Could you be threatening me?"

"Not at all! I'm like you, Uncle Gerard, I'm only trying to point out the dangers."

Resolutely he walked away from the table, a most peculiar expression on his face. "I'm leaving in exactly ten minutes, Simon. Are you coming with me or are you taking your own car?"

"I'll come with you," Simon said instantly with considerable sympathy. "There are things we need to discuss."

After his father had left the room Simon lingered for a moment longer. "It's hard to go against the strength, pet. You'd better pick your side."

"I have already."

"Then don't say you weren't warned. You know, Jaime, you're an endless temptation until you open your mouth. Women aren't cut out to be tycoons and they never will be."

Jaime flared up. "Don't you believe it! It's only now that women have come to take a great pride in their talents or even been allowed to. We've arrived and we're here to stay. Don't worry, it's no big disaster. It's the men who have to answer for the state of the world as it is today—no temptation for a woman to bring children into it."

"You're irrational, over-emotional!" Simon accused her, sounding quite overwrought.

"Believe that and you'll believe anything! Run along, Simon. Don't keep your father waiting. I notice you're exceptionally dutiful, or is that the impression you want to create?"

He shrugged and a very hard expression came on to his face. "You're a very clever girl, Jaime. I can almost admire you."

"I know. I'm hoping my mind will cancel out my other attractions!"

"I doubt it! Lunch?"

"No, thank you."

"You'd better leave Quinn Sterling well alone. Either Sue or Leigh would scratch your eyes out."

"A jungle, is it not?" she said.

"And it's you who'll finish up licking your wounds!"

Jaime forced herself to smile at him. "You've got the slogan the wrong way round; *Right* is might!"

"Boy, are you the new girl!"

She nodded. "I suppose I am, but that's the way I'm going to do it."

"Then you won't worry us. Ever hear the sad tale about Honest John Sterling? A very aristocratic and highly ethical man. Given his head Honest John would have ruined us, by cleaning up here and there, instead Grandfather brought him to his knees."

"Apparently Quinn's sorting that one out!"

"You're quick to defend him, aren't you? He doesn't need you, little girl. Quinn is unique among the Sterlings. A brilliant, complex man with tremendous energies, infinitely tougher than all his ancestors put together."

"You sound as if you admire him, in a grudging sort of way," remarked Jaime.

"He's bringing the Corporation on in leaps and bounds."

"Then shouldn't you go down on your knees and thank him?"

"That's likely!" Simon jeered. "Remember the name dear, *Hunter* Sterling? Quinn might start demanding an entirely different arrangement. Sterling Hunter, or maybe just plain The Sterling Corporation. Get my drift? Well, so long, kiddo. Enjoy yourself, though you're going to make it hard on yourself every step of the way."

"Water off a duck's back!" said Jaime, looking right back at him.

"You must like trouble," Simon said unbelievingly, "and I'm telling you, you'll get just that."

"I know, but listen, Simon, it's not really clever to make threats." Jaime's heart was racing and she felt sick inside. The trouble was, though she found it easy to fence with words, her relatives had the edge on her in every department. They were ruthless and wolfish and hard as steel chips. She was actually a fool to cross them, rushing into verbal combat when she couldn't even guess at the real weapons they might use against her. The only friend she had at Falconer was her grandfather, a man with a serious heart condition. She could never use him as her supreme weapon. One spasm of anger or retaliation on her behalf might kill him. All she could do was use him as a bluff. So heartless themselves, the family might consider her equally ruthless to gain her own ends.

It was with the greatest relief that she heard the front door slammed shut as if in a massive protest. Uncle Gerard was furious with her. He would have to be careful to avoid a bad migraine. In another half-hour, she would ring through and make an appointment to see Quinn. Her grandfather was no ordinary man. He had done many things that couldn't possibly have been right, but now he was old and sick to death, absolutely beyond touching. Quinn probably had very good reason to hate him, yet she was quite sure he didn't. Quinn's purpose was resolute. He was brilliant and super-efficient, thunderously formidable on occasions, but he wasn't cruel. Somehow he had managed to retain an element of pity for her grandfather. She had seen it in his eyes.

Jaime sat very still at the table, a strange pallor under

her skin. She was sick and shaken, but she wasn't feeling the full effects even yet. A vivid picture of Quinn began to move behind her eyes. His sombre dark face was smiling, a light passing across it, softening his beautiful, well defined mouth, faultless white teeth, brilliant black eyes with silver points of light at the centre. She saw him very clearly. He might have been sitting opposite her, one lean brown hand reaching out to her. She relaxed her rigid spine and all at once she began to feel better.

CHAPTER FIVE

JAIME CROSSED the foyer of the Hunter Sterling Corporation Building, making for the nearest lift. She was right on time, though she had found it necessary to use her grandfather's name to get through the armada of telephonists, receptionists, and private secretaries that surrounded the Corporation's top executives in an elaborate defence system. It galled her that Jaime Gilmore had cut no ice, but it was imperative she see Quinn. As Sir Rolf Hunter's granddaughter she had found it wondrously easy to speak to him, but not so easy to see him. He was tied up all morning and told her very briskly that he would meet her for lunch. She had hung up swiftly, but even then he had beaten her to it. It only took her a moment to assimilate the fact Mr. Quinn Sterling's office was synonymous with the Holy of Holies. To be able to see him at all was some small comfort.

By the time she reached the top floor, she found he was further buffered by an anteroom. His secretary, an immaculately groomed brunette in her late thirities, was busy on the phone, but she went through the usual pantomime of smiling and mouthing silently to Jaime to take a seat. After a moment she replaced the receiver and enquired warmly:

"Miss Gilmore?"

Jaime said that she was, aware that she was getting most meticulous head-to-toe inspection for possible re-lay to the rest of the typing pool. It didn't make any difference, but still she didn't really like it. One was supposed to look only briefly, then away again, not this show of undivided attention. She decided to return this frank stare, then the secretary picked up the intercom phone and rang through to Quinn's office. Another minute and he was there, opening the door, no smiles but the same brilliant alertness, thanking "Betty" and showing Jaime through to his office, pulling forward the nearest chair.

"I've just got to make one more call, then we'll go. How are you, you look a little pale?"

"I didn't aim to be," Jaime said wryly. "Make your call, Quinn, I'll admire your office. It's very, what's the word?..."

"Impersonal?"

"Not at all. It's more like a home away from home. Very contemporary and tailored. Perhaps you could do with a few paintings on the walls."

"See to it for me." He was walking around to the other side of the huge custom-made mahogany desk with its crystal and chrome desk appointments, his dark face utterly preoccupied.

"Are you serious?" She couldn't tell at all.

"Yes." He looked back at her, obviously having to transfer his concentration to her question. "You can handle it, can't you?"

"Of course. What price range?"

"Round the two thousand five hundred dollar mark. No more. Abstracts. Concentrate on the young up and coming."

"I should get into this myself!" Jaime said, smiling at the thought.

"Can you?"

"A few people have been kind enough to say I needed encouragement.

"Notably not your father."

"That idea had already taken root in my own mind. You didn't plant it."

"Don't flash your eyes at me, Jaime. Perhaps he didn't relish the idea of competition from his own daughter, which is what he might have got!"

"Oh well," she said guardedly, "it's neither here nor there anyway. We were discussing your paintings. Leave it to me. It will be a great pleasure. More, *exciting*!"

"Good girl!" He picked up the phone and immediately tuned out on her. Very shrewd was Quinn, and he had only met her father the once. She studied his handsome, downbent, frowning face, heard him ask for a Mr. Brian Donovan, then she turned slightly in her camel-coloured suede upholstered chair, giving her attention to the scale of the room and the size of the walls. It was a very large office, with a long sofa flanked by contemporary chrome and leather armchairs with a chrome and glass table in front of this seating arrangement, well away from the desk area with its opposite wall of mahogany cabinets which came about waist-high. The room would take, comfortably, two large canvases, one above the rust-coloured sofa, another above the long line of cabinets. A flood of natural light streamed in from the lightly curtained window wall at the back of the desk. She shouldn't have too much trouble with her selection, there were many brilliant young artists to choose from.

She was still deep in thought when Quinn finished his call. He marked his desk calendar, then looked across at her intent face for a moment. She looked a dream as usual, very young-sexy-chic, but she *was* pale, and a number of possible explanations occurred to him.

"How are you coping with the family?" he asked, without compunction.

"You've half guessed it." She turned back to stare at him coolly. "A fight all the way."

"Then it's time to get you out from under their feet!"

"That's what I'm here to talk to you about."

"What happened this morning specifically?" he asked.

"Why?"

"Jaime," he said impatiently, "you're the very picture of health, the spirit of youth if you like, but this morning you're so pale, I get no pleasure from commenting on the fact."

"Damn you, Quinn," she said a little breathlessly, "you're making me feel unattractive."

"That wasn't my idea. I'm nearly nerveless, you're so beautiful. Are you going to tell me, or do I have to wait for hours?"

"After lunch, maybe," she promised.

"In that case, we'll go out!"

He stood up and came around the desk to her, his eyes going over her, the gently tailored little blazer suit, her new hair-style that made the most of her lush fall of hair; a kind of sophisticated pageboy, glossy and perfectly cut, just clear of her shoulders. At the moment, with her head down, it was swinging in a shining dramatic curtain over one cheek. He leaned forward and tilted her head up, holding it there.

"Hello, Jaime."

"Hi, Quinn!"

"You sound about ten years old."

"Can you really spare the time?"

"No."

With his hand under her chin she was forced to meet the gleaming mockery of his eyes. They spelled out a kind of breathless excitement, an element of danger for her, and she was beginning to react. There was nothing calm or ordinary about Quinn. He was a superhuman and very hard to handle. In fact she was sure she couldn't handle him at all. "I have a funny feeling you're trying to hypnotise me," she said with a wavering intensity.

"No," he said briefly.

"All right, go ahead."

"Not here, Jaime."

"Not anywhere! I won't surrender. Go on, laugh, but I tell you I mean it."

"You look pretty intolerably pressured. Coming?"

"You know quite well I want to."

He leaned forward and almost lifted her to her feet,

and the worrying thing was he could make her tremble, her initial sensations beginning to multiply by the second. She tried to smile at him, but the veiled intensity was shining out of her eyes. It was unsuitable and ruinous, but Quinn Sterling was dangerously fascinating to her, and she communicated her feelings with a youthful lack of control.

"I thought I could see you without kissing you, but I can't!" he said with sardonic self-mockery.

"Why not?"

"To be honest I don't know. I don't always do things I want to do. You seem to be swaying my better judgment."

"That's ridiculous."

"Yes, isn't it?" He ran his hand down the side of her neck and she was shocked at the trail of fire it left. Jaime was trembling now and with certainty he knew it, his touch sealing them both off in a private world. There was no one in the whole building and she was committed irrevocably to letting him dictate this awesome excitement. She shook her head and her hair swirled about his hand.

"I'm not used to this, Quinn."

"What's wrong with it?"

"We haven't a thing in common."

"Put that out of your mind for all time. It simply doesn't apply!"

"Well, it doesn't strike me as a very good idea. We're business partners, remember?"

He greeted that with an involuntary, disturbingly attractive laugh. "Would you do me a favour, Jaime?"

"What?"

"Just shut up. It won't be half as bad as you seem to expect."

She recognised that herself with awful clarity, the blood tingling in her veins, his dark face going slightly out of focus as if she were a little drunk. If he touched her she would precisely melt. She felt so weak and yielding, it was really the time to pray, but what would she be praying about, when it was this she so ardently desired?

"You mean it, don't you?" she half-whispered.

"I'm afraid so," There was laughter in his voice that was quickly banished as soon as his mouth touched her own. It seemed essential for them to draw together as closely as possible until Jaime wasn't even sure she could move away from him again. The pleasure and faint pain he was inflicting on her was exquisite, a hard and ravishing, brilliantly provoked sensuality. Her body couldn't lie. Her mouth couldn't lie and she was responding very naturally and quite passionately to his consummate skill, making a suicide of her vow of non-surrender, thirsting after this complex and fascinating man. His ability to arouse her was fantastic and it was also alarming, even if he released her abruptly as though unwilling to prolong these impossible moments.

When she opened her violet eyes he was studying her closely. "It's all right, Jaime, it's all over."

"I think I'll kill myself!" she said dramatically.

"I'd never let you. You wanted it, I wanted it. Now we'll go out and have lunch. I've booked a table at Carlo's."

"It's crushingly expensive," she warned.

"And what's that to do with you?"

"Nothing."

"I believe you."

"I just spoke out of my habitual thrift."

"I know, but I'm paying the bill. Besides, the food's superb and it's very quiet. I hate noise and being stared at when I'm attempting to put a bite in my mouth."

"I wonder you're not used to being stared at. It's only just this minute struck me, but you're a very handsome man. An hidalgo with black eyes and black hair and an easy accustomed arrogance."

"Thank you, Jaime. I wasn't looking for a compliment."

"You've got one."

"As long as you mean it."

They had fallen into their usual light banter and her heart began to slow its mad racing. For a few moments there, his personality had engulfed her completely, so much so that the touch and the scent of him still clung to her. Now he had switched roles again from the intensity of a lover who knew intimately the very texture of her skin, to a charmingly domineering, much-older-and-wiser-than-you-are mentor. This way, at least, she could control her own body and mind, not give herself over to the tormenting, dazzling Quinn Sterling.

At Carlo's their host came forward beaming, clapped his hands together, and made pleasant conversation, showing them to one of the beautifully secluded alcoves upholstered in plush velvet; an aura of everything in the very best of taste, the line crisp as snow, the flowers small and pretty and freshly picked, a paradise of a restaurant if one had the financial standing to pick up the bill. Jaime, on her own account, would never have ventured through the front door. The world of affluence was new to her and she was deeply suspicious of high prices.

The food, however, when it came, was so delicious, the wine list so illuminating, that her ever-present conscience about the world's starving millions was momentarily lulled. This was her opportunity to speak to Quinn, to have his night-black eyes touching her lightly, with such infinite skill to sway and excite. They weren't even through the Sydney rock oysters with a cold Chablis before she knew she was going to tell him everything, very clearly and sharply as though it was all happening right under his eyes.

He listened in complete silence with no prompting, and simply contented himself with getting all the facts and not firing her justifiable sense of anger and alarm.

"That's it!" she said when she had finished, her blue-violet eyes blazing in her small face.

He gave her an odd smile, laced with his own well-projected smouldering. "Extraordinary, Jaime! I could almost enjoy your tale, if it weren't for the fact you're too young to suffer their enmity."

That silvery flicker in the centre of his eyes frightened her. "It might have been just a lot of hot air," she ventured, seeking not to tone down her own perfectly accurate account.

"No, Jaime," he said, deadly quiet, "you'd be making the biggest mistake of your life if you thought that."

"I don't really. Uncle Gerard looked as if he could cheerfully have choked me. At least he put a lot of effort into the impression."

"And Simon?"

"I think Simon has plans for me."

"How?"

"You said it yourself, cousins marry."

"I think it's a dangerous practice myself."

She shrugged. "The lesser of two evils. They can't really put a weight around my neck and drop me into the harbour."

He was looking at her with astonishing attention, so hard and alert that Jaime, unused to his boardroom face, found herself blinking. "And I'll tell you why," he said tersely, "you're the jewel of the family, the very apple of your grandfather's eye. They're not going to shed many tears when he goes, but they don't dare risk angering him now. They could only stand to lose. You see, little Jaime, you're much too important a person."

"That doesn't prevent them from firing away at me when Grandfather is out of sight."

"No," he said grimly. "I must tell you I regard it as a measure of your courage that you're mentioning me at all."

"They hate you," she said simply. "Perhaps more than they hate me."

"I've worked hard enough for it!" he said, and smiled.

"They're not too happy with my silly ambitions either."

"Which, incidentally, is what I really want to know about. Tell me, Jaime, are you still interested in becoming a career woman, which means working very hard?"

"I'm not a piece of prized porcelain!" she said, looking bewilderingly delicate and worthy of a glass case.

He seemed to think so too, for his faint look of tension relaxed. "Yet that's exactly what your grandfather wants and expects of you. Your future is secure. You don't have to work at all."

She stared at him a little helplessly as though he had withdrawn his support. "Why are you talking like this?"

"You've had over a month of wealth and comfort. It's assuredly yours for life if you toe the line."

She looked down at the small, perfect centre-piece, the intermingling soft pastel shades. "It might sound absurd, but wealth and comfort aren't among my goals for life. By-products maybe, not even necessarily. The thing is, I'm no good at wasting my time and whatever talents I've got. I don't want to get up about ten and sit around the pool all day sunning myself until it's time to dress and go out for the night."

"A lot of people would be glad to put up with it," he observed dryly.

She glanced across at him sharply, her violet eyes electric. "Is our deal off?"

He threw up his hands, his teeth dazzling white in his handsome dark face. "Jaime, Jaime, the times I've seen that warring glance! You're like the old man, did you know that?"

"Oh, shut up!"

"You are!"

"What does that mean, I've lost an ally?"

"Just a sprinkling of his drive would take you to the top."

"I asked you a simple question, Quinn Sterling, my friend or my enemy. Are you still with me?"

"That depends, Jaime, on what I get back!" he said, and his words weren't merely sounds but a series of shivering caresses.

Curiously her body was curving towards him. "I know that doesn't mean what it sounds like," she said, wondering again at his mysterious and absolute power.

"No, it doesn't!" he said crisply as though he had just changed his mind. "Such a pity you're not ten years older."

"*Please*, Quinn!"

He thought for a moment, his face losing its expression of mockery finely edged with sensuality. It tautened into the exact world of big business. "I'm not a fool, Jaime, and I don't entertain angels unawares. To answer your query, I'm with you all the way. By the sound of it I'll lose money if I'm not. I've even lined up premises for you, and a staff of three. Now I have your assurance you're ready to start work, I'll go ahead and register a company with a working capital of, say, twenty thousand dollars."

"That's a lot of money!"

"It's not, but it will start you off. First we'll see how well you shoulder responsibiity, then we'll think of expansion. I know you've got sensational legs and you'll have to use them, charging around with samples, seeing buyers, shops, boutiques, department stores, that kind of thing. I imagine you're going to make up a small collection—you might at this stage have to model them yourself. You'd be ideal!"

Her eyes were fixed on him, captivated with the whole idea, blazing with a youthful intensity to succeed. "I have my designs already worked out. They're aimed at the young fashion-conscious with not a great deal of money. Someone like myself who likes to look good and can't spend a fortune. I'd prefer to do everything myself for a while. Detail is so important. What about this staff?"

"Excellent women, I'm sure. They're only too pleased to line their pockets at any rate. I'm sure you'll find you can delegate the assembly of the garments to them, but I'll leave you to handle all that. One of them is a graduate from the Institute of Technology. The other two, older women, have worked for various fashion houses. None of them have the verve or the flair to get going on their own, but they'll be just what you want in the way of a team. In time you can do the designing and the organisation of the cutting sheets and let them do the making up."

Jaime picked up her wineglass and drained it, knowing she was being rash, but lured on to a wonderful new horizon. "Where are the premises?" she asked.

"Double Bay."

"Classy?"

"Sort of. A most agreeable place to start, anyway."

"How am I going to thank you?" A surge of rapture was on her, colouring her flawless skin and flooding out of her eyes.

"*Succeed*," he said, and resisted the strong impulse to give her quite a different answer.

"Oh, I will!" she promised, reaching over and touching the tips of his fingers.

"You're very brave in a restaurant."

Their eyes met and the seconds spun out endlessly. "Don't play games with me, Quinn."

For answer he imprisoned her wrist.

"Tyrant!"

"Partner!" he said, watching her from under hooded lids.

The silence lengthened until a pulse began to beat at the base of her throat, a little frantically, and her thick black lashes fell on her cheeks. "If you let me go I'll tell you something else."

"I'm not hurting you," he said.

"Yes, you are. It's strange, but you are."

"No other way is possible, Jaime!"

"I knew the moment I laid eyes on you you'd affect my life," she said inconsequently.

"I'm not demanding anything, am I?"

"You're a very clever and perceptive man, Quinn. Perhaps you're trapping me into something."

"Keep that up and I really will hurt you."

She lifted her head and saw his bitter, beautiful smile. "I'm sorry."

"I want to make love to you, Jaime. Now."

"For everyone to see?" she said, with her own incurable desire.

"I thought we were on an island."

"Would you then?"

"If you can say that you know nothing about me at all."

Her hand under his trembled convulsively and he released her as though suddenly contrite or at least mindful of her youth and innocence. "Relax, Jaime. These are only words. I won't lose track of the fact that you're only nineteen going on twenty."

"An open book for you to read," she agreed bitterly,

"I *am* hurting you, aren't I?"

"I told you that. Right at this minute you could lead me anywhere. I suppose that's because I'm a woman, but I'll grow up."

"Stop it!" he said pretty forcefully, but quiet, "or I'll abandon the rest of the afternoon just to see that you do."

"I'd say no."

"*You'd* say no! You said it yourself, Jaime, I could fashion you into anything I want."

In her heart she knew this was true, and if it was true then she loved him. He was now an integral part of her. To have come so far in so short a time! One would have to believe Shakespeare. She had been marked out from the beginning to love Quinn Sterling. The tears came into her eyes, making them glitter like gemstones.

"Jaime!" he lingered over her name as though he loved her too, which was impossible. "I swear if you cry, I'll just pick you up and walk out of here."

"What about all these people?"

"They wouldn't stop me."

"I don't suppose they would. I think I'm a little sick with you, Quinn," she confessed with complete self-abandonment.

"Don't despair, you'll get over it."

"Is it so obvious?"

"These things are always mutual, Jaime. Do you think I can forget the sweet taste of your mouth? I don't delude myself about things like that, but you're just a child starting out and I'm determined to give you a start. If you've got any sense at all you'll tell me your other news."

"It's about Derry," she said, trying to concentrate. "I rang him the other night. May I have another glass of wine, Quinn?"

"No. Go on." He relented slightly and half filled the tulip-shaped goblet. "You speak of him as though you're the parent."

"I have a very responsible nature."

"Yes," he considered. "In a lot of ways you're very mature for your age."

"But not mature enough?"

"I regret it as much as you do, but cradle-snatching isn't in my line."

"Then I'll tell you about Derry. He has a showing coming up in December. He's well and he misses me, and he's getting married again."

"Good God! I thought you said that would never happen?"

"I may be a lot simpler than I thought. In fact it looks very much like it. Derry has decided he can't do without household help, or so he told me, and he doesn't see me coming back."

"Tavia?" he asked simply.

"I believed so myself, but no. Her name is Gayle and she's seven years older than I am."

"Then you'll be delighted to meet her."

"No," she said firmly.

"Too much of a surprise?"

"It shouldn't be, but it is."

Quinn regarded her for some little time. She looked faintly disconsolate and he felt an unaccustomed, betraying tenderness. Her hair fell like thick silk on to her shoulders and her small elegant features had a rare delicacy and strength intermingled. Perhaps it was the expression more than anything, the intelligence and character that shone from her eyes. She had appointed herself her father's keeper and she had taken the job seriously. Now she appeared to be blaming herself for her father's suspected aberration. His voice when he spoke was cool and impassive, on neither side.

"Your father is a very attractive man, Jaime. He has charm and talent. I'm sure he could have made more of a mark in the art world had he really tried."

"I know he could," Jaime said sadly, "but he's incurably lazy."

"Gayle might help there. I know you find it hard to comprehend, but sometimes a wife can accomplish far more than the most conscientious daughter. For example, Gayle may have a child. Raising a family takes money."

"Not much was spent on me," she pointed out.

"And you've done nicely enough without. Aren't you happy for him?"

"Of course I am! I just hope he's doing the right thing."

"Naturally, but a young wife might be particularly pleasant."

"What a pity he's not like you!" she said faintly caustically.

"Shame on you, Jaime!" he said solemnly. "You scratch nicely when you're brushed up the wrong way."

"It's ironical, though isn't it?"

"It's life. Don't worry, Jaime, your father has always fallen on his feet and will continue to do so until the end of his days. Some people have that gift."

"Then I'm happy, and I hope he makes Gayle happy too."

"She does have the whip hand. She's young. Your father will put himself out to keep her."

"If I was really honest I'd say I was a little hurt," she admitted.

"Your honesty, Jaime, makes you a very interesting person. As well you're beautiful and you're generous. You'll attend your father's wedding happily. I'm only hoping for an invitation."

"I'm sure you'll get one—he sent his kindest regards. None to Grandfather and not a mention of the rest of them. There's no love lost there." She glanced up and caught sight of a small group of people coming into the restaurant. Two of them she knew. "I thought you said this place was quiet?"

"And it isn't?"

"Leigh and a friend just came in. They're heading this way, quite unmindful of Carlo's directions."

"A stroke of unlooked-for bad luck. Don't panic, Jaime. No one is going to attack you when I'm around."

"Possibly, I wouldn't know. Leigh is kind of gone on you, isn't she?"

"A wreck." His black eyes wandered over her. "I've just had a brainwave. As a kind of cover would you consider getting engaged to me?"

"The best plan in the world!" she said absently, used to his amiable nonsense.

"When do you think we should announce it?"

"Why not now?"

"Right!" he said with rapier-sharp alertness, one black eyebrow lifting in appraisal. "And I couldn't have chosen a more dazzling fiancée, a little on the young side, though I'd be the last man to hold such a child to her promise. Think of it as temporary protection for both of us."

Something in his tone made her look away from the advancing party and right into his sparkling black eyes. "Quinn?" she asked distractedly, her breath catching.

"Leave it to me," he said firmly. "I've got your very best interests at heart, not to mention my own. Ah, Leigh, Carolyn!" He stood up suavely, the most charming false smile on his chiselled mouth.

"Why, hello there!" Both girls stopped at the table, Leigh acknowledging her cousin with a gleaming gaze, Carolyn smiling, enjoying every moment. Both of them looked directly back at Quinn, intensely handsome with a magnetism no woman could fail to recognise. "And what are you two doing here?" Leigh demanded, tossing her blonde head.

"*Shall* we?" Quinn asked, capturing Jaime's distracted gaze.

She sat there, speechless and completely unresolved. Had he gone mad? He had, for he began to explain himself to the two girls. "Actually, Leigh, Carolyn, you interrupted an extremely tender moment. You know my fiancée. You must admit she's beautiful—and clever, which isn't strictly necessary."

An earthquake couldn't have rocked them more. Leigh visibly lost colour, and her hand went to her throat as though her white jade pendant was choking her. "You're joking!" she said, wildly in need of reassurance. "I know how you like to throw people into an uproar!"

"Call it what you like," he said pleasantly, "but Jaime and I are unofficially engaged."

"You can't possibly mean it."

"The announcement will be made in a day or two."

"*No!*"

"I'd say yes!" Carolyn contradicted her friend dryly.

"Have you told anyone else? Grandfather?" Leigh said desperately, a kind of venom creeping in.

"Not as yet," Quinn answered for the unnaturally silent Jaime.

"You should have found out first if it was all right with him," Leigh persisted.

"We'll call him later on and ask. Jaime, darling, I don't like to hurry you, but I'm due back at the office. We'll skip coffee if it's all right with you."

"As long as you make it up to me this evening," she managed, falling back on her experience with the school dramatic society.

"Harping already?" he responded. "What a wife you'll make!"

Leigh couldn't smile, couldn't speak. And Jaime felt her heart move out in pity. She was genuinely sorry to see her cousin so stricken. None of this was really penetrating her own mind; Quinn was a skilled manipulator of people, but surely he didn't have to go to extremes? If he was setting a trap to catch her, she had fallen right in. On the other hand, it was reasonable to believe that he was acting for the best. A fiancé was an acceptable guarantor in a business project.

They were all on their feet now, with Leigh looking like a witness to some appalling disaster, yet she kept doggedly on. "I won't congratulate you," she said in a throttled voice, her eyes on Quinn's face, "because you're making a frightful mistake!"

"Please, Leigh!" Carolyn said, seizing her friend's hand.

"Do go on!" Quinn nodded his arrogant dark head, not in the least sorry for her.

Leigh responded, her lips scarcely moving, seeing and hearing no one but Quinn. "You can't!" she said

pathetically. "It's not possible. You're up to something
as usual. You spend your entire life trying to outflank
and outmanoeuvre everyone."

"Don't be absurd, Leigh," he said dryly, "I don't
try. It really works."

"My God, and you know how I feel about you!"

"Please, Leigh, no scenes here!" Carolyn begged.
"There are people we know here."

"There could be millions for all I care!" Leigh
threatened, her pale green eyes flaming.

"Perhaps," Quinn said gently, "your mother might.
I can't see all that clearly, but two of her dearest friends
are over there. You missed them on the way through."

"*You* did this!" Leigh transferred her burning acid
glance to Jaime, her face working.

"No, Leigh."

"For heaven's sake," Carolyn gritted, "we aren't
children. There's no need for a brawl."

"Yes, and if you don't move Leigh along it would get
worse," Quinn warned her gently. "It's strange, but I
thought you would be pleased."

Leigh's eyes were seeing him again and Carolyn suddenly got her hand under her friend's arm with such
strength and determination that Leigh found herself
being borne away against her will.

"What a pity!" Quinn murmured. "I'd like to have
heard the rest." He took several notes from his wallet
and placed them on the table, weighing the edges down
with a bread and butter plate.

Jaime watched him, unable to match his poise but

feeling she had to pass a remark. "You're cruel!" she whispered.

"What was that?"

"I said you're cruel."

"So I am," he agreed brightly, taking her by the arm and steering her towards the door. "I should have damned well got engaged to Leigh or even Sue. It just so happens I chanced on you."

"You're insensitive," she continued, low-voiced, staring straight in front of her. "To choose this moment. You know she loves you."

"Rubbish!" he said violently.

"Well, she thinks she does, and no one told her not to. It's unbelievable!"

He said nothing until there were well clear of the restaurant, the full sunshine beating down on their heads. Then he looked at her in a hard and controlled way. "Stop acting like your cousin, Jaime, or I'll break off our engagement."

"I can't see how you can," she retaliated instantly. "I'll sue you. Breach of promise."

"That's my girl! That kind of thing is important."

"It *has* to be!"

"It so happens I think we'll enjoy it."

"And when it's all over?"

"You'll be a much better girl for it."

"So *you* say!" she said dryly, her heart fluttering. "Anyway, I think I know what's in your mind."

"Do tell me," he invited, and looked so easy and relaxed that she really wondered.

"I somehow fit into your plans," she suggested rapidly. "I mean, I'm useful to you."

"I thought it was the other way round, but never mind. I certainly desire you, Jaime."

"Not *that*!" she said, her head spinning. "And don't you dare laugh. I feel giddy."

"The wine. I did try to stop you. The thing is, I do need you, Jaime. You *do* fit into my plans and yes, I won't deny it. You're so shrewd you see through me."

"And it was all premeditated?" she persisted.

"No, more of a spur-of-the-moment thing. For all we know you could head a multi-million dollar fashion house some time in the foreseeable future. That's what you want, isn't it? A fiancé seems a small price to pay."

"I want to put Australia on the map," she said with a glorious vision. "I want to dress my own country-women superlatively well. Maybe our children too. I have great ideas for the kids as well."

"Bravo! There you are, Jaime," he said, resonantly congratulating her, "and they don't call me a tycoon for nothing either. Why, a girl like you could go zoom to the top and I'm going to be there when you arrive."

"And that's all there is to it?" She was so giddy that she couldn't for the life of her see how she would get home.

He smiled. "Must we discuss this in broad daylight? I'm seeing you tonight, aren't I? I'll call at Falconer and confront the Old Man. The rest don't matter."

"It should be an eventful evening," she said vaguely. "Just don't drink anything Sue-Ellen might pass you."

"It's comical, isn't it?" he asked charmingly. "Three beautiful girls all anxious to marry me."

"Two," she corrected sharply. "I'm not marrying anyone for years yet. I'll be much to busy. I mightn't even marry at all."

"I know exactly how you feel." His tone was warm and sympathetic. "Just don't leave it until that shining black hair turns a nondescript grey."

"Not these days," she said, reacting seriously. "No one need put up with a single diabolical strand."

"Just be quiet for a moment, would you? My own head is starting to whirl." He was regarding her closely, then he suddenly caught her shoulders and almost turned her into his arms. "By the time you get home you'll find the glad tidings have gone before you. Not all the angels are in heaven. I'll tell you what I'm going to do now, I'm going to drop you off at my unit and you can spend an hour or so there. You'll be quite alone and there should be plenty to interest you. No doubt you'll want to suggest a few telling changes, curtains and slip covers and so forth. Take a cab home at about four. I'll give you the money..."

"I don't want it!"

"Will you *be*? When you get there, just keep saying Quinn will be calling this evening. Got it?"

"Got it!" she said like an automaton. "Quinn will be calling this evening. Where are we going, by the way?"

"Do I detect a definite pick-up of interest? I think we'll have dinner with Grandmamma. Rosemount isn't Falconer, but I like it a whole lot better."

"Rosemount is beautiful."

"My grandmother is content with it. She won't hear of any improvements or changes. The house speaks to her of the old days, happier times. I can't think of many myself."

"Maybe you're neurotic?" she suggested.

"Oh, I love that!"

"A very smart neurotic, self-sufficient and secure, but complex nevertheless!" She looked at him, her beautiful thoughtful eyes on his face. "Are you going to tell your grandmother of the master plan? I couldn't bear to deceive her or Grandfather. I've become very fond of him. He's my grandfather whatever he's done, and he's done a lot of good as well as pulling a few people down."

"He has, you know."

"Done a lot of good?"

"Forget it. Don't take any notice!" Quinn's face was intensely alive, darkly, vividly handsome, the sombre look completely dispelled. "Surely you're content to be engaged to me for a while? I assure you I'll act the part."

"The point is, I don't want you to!"

"You haven't yet mastered the outright lie. We do *not* propose to deceive anyone, Jaime. We *are* getting engaged, and who knows, by the time you're ready to consider marriage I might have sufficient life in me to consider it myself. That way we won't break up what I'm sure will be a most promising and rewarding business relationship."

His hand had fallen on her shoulder and she twisted her head up to him. "You're an expert at this kind of thing."

"Yes, I am. Anyway, Jaime, at this particular point of time, I don't think you could survive in the cruel world without me. I represent protection for the working girl, and believe me you need it. Your father is too far away and content to stay there and your grandfather is beginning to die right in front of our eyes. It's not necessary to mention your other relations. One other thing," he said coolly, "you may take it as gospel that I won't attempt to seduce you."

"I couldn't be tempted," she said, shocked so much that the words left her throat with a stammer.

"We'll debate that at a later date. Just when I'm ready to kiss that petal-smooth mouth."

"A kiss is not consummation."

"No, but can't you see where it could lead? Anyway, Jaime, we have an agreement."

"Until it's broken," she amended.

"I happen to want to stick to it. I swear I only wish to cherish and respect you, little Miss Teen."

She gave a muffled little sound that could have been interpreted as outrage. "I don't care a damn about that. I'm determined to match you."

"Thank you, Jaime," he drawled, his brilliant gaze very lazy and misleading.

"It wasn't a compliment."

"Yes, it was. You know it was. You're half way to being in love with me already."

"I must be if you say so."

"Get in the car like a good girl," he said crisply, "I can't stand around talking nonsense all day. I'm like a general, I always have to be around for briefings!"

"You're brilliant!" she said, trying to bury her sparkling female antagonism.

"I expect you're quite right." He almost pushed her into the car, and she had to clench the dashboard to prevent herself from hitting him.

"Come, come!" he said, and caught her fist. "That's no way for a fiancée to act."

"I'm wishing I'd denied it."

"No chance of that!" he said softly. "You're right up to your neck. Who else is there to back you in Just Jaime?"

"That's a great name!" she burst out involuntarily, her violet eyes dilating.

"And it's part of the deal."

His dark face was very close to her and unconsciously she brought up her hand and touched her mouth in concentration, as if the feel of his mouth was engraved upon it. It proved fatal, for he bent his head swiftly and covered her mouth with his own. "Does that solve the mystery?"

Lights seemed to be dancing all around his head and she couldn't tell if she was showing the tumultuous shock of feeling she was experiencing. "You scare me," she said truthfully. "I shouldn't have expected no strings to be attached."

"That would have been too damned childish! Consider yourself engaged. Maybe I've been plotting to get you all along."

"For God's sake, why?"

"Oh, come on now, Jaime!" His expression was hard and mocking and charming all at once and some-

thing else, and seeing it she quailed. Possessive. She
would have to spend her time as his fiancée until he
decided she was no longer necessary to his schemes.
The only possible answer was to go home, but she
wasn't going to do that. *Just Jaime* would be her distin-
guishing label. She too could have plans, and this arrogant, challenging, absolutely fatal man would lend her
his tremendous vigour and organisational know-how.

She was filled with a remarkable energy, but managed to fall asleep at Quinn's very luxurious home unit
that had a superb view of the harbour and the city lights
by night. Because she felt generous Jaime had by then
decided she couldn't change a thing, except maybe the
repositioning of a Persian prayer mirror to the entrance
foyer. Quinn had superb taste, and equally important,
he was going to help her.

She couldn't scorn his offer to become engaged to
her. He was a fantastic man and one couldn't expect
such a man to be without complications. She didn't
want to think about it, but it was obvious she would
have a few dreadful moments. Indeed, the best laid
plans often went astray. The only way out of tension
was a delicious daydream.

CHAPTER SIX

THE FIRST PERSON Jaime saw when she got back to Falconer was Georgia. She swept down the staircase, her green eyes sharp enough to drill a hole through an unopened door, her voice icy with dignity.

"Your grandfather is waiting for you in the library," she announced.

"Good for him."

"You haven't a hope of pulling this off, you know that, don't you?"

"Pulling what off?" Jaime stalled.

"This phoney engagement!"

"What's it to do with you?"

"Everything!" Georgia maintained broadly. "My daughter has been in love with Quinn Sterling for years!"

"Well, these things happen. I'm sorry for her, of course, but really Quinn doesn't feel that way about her."

"What would you know about it?"

"Take my advice."

"He's only using you!" Georgia said in a low voice.

"It's no good Georgia; extraordinarily enough I don't mind."

"You don't mind being used? How humiliating!" Georgia paused, trying to control her rising tone. "You're not in trouble, are you?"

Jaime shook her head. "What are you thinking of organising? No, Georgia, I leave trouble alone."

"I was under the impression you were causing a great deal of it!"

"It's not a crime to get engaged, is it? Some people might wish me well!"

"I wish you the very reverse!"

Jaime looked at Georgia's handsome face curiously. "Why? *Why* do you hate me? It seems mindless."

"The fact remains you're trying to wreck this family. My daughter's happiness."

Jaime sighed. "Excuse me, won't you? You did say Grandfather was waiting."

"And don't you dare upset him," Georgia cried.

"Would you mind? I had the distinct impression you're all waiting for him to die!"

"You detestable creature!"

"Not detestable at all—smart. I also care about my grandfather, which you don't."

"You just wait until my husband gets home!" Georgia said through clenched teeth.

"Ring him," advised Jaime crisply.

"I already have."

"And who rang you? Leigh. She's in love with Quinn as well. It's almost like an epidemic."

Georgia stared at her, her eyes glassy. "You'll wish you never came to Falconer before I'm finished with you."

"Lovely! Get out of my way, Georgia, I'm not going to stand here and swap insults with you. You have everything and it's not enough, and you've taught your children no better. You're a greedy, ugly woman!''

"I was a legend in my girlhood!'' Georgia shouted, her throat flushing and her hand tearing at her caftan.

"I don't mean your looks,'' Jaime said wearily. "I mean the real you, inside. You know, where you live. You lack something vital—charity.''

"It's time we got rid of you!'' Georgia said, stepping nearer, a tall and a strong woman, three stone heavier than Jaime.

"Not a chance,'' Jaime said breezily. "I like mixing with the real élite. It's so ennobling!''

While Georgia paused to take breath, Jaime went quickly round her, and on to the library. It was a wonderful room, which housed a valuable collection of books in arcaded ceiling-high recesses. It also incorporated her grandfather's study, and the cedar tables and smaller cabinets held the trophies, the awards and the honours, the great pile-up of personal memorabilia her grandfather had accumulated during a long eventful lifetime. Rolf Hunter wasn't just one man but a number of men, and even his enemies acknowledged his confounded excellence.

Today he looked frailer than usual, his relatively unlined and tanned skin almost blanched. Jaime threw her handbag down on an armchair and went towards him, her hands outstretched. He took them and she bent over him to kiss his cheek. "What's the problem?'' she said in her habitual forthright way.

He looked at her without his customary enthusiasm. "Georgia has been babbling endlessly to me about some engagement."

"She had no right to do that."

"She has some rights, Jaime," he said forcefully.

"What are they? None so far as I'm concerned. You don't look very comfortable there at the desk, Grandfather. Come over to the sofa, then we can both sit down."

"Perhaps I will, as I'm determined to continue this discussion."

"You're not delighted?"

"It's true then?" He shot her a baleful look from under his thick brows.

"Sit down," she said calmly, and waited for him to do so. "Yes, it's true," she murmured, sinking down beside him, "but I wanted to tell you that myself. Quinn, in any case, is calling on you this evening."

"Indeed?"

"I thought you admired him, Grandfather? You sent him to find me when you sent no one else."

"You don't know Quinn, my darling."

"Of course I don't. Do any of us know anyone? Tell me about him. Your view!"

"He's everything we do know. Brilliant, compelling, ambitious. He's the biggest persuader I know and he's willing and able to work superlatively hard. Actually he's been able to run rings around my sons for years now and he's only thirty-four now. There's no question he hasn't a great future, but he's deep. A very complicated man. For example, he's taken over my business right from under my nose. These days I'm content to sit by and watch human nature at work. I'm too old now to stop him and my sons wouldn't know how. I'm wondering now what his exact interest is in you?"

"Perhaps he loves me," Jaime ventured.

He nodded. "Of course. You're a very beautiful girl, yet still I wonder. It's not the money, it's not even the power. It's something else with Quinn. Family skeletons. They keep rattling. He'd use you if he had to."

"As a matter of fact, Grandfather, he's helping me. I don't know if you notice my clothes?"

"Of course I do!" He looked at her in astonishment. "What have your clothes to do with it? I must say I've wondered how you got the money to pay for them before you came here."

"I made them."

"One would never know!" He turned sideways to stare at her, nibbling on his lip. "It seems to me an expert couldn't do better."

"I am an expert in my way," she explained. "At least I want to be!"

"Aren't we straying from the track?" he enquired.

"Not really. You see, I'm going into business."

"You're *what*?" Matchless at taking shocks in his stride, he couldn't hide his objections.

"I'm like you, Grandfather!" Jaime said, trying to go carefully. "Quinn only pointed that out to me today."

"What kind of a business?" he demanded uneasily.

"Fashion. I want to design women's clothes."

"Oh, really, Jaime!" he said impatiently, and somewhat relieved. "It's not necessary for you to do anything. Enjoy your life!"

"I could only do that working. Surely you understand?"

"No, I don't!" he said sourly. "It's a man's lot to work for the sum of his days, not a woman's."

"Oh, Grandfather, you know very well that's not true any more."

The handsome old face was glowering and one hand began to move jerkily. "That's why women are so unhappy today. They don't know their place. They weren't unhappy in my day."

"Perhaps they weren't allowed to say so," she suggested. "No one listened or cared!"

"I don't want to discuss it now, Jaime. Still, you mustn't think I'm not interested. Give yourself time. You love being here, don't you? You care about me. You can have anything you want—just name it. Not everyone finds work a pleasurable activity."

"You did and so will I!"

"Forget that, Jaime!" he burst out irritably. "You give me a long story about wanting to work when I want to press on about Quinn. I don't like this engagement. You're much too young."

"We're not rushing into anything, Grandfather."

"It seems highly suspicious to me and knowing Quinn I'm right to be alarmed. Soon he'll have everything, including you. He idolised his uncle Nigel, did you know that? A very charming young man was Nigel. Charming but not practical. I never knew anyone who wasn't utterly taken with Nigel. He was a gentleman, the only one of them who wasn't a revolting aristocrat. He was lovable. Good—too good perhaps. I promoted the match between your mother and Nigel; he adored her, there was no other word for it, and he was prepared to extend the love that was in him to me. I've never known anyone else like him. Quinn isn't like him at all. He's more like his grandfather. Quinn can be as hard as nails. Nigel was too sensitive, too human, for his own good. I suppose you find it hard to comprehend?"

"No, his mother speaks of him in the same way."

"Margo? She's always looked right through me, yet she loved Rowena. Between them, Rowena and Nigel, they nearly killed that old woman, but she managed to survive as I did. What Quinn has in mind I don't know, but be on your guard. He's going to be a great man one day, but I prefer him not to have my granddaughter."

There was an intense, close look on Jaime's face. "So you don't think he could love me for myself?"

"The human mind follows some pretty tortuous paths. You've looked into his black eyes, haven't you? They're fathomless. With you one can see right through to the soul. Paradise itself couldn't have a more heavenly blue. You're mismatched—Quinn is a very clever man, mature, and he's been around. You're just a child. You're courageous and gay, but that's nothing. I could give you the names of a dozen women who have flung themselves at his head, and that doesn't include my own granddaughters, spoilt silly little beggars. Things are complicated enough, Jaime, without your thinking of Quinn Sterling."

"I didn't think about it, particularly, Grandfather. It just happened."

"All right, I can understand that! God knows it's clear enough what you see in him, but break it off."

"I'm not sure I can do that!" Jaime said strangely. "I love him."

"You're *in* love with him," her grandfather pointed out heavily. "Of course I know that. He's a handsome devil—they all were. And that's it. He's Philip's grandson. He looks at me sometimes with those probing black eyes and believe me I don't know who he is for a minute. But Philip was never ruthless; Quinn is, or he could be."

Jaime nodded. "All right, I can see you're serious and I can see that you're worried. I've come to love you, Grandfather, as though I've always lived here with you. I don't want to hurt and upset you. There's been enough hurt for all of us, but I love Quinn too. I promise you I don't consider that reason enough to marry, I won't rush into anything. You could be right. I know Quinn's a complicated man. If I said I didn't have doubts about him, I'd be lying. Time will tell. I'm going to become engaged to him for a while anyway. I might as well tell you the rest. He's willing to back me in a business."

He caught her eyes steadily, looking tremendously alert. "Has he gone into it?"

"You know Quinn."

"Then you should be particularly proud of yourself. Quinn doesn't back losers. Couldn't you have come to me? Why Quinn Sterling, for God's sake?"

"You've been ill, Grandfather, and you said it yourself, you're content to sit back these days, and that's as it should be!"

"Leave that part of it aside, if you don't mind. You should have came to me."

"Would you have listened?" she enquired.

Unexpectedly he chuckled. "Well...not for some little while. Good grief, child, you've only just come back to me. The question of earning your own living doesn't arise. I've made millions, and I can't take it with me. I've left you secure for life. There's no law that says you've got to have a job as well."

"We make our own rules, Grandfather. I'm a doer. I can't sit around and let someone else create and direct my environment. I think I have something to offer. I believe in myself. Didn't you believe in yourself?"

"I made Hunter Sterling what it is today."

"Wasn't Philip Sterling entitled to some of the credit?" she asked.

"We're not talking about Philip Sterling, young lady. We're talking about his grandson, and let me inform you that Quinn is absolute in his intention to take us all over. Maybe he's getting back at me through you. You're the only weapon anyone could use against me. You're all I care about."

She shut her eyes, her voice so quiet that he had to turn and look at her. "How can you say that, Grandfather? What about Uncle Gerard, Uncle Vivian, my cousins?"

"You sound horrified," he said, his eyes on her face.

"I am. Don't you care for them at all?"

"I suppose I should, but God damn it, I can't! Why should I? They don't care about me. They're all waiting for me to die as though they haven't got enough already. I've always been one-track and I suppose I'm not exactly an admirable person. I've loved my work, I loved my mother. I loved my daughter, and you're Rowena all over again. In a way I can't explain it's exactly like having a second chance. You've even a bit of me in you, I can see it myself. He's a shrewd devil, Quinn—diabolical. I've always recognised his perception. The only possible way he can hurt me is through you. The only way he can avenge his family is through you. I don't want you to marry him."

"It may never come to that!" Jaime said, caught into this dilemma.

"Then why bother to get engaged? If you're serious about this business venture, I'll put up the money. Surely you know you had only to ask?"

"I do know it, Grandfather."

"But I'm dying, is that it?"

"Don't say it!" She covered his mouth with her fingertips. "Don't say it. With care you'll live for years yet! You'll see me make a success of myself. You won't see Quinn Sterling ruin my life. I won't let him!"

"Yet you love him?"

"If what I feel for him is real, yes."

"It mightn't be enough," he warned.

"Then we'll find out in time. I give you my solemn word I won't rush into marriage."

"He has you plainly infatuated. I wish to God the boys were like him. Simon and Brett might make out—

at the moment they're just nothing. They've had too much. Too much has been given to them and I'm to blame. I had nothing in my youth but conflict. No family. No money. I don't know how many jobs my poor mother and I held down to get me through university. I had a first-class brain, that helped. Philip Sterling befriended me. The Sterlings, of course, were right out of the top drawer. Still, he was a good fellow. A brilliant engineer. Too moral, of course."

"Can anyone be too moral?" Jaime asked, her eyes flying open.

"In business, yes."

"You look calmer, Grandfather," she said quietly. "Do you feel it?"

He gazed at her thoughtfully with his steel-grey eyes. "I can see you're not like your lunatic cousins, Sue-Ellen and Leigh. You won't let him make a fool of you. I couldn't drink the cup of bitterness again."

"Talk to him tonight?" Jaime begged, and took her grandfather's hand, feeling the fine tremor in it.

"Yes, I will. We seem to be moving over the same old chessboard. You'll upset Margo, you know—a natural reaction. It's easy for you young people to talk about love; one is extremely lucky to know love and have it returned in a long lifetime. We're all beggars most of us, turned away from the table. Not even the crumbs. Still, I'm not infallible, it may be a splendid match. At the moment, however, that's not possible for me to admit. If he hurt you I'd kill him or have him killed."

"Don't speak like that!" Jaime begged, frightened and with reason.

"What would you have me say?"

"I'm not so foolish or so weak that I need someone else to fight my battles. I mean it, Grandfather, I can handle Quinn, or I'll learn how to."

He glanced away from her as though sick to death of the whole thing. "It's child's play for a man to pretend he loves a woman. Stupid creatures, women, I've always found them so and I've had plenty of them in my time. A series of meaningless relationships."

"That's the secret, Grandfather," Jaime said, her violet eyes saddened, "one must be able to give love to receive it. To be prepared to suffer to gain much. You love me because you see my mother in me."

"I see you in me as well. Why, damn you, I love you more than I loved Rowena. There, I've said it!"

Jaime glowed. "You're not ashamed of it? You're not frightened to love me, to commit yourself?"

"I'm beginning to feel shame for a lot of things. That goes to show you how old I really am. All right, my darling, I can't pretend I'm joyous about this engagement, but I can play games as well as the next man, maybe even better than Quinn Sterling. I'm not dead yet. You're the prize and we both want you."

"That's funny!"

"Very. A contested claim," he said dryly.

"I love you both."

"And if he doesn't love you, I ought to find out about it and I will. Yes, it's funny all right. History repeating itself, only I'm not handing you over."

"When I came in you looked tired." Defeated, she

thought to herself but could never say. Now her grandfather looked vigorous.

"I'm not tired at all!" he said, supporting her.

"Good. I have a wonderful vision of you as a young
man, tremendously handsome and alert. A real power-
house. No wonder you understand Quinn."

"Get me a drink," he ordered.

"Are you allowed it?"

"Just one. Whisky with a little water. It's over there
on the sideboard. What time is he coming?"

"We're having dinner at Rosemount, so it will be
before then."

"Good. I can't wait. He thinks he has an insurmountable advantage, but we'll see!"

"No tricks, Granddad!"

"I won't say. It's never been my policy to give away
secrets."

Jaime, busy pouring him a drink, glanced back over
her shoulder and they both smiled. It wasn't until later
that she began to be plagued with doubts. When it
came to summing up his fellow man Rolf Hunter had
never been far wrong, so regardless of her feelings she
had to listen to his fears about Quinn. What did Quinn
Sterling, with the world at his fingertips, want with
her? She had said she could handle him. The difficulty
would be doing it.

CHAPTER SEVEN

A MONTH LATER, the engagement still hadn't been made official, for Sir Rolf had found a very good reason to send his top executive and director to Japan for a series of important business talks. When he put himself out it was clear that Sir Rolf's word was still law. In any case their Japanese friends were showing considerable interest in Hunter Sterling Exploration and were pressing for the talks. It went without saying that Quinn was the right man to head the delegation and it didn't need Sir Rolf's firm assertion to convince Jaime that this was right. Uncle Gerard had gone as well, so she was spared his knife-edged remarks over breakfast. She had only seen Quinn once alone after that dinner at Rosemount. Her grandfather had been right about Margo Sterling's reception of their news; she had been shocked and genuinely worried, as though there was little chance such a match could come to fruition, let alone guarantee anyone any happiness.

Under the circumstances Jaime didn't find this attitude surprising, but Quinn had handled both of them with great charm and persuasiveness, talking most of the while about Jaime's plans and aims for her own company. At the end of the evening, Mrs. Sterling hadn't seemed nearly so stricken, but it was obvious that never in her wildest dreams had she considered a marriage between them.

Jaime was the loveliest young creature she had ever seen, a more spirited, purposeful version of her mother, but a child still, one who had had no chance to mature, and in that Margo was wrong. Jaime's temperament, the events of her life, the solitude and frequent setbacks, had strengthened her backbone and decided her character. Jaime was a woman and she was able to cope with her new life far better than anyone imagined. Because she looked so young, so eager, so physically fragile, it didn't mean she hadn't learned how to survive and better, meet challenges. Quinn Sterling was the biggest challenge of her life, a frighteningly self-sufficient, self-assured man, but he couldn't force her into anything she didn't want. She was dedicated to making a success of herself, though she had to admit Quinn took her aspirations and burning ambitions quite calmly. She was no shrinking violet and if she wished to set the world on fire he was prepared and willing to help her. He had a great eye for talent in any field and considered it a precious commodity to be sponsored.

So brilliant and uncommonly successful himself, he would never fall into melancholia if he happened to marry a woman with a few grandiose ideas herself. Life would have to be exciting with Quinn, and there would be no room in it for a less than interesting life's partner. All the time he was away Jaime was so busy that she had to wonder how she found the time to miss him, but she did. Some vital part of her was a prisoner to Quinn;

still she launched into her collection, involving herself with her team to such an extent that they were beginning to find words unnecessary, the same beautiful thoughts communicated through fabric and the feel of it, until finally Jaime was ready to show her small range to selected buyers. They had all expected it to be a series of triumphs, but it didn't work out that way.

By the time Jaime got back to the shop, she was so upset that she would have burst into tears, only she didn't have the energy. The collection that had sent Di and Marike and Jill into raptures had somehow looked terrible to three leading boutiques. The fourth, admittedly less exclusive, had found the garments attractive, in fact the buyer had just stopped herself from going into a rave in case she shot the price up. Anyway, she had placed an order. The rest had hated the entire range, but then they couldn't keep themselves from inspecting each garment very closely. There was something strange about the whole thing.

Jaime knew she was young and unknown and she had taken that into consideration, yet it was more like a planned refusal. "The garments might sell anywhere else but here," type of thing. The saleswoman at Claire's had changed her tune dramatically the moment the manageress declared her attitude. Up until then Jaime had almost chalked up an order. It didn't make sense. It was almost as if she was being undermined.

According to her team, and they were experienced, knowledgeable and very fashion-conscious women, Jaime's collection was a winner. They had greeted her designs with an overwhelming vote of confidence

ready to follow her anywhere despite her youth and inexperience assuring her that the made-up garments
would gain the *Just Jaime* label a reputation and lots of
orders, perhaps make them all rich. Marike, a few years
older, with a diploma in fashion design, was already a
good friend and sincere admirer of Jaime's very adequately demonstrated gift. They had given her endless
encouragement and she had let them run on, more
than satisfied with their individual abilities, and already
thought of them as important to her and was pleased to
be able to repay them for giving of their very best. It
was then more of a shock to learn that at least three
buyers took the extreme view. Such a dismal collection
wouldn't even go over in Siberia.

With the inbuilt conviction of the truly gifted, the
confidence in the face of severe criticism, Jaime found
herself more sick and puzzled than disheartened. Her
garments were far better made than most that were
selling well in the stores, potential winners. Too bad
they weren't going over.

She was so tired, so footsore, that she almost dragged
herself through the showroom to the workroom beyond.
In just on a month she had lost weight, so that every
contour of her face and body appeared so much more
delicate. She had even resorted to multi-vitamin pills,
something she had never done before. It was past five,
yet all three were waiting for her as if it was an occasion.
One look at her face told the tale.

"I don't believe it!" said Di, always the spokes-
woman.

"Me neither!" from Jill.

"What happened?" Marike asked, slightly annoyed with Di and Jill.

"Nobody was buying. Oh yes, Ultra Chic placed an order. A good one. The other three, Sally K., Dina's and Claire's, found the whole range upsetting. Brilliantly put together, the whole lot of them nearly took the garments apart, but they wouldn't consider selling them."

"Sit down!" Di urged. "If you get any skinnier you won't be able to model them."

"You're not happy about something?" Marike persisted.

"No." Jaime's blue-violet eyes were thoughtful. "Maybe it's a weird idea, but I think we're being got at."

"Who would do a thing like that?" Jill moaned, striving stoically to think of someone.

"What about your dear aunty?" Di suggested. "I know for a fact she could make or break a few of the very exclusive boutiques. You won't trade on your name..."

"No, I won't!" This emphatically from Jaime.

"Don't get uptight, dear," Di said soothingly. "I'm only suggesting a possible line of sabotage."

"And you could be right. I've heard about such things. In which case how do we go about setting things right?"

"Listen, my dear," Di said with sublime confidence, "the range is superb. You're a very talented girl and we're pretty stunning ourselves. Would you like me to put the word out on the streets?"

"What word?" Jaime asked rather wistfully, accepting a cup of coffee from Marike's kind hands.

"Who you are, dear!" Di said patiently.

"I'm Jaime Gilmore. Just Jaime."

"And you can guarantee your dear aunty told them just that. No mention that you're Sir Rolf Hunter's granddaughter or anything like that."

"If she was trying to stop me she'd certainly keep it quiet. Don't worry, Di, we can do without them. Their prices are too high anyway. I saw an imported rag on a model for six hundred dollars. Those kind of prices would destroy my very aim!"

"Be that as it may, with your talent the customers will pay. Let me drop a fact or two in a few pertinent ears. One doesn't like to trade on a name, but everybody does it."

"I'm going to trade on my own ability—at least until I'm quite desperate," said Jaime. "Let me line up the department stores. Georgia can't buy them, or can she?"

"She's a very influential woman, which as you all know counts in this rotten world!"

"Well, it's Friday and well past knocking-off time. Monday I'll be ready to come back fighting!"

"Atta girl! The first step or two is pretty hard," Di said fondly. "I've been closely associated with this game for twenty years now. It's no secret that contacts are important. If I were you, young lady, even allowing for the fact that you have a genius for design, I'd get that beautiful face into the glossies as Sir Rolf Hunter's granddaughter, starting out in her own business. The implications are enormous."

"I'll never get the Communist vote!" Jaime said, and laughed for the first time that day. "I don't like it, Di. I want to make it on my own!"

"You nearly didn't today, thanks to your aunt."

"We're only assuming Georgia had anything to do with it," Jaime reminded her.

"You did tell me Sue-Ellen had your design sheets on purpose!" Marike pointed out, her piquant face disliking the idea but not rejecting it.

"So she did."

"Then I don't think there can be any doubt about it."

"Maybe not!" Wearily, Jaime brushed her hand across her eyes. "I never think when I'm as tired as this. Let's all go home."

"Just you remember we're right here behind you."

"Thanks, Di."

"Shall I lock up for you?" Marike asked.

"Gosh, I forgot to tell you, Mike is waiting outside!" Jaime swept to her feet trying to look as if she was capable of locking up her own premises. "All of you, thanks for everything, I'll reward you in time—now get out of here and have a nice weekend. Jill, take those flowers, they were only fresh this morning. Tell your mother they're a present from me."

"Gee, thanks! Usually we have a few nice little daisies, not these beauties. How can you afford them?"

"I didn't," said Jaime. "They were sent to me—

a persistent admirer. That's the second lot this week."

"I wish someone would send them to me!"

"Why, bless your heart, they will. On your next birthday." Di rustled up a few sheets of tissue paper and wrapped the masses of beautiful carnations, presenting them to the very pleased Jill. "See you, Jaime. Take care now."

Jaime smiled and waved them all off, pretending an energy she didn't feel. For the first time it occurred to her that one could be dedicated and still feel terrible. The last month had taken a lot out of her, though she had been wondrously happy and fulfilled from time to time. This was possibly the aftermath. It happened, the unresolved tensions. She didn't want to, but she immediately thought of Quinn. She had wanted to please him with a full report of some modest success, but not after a day like this. If there was some plot going against her it was clear it had worked. Well, what had she expected, miracles? Ultra Chic were largely taken with the range; it was a start. On Monday she had two appointments with the leading department stores. She had to look forward.

At that moment she only succeeded in looking impossibly overworked, very young and dangerously fragile. She rested her elbows on the cutting table and looked away out of the window. There was no view to speak of, not the magnificent harbour vistas of Falconer.

Her grandfather didn't wish her to pursue this career of hers. Was it possible he was making things hard for her in the mistaken belief that she would fall back on him alone? He was capable of anything to suit his own ends. He harped constantly on the way she was cooped up in a workroom instead of being out in the sunshine enjoying herself. Sue-Ellen had the most glorious tan from hours in the pool or the surf. Jaime in a month had lost her pale golden tan to a clear ivory. It only served to accentuate her increasing delicacy.

Her chin in her hands, she considered her grandfather's remarkable record of interference and intrigue. He could force her out of business if he wanted to. He had become extremely possessive and jealous of her ambitions that denied him her time. Sabotage, every way she turned. Georgia wouldn't hesitate to injure her in any way she could. What few moments they had had together hadn't been pleasant. Sue-Ellen and Leigh were livid, mutually supporting, in their open contempt and rage over her supposed engagement to Quinn.

One month and still not a word from him. He was real and he was powerful and he would want to know how she had slipped up. At least he supported her, or did he? If she couldn't trust Quinn, she couldn't trust anyone. He was too big a man to crush a mere girl, non-starter in the power stakes. She let her head slide down on to her hands, shutting her eyes. She wasn't looking forward to the weekend. The only peace she could find these days was at Rosemount. It was very easy to talk to Quinn's grandmother; she was a highly cultivated woman, and her fashion judgment even for the young sophisticates was perfectly sound. It wasn't even necessary to explain things to her, and importantly she had given her sincere seal of approval to the

Just Jaime collection. If she didn't move soon she would fall asleep at the table...

QUINN, leaving his parked car, saw Diane Collins waving frantically from the window of a parked car across the street. He walked across to her without hesitation, though he was anxious to see Jaime.

"How goes it, Mr. Sterling?"

"Fine, Di, and you? How are you, Jill, I didn't see you there." He bent his tall, lean frame to look into the car. "How's Jaime?"

"The girl genius. You said it for us. We'll go ahead and repeat it."

"That means she's got your approval."

Di smiled. "Not a single complaint. She's working too hard, and there's precious little of her. Apart from that we want you to know you let us in on a good thing. I've been in the business twenty years, and seriously, Jaime makes it all worth while."

"Can I repeat that please?"

"You sure can. We won't hold you up, we just wanted to say hello!"

"I'm glad you did. Jaime still inside?"

"The last one as usual."

"I'll see she's through. When this collection's launched we'll have a party."

"How's Tokyo?" Jill asked, smiling.

"Worth every minute, but it's good to be home."

"You look like a man who got results."

"Thank you Di." He smiled at her and for a moment Di had to support herself in the seat. Never, even in her early days, could a man drive her nuts, but then she'd never met a man like Quinn Sterling and he wouldn't have looked at her. Still, the smile was nice, like a sweet shudder up the spine. She nodded to the equally smitten Jill to start up the car, and with many waves and smiles they were off to the weekend routine. Work was more interesting these days and a party was something to look forward to. If Quinn had promised them one, he would stick to it. Both women automatically began thinking about what they could wear. Perhaps Jaime might dream them up a design. They just flowed out of her in an unquenchable stream, and she knew exactly how to hide figure faults.

Quinn looked around the tastefully decorated showroom, then walked through to the workroom, a slight frown on his face. He was just about to call out: "Jaime!" when he saw her.

Not the vibrant young beauty he had left with a passion to conquer the fashion world, but an exhausted young creature, her glossy black hair spilling around her in silky confusion, the only side of her face visible newly pale, without any colour whatever, a gleaming ivory. Her thick black lashes and delicate arching brows made up this black and white etching, for her vividly blue eyes were closed. She looked so vulnerable, so utterly spent, that he felt a quick surge of exasperation. It was all very well to make her mark, but she didn't have to make it in a month. That just proved what a child she was!

"Jaime!" he said crisply, with a faint anger.

She didn't answer.

He went around the table and shook her, expecting

instant arousal. She had to be very tired, for she didn't spring to life, but tilted her head back very drowsily, her violet eyes opening, flower-fresh but still immersed in some fantastic world of her own.

"Jaime!" he said again, his hand sliding down over her back and closing at her too slender waist. "Wake up!"

"Quinn!" she said in a hushed voice, her gaze now trapped by the sight of him, the warm strength of his hand. "What are you doing here? We didn't expect you until next week."

"Your grandfather knew perfectly well when I would be home."

"He never told me. Worse, *you* never told me."

"Did you really want to know?"

"Oh yes!" she said unguardedly. The sight of him seemed to be twisting her heart over. She wanted to tell him he had haunted her subconscious, except for certain times at night when she ruthlessly had to eject the conscious thought of him from her bed, but she was far from being in control of herself. The sight of him was so unexpected that he might well have been part of her dream. Her deep exhaustion, perversely, was unintentionally provocative. She was half lying back against him, her eyes resting with tantalising softness on each separate feature of his face. "Hello, I missed you."

"You say that very easily."

"It's true."

"Wake up, Jaime," he said, moving to lean back against the table. "You look unbearably desirable."

"More so than the geishas?"

"Now how would *I* know?"

"You have a very worldly air."

"Jaime darling, when in Tokyo, I'm totally committed to business."

"And here?"

There were diamond points of light in his jet-black eyes. "Do you mean to be so provocative, Jaime?"

"You're my fiancé, aren't you?" she asked with mischief. "You said you were going to act the part very suitably."

"Did I say that? I'm *not*. You don't look fit enough for a little sweet violence. Perhaps later on tonight."

"I think you should kiss me now," she said plaintively. "I've had an awful day."

"I can see that! I'm ravenous myself, but I can wait. Right now, I'm going to take you home."

She stretched her arms luxuriously above her head, arching the slender creamy column of her throat "I could do with a nice, scented time-wasting, relaxing bubble bath!"

"Don't say another word!" he said dryly, "I have to draw in my breath just thinking about it. Stand up, Jaime, and let me have a look at you. You seem to have shrunk."

"What there is is real. I seem to be aching for you in some odd way."

"You shouldn't talk like that," he warned. "It's dangerous."

"Why?"

"Why? Surely you know, Jaime. You don't have to plead to be made love to!"

"Then why don't you?" she asked with a strange insistence.

"You're in too much of a hurry. I'm taking you home."

"All right, I won't ask again!" she said haughtily. "I'm so tired I don't even know what I'm saying. In fact I'm not even properly awake."

"Don't give up hope!" he taunted her, steadying her swaying figure.

"Keep your kisses for ever, Quinn Sterling. I don't want them."

"Yes, you do. Fiercely!"

"But then you're so conceited," she riposted.

"Very neat, Jaime, but it's not true. Come here. No tricks, I just want to look at you."

She stood up straight and held up her head. "Well?"

"Quite possibly you're even more beautiful. That's odd. Are you sure you want that badly to be a success?"

"What's success, for God's sake?" She really was swaying and he caught her shoulders and drew her gently against him, making no attempt to lower his head.

"I think I might have to carry you. You might have warned me you haven't shoes on. Your height shocks me. I'll pick you up about eight—that will give you a little time to sleep in your own bed. Anywhere else would just add to our dilemmas. You're doing quite enough of that."

"I'm not!" she murmured, deciding to stay where she was for the duration.

"You know you are!" He suddenly swept her off her feet, cradling her lightly. "God, Jaime, you're no weight at all, but at least you have some shape left."

"Don't look at me like that," she said drowsily.

"Why not?"

"I think you're only pretending about those geishas."

"I have an ivory-skinned geisha of my own. What happened to that Gold Coast tan?"

"Ask Grandfather. He's very resentful of the time I've been spending away from him."

"I know, I spent over an hour at Falconer. This will be my second trip today. He's very shaky, the Old Man, very frail. It seems to have happened overnight. It hurts me in a way to see him so diminished. You can't imagine what he was like."

"Yes, I can. Grandfather thinks you're trying to hurt him through me."

"How is that?" he asked sharply.

"You're hurting me, Quinn."

"You deserve it."

She linked her arms around his neck to balance herself. "Are we still going ahead with this engagement?"

"More than ever. You fascinate me, Jaime."

"There are shadows around you Quinn," she said a little sadly. "Don't think I can't see them."

His expression changed from a sensuous charm to a dark arrogance. "Who's been talking to you?"

"*Everyone*. No one, including your grandmother, thinks I'd make you a suitable bride."

"How mistaken can they get, when in fact, in some

ways I find you flawless. Satiny skin, violet eyes, black shiny mane, even that condescending little smile. I might as well kiss you at that."

"Oh no, you won't," she said, struggling so wildly he dropped her to her feet. "I'm myself again."

"Well, make sure you stay that way. You couldn't decide who you were a few moments ago. I would have thought you were mine."

"It's better and wiser that I be myself!"

"Where would you like to go tonight?" he asked, his eyes searching her face with a turbulent brilliance.

"Oh, let's just go for a drive."

This for some reason started him laughing, such a warm, disturbing sound that Jaime turned to stare at him with surprise, then a terrible suspicion. "On second thoughts, we'll stick with the bright lights."

"But, Jaime," he said lightly, "I promise you I'll treat you like a hideous, well-loved great-aunt."

"Have you a great-aunt?"

"I had one until recently. I believe she was a glorious beauty in her day."

"I'm not surprised. Being hideous isn't one of the Sterling misfortunes. You look remarkably well after your long trip."

"And you look extremely touching just coming up to my heart, but collect your things. It doesn't pay to push yourself to the limit and I don't think you can stand up much longer."

The room seemed to be swimming around her and her eyes looked dreamy and bemused. "I don't seem to be asking you any of the important things. How was the trip?"

"Extremely successful, thank you, Jaime." He moved over and checked on the windows. "A deal has been arranged with very favourable terms for us. We have a few more talks with the government, then we can go ahead. I might ask you the same question. How's Just Jaime?"

"I'm not ready to talk about it," she said, drooping disconsolately and letting him complete his circuit of the premises.

"Then we can easily talk about it tomorrow or the next day. I didn't expect you to wear yourself to the bone."

"But I've been full of enthusiasm!" she said urgently. "Everything was going so right, yet today three potential buyers knocked me back. It wasn't what I expected. The girls were pretty impressed and they don't impress all that easily, especially Di."

"What buyers?" He came back and looked straight at her, a bracing look that made her pay attention. "Give me a list of them. It sounds as if it could be a little elementary or crude blackmail, in which case you're far from sunk. Your grandfather is sour on the whole thing; ferocious, but kindly disposed towards you. I told you, remember, he wouldn't want you to work at all."

"Damn you, Quinn, it was to *you* I came for help. I'm a lot smarter than you give me credit for."

"And I'm glad of it. One little problem you can't thrash out by yourself: when are we going to celebrate our engagement? The Old Man has put us off long enough.''

He was focusing all his attention on her and Jaime reacted with a young girl's uncertainty. "Talk to me, Quinn. You don't really talk to me. You didn't even send me a postcard.''

"No time, but I remembered you. You have the right skin for pearls. A swan's neck. Stop staring at me.''

"Surely you don't think Grandfather is behind it?''

He shook his head. "No, he's gone quite soft on you. I'm sure it's making the family envious.''

"You're on my side, aren't you?''

"Indeed I am.''

"I wish I could be sure of it,'' she sighed.

"You damned well should be!'' he said tersely.

"Well, I'm not. I'm vaguely uneasy about you, Quinn. Your motivations.''

"Oh, be fair!'' he said lazily. "I'm merely trying to protect you.''

"It has to be that. I can't flatter myself you've fallen madly in love with me.''

"I told you—mutual protection. I'm tired of being chased by panting females and I'd feel quite safe with you. At least you've given me your solemn promise not to consider marriage for years yet, if at all.''

"And what's wrong with that, you mocking man?''

"Nothing. Let us say at once I'm taking refuge behind your stance. This way we can have the best of both worlds.''

"Don't make *that* mistake!'' she said, swiftly gathering up her things.

"It was just a thought." He came after her and turned off the light. "It might save us from boredom."

Jaime turned pensively, her head still tilted, her eyes an indescribable mixture of blue and hyacinth. "I'm never sure of the exact colour of your eyes. Did you ever consider I might be serious?"

"No."

"All right, then! Let's check my intentions. I'm just your backer-advisor-sometime-protector. Valued, I hope. I wouldn't want you to think of me any other way. Is that the key you're hiding?"

"Yes."

"Give it to me. Now I'm going to try and get you out to the car. You look like a child who ought to be picked up and tucked into bed."

"So you keep telling me. I must look pathetic."

"No, you're terribly attractive to me as you must know. But I have this unshakeable grievance against cradle-snatchers. I've talked to you about it before."

They went out in the street now, and she lifted her face urgently. "I'm twenty. In another year I'll be twenty-one. Then what?"

"We'll talk about it then. I'm not prepared to act until you're at least thirty. Does that please you?"

"Indeed yes! I expect you'll be married yourself by then."

Quinn steered her towards the car, then leaned forward and opened the passenger side. "She'd have to be pretty exceptional. I haven't had the faintest urge up until now."

"Nobody worthy?" she enquired.

"Nobody pleasant enough. You're a little cat yourself. Hop in and curl up."

"Of course!" she replied sweetly, and instantly complied, settling back and crossing her long slender legs. She never quite knew what was happening to her when Quinn was about, but he made her come frantically alive. Her skin was electric with an unbearable sweet tension, an enormous excitement that made her feel giddy like a deep draught of mountain air recklessly taken and held.

Quinn got in beside her and gave her an odd, considering little smile, a combination of tenderness and taunting. "Tell me what you're thinking about this minute?"

"No. I refuse to indulge you." Her heart was beginning to drum wildly and she turned her head to look out of the window.

"All right," he said easily, "but don't think you can lock up your thoughts. I can see right through to your soul."

"Then obviously I'll have to keep staring out of the window!"

"You'll turn to me of your own accord. I can wait!" He switched on the ignition and the big car purred into life. They crawled out of the narrow street until they turned on to the main road, then they picked up speed. It was a powerful and very expensive car and it was deeply comfortable so that after a minute, Jaime relaxed her rigid spine.

Quinn glanced at her briefly and laughed. Her blue-violet eyes seemed to be imploring him, revealing and very beautiful. He put out a hand and lightly touched her cheek then he gave his total attention to the road. Jaime, totally relaxing still, didn't delude herself. There was no escape from Quinn, for wasn't she his latest acquisition?

CHAPTER EIGHT

FALCONER was a blaze of lights and Vivian Hunter's car stood in the drive some little distance from the gold Mercedes belonging to "Robby" Burnett, Sir Rolf's close friend and personal physician for over twenty years.

"Something's wrong!" Jaime said with the first dreadful premonition.

"It may not be anything, Jaime. Try to keep calm." Quinn swung the car round to the base of the stairs, his dark face inscrutable, but Jaime barely waited for it to come to a complete halt before throwing open the door and jumping out. All her senses were working overtime. The doctor's car alone seemed an unbearable menace. Quinn came round to her and grabbed her arm, restraining her, but already his sombre dark face was revealing his own forewarnings. "We'll go quietly, Jaime. You mustn't lose control. Your grandfather was quite all right this afternoon. In fact, he was the best I've seen him for a long time."

"He wouldn't be proof against another heart attack."

"We'll go in," Quinn said quietly. "Your Uncle Vivian is here." That it itself argued a relapse, but he didn't mention it. Jaime's desperate young face was hurting him.

"He could be dead!" she whispered, visibly trembling.

"The end has to come!" he said rather harshly. "It was a miracle he rallied the last time."

"I think my heart will break!" She was gasping, her eyes filled with tears.

His arm came round her shoulders, the fingers biting into her skin. "You feel everything so intensely, Jaime. Your grandfather isn't afraid to die. He's very tired. I think he only wished to live long enough to see you."

"I don't want him to die."

"There's an end for all of us, Jaime, and we have to be prepared for it. Come, you're not alone!"

They found the entrance hall brilliantly lit and beyond they could see into the drawing room where the family was assembled. Everyone looked mortally stricken; whether by the threat of death and its bitter promise for all of them, or now, at the end, a sense of family and respect.

Gerard Hunter was standing in front of the fireplace and he turned his head towards them. "My father has had another heart attack. He's not expected to live the hour."

"Can I go up to him?" Jaime cried, in a frenzy of distress.

"No, Jaime, you cannot! I think you've caused quite enough harm already."

She almost reeled, but there was more.

"You think you're one of us, but you're not!" he continued dully. "My father wouldn't wish to see you."

With her quick nervous recoil against Quinn's shoulder she could feel the icy rage in him and she knew without looking at him his black eyes would be glittering. "Spare her your poison," he said in a low, cutting voice. "Jaime has given your father the only pleasure he's known in long years!"

"Please, Quinn!"

Both men ignored her. "I would expect you to take that view, Sterling!" Vivian Hunter said sneeringly, but his heavy handsome face flushed a dark red.

"I haven't the brutality to be more honest at this time!"

Georgia, seated behind her husband in an armchair, suddenly began to moan helplessly. "Must we make things worse? Have a care, Gerard. We may all be disinherited for all I know. Grandfather is much to far gone to see you, Jaime, and it would only distress you to see him."

"I'd like to go up."

"*No.*" Georgia buried her head in her hands. She looked genuinely besieged with anguish, overwhelmed by the thought of her father-in-law's imminent death. He had always been there, manipulating their lives. It didn't seem possible that he could be human enough to die. She was suffering from a guilty conscience as well, for she had been out all day and she had often wished him dead of late. It was puzzling now that she could be so truly torn.

Vivian Hunter, at the head of his family group, stood nibbling his luxuriant moustache, the only thing that marked him from his brother to the casual eye. He was determined now not to fall out with anyone. He was discovering too for the first time in years that he loved his father—more, worshipped him for the financial giant he was. Not that his father had ever loved him, and with a kind of deeply driven sense of inferiority he had learned not to expect it. It was now an added punishment that he had seen so little of the old man of late. The years since his boyhood were flashing past his eyes at a frantic pace, his father dominating every one of them. Now he was going, perhaps gone, an old man with nowhere to conquer. A giant no more. Evelyn, his wife, was crying quietly and he patted her shoulder, the first time he had done that in years. She didn't draw away, which was unusual, but rather seemed to be comforted by it so he continued in this mellow, melancholy vein.

Robby Burnett was suddenly in the midst of them, scanning their faces. "The position is grave. He's conscious, but not for long. Jaime, would you come up? Quinn, you might come with her."

"It doesn't really matter about the rest of us, does it?" Gerard Hunter called bitterly.

"I'll call you all in a moment!" Robby merely replied. "It's Jaime he wants to see, and she'll need somebody. None of you seems to qualify."

The doctor turned away, his eyes flashing. He was infinitely upset himself and finding it difficult to hide. Rolf Hunter has been his closest friend and a brilliant mind. He knew perfectly well what a lot of people said about him, and he even believed some of it, but Rolf was his friend to the death. Rolf's sons he had never liked, but they had suffered on their father's account, terribly perhaps, and this thought made him turn back and lift his hand to them as though exonerating their sins.

"Pompous old goat!" Sue-Ellen hissed when he was out of earshot.

"He is your grandfather's friend!" Georgia pointed out severely, still feeling virtuous.

"Yes, and so is Jaime. I think we should all be worried."

"*I* am!" Gerard Hunter maintained heavily, beginning to pace up and down.

"Didn't Father ever reveal to you the contents of his will?"

"No, he didn't!" Gerard suddenly roared, rounding on his brother.

"Well, we'll never be exactly broke!"

"You've always been a fool, Viv!"

"Yes, that's so!"

"Don't agree with him, Dad," Brett protested. "Stick up for yourself!" he admonished, emerging as his father's protector.

"Shut up!" his uncle said cruelly. "When we want to hear from you we'll be dead ourselves."

Brett muttered something unprintable and Sue-Ellen gracefully collapsed into the armchair opposite her mother. "This is marvellous, isn't it, and so typical! We sit here feuding while Jaime grabs the lot!"

Her mother was coming out of her reluctant trauma. "Oh, for God's sake, Sue!"

"Oh, don't persist with the act, Mother. We all knew this was going to happen. Old Robby warned us ages ago."

"You're so young and so terribly cynical!" her mother wailed tearfully. "I don't even think I like you."

"On the other hand, this tearful mood will pass. I'm sorry Grandfather is dying. I really am. Please note that I don't wish to go up to the sickroom. The rest of you can. But certain thoughts occur to me. Jaime could get the lot and Quinn, the smartest operator in the business, is poised right there to carry her off—the lily-white prize. He's always been a great one for keeping ahead of us. Look at all the time Simon and Brett put in on her. The results, scorn from those burning blue eyes; Quinn only had to look at her. I tell you he's clever."

"And he's incredibly sexy!" Leigh said from the depths of her jealous despair. "At any rate she'll know by now that she's not another Chanel."

"And what is that supposed to mean?" Gerard Hunter glared at her in the fraught pause.

"Oh, just a little plan we cooked up together," Sue-Ellen said uneasily.

Her father's eyes narrowed unpleasantly. "Don't confuse Jaime with Sterling, you little fool! He's back and he'll put paid to any of your bitchy little schemes—and what's more you'll have to pay for it. *I* won't!"

"Now, now!" Georgia exclaimed, not daring to continue this line of discussion. "Would you mind terribly if we all be quiet?"

"My mother, are you going to pray?" asked Sue-Ellen.

"No, that wouldn't be right."

"Why not?" Evelyn Hunter suddenly cleared her throat. A little afraid of Georgia and her daughter, she now felt disgusted with them. "It's obvious we all regard prayer as something shameful. That might account for our lack of integrity."

"Oh, excuse us," Sue-Ellen murmured caustically. "There's nothing worse than a convert." She got up and walked to the beautiful bay window, looking out. "How gloomy death is! How chilling! It's easy to see why people like to live dangerously and die young. I couldn't bear to grow old and sick. Grandfather from the height of his powers to this—a frail and haggard old man. It's an outrage. I wonder how Jaime is going? The King is dead, long live the Queen. In the meantime we all feel ill!"

TREMBLING, and trying desperately not to cry, Jaime approached the huge four-poster bed where her grandfather lay dying. She had known him for so little time. He had ignored her for almost all of her life, so she could have been expected to feel little more than compassion, the trouble was, she loved him and had loved him on encounter. Ruthless and egocentric though he was, she wanted nothing more than to have him stay with her for ever, when finally she had to admit, as she leaned over his bed, he could stand no more.

His eyes were shut and she was terrified he might be already dead. Then his hand moved on the covers and he seemed to be training all his concentration into opening his eyes. The man who had founded a splendid and flourishing corporation looked appallingly frail, more dead than alive, curiously small and pathetic for a man who stood at more than six feet. Jaime struggled to keep back her tears, but they spilled out of her eyes and one sparkling diamond splashed on to her grandfather's hand. The handsome old face was all bone now, bloodless, the silver hair stiff around his skull. It was too much, and she had never seen death before. She was tempted to bury her face in her hands to hide from the common dread, to somehow cover a whole world of regrets, but she was committed now to witness her grandfather's death. It was absolutely the most dreadful moment of her life, and the anguish was in her face. She could not bear it if he had to endure agony.

Quinn and the doctor stood close together at the far side of the room. Both of them had forgotten everything except the sight of the dying man and Jaime's tortured young face. Quinn, who had reason to hate, immediately forgave all the things that had been done to his father and his father before him. It didn't seem to matter now.

Jaime looked breakable in the restrained lighting, the concentrated essence of womanly sorrow, the lamp striking purple tints in the silky masses of her hair. He had brought her here to this. She was so young, so intensely *feeling*, he might have spared her. Her life hadn't been easy and her relatives had done everything in their power to make her uncomfortable and unwelcome since she had arrived at Falconer. But there was nothing weak or unstable about her. She had the old man's brilliance without his ruthlessness, the old man's strength without the coldness of temperament that had kept his sons and his grandchildren going beggarly for a sign of heartfelt affection. What did it matter now anyway? Man was born to heartbreak. Quinn might want to spare her, for the sight of her was tearing into him, but he knew it was impossible. Jaime would have to suffer. There was a price to be paid for everything.

A second or more later, with an indescribable effort, Rolf Hunter opened his eyes, striving to raise himself from the pillows. He was frowning, trying to see through the awful fog before his eyes as he stared straight in front of him. Jaime moved and he rasped out a single word, his face clearing miraculously, lighting up so that Jaime began to whimper in her throat.

"Rowena!" he said, pushing up, and it was impossible to mistake the loving ecstasy of his tone, the pride and the utter belief that he was face to face with his daughter.

Jaime looked down at him, taking his hand and easing him gently on to the pillows. "I'm here, Father. Don't worry, I'm here to look after you."

He rested back, his head turned to her, staring at her with shining eyes. "Rowena!" he said again, marvellously eased.

Jaimed lifted her head to find Quinn. She wasn't Jaime at all, but her mother, and she was content that this should be so, for it granted her grandfather a strange serenity. The expression in Quinn's black eyes descended on her like a benediction. She would never doubt the depths of his nature again. He cared for her in some way.

She sank to the floor, kneeling now beside the bed, stroking her grandfather's hand. There was the faintest smile on his mouth, every line of pain on his face eased out. She relaxed her head for a moment, even hopeful of some immense recovery, so that the doctor's words hit her like a blow:

"He's gone!"

Jaime threw up her head and saw that this was so. All her own breath seemed to leave her. It was impossible to mistake death, the emptiness. "Oh, God!" She dropped her head on to the bed and burst into uncontrollable weeping for her grandfather's parting soul.

"Jaime, Jaime, don't. I can't bear it!" Quinn moved forward quickly and lifted her bodily away from the bed, feeling the throbbing pain in her, while Robby Burnett, his face puckered, leaned over and closed his friend's eyes.

"Go to them, Quinn. Tell them, I can't."

"In a minute." Quinn looked down at Jaime. He was cradling her like a child, unable to see her face buried so infinitely touchingly against him. Her teeth were chattering and she was shaking vehemently, when outside it was a blissful summer's night.

"I'll give her something," Robby muttered over his shoulder. "Poor old man. Poor, poor old man. Goodbye my old friend. If any one of them says the wrong thing to me I shall strike them, and I've never hit anyone in my life."

Quinn hesitated for a moment, then he lifted Jaime
in his arms and carried her towards the door. "I'll take
Jaime to her room, then I'll go down. I don't want her
exposed to them. They'll be cruel even in their pain."

"Margo will look after her," Robby said quietly.
"Take her there. I can make the arrangements here."

"Thank you, Robby."

"Listen, Quinn!"

"Yes?"

"You're a good man."

"I've been...lots of things!"

They looked at one another in silence across the
great bed. "I know the old stories. I say what I mean.
You're a good man. Be kind to that child—hardly bearable the way the old fellow thought she was Rowena."

"Yes, Rowena, offering pardon!" Quinn said sombrely. "The only one who ever held a place in his heart.
He never did see Jaime as she really is, only an extension of his daughter. Still, it gave him peace at the end.
Or peace of a sort."

Quinn glanced at the bed again, his dark face set,
then he moved out through the door with his slight
burden. The quivering slender body moved him pro-
foundly. He couldn't leave her here to the tender
mercies of the Hunters. With her grandfather gone,
Jaime had no other friend in the house. He would take
her to Rosemount. His grandmother would know how
to console her grief. Never callous, he began to feel the
great silence of the house. Death communicated its
own message. The heirs of Sir Rolf Hunter would be
no less stricken than Jaime; all of them the old man

had starved of love, hardened in every possible way, so it would be necessary now to show a little of Jaime's compassion. For all of them it was the end of an era. Rolf Hunter had been an unforgettable man.

THE WEEK that followed her grandfather's funeral would always have a place in Jaime's memory. His death had stunned all of them, but immediately the will was read they all began to recover, determined to make a fight of it. It had been expected that Jaime would be richly rewarded beyond her deserts, now it seemed Sir Rolf had made an unforgivable welter of it. To the amazement of everyone, he had left her Falconer and the entire contents of the house, including the magnificent art collection. Add to that a massive bundle of shares in Hunter Sterling Exploration and Hunter Sterling Land Corporation, and it was the final crack on the head.

Even at Rosemount Jaime was made aware of the family's impotent rage. It was hell, and there were necessary meetings and coldly abusive phone calls. She was torn in all directions, because she didn't want Falconer nor a fortune. As Sir Rolf Hunter's heiress, her name and photographs had found themselves into all the papers, giving of all things the Just Jaime label an enormous if temporary boost. Di, with a single phone call, had assured her of this. Jaime Gilmore might have been a nothing, but the late Sir Rolf Hunter's granddaughter was quite a different matter. The boutiques that had scorned her now could spare her all the time in the world, but she promised them nothing.

Her father had not attended the funeral. He hadn't even expressed regret when Jaime rang him that first evening at Rosemount. All he had promised was to defer his pending marriage until Jaime was free and able to travel up to Queensland. The tears running down her paper-white cheeks, Jaime didn't have it in her heart to upbraid him. It would have been hypocrisy for her father to have said he was sorry, but it seemed proper to stick with the nice old-fashioned idea of murmuring a few sympathetic words to the living. Derrick Gilmore had always loathed and detested his father-in-law: Jaime had loved him. Their views could scarcely be compatible. At the time Jaime had not been aware of her stunning inheritance, so she had given her father no news that interested him, so that finally when she hung up she wondered why she had rung at all.

"He wasn't in the least sorry," she had murmured to Mrs. Sterling, and Margo Sterling had touched her head gently with a wry: "I daresay!"

The days passed, of course, but Jaime was never to forget them. Quinn, however, was Quinn, always going forward, never back. She couldn't have done without him, for he soon put an end to all the harsh words that were offered to her by her relations. She could never have borne them unflinchingly without Quinn, for he seemed to find her a quick way out of all her difficulties. He had now taken on the role of conscientious and supremely capable big brother who went right out of his way to dispose of all her problems, as though she were a precious and incompetent semi-invalid, which for that week she was.

When she began to recover she approached him
about Falconer. He spent most of his evenings at Rosemount, which delighted his grandmother, but Jaime
had never seen him alone. It was a deliberate manoeu-
vre and she had forewarned Mrs. Sterling so that the
lady retired early, allowing Jaime to corner Quinn's entire attention. The night was a blaze of stars, the breeze
coming in off the water, so they sat in the semi-dark of
the verandah to escape the heat, Jaime on the cush-
ioned lounger, Quinn a few feet from her, madden-
ingly relaxed.

"Quinn," she said purposefully.

"Hmm?"

"There's something I want to talk to you about."

"Oh, my God!" he said.

"You told me to tell you if there was anything
bothering me."

"It's plain there is now. Go ahead, my lady!"

"About Falconer..."

"Lordy!" he interjected, his teeth a flash of white in
his dark face.

"Are you going to listen to me or not?"

"Baby, I'm so tired," he sighed.

"Are you? It doesn't seem possible, you're such a
miracle of energy."

"It just happens I am."

"Then come and sit beside me."

"No, thanks, Jaime. You said you want to *talk*."

"I don't want Falconer!" she said bluntly. "It's too
big, it's too beautiful, it's too valuable. It could only
hold unhappy memories for me."

"How sad. Tell me, what do you intend to do with it?"

"Practically anything but live in it."

"May I make a merciful suggestion?" he enquired.

"Please do."

"Sell it to your Uncle Gerard for a fair price. It's always been his home, you know."

"Are you trying to say that Grandfather was unfair?" she asked.

"Not *trying* to say, darling girl. With time and forgetfulness I might change my tune. Obnoxious as Gerard undoubtedly is I feel sorry for him."

"So do I. In fact, I don't know why I didn't think of it myself."

"These haven't been great days for you. Tell me, what do you weigh now?"

"You'll still be able to carry me," she told him.

"Much more important, I might be able to make love to you. You look like a little girl, all curled up there. Shall I approach your nice uncle?"

"Would you?"

"I have to work with him. It isn't easy. There's no way of knowing how he will react initially. But I'm sure it will eventually be arranged."

"That's the house," she said.

"And there's more?" Quinn asked wryly.

"Uncle Gerard is a very rich man. I can't feel *too* sorry for him. The art collection, the *Australian* art collection, I have definite ideas about. It's a complete history of our art from the colonial days to the outstanding artists of our day. I don't feel entitled to hoard it up like a miser with his gold. It's part of the national heritage. I would like everyone to see it. What did you say?"

"Nothing!" he said blandly. "I'm just numb. Keep going, Jaime, I'll just sit here and admire you."

"I think I'd like it to go on permanent loan to the national art galleries."

"That's spendid. I think you'd better keep the Renoirs and the Picassos."

"I'm serious, Quinn," she rebuked.

"So am I. You're the only benevolent Hunter I've met. A strange child in a strange land. What about the fantastic assemblage of antiques?"

"I thought I'd let each member of the family select a favourite piece. I want the Oriental vases and the portrait of my mother. What's left can go up for public auction, and the proceeds can go to medical research foundations. My mother died in childbirth. It was touch and go for me, I believe. I'd like some of the money to be set aside for that kind of thing."

Quinn sat up. "I said I was tired, but you seem to have brought about an incredible renascence. Is it possible you want to finish up with nothing?"

"I have all those shares," she pointed out.

"So you do." He rocked back precariously and put his arms behind his head. "God knows what the old man would have thought of this."

"He wouldn't have approved?"

"He was never known to give anything away that couldn't go down as a tax deduction. You're undoubtedly the finest, purest Hunter I've known."

"I wanted to talk to you about it," she confided.

"Is that why Grandmamma went to bed?"

"We talk practically all the time. No secrets."

"Yes, you're no longer the child of Rowena. You're Jaime, and Jaime wouldn't let anyone suffer."

"Don't entangle me in all the sad, old stories," she said. "Are you sure you know who I am?"

"Jaime, the witch," he responded.

"Within limits. I can't even get you to sit beside me."

"No, you can't!" he said crisply. "I've seen all your fearful little violet-eyed glances, the ideas they've put into your head. Black-hearted Sterling carrying off the heiress. The powerfully cruel eagle with the pathetic little lamb."

"You have been mentioned, yes," she said truthfully, trying not to remember exactly what was said. "There's no need to even go on with the engagement."

"Particularly when you're going to give everything away!"

He sounded so vastly ironical that Jaime swept off the lounger shaking with the urge to hit him. "Oh no, you don't!" he said, catching her around the waist. "You're my business partner anyway, and you're going to make me rich!"

"You *are* rich. That's the only thing that confuses me, but some men are power-mad." She was facing him, speaking softly but intensely, his fingers hard about her waist.

"No news, Jaime. I'm power-mad at the minute!" In seconds he pulled her down on to his knees, making it seem the most natural, the most dangerous thing in the world. "You're absolutely determined about all this?"

"Absolutely."

"But you decline to go on with the engagement that never had a chance to get off the ground?"

"I have certain information that you're just using me!"

"There is that possibility," he said suavely.

"Thank you, Quinn, for admitting it."

"I'm not admitting anything. I'm trying to agree with you. It's what you want, isn't it?"

"Would you please let me go?"

"Definitely not. I was a fool not to have thought of it before, but you seemed so fragile."

"Is it true?" she insisted.

"What?" He stared into her flower face. "Oh, I see.... Am I using you. What a dreadful way to put it! For one thing, Jaime, I can't resist you, but I wouldn't be telling the truth if I said I was unmindful of the advantages. My maternal grandmother was French. Doesn't that mean something to you? Marriages of convenience and all that, sensible, long-lasting arrangements. That appeals to me. Besides, you're going to be famous."

"Depend on it."

"Oh, I am. I never back long shots. I like that dress. It shimmers in this light. Yes, you're going to be the designer to end all designers. They're my pearls, aren't they?"

"Yes, they are!" She shivered as his hand touched her bare skin.

"They're the new length, or so they told me," he observed idly, "and they look good with a deep V. You're so beautiful, Jaime, you were bound to complicate things."

"If you're not going to let me up do you mind if I make myself more comfortable?"

"I'm hoping you will, because you're not going anywhere. I mean it—relax. You'd do anything for me, Jaime, wouldn't you?"

"I never at any time said that!" she half whispered.

"But you mean it, don't you?"

She rested against him, her breathing deep and urgent. "Do you know what Grandfather once said to me? There's nothing easier than pretending to love a woman."

"I'd find it equally impossible to pretend I wanted a woman when I didn't. Your grandfather was a wicked old man, God rest his soul!"

"It happens, though, Quinn," she said gravely.

"Shut up for a while, would you, because I'm quite normal and you're the most desirable creature I'm ever likely to meet."

"Are you saying that with a thread of self-contempt? You have such a voice for inflections. You can manage to convey anything."

"I said, let's not talk. Turn your head up, Jaime. I don't want to hurt you."

"I have a feeling you will soon," she sighed.

"And that's bad? It seems such a long time, Jaime."

"Yes." She spoke so softly her words just melted into the darkness. Maybe she didn't even say them, but felt them. It had seemed an eternity. Her smile had faded and her face was very still.

"Nowhere to go, Jaime?" he murmured with low mockery. His hand that encircled her nape suddenly slipped under her chin, forcing her head up. "Your skin is as luminous as that string of pearls or the soft summer moonlight. I knew at the beginning where it would lead to!"

She was silent, just staring up at him, seeing the sparkle of his eyes in the scented gloom. Then all at once she was trembling violently, with a desire she couldn't hide. He gathered her right up against him with a hard deliberation, lowering his head on a shattering path to her mouth. Her breath fluttered and she was pervaded with such urgent sensations that it was like some powerful rising storm, a quickening she couldn't control, with only Quinn holding the key to whatever path they were travelling. The very darkness seemed to be burning, crackling with a mounting intensity.

"Jaime!" he said barely audibly, twisting his hand through her hair as his mouth lifted a little, lingering, learning every contour of her face and throat. She was just a slender blur against him, her heart pounding heavily. If he wanted her to believe he loved her, he was succeeding. All she could think of was recapturing his mouth, moving her head blindly, as if the most totally important thing in the world was to seek the source of such exquisite excitement.

They might have been at the very core of a pulsing circle ringed with fire, the breeze cooling her heated skin, but never the echoing wildness in her blood. His mouth was warm and hard, faultless in its task of arousal, his hands positive, insistent, caressing, sure of her, sure of fashioning her into whatever he wanted. If it was folly to be taken over so completely, it was something she wanted too badly to resist. There wasn't a shadow between them but a remorseless passion, Jaime's head thrown back in a beautiful abandon, his hand caught in her hair, while he continued to kiss her in a brilliant devastation.

"Jaime!" He lifted his head slowly, his breath uneven.

"No, don't stop."

"I'm just tormenting both of us."

"I don't care!"

"I do. Believe me, I'm going to take very good care of you."

"Oh, *why*?" she said, sounding mortally deprived and not in the least thankful.

"In this case, because you're just twenty years old!"

"Does it ever occur to you I'm a woman?"

"What a fool question! That's what's causing all the trouble. Sit up and behave. I want to go on with this quite shockingly, but we've done enough dallying for now. Let's go inside." He lifted her off his knee with tremendous decision and stood up.

"God, how confusing!" Jaime groaned. "Here I am maddened with passion and you're as retiring as an inoffensive, sanctimonious parson."

"I should ravish you for that!" he said, and dropped a violent kiss on her mouth. "I'm a gentleman by nature, Jaime, just don't keep flinging yourself at me."

"I never get the chance," she said derisively.

"I wouldn't care, but first you have to tell me, do you love me?"

She stood looking up at him. He didn't seem serious. "You might just as well ask me if I trust you!"

"Of course, I forgot. You don't!"

"Quinn?" She drew nearer him and touched his sleeve, dismayed by the hard note in his voice. "I was only fooling, you know."

"You fool too much!"

"So do you."

"Yes, I suppose so. You look like a girl who's practically been kissed senseless."

"Which was considerably less than I felt like."

"You are modern, Jaime!" he drawled.

She moved back a step and he followed her. "I said *felt* like. Feelings aren't actions."

"Really? Perhaps we'd better stay here and explore this dazzling new world we've just found."

"No, we'll go inside and I can see your black scowl!"

In the hallway Jaime turned her head back over her shoulder. "Do you think you'll be able to make Derry's wedding? He does so want you to come."

His dark face was very handsome, very seeking and alive. He adjusted the collar of his shirt, a faint smile on his mouth. "Bless him! And to think I didn't know him all these years!"

"Sometimes I hate you!" she said truthfully, but she smiled, her violet eyes very soft and tender.

"That's good!" He reached out and touched her cheek. "I don't like you either, from time to time. As for Derry, maybe I can escape for the weekend. I'll certainly try. When are you leaving?"

"Wednesday. I thought I'd have a few days as a sort of pick-me-up."

"Believe me, you don't need one. *I* do!"

"Alcohol's not the answer, Quinn," she said with sweet maliciousness.

"It might be tonight. Get me a drink, you violet-eyed witch. I deserve one!"

CHAPTER NINE

JAIME TURNED to answer yet another battery of questions. The ceremony was over and the fifty and more guests were revolving around the gallery where the reception was being held. The air was buzzing with conversation, as far as Jaime could make out, mostly about her. Overnight she had become a celebrity, the ornament of the evening, and she had dressed the part with beautiful unaccustomed extravagance in black silk chiffon printed with huge roses and peonies in Persian blue and rose, with gold and silver leaves. She had designed it as a one-shouldered toga and Di and Marike between them had run it up for her. She wore nothing around her neck, but silver pendant earrings set with turquoise and pearls. It was now her enormous responsibility to dress the part if she wished to add lustre to her own label.

Most of the guests were known to her except for Gayle's friends, the artistic community that lived and worked on the beautiful Coast, and a few of her father's best clients. They had been dumbfounded to read her story in the papers, but now they were ready to talk about it. To spring into the national spotlight with Hunter Sterling, one of the biggest enterprises in the

country, and Sir Rolf Hunter Jaime's grandfather—it
had come as an enormous shock to everyone. Derry
had never breathed a word and he was a colossal gossip.
That he had kept such a secret to himself seemed unbelievable.

Jaime was besieged from the moment she arrived.
What was life like at the top? After a while she began to
feel a prisoner of her newly glamorous background,
though she tried to sparkle and look interested, assuming what would later become her public face. Gayle was
the real surprise. Knowing her father and his predilic-
tion for good-looking women, well covered if possible,
she had been unprepared for Gayle's tall, thin figure,
the soft copper hair and the goodly sprinkling of
freckles. Gayle would never entrance the senses, but
she was intelligent and articulate and made the most of
herself to the extent that she appeared attractive.
Somehow her father had had the good sense to see
through to the essential Gayle, with her clean, strong
mind and her ability to inspire contentment.

It had come as a tremendous relief to Jaime to discover that Gayle was very much in love with her father.
The marriage ceremony, to Jaime's further surprise,
was performed in a church and it was heartening to see
her father take it all very seriously when they had had
many an argument on religion. His views had been
quite straightforward then. In a very short time Gayle
appeared to have worked wonders, and from the look
of happiness about them tonight, things could only go
on improving. Gayle at their first meeting had been
very nervous under her nice easy manner, but Jaime

found her pretty nearly perfect and said so. Gayle loved her father, and from his attitude he appeared to regard her warmly in return. Jaime could only be happy for them. In her own quiet way, Gayle was also sharpening his ambitions, and had become very involved in the art scene herself since her arrival on the Coast, and Jaime felt almost breathless to see what this new stimulus would lead to.

Derrick Gilmore was a very good artist, the trouble was that his whole life had been drastically upset and altered as a young man, robbing him of any real incentive. Jaime, though he would never have told her and foolishly imagined she didn't know, reminded him unbearably of Rowena. Though she had inspired his best work, her portrait, and he loved her, her presence never eased Rowena from his conscious mind: Rowena and her father, Rolf Hunter, for whom he had always felt such hatred that it swamped him. Gayle, who he feared he hadn't even noticed at the beginning, was steadily changing his attitudes to everything. He was almost tranquil and looked incredibly youthful, as some fair men remained for a large part of their lives.

It gave Jaime great pleasure to see her father looking so well, and if she had to surrender him to another woman, she could feel truly glad about Gayle. Tavia, now, would have been another matter, and Tavia surprisingly had been invited and came to the reception but not the ceremony. It was the unanimous opinion that Derry had been fortunate to win such an attractive and intelligent young wife.

It was a Friday night. It was a party, they were enjoying

one another's company enormously, celebrating the
marriage of a dear friend. No one seemed in the least
inclined to go home any more than Gayle and Derrick
wanted to depart. The leading figures of the artistic community were there, the painters, the potters and the
craftsmen, so they were content to raid the excellent
buffet, grab another drink and return quickly with their
own pertinent or controversial comments. Not a soul
looking at Jaime, so beautiful and argumentative, could
have guessed at her other preoccupations and the bitter
disappointment she was feeling. The blazing anticipation
with which she had dressed had given way to a becoming
loss of confidence in her powers of seduction. It had
been an enthralling idea to think Quinn might be slightly
in love with her, and the thought had her so buoyant that
she was floating, now with every passing minute it
seemed she was wrong. He had never left Sydney,
though he had sent a handsome present that endeared
him to Gayle from a distance. Meantime Jaime was discovering she was leading two lives, stimulating the conversation and mourning Quinn's absence. She couldn't
enjoy herself no matter what anyone thought, but she
owed it to Derry and Gayle to scintillate.

The gallery was overflowing with people, yet she
might have been alone on a desert island. Gayle, catching sight of her momentarily betraying face, excused
herself from her group and started towards Jaime, who
clearly heard not a word her highly entranced companion was saying to her. Gayle smiled at him and waved
him away, taking Jaime's arm.

"You're the sensation of the evening. Our celebrity."

"Possibly," agreed Jaime.

"Also you're so extravagantly beautiful I'm frightened to stand beside you. The only thing is, I'm a good reader of faces and I just caught your expression."

"I'm enjoying myself, Gayle!" Jaime protested smilingly. "I would never have missed your wedding for the world."

"I know you really mean that, Jaime, and it means a lot to me. Your friend, Mr. Sterling, can't be coming."

"It doesn't seem likely now," she agreed.

"I imagine he's an extremely busy man."

"I can't pretend that's not true."

"You're pretty badly in love with him?" Gayle suggested, risking getting put in her place.

"Is it showing?" Jaime said wryly.

"Only to me perhaps, being very much in love myself."

"Ah well," said Jaime, "don't let it throw a shadow on us. Derry looks very happy, Gayle. Thank you for that. I think he can do with a new family background. He was never happy with the old."

"No, and he kept remarkably quiet about it. Odd in Derry. The whole story is fantastic. I expect you can't believe it's happening, Jaime."

"The money doesn't mean very much to me, Gayle."

Gayle nodded. "No, I don't think I'd want too much money myself. Great wealth must be frightening. You up there with everyone resentful and envious trying to pull you down. One would feel so exposed. Tavia's being very friendly, isn't she?"

"Tavia's a deep one."

"She was very fond of your father."

"Indeed yes!" Jaime murmured, wondering if Gayle knew exactly how fond. "You've shown some skill interesting him in marriage."

"I'm an old-fashioned girl!" Gayle smiled. "Even Derry had to see that. Anyway, he didn't see it coming until it was too late."

Derry, however, saw their smiles and he came towards them, slipping an arm around each one of them. "How are my girls?"

"Some people have all the luck!"

"Don't they now!" Derry bent his head sideways and kissed Jaime's cheek. "You look extremely beautiful tonight. What an exquisite piece of material!" he added with the artist's eye. "You've handled it just the right way—simply. You seem to have grown up and gone away from me."

"No, Derry!" Her beautiful eyes were very tender. "We'll always be just as we are now!"

For a moment her father stared into her face, completely in the grip of the past. Gayle's smile wavered at the strained intensity of his gaze. "Darling?" she said, but he never even heard her.

Those very words had been said to him twenty years before, and he had never seen her alive again. For a second he was forced to relive the old tearing agony, the blind, hopeless, never-ending alleyways of pain. Straight out of heaven, right into hell, and everyone expected him to shine. He had been left aimless, *aimless*, for twenty long years. Jaime, familiar with that hard tormented look, wasn't surprised or upset when he dropped his arms abruptly and walked away from them.

"What happened?" Gayle asked in bewilderment, turning slowly towards Jaime, her amber eyes frightened.

"Nothing to worry about, Gayle!" Jaime said kindly.

Gayle stood twisting her wedding ring, and tried to regain the golden glow of the evening. "Can't you tell me? I've never seen Derry like that before."

"There's nothing to tell. Derry was seeing a ghost, perhaps. Do you believe in them?"

"If they looked like you, maybe. Your mother was a very beautiful woman, wasn't she?"

"She died when I was born," said Jaime. "I have no memories of her, Gayle, only a portrait. It could be me."

"And Derry never told me. All that part of his life he's kept rigidly bottled up, locked away inside of him."

"If it's any consolation to you, Gayle, he never told me either. But what are you looking so melancholy about? These isolated little incidents pass. You won't experience them at all when I'm not around."

"I suppose we're never free of the past," Gayle said, meditatively.

"I'm sure now that's right," said Jaime, thinking of her grandfather's last moments. "The thing to do is subordinate it, and you're just the girl to do it."

"Eventually!" Gayle said wryly, struck with a problem she hadn't been aware of.

"You love my father, don't you?" asked Jaime.

"Oh yes!"

"Well then. Whoever claimed anything was easy— and just to prove life goes on, here comes Derry again!"

He came back to them smiling, as if nothing at all had happened; no explanations, just a lift of his elegant hands. "Gayle, my love, you've got to come right over here and settle a point. Jaime darling, excuse us for a moment. Gayle can talk like a bibliography on any painter you can name in any part of the world."

For a second Gayle didn't respond, then she wound both her arms around her husband's sleeve. "Can you give me a clue?"

"Local."

"That's easy!"

Naturally Jaime's earlier admirer saw the moment to return bearing two glasses of champagne. Jaime accepted a glass gratefully, very nearly on the point of tears. Weddings were emotional events and her father's momentary lapse had assuredly upset Gayle, though she had tried to rally. Her companion was telling her she had the most beautiful eyes in the world; one hand held up the wall behind her, trapping her, bent slightly towards her, viewing her steadily. She couldn't remember what his name was. It could have been Eric or it could have been Ian. It emphatically wasn't Quinn.

Then slowly and painfully Quinn's dark handsome face began to superimpose itself on the tanned pleasant face of the man before her. Jaime found herself staring, the pupils of her eyes distending, in turn disturbing her companion to such a degree that his hand trembled. He had settled on Jaime the moment he had caught a glimpse of her in the church, long before he knew she was a very wealthy girl. Now with her blue-violet eyes intent on him, he almost passed out. What was so astonishing was that a friend had just told him he was wasting his time. A girl like Jaime with money as well was out of this world. Certainly out of his reach. Now her beautiful violet eyes were trained on him, confusing and exciting him. The next second he realised she wasn't even seeing him, for she blinked rapidly.

"That's the strangest thing!" she said uncertainly.

"What?" he asked, baffled and disappointed beyond mere words. This time her eyes went beyond him, widening, and the colour swept into her lovely face, like a fire suddenly lit inside of her.

"Oh, excuse me," she said with a gentle, eager rush. "A friend of mine has just arrived."

Ian Gibson turned his head, of course, and his hopes were killed dead, pathetic now as it happened, and he wasn't a bad-looking man. Gayle and her new husband were greeting the smoothest, most sophisticated-looking character Ian had ever seen. Very tall, very lean, a classy dresser, his head tilted towards Gayle, who was blushing and laughing; a careless, handsome arrogant devil, slightly foreign-looking, with black eyes that now lit on Jaime. The miracle of a girl in her delectable dress, the girl who had seemed so young and eager, was now greeting the stranger with an equally

cool, sophisticated poise. Obviously they belonged together and Ian felt desperately envious. Quite a few
people had broken off in their conversations to stare
and Ian caught the name Sterling.

Of course, that explained it. A man who looked and
talked like that just had to be somebody, a real big
wheel. Ian couldn't figure what lots of money did, but
it did. For the first time he began to pay attention to the
girl he had come with, who wasn't tearfully sad anyway.

With the arrival of Quinn, and the consequent introductions, the reception gained a valuable new impetus.
He was stared up and down, devoured by the women,
and suffered it all with great charm, never once passing
his hands in front of his eyes as Jaime did on more than
one occasion. With a harsh stab of reality and no sense
of resentment, she was made to stand back and observe
the immense sexual attraction he held for other wom-
en. There was no question of anyone going home now
unless Hugo, who owned and ran the gallery, turned
out the lights, and he obviously didn't want to. Contacts were important and "good old Derry" had an
heiress for a daughter and a friend in Quinn Sterling of
Hunter Sterling, who had kissed the tips of Gayle's
fingers the moment he arrived, making that new bride
swim with pleasure. It had to be some Gallic blood in
his background, Hugo reasoned. He'd never seen
another man do it quite like that, except maybe Charles
Boyer in those old movies.

Shortly after midnight, Gayle and Derrick decided to
leave and after that they all got away fairly swiftly. With
the newlyweds staying overnight at the best hotel on

the Coast, Jaime was free to go back to the beach house. With Quinn so very much in demand, she had scarcely spoken two consecutive words to him. Indeed, although his brilliant eyes strayed over her frequently, he had seemed another person, considering her memories of their last meeting. It was impossible to read what went on behind those pitch-black eyes, and now with all her confidence abating she wasn't even going to try. She might have looked her very best and made all that effort mostly for him, yet he looked extraordinarily unmoved, quite relaxed, with no more than an ordinary passing interest in her appearance. He was scarcely to be borne unless he was a split personality.

Over the short distance home in the hire car she didn't even look at him, or turn her head. He had explained his delay, of course. His position gave him any number of excellent alibis. Who could be certain if he saw the Minister or not? If he did, it was very good of him to come anyway, and if he didn't he had only just made it. Her mood of rejection and despondency had set in accompanied by the moral post-wedding-reception blues. Marriage wasn't always the answer. She only hoped Gayle would bring an illuminating quality to hers. Her father wasn't an easy man to know, and that summing up wasn't only limited to her father. She was just thinking Quinn was a stranger.

"Are you going to invite me in?" he asked smoothly, the moment they arrived.

"Are you certain you want to?" she said coolly. "I thought this was a mercy mission."

He ignored her. "I'd like some black coffee, thank

you, Jaime. Maybe a sandwich. I missed lunch and dinner, you know, all on your account.''

''Did you really?''

''Is there absolutely anything you'll believe of me? To the good, that is!''

She fumbled with the front door key and his hand shot out and took it from her, inserted it into the lock and turned the spring. Jaime swept ahead of him, switching on the lights. There was a wild carnation tint over her delicate cheekbones, not just a blusher, but quickening blood. In a few days with the glorious wash of sun, her skin had turned to a gleaming gold again, and the devastating excitement she was feeling coloured her eyes almost purple. It was vastly foolish the way she let Quinn agitate and upset her.

She put her evening purse and her floating chiffon stole down and went to the sliding glass doors that led on to the balcony and provided an incomparable view of the ocean. A moment more and the lovely sea breeze came into the room, with the fresh tang of salt fluttering the curtains. She glanced back at Quinn almost defiantly and caught him regarding her with a certain amount of dark arrogance.

''I learned a lot tonight,'' he said in an attacking voice. ''You're fairly provocative with everyone.''

''You're mad!'' she responded. ''I'd have to try desperately to remember one face!''

''How about that chap—Gibson, wasn't it? The one who had you pinned to the wall when I arrived.''

Jaime's delicate nostrils flared and her eyebrows shot up. ''I should be able to remember him, but I can't.''

"I'm surprised to hear that. You were certainly staring up at him very agreeably."

"You couldn't be jealous?"

"No," he said contemptuously with the cool arrogance that exasperated her and threw a corresponding switch in her.

"Do you really want that coffee or a fight?" she demanded.

"You're very aggressive," he said narrowly, his black eyes glinting.

"I waited all evening for you!" she burst out, surprising herself. She hadn't meant to say that.

"I *told* you," he said impatiently. "It was impossible to make the early flight. Swinging a big business venture doesn't go hand in hand with pleasing oneself!"

Jaime shook her head as if she didn't want to discuss it any more. "I'll make the coffee. We've chicken and ham. Which?"

"As a matter of fact, both. There was very little left of that buffet."

"Yes, I know, and it cost the earth!" Jaime said, suddenly distressed on his account. In fact a wave of remarkable, inexplicable desolation came over her. She dashed her hands in front of her eyes and turned away. She felt she had to. There was no denying it. Quinn unsettled her so badly that just being alone with him gave her a bad time.

"What damn game are you playing now?" he demanded, covering the distance between them with devastating speed. He swung her about and stared down into her face.

"I'm not used to being manhandled!" she said shortly.

"Then there's no time like the present. Forget the blasted coffee. I'm not in the mood anyway."

"Why are you so angry?" she challenged him, her blue eyes blazing.

"Aren't you?"

"Yes, I am, and I don't know why. I hope Derry's going to be happy. You scarcely said two words to me all night."

"You're very demanding, aren't you?"

"Quite possibly. I thought you enjoyed my company?"

"If so I'm not the only one."

"You're jealous!" she accused.

His lean fingers bit into her shoulders. "If it were only that simple! There's a considerable difference between being jealous and wanting to turn you over my knee. You need taking in hand, Jaime. You're too beautiful for your own good, and you're so vital that you really affect people. You're going to need a strong hand and a man a lot older than you. No ordinary run-of-the-mill young man would do. You'd lead him a sorry dance!"

"And you're the man with a difference, I suppose?"

"Careful, I'm not playing."

"As a matter of fact neither am I," she retorted. "You're pretty remarkable at that. To think I was in the odd position this afternoon of longing for you to arrive! Now you're here you just want to snarl at me."

"I'll show you what I want to do!" He lifted her

clean off the floor and walked backwards with her to the couch, pinning her body.

"What's got into you?" she asked faintly, thinking it advisable to retreat.

He dismissed the violet alarm of her eyes, threading his hand through her hair experimentally, whether to pull it or what, Jaime couldn't tell. "You're untamed, aren't you?" he asked abruptly.

"I prefer to be," she said clearly.

"Since it's not going to happen for very much longer, make the most of it."

"How's the family?" she flashed at him. "Leigh and Sue-Ellen?"

"Coming right out of it. I saw Leigh briefly yesterday. She looked a picture. She was in to see her father."

"I'm sure she continued down the corridor to you."

"As a matter of fact she did."

"Well done, then!"

"I'm not used to young women like you," said Quinn, his eyes sliding down the length of her, the slender young body, the exquisite long legs outlined by the tautened chiffon.

"Then you should be glad of a little variety!" she said shakily.

"I wasn't looking for trouble."

"Neither was I."

"You've got it!" He looked hard and reckless, though she was seeing his face through a shimmering haze.

"It's fairly obvious I bring out the barbarian in you," she blurted.

"What little there is. But yes, I agree. There's something about you that makes me want to hurt you. Move your hand away from your face. What is it, some kind of protection?"

"I won't!" she said firmly.

"You have noticed I'm stronger than you."

"You're a bully as well!"

"Now and again. You'll only get hurt struggling, so stop it. I haven't time for it anyway. Argue as you will, you love me!"

"No."

"*No?* That sort of an answer needs proving. Such an exquisite dress. What a pity to crush it!"

"You're perfectly well aware it's uncrushable."

"Is that an invitation? Well then!"

"Don't you dare touch me!" she said wildly, safe if she kept talking.

"Face it Jaime. I'll do anything I have to to get you!"

"Aren't my feelings important?"

For answer he took hold of her in a hard practised manner. "There's got to be one boss, and we're going to settle this, my poor frightened baby. It's unfair to take advantage of you, but I have to. I can't even understand myself these days!"

"You'd better!" she warned with her very last breath of resistance. Her blood was on fire, answering the violence of emotion in him.

He grasped the back of her head very deliberately. "Let me look at you. Just who *are* you anyway?"

"I'm Jaime!" she said passionately, to establish her identity once and for all. "Just Jaime, and I don't mean any blasted label!"

"You're mine!" he said with no trace of ardency but implacably, twisting her head back and kissing her mouth violently.

She began to struggle, slipping sideways on the couch so that Quinn was half leaning over her. "Go on, deny it. If you want to, you'd better do it now!"

A volcanic hard recklessness was upon him, a queer tautness in his expression. "No, I don't want to!" she whispered, visibly relenting. There could be no other way for her. So deeply in love, she was now trying to subdue the antagonisms she had invited. She was unaware of the radiant tenderness that invaded her eyes, the soft natural yielding of her body. It came so suddenly, this surrender, that it completely flooded her being.

Quinn didn't move for a second, his black eyes anything but tranquil. There was a devil in him and she had aroused it. Now she was looking shatteringly submissive, a contrary little enchantress, as fragile as a flower, as brilliant as a jewel. He didn't trust her, but the compulsion to make love to her was taking control of him.

Jaime drew in her breath, lifted her arms and linked them around Quinn's neck, forestalling his anger. "Don't look at me like that. You frighten me."

"Do I?" The glittery look eased just a fraction. "I'm sorry. Quite easily I could strangle you and I would, only I've wanted you from the very beginning."

"You'd better have me, then," she said gently. "Don't you think so?"

"Who'd want to marry you off so soon?"

"It was bound to happen. Predictable." All the while

she was lifting her mouth to his, overcome by a sweet and piercing exultation. It was wondrous to take the initiative, but it wasn't for long. One moment he held back, then he forced her head back against his shoulder; kissing her with a driving need he didn't bother to hide. It was scarcely endurable, the soft searing sensations speeding through her, the beautiful, terrible rhythm of it all. The mysterious knowable, unknowable world of Quinn.

She was lost and any other consideration never even surfaced. When he freed her mouth briefly, she murmured broken little endearments, indulging herself endlessly, telling him in every way possible that she loved him. She was so ravishingly helpless, yet so flamelike, that soon there was nothing else for Quinn to do but pull away with the kind of steely strength that marked him.

"I think it's time for me to go back to the hotel," he said, grasping her hair.

"Darling, you're here with me."

He drew away from her treacherous sweetness, sat up and pushed her filmy skirt aside.

"Oh God, I don't know what to do about you!" Jaime moaned.

"You won't have to for long. We'll see Gayle and your father off tomorrow, then we'll go home."

She leaned over, burrowing her head against his side. "That's a tumultuous back-to-front proposal. You told me you wanted to marry me, but you haven't said you loved me."

"Yes, I know."

"Are you going to?"

"I'd never get back to the hotel," he said dryly, not nearly so calm as he appeared.

"Who cares?" she said, and flung her arms around him, hugging his taut frame, feeling the indecision in him then the final rejection.

Quinn stood up, turning away from her, straightening his tie as if he were about to go into a Board meeting. It was time to gather himself. She was startled at the way he could turn such powerful emotions on and off when she could hardly stand because she was trembling so violently.

At the door he relaxed, sliding an arm around her and dropping a brief parting kiss on her head. "My beautiful Jaime. You must be tired and I've kept you up too long."

"And you didn't get your coffee."

"Judging by your earlier reactions you might have thrown it at me." He held the door, looking out at the sparkling stars. "What a beautiful night!"

She slipped herself under his shoulder. "I feel as though you've pulled down a star for me."

"You deserve another kiss for that," he said tautly. "I'm not earthbound myself."

"Out of the question when you want someone so badly!"

"Jaime?" he said against her mouth.

"Yes?"

"I love you. You're what I've wanted all my life."

"That sounds sweeter to me than the lovely music of the sea."

"Just one thing. You'll never escape me. That I swear!"

"Who said I'll ever want to?" she whispered, shocked.

"It pays to know what you're getting into. I'm the man in possession, remember that."

"And don't think I'm going to wait long," she murmured.

"You won't have to. Whatever life holds for us, we're ready. What happens to you, happens to me. A partnership no one is going to dissolve!"

Beyond them the white sandhills were lit to a radiance. The surf rolled in, unstoppable, rushing up on the sand like long bolts of silk. So inevitable the tide. So perfectly ordained Jaime's destiny.

TOUCHED BY FIRE

Touched by Fire
Jane Donnelly

Because her mother had firmly believed that Leon Aldridge, art-gallery owner, had been the factor in her father's decision to leave his family to pursue a painting career, Fran Reynolds was prejudiced against him.

Now, for her uncle's sake, she was forced to be friendly with Leon, and little by little as she got to know him, she found her dislike fading away. But falling in love with him was another matter entirely.

For one thing, though she found her mother's beliefs unfounded, Fran also found that she'd given her heart to a man whose nature was as cold as ice!

CHAPTER ONE

"I DON'T CARE if your Uncle Ted does need you," wailed Fran's mother. "I need you more."

Fran Reynolds caught her stepfather's eye over the breakfast table and they exchanged grins. He was a super stepfather, with his patience and his kindness, and this prosperous farm in the Yorkshire dales had been a grand place to grow up in. But Fran loved her uncle too, and his letter read like an appeal for help.

Uncle Ted, her dead father's brother, phoned and wrote regularly. He always came to stay on the farm for Christmas, although he wasn't a countryman in the Yorkshire sense of the word. He developed a hacking cough when the winds were too keen, and he missed his books.

He had been happiest when Fran visited him. Once she had gone down with her mother, and stayed in Edward Reynolds' flat over his shop, but that hadn't been a success. Isabel Martin had wept for Peter Reynolds so that Fran was only thankful that Jim wasn't with them.

Jim Martin had married Isabel Reynolds, a pretty widow, knowing that the great love of her life was her first husband; even though Peter had deserted her and Fran a year before he died. He took her on those terms, he was an easy-going, undemanding man, but it would surely have hurt him to see Isabel walking past the little house where she had once lived with Peter, declaring that that was the only place she had been truly happy.

Fran, fifteen at the time and as fond of Jim as though he had been her real father, had said to Uncle Ted when she and her mother got back from that walk, "I think I'd better take her home. I don't think this holiday is going to do her much good."

They had returned to Yorkshire and the farm four days ahead of schedule and Jim had welcomed them back. Jim was a rock, an oak tree. There was all the security any woman could want with Jim and, whatever she said, security was the thing that made Isabel happy.

In Boddington Farm she wanted for nothing, and Jim didn't mind the painting that hung on the living-room wall. Newcomers would look at it and then Isabel would say, "My first husband painted it. He was Peter Reynolds, the artist."

Even if they hadn't heard of Peter Reynolds there was such pride in her voice that they often pretended they had. The women at any rate nearly all said, "Was he really?" and admired the painting.

It was striking, a restless study of hills and storm clouds, showing a talent that might have made his name if he hadn't gone swimming off the coast of Sicily and drowned, just when his pictures were starting to sell. If he had stayed with his wife and daughter he would probably have lived longer, so his bolt for freedom, to paint to his heart's content, had been a tragic mistake.

Fran had missed him desperately when he first went —
when she was twelve years old. She had come home
from school one day to find her mother distraught, sobbing, "Your father's gone. He's gone away and left
us."

He had always hated his job as a draughtsman with a
local firm. In his spare time he had always painted, and
talked of the places he would visit one day, the pictures
he would paint. He had gone to find the places, travelling alone, and his brother Ted and Fran had had a
grim time with Isabel.

What had hurt Fran most was that he didn't write.
She had had a sneaking sympathy for him because, in
those days, her mother hadn't had any sympathy at all
with his dreams. Fran didn't blame him for going away
to find out whether he was a great painter or not. It had
seemed romantic to her at first, just like Gauguin, but
she hadn't believed then that he was really cutting
them out of his life.

They weren't badly off financially. He left them the
house and all that was in his bank account. That wasn't
much, but he sent a little money every month. But he
never wrote a letter nor sent an address.

Isabel grew bitter so that no one dared mention his
name, although his brother Edward lived in a state of
perpetual apology, always trying to make up to Peter's
family for Peter's desertion.

Edward was unmarried himself, and he did his best
to be the man about their house, dealing as best he
could with each difficulty that arose. He tried to comfort Fran, insisting that her father would return, and at

first she believed him. But there were no letters, not even a card when she was thirteen, and two weeks after her birthday Peter Reynolds was beyond return.

When he died Isabel forgave him. Her bitterness dissolved and he was her own dear love again. She was still mourning him when she went on holiday to the Lake District and met Jim, charming him with her soft feminine ways and her air of needing looking after.

Jim Martin was a big man with a big heart. Before the holiday ended he had asked Isabel to marry him, and he travelled home with her to break the news to her daughter and her brother-in-law and her friends.

It was less than six months since Peter had died, and Isabel was not sure how people were going to take this, but although she told everyone that she could never love any other man as much as she had loved Peter she realised how lucky she had been to find Jim.

So did Fran. She liked and trusted him on sight, and Ted was so relieved that Isabel was no longer his responsibility, and that the man she was marrying seemed such a decent fellow, that he didn't realise at first that Isabel's marriage would take Fran away from him.

Ted liked Isabel. He thought Peter had treated her shabbily and he was glad she was getting a second chance at marriage, because she was born to be a wife, just as Edward—and Peter, it seemed—were born bachelors. Isabel could never have managed alone, and Jim Martin would make her a good husband, looking after her, and always being there. No danger of Jim ever packing his bags and clearing off.

Ted was fond of Isabel, but Fran was the apple of his

eye, and when Isabel and Jim took Fran away to live in the lovely old farmhouse, he felt lost and lonely himself for the first time in his life.

Fran missed her Uncle Ted as much as she had missed her father, but the new life was a good life, and Jim treated her as a daughter during the years she grew from a gangling bright-eyed schoolgirl, with a mop of red hair, into a tall slim young woman who turned heads wherever she went.

The hair was still red, but long and silky. She wasn't as pretty as her mother, but she had an enchanting smile and green eyes with thick dark lashes, and she knew how to use her assets. She brightened up the office of the estate agents where she worked, and the junior partner, who was fairly young, not bad looking and not married, was always asking her out.

That pleased her mother more than it pleased Fran. Fran was twenty-two and her mother was anxious for her to marry and settle down. Fran didn't take life seriously enough for Isabel, because life was serious and finding a nicc man was the most important thing of all.

Her mother approved of most of the men Fran brought home, but up to now Fran had had no urge to walk down the aisle with any of them, and certainly not with Arthur Deane, the junior partner, although he was eligible enough if that was what you were after.

Lately Arthur's friendly overtures had become rather more than friendly, and Fran had discussed the problem with Jim, whose advice she valued although they both pretended that her mother was her closest confidante.

Her mother would have told her not to be too hasty,

reminding her that one day Arthur would be the senior partner of an old-established family business. "Don't be so impulsive," her mother would have said meaning— this one is a prospective husband and no wanderer, and where are you going to find a steadier man?

Fran's impulsiveness worried her mother. Peter had had the same red hair, and been too impulsive for his own or anyone else's good. More often than not Fran took her emotional tangles to Jim rather than to her mother. Jim was less anxious to see her married, and less bothered about eligibility.

Last Sunday, as they'd walked together over the hills where the sheep and lambs were grazing, she'd said, "I've got a problem. It's Arthur. He's getting serious."

"Don't you want him to be serious?" Isabel had drawn Jim's attention to the way Arthur looked at Fran when he brought her back home in the evenings, how anxious he was to let them know that the business was thriving and that he was ready to settle down.

"It won't be long," Isabel had said happily, "before he'll be asking you if he can ask Fran to marry him."

Jim had thought he would be well advised to ask Fran first. *"No!"* said Fran explosively, and Jim supposed that was the end of that.

"Then what's your problem?" he asked.

"Mother," said Fran. "You know how she'll fuss if she finds out."

Jim chuckled. Indeed he knew. "Has he asked you to marry him?"

"Not yet, but the signs are there," said Fran dourly. "And if he does I might have to leave the office. It could be awkward staying on and jobs aren't two a penny these days, are they?''

It wasn't likely that Fran would be unemployed for long. She had first class secretarial qualifications, but she would be turning in a steady job as well as a steady man, and her mother wouldn't like that at all.

Jim liked it when she asked his advice. "If it gets that awkward," he said, "there's plenty of paper work here to keep you busy until you find something else, and I'll tell your mother I don't think Arthur's right for you. You'll soon find another job." He looked at the sparkling young face. "And another lad," he said.

"Bless you!" Fran flung her arms around him and kissed the weathered cheek soundly. Jim could stand between herself and her mother's exasperation like a solidly built wall. He just smiled and let it all blow over. "I like my job," she said, "if I could just cool it with Arthur."

Jim chuckled at that, because this stepdaughter of his was not a cool girl. She was gay and generous, openhanded with money and with affection. Arthur was not by any means the first man to fall for her, but he was her employer and since she had begun to make excuses why she shouldn't see him out of working hours he had shown a jealous streak.

He wanted to know exactly where she would be going, what she would be doing, and when the phone rang on Wednesday evening she had been pretty certain it was Arthur, checking up on her.

She had told him she was washing her hair, and so she was. It might be a hackneyed excuse, but it was

true, and as there was no one else in the farmhouse at
the time she put down her hair dryer and went to
answer the phone with a towel around her shoulders.

Her, "Hello," was guarded. She hoped he wasn't going to suggest coming round to keep her company.

"Fran?" said Uncle Ted. "It is Fran, isn't it?"

She began to smile. "Did I sound very grumpy?"

"You did rather. Is everything all right?"

Her mother and stepfather were out for the evening at
friends. She sat down on the old wooden armchair by the
phone table in the hall and hugged the phone to her.
Dear Uncle Ted! She always enjoyed talking to him. She
wished he lived nearer because he was a lovely erudite
man, gentle and courtly, full of learning although he
lacked Jim's down-to-earth common sense. She had always had a feeling of protectiveness towards Uncle Ted,
even in the long-ago days when he was trying so hard to
make life easier for herself and her mother.

She said now, laughing to reassure him, "Boy-friend
trouble, I thought that was who was phoning."

Uncle Ted knew about her boy-friends. She kept in
touch, and at Christmas, when he was an honoured
guest, they talked and talked together.

"Which one is it this time?" he asked her.

"Arthur Deane. I work for him, and he's getting too
serious by half." It was in recent weeks that Arthur had
staked his claim so firmly. She hadn't written or
phoned Uncle Ted for a while so this was news to him.
"Trouble is," she said, "I can see myself being out of a
job, drat the man."

He sympathised with her, and she told him the rest

of the family news. Everyone was well, everything was fine, and how was he?

She had heard him coughing as he talked, and now a paroxysm delayed his answer before he said, "Not too bad."

"You're coughing well."

"Ah yes, that. I'm waiting for the summer. Talking of the summer, have you all fixed your holidays?"

"Mother and Father *are* going to the Canaries." They had had the travel brochures at Christmas, the holiday discussions had been starting then, the bookings had been made a couple of weeks ago. "I haven't fixed anything, how about you?" asked Fran. "How about you coming up here?"

"How about you visiting me?" he said promptly. "It's nearly three years since you did."

"Really? That long?" While she was at school and commercial college she had always gone down to Uncle Ted's during her summer holidays. Alone, after the one disastrous time when her mother had accompanied her. She had enjoyed pottering around the flat, helping in the shop, but she supposed it was about three years since her last visit.

"That long," said Uncle Ted. "I wish you'd come."

He had mentioned it at Christmas. He always did. Inviting them all, any time. But somehow she got the impression now that he was feeling depressed, and that was why he had rung tonight. She said immediately, "I'll get a week's holiday just as soon as I can, and I'll come down."

"You mean that?"

"As soon as I possibly can."

There was silence for a few seconds. Then Uncle Ted said, "I'll be waiting for you."

She almost joked, "Don't count the days," but she didn't think he was smiling. She said, "You take care of yourself. In the morning I'll use up my last bit of influence with Arthur to get my holiday brought forward."

"Thank you," he said quietly. "I'd appreciate that."

Her mother and Jim were late back, but at breakfast next morning she told them, "Uncle Ted phoned last night and I've promised to go down for a few days."

"It should be a nice change for you," said her mother, pouring tea and watching Fran's breakfast plate. Often as not Fran skipped lunch or settled for a bun in a coffee bar, so Isabel insisted on a cooked breakfast, preparing it herself and putting it down in front of Fran, who would have preferred toast and honey.

"He sounded low," said Fran, "and he was coughing badly."

Her mother smiled tolerantly. "Ted always was an old woman. Peter used to say he should have been a maiden aunt."

"Maiden aunts are very trendy these days," Fran teased. "They're the ones who've got the best of both worlds." And her mother frowned, not sure how to deal with that heresy.

Fran fixed her holiday to start in three weeks' time. She explained that her uncle had phoned, and there seemed no reason why she shouldn't go. Business wasn't that brisk.

Arthur knew about Uncle Ted. Everyone who knew Fran did, the two men had met last Christmas, but for all that Fran got an old-fashioned look from Arthur when she asked for some of her holiday leave right away to visit her uncle.

"That's where you were born, isn't it?" said Arthur. "Do you still have plenty of friends down there?"

"Not many," she said. "It's years since I was there, and then it was only for a few days."

"No loyal old sweethearts?" smiled Arthur.

"No, worse luck," said Fran lightly.

She resented this prying, although it was ridiculous. She might have said, "I don't have a lover in those parts. There's a nice man who works in the galleries next to the crafts shop, and there's also the only man I've ever detested. There's always the risk of meeting him when I go visiting Uncle Ted."

But she wasn't close enough to Arthur to be telling him things like that, and she never spoke about Leon Aldridge to anyone if she could possibly help it.

She wrote to Uncle Ted that day, with her date of arrival, and their letters crossed. His came with next morning's mail and she scanned it quickly, then bit her lip and started again, reading slowly, weighing up all the implications.

If you weren't familiar with the crabbed handwriting it took some reading, but Fran knew this writing nearly as well as her own.

"Since I spoke to you on the telephone," Uncle Ted wrote, "I've been thinking over what you told me about the possibility of your leaving your job. I presume you have nothing else in mind, and I wonder if you would consider coming here and helping me. These days I'm quite feeling my age."

He was quite a bit older than her father, but he must still only be in his fifties. She read on with a growing conviction that this was not just a suggestion to deal with her problem. She knew that Uncle Ted would have welcomed her any time, but this letter seemed to say more than appeared on the surface.

Her mother was at the stove, presiding over a pan of frying eggs. Jim sat at the table, opening his mail, and Fran pushed the letter across to him. "Read this," she said.

Her mother turned at that to ask, "What is it?" but Fran didn't answer immediately. She waited until Jim looked up from the letter, then she said,

"Uncle Ted's suggesting I go and stay down there and help him run the craft shop."

"What?" The egg slipped from the scoop back into the pan, and while she was retrieving it Isabel gave a snort of derision. "What a stupid idea! He must be going senile."

"I think he needs me," said Fran quietly.

Her mother put the egg on the plate and the plate in front of Fran and said, "I don't care if your Uncle Ted does need you, I need you more."

Fran and Jim smiled wryly at each other, and Isabel knew they were laughing at her a little. She said shrilly, "You've got a job here. You've got Arthur here."

She had to be told if Fran was going to take up this offer, and Fran said, "Sorry, Mother, but I don't want

Arthur, and if I turn Arthur down I think I'll have talked myself out of the job."

It was too much for Isabel, so early in the morning. She sat down in her chair at the table and slumped back croaking, "Jim, tell her, stop her!"

Jim said mildly, "She wouldn't be emigrating."

"Give me the letter." Isabel leaned forward and took it, blinking and peering because she had no patience with illegible handwriting. It was short enough, and she said snappishly, "If he needs an assistant I'm sure he can find one."

Fran said, "It's a funny letter."

Isabel tossed it down again on the table. "It doesn't make me laugh."

"I mean it's odd." Her mother had known what she meant. Fran hunched her shoulders. "I can't explain it, but I feel I ought to be reading something between the lines."

She looked appealingly at Jim; her mother had no sympathy for any message that hadn't been plainly spelled out. Jim was stolid and unimaginative, but he was very practical and he suggested, "You could go down for a month and see how you go on."

It was such a temptation to get away from Arthur that that might be why she was telling herself that Uncle Ted needed her so badly. But if he did a month would show it, and it would be fun to give a hand in the shop. She had always worked in offices, but perhaps the time had come for a change. She said, "I could do that, couldn't I? I could hand in my notice this morning," and her mother shrieked at her,

"*No!* Oh, you're so impulsive, you never stop to *think*." She banged the table with her clenched fists, her face crumpling like a child's. "Now you've decided to walk out and leave me too," she wailed. "Just like your father did."

That wasn't true. Fran had been a deeply caring daughter and still was.

"Steady on, now," Jim began, and Isabel turned on him.

"You don't understand, how can you? I don't want Fran going away, working in Ted's shop. I hate that shop, next to the galleries and that terrible man. I couldn't even go to see her there."

"Steady on, old girl," said Jim, and Fran recognised his little signal that she should get out and leave this to him. She jumped up and her mother said automatically,

"You're not going to work without your breakfast."

"Plenty of time for that," said Jim, although Fran never gave herself any time to spare in the mornings.

She stood outside the kitchen door for a few minutes. She heard her mother's high-pitched voice, but it was a stout door and Jim's deep voice didn't reach her. She would have to put her ear to the wood to get the drift of the argument, and eavesdropping seemed rather mean, even though she was the one under discussion.

There wouldn't be a row going on. They never rowed, because Jim never argued; not like the old arguments in the old days between her mother and her father. Jim was always good-tempered, but this was taking time, and Fran took her camel coat off the hall-stand, collected her tan-coloured handbag from the living room, and went across to the garage.

She drove her car out and sat in it, watching the house and waiting. She didn't want to be late for work. If she was handing in her notice that would be rather adding insult to injury. But she had to hang around until Jim came out and told her whether her mother was reconciled to her leaving or not.

Suppose she wasn't? Suppose she carried on like she'd done when Fran's father had left them? She'd just said, "You've decided to walk out and leave me, like your father did," and Fran could remember how dreadful the days that followed that desertion had been.

Uncle Ted had been wonderful then, and now of course there was Jim. He'd tell her that she wasn't losing Fran, that there was no comparison at all. Fran also hoped he would tell her to count her blessings.

She turned on the little radio she usually carried in her car, and listened to music and time signals and bright D.J. chatter, until she saw the back door open and Jim come out into the yard. Then she wound down the window and called as he walked towards her, "How is she?"

He was grinning. "Ah, she'll be all right," he said. His eyes were kind and tenderly amused. "It came as a shock to her, she thought things were coming on nicely between you and Arthur Deane. Do you want to go and work for your Uncle Ted?"

"Yes, I think I do." She would miss Jim, and her mother of course, and the farm. She said, "Like you say, I can go down there for a holiday and see how it works out." She pulled a face. "I don't know why Mother's making such a fuss. She'd be thrilled to pieces if I got married and moved out."

"But you'd be settled then, wouldn't you?" said Jim sagely. "She'd know where she could find you and it wouldn't be more than a few miles away." Isabel was watching them through the kitchen window, and Jim said quietly, "She's never forgotten that your father walked out. That's why she's so possessive about you."

She was possessive and she had been hurt, but ever since she had married Jim she had been cherished, and Fran said hotly, "She's probably had a darn sight better life here than she'd had if he'd stayed and she'd never met you."

She wasn't concerned at the moment whether it was true, but her stepfather had always done his best for both of them and she was grateful; and she knew that her mother was, although she couldn't let the memory of her first husband die.

"You're a good lass," said Jim.

And he was a good man. "You'll take care of her, won't you?"

"Don't I always?" He took his pipe out of his pocket, he looked right with a pipe, puffing contentedly. "And she takes care of me," he said.

"Of course," said Fran. Her mother loved this attractive old house, the money to be comfortable and buy pretty things. She loved fussing over Jim and Fran, preparing attractive meals, having her friends round for coffee. She was not made for hard times and Fran was leaving her in good hands.

Jim stood back as she started up the car. "Now I've got to break the news to Arthur," she said as she went, and she left him chuckling.

This was the town she knew best of all. She had finished her education here, gone through a couple of earlier office jobs before moving on to Arthur's firm twelve months ago, and she had always been happy. There had been little miseries, of course, little downs, but on the whole she had been very happy, and she could have stayed here and made this the centre of her life for the rest of her life.

But she had welcomed the chance of escape in Uncle Ted's letter. She needed a change, although explaining that to Arthur might be tricky.

The estate agents had attractive bow-fronted windows, and a big light reception room, with an artificial flower arrangement in an alcove; and Mrs. Lowndes, who had been here for thirty years, behind the counter.

She and Fran said good morning to each other as Fran hurried through the door behind the counter that led to Arthur's office. Fran's desk was in here, and so was Arthur, because she was ten minutes late and he was always punctual.

He glanced at his watch as she hung up her coat, but made no comment about the time. He was surprised, that was all, she was usually here on the dot too. He expected her to say that her car had given trouble, or explain what had held her up.

She sat down at her desk and he was still looking inquiringly at her when she turned to face him.

Arthur was plump and smooth, and would grow

plumper and smoother with the years. Fran could see why her mother fancied him for her. He wasn't built for running away.

She was a little nervous about the scene that was coming, and she took off the cover of her typewriter and fiddled with things on her desk as she told him, "I had a letter from Uncle Ted this morning."

"The one you're going to stay with?"

"I've only got one uncle." He knew she had, but she need not have snapped even if she was nervous, and she said quickly, "Yes, that one. Well, he wants me to stay and help him run the shop."

"Stay?" Arthur's shiny receding brow crinkled. "How long?"

"Er—permanently." Whatever happened she wouldn't be coming back to work here.

"But you're not a saleswoman." He sounded as though this must have been overlooked and someone should point it out.

"I can learn," said Fran.

"But you're a secretary."

"There'll be letters and ledgers down there."

The news was sinking in. After a moment or two he said, "I'll never be able to replace you." She presumed he was talking about work, he was looking worriedly at his "In" tray and she said reassuringly,

"Of course you will. I'll get all the files and correspondence up to date and you'll advertise and—"

"But what about *us*?" He pushed back his chair and stood up, the colour rising in his smooth skin, stammering a little. "I thought we—you know how I feel about you—" He gulped and got out a complete sentence, "If you're going away I think we should make it official."

He hadn't actually asked her to marry him before, but he had brought up the subject more than once. He probably believed they had an understanding, although Fran had always avoided an outright declaration.

She stood up too. "Don't let's be hasty," she said. "I don't think this is the time to come to any decisions about anything."

He came from behind his desk. "Fran—" he began, and she kept her desk between them, moving round so that she was well out of his reach. He could hardly chase her round it, if he did she was quicker on her feet than he was, but she didn't want to bruise his ego.

She said, "We're very good friends, aren't we? Let's keep it that way, shall we?" and he stopped circling the desk. He looked at her and sighed, and then went back to his chair, sat down in it heavily and sighed again.

"You're determined about this?" he asked her.

"Yes, I am."

"He wants you to go down there, does he?"

She sat down too. "Yes, he says he's feeling his age." She prattled on, "It's a smashing little shop. Everything in it is made by local craftsmen. There's something of everything: carving, metal work, things made of glass, pottery, even toys. There are handwoven skirts and scarves and cloaks. No paintings, but everything else."

Her father had sold some of his early pictures in the crafts shop, but Uncle Ted wasn't an art dealer.

"And you're all the family he's got?" Arthur was asking.

"Yes." She offered an explanation that she hoped he might accept. "I have to go. There's really no one else he can call on."

"So it'll come to you eventually," said Arthur, and Fran stared at him.

"You mean I'll inherit it?" She had never thought about that. Please God, that was twenty or thirty years away.

"So I suppose you want to help keep the business together." He looked at the door as though he was checking it was still shut, then leaned forward, speaking softly and confidentially. "As a business man may I give you some advice?"

She wondered what an estate agent would know about running a crafts shop, but she said, "Please do."

"I'd stay with the farm if I were you." He gave her a cagey little nod. "I'm not saying that Mr. Martin would ever turn against you, but you are only his step-daughter. As long as you're here you're the one he'll leave it to, but if you go away there's always the chance—"

Fran couldn't help it. Laughter was bubbling up in her, and her voice shook with suppressed giggles. "You are planning ahead, aren't you? You've just killed off every living relative I've got!" The pink in his face turned pinker with embarrassment, and she told him, "I reckon my stepfather will outlive you, and my mother wouldn't be flattered to hear you think she's got one foot in the grave."

He began to bluster, "I never said anything of the

sort." But it seemed that one of her charms for Arthur Deane was the fact that she was the stepdaughter of a prosperous farmer.

She said, "I do like a practical man, but this is ridiculous."

She wasn't hurt, because she had never for a moment thought she was in love with Arthur. She had enough self-confidence to find this funny. The cheek of the man! The mercenary little prig.

I should worry about you, she thought. "A week's notice, then," she said.

SHE DIDN'T TELL her mother why Arthur felt she should be staying here, her mother would not have been amused, but she told Jim when she got him alone for a few minutes that evening. Her mother was on the telephone in the hall, talking to one of her friends, and Fran said, "Arthur thinks I'm a heiress, but if I leave here you'll cut me off. It's the farm he's after, not me."

Jim chuckled. "I don't suppose he'd mind the farm, but it's you he fancies. He very likely thinks he's looking after your interests. You could tell him you'll get the farm some day, for what it's worth, but I'll probably outlast him."

"That's what I did tell him." Through the not-quite closed door she heard the phone jingle as her mother put down the receiver, and finished quickly, "That you're going to live longer than he is, so see you do or you'll make me out a liar!"

Isabel's friend had been commiserating with her on Fran leaving home, and Isabel came back into the

room to say again what she had been saying all evening:
"How can you possibly move out in a *week*?"

"I could pack all I shall need in fifteen minutes,"
said Fran. "I could be back here in a matter of hours
for anything I've forgotten."

But the move wasn't quite as easy or as simple as
that. She wasn't going far, nor to strangers, but it was
still an uprooting. Her way of life would be changed.
She would have to make new friends and compared to
the solid comfort and security of family life in the old
farmhouse she would be out on her own.

She spent most of the week saying goodbyes, and the
days flew by. Her mother had now decided that this was
a holiday and nothing more, but somehow Fran didn't
think so. She felt she was making a real break, although
she could get back here without any trouble, any time.

Her mother waved her goodbye, calling, "Phone us
as soon as you arrive, and we'll see you in four weeks.
Have a lovely time."

It was a pleasant drive, and a straightforward route,
although it was three years since Fran had taken it. She
had been nineteen then; her little second-hand car, a
birthday present from Jim and her mother, was still going strong today and she hoped it would stay good for
another year or two.

She was looking forward to seeing Uncle Ted, his
shop had always been something of a treasure trove in
her mind. Although she hadn't inherited her father's
artistic talents of course she loved beautiful things, and
working among them should be more rewarding than
tapping away indefinitely on a typewriter.

She had no fear of loneliness, she had always been able to make friends, and as the music played on the little radio on the seat beside her she hummed the tunes, and the sun was shining and everything looked bright.

She had probably exaggerated that uneasy feeling that Uncle Ted's letter had given her. When she'd phoned and told him she was coming he had sounded delighted, no longer depressed, and why should there be anything the matter? She was getting fanciful.

She reached Stratford-upon-Avon around four o'clock in the afternoon. It was market day in town, the centre of the square was filled with stalls and the traffic edged slowly round. Next Friday she would be able to come shopping here, and she scanned the faces of pedestrians, not expecting to recognise anybody—at least three-quarters were tourists—but she might see someone she had met on earlier visits to Uncle Ted, or even someone she had known when she lived here.

Uncle Ted's shop had one of the best positions in town. It was a small part of a rather spectacular black and white Elizabethan house, set back from the road by a flagstoned forecourt. The downstairs windows were no longer leaded, but clear now for display purposes. In the biggest windows paintings, and an occasional small piece of sculpture were shown, and the name on the windows was "Aldridge Galleries".

The crafts shop was at the far end. In front of it were roughly hewn tables and chairs, garden furniture, in natural wood. The crafts shop had always looked cheap and cheerful compared to the galleries. Customers entered by a side door instead of the impressive central door that led into the galleries. Parking was through an archway this side of the house as Fran turned off the road.

As she did a tall man came out of the gallery, and stood looking at her car, then at her. He was wearing beige trousers and a blue denim shirt, casual wear, but he was arrogantly elegant. His straight fair hair flopped a little over his eyes, and his eyes she remembered were Arctic blue. She had never seen eyes colder than his remembered eyes.

They faced each other, with no sign of recognition, then Fran jerked round and fumbled a gear change, furious with herself. She got the car through the archway and drove to the far end of the courtyard where Uncle Ted's old Austin Cambridge was parked.

When she switched off she sat for a moment, her stomach churning as though she had stepped into a lift that had dropped too fast.

He hadn't changed. She had seen him the last time she was here, briefly of course, accidentally. He must have recognised her now, but she hadn't expected him to acknowledge her. They never had had anything to say to each other.

She shuddered. Leon Aldridge, waiting for her. No, of course he wasn't waiting for her. It was coincidence that he had walked out of the door as she turned into the forecourt. But there he was, even before she'd got out of her car and set foot on what was going to be her home territory. If she had been superstitious this would surely have been a black omen.

CHAPTER TWO

THERE WERE no customers in the crafts shop when Fran went in by the side door, to the faint tinkle of the bell, and Uncle Ted came out of the office. He was a tallish ascetic-looking man with a slight stoop, and the joy in his voice when he said her name made her drop her case and run to him, hugging him close.

"Am I glad to see you!" she said.

"You came." He held her at arm's length, looking at her. "Even after you rang and said you'd be here I could still hardly believe it."

"Oh, I'm real enough." She hoped it was the muted lighting of the shop that was making him look haggard. "You're thin," she said accusingly.

"Of course I'm thin." He had a nice lopsided grin. "I've always been thin."

Yes, he had. Perhaps she was comparing him with her stepfather, who was built on a much heftier frame. All the same she said, "Do you get enough to eat?" then laughed, "I sound like my mother!"

Uncle Ted collected her case, as she walked up the stairs to the landing of the little flat ahead of him. "I thought your mother might stop you coming," he said.

"She wasn't enthusiastic," Fran admitted. "I must

phone them tonight. Oh, this is nice. Is it really three years since I was here?''

The living room was comfortable, with rather dilapidated furniture. Two old wickerwork armchairs were one each side of the fireplace, exactly as they had been as long as she remembered. The ceiling was beamed, the wooden floor was covered with rugs, and there was a lot of clutter about. ''Will you mind if I tidy up a little?'' she said. ''If there are going to be two of us in here.''

He put down her case and swept out his arms. ''You can sweep it all out of the door if you like. You can do anything you like with it so long as you stay.''

''I wouldn't dream of anything so drastic.'' She sat down and bounced on the sofa. ''It's good lived-in stuff, is this. I used to jump up and down on this when I was a baby, didn't I?''

''You were an energetic child.'' He smiled nostalgically and the shop's doorbell rang again below. ''You know your room, don't you?''

She should know it. It was off the same landing as the living rooms. Uncle Ted's bedroom and a storeroom were up another flight of stairs, under the eaves.

She took her case into her room while he went down into the shop. It had always been a pleasant little room, with white walls and light wood furniture, but today it smelt of fresh paint. The walls were pale green and there was a vase of daffodils on the chest of drawers.

Uncle Ted had worked hard to pretty her room. The kitchen-cum-diner had a savoury aroma, and he had laid the table for two. When she opened the oven door there was a casserole inside. Everything had been prepared to welcome her, and she went down into the shop as the customers left. "I love my room," she said, "and the flowers."

He looked pleased. "Good sale?" she asked, as the door closed behind the customers.

"Every little helps."

"You'll have to show me around the stock." She picked up a pink glass paperweight with a price ticket on the bottom. "Is everything marked?"

"Most of them. I think I'll close early tonight. You probably want to have a wash after your journey, and the food should be about ready, so I'll see you upstairs in about ten minutes."

She washed hands and face, put back a light dash of make-up, and when she took the casserole out of the oven and lifted the lid she found that it was cooked to a turn. Casseroled pork chops, smelling of herbs, mushrooms, and onions, and baked potatoes in their jackets on another tray.

She served them both and they sat down to eat. As she tasted she said, "You're still a good cook, and I was wrong about you not having enough to eat."

"I didn't bother much when I was on my own." He was eating with an appetite now, beaming and contented, and Fran realised just how lonely he must have been.

She had never thought of him as lonely. He had always lived alone. He had bought this shop when he was a young man and he had always been here. But perhaps the passing years and his not-too-robust health had taken the gilt off solitude.

He was so glad to have her here and she chattered

about things that she thought would interest or amuse him, including Arthur's suggestion that she might lose the farm if she didn't stay put. "How about that for keeping an eye on the main chance?" she grinned, "and I thought it was me he was crazy about!"

Uncle Ted didn't smile until he was sure there was no hurt in Fran's smile, then he did. He was smiling when she said, "That's put me off men for a bit. And talking about men I can do without, guess whose was the first familiar face I saw when I arrived this afternoon." Uncle Ted shook his head. "Leon Aldridge." She said that as though it was the name of a mass murderer, with an exaggerated grimace of distaste. "Yeuk! Is he here much?"

There were Aldridge Galleries in London, New York and Rome, but this was where the Aldridge home was, a couple of miles down the river on an island all its own.

Uncle Ted had stopped smiling. He said quietly, "He's away next week."

"That's something," said Fran cheerfully. "Just as I was driving in he came out. Why him now? Why not a customer or one of the staff? I crossed my fingers in case it was a bad luck sign."

"Did you speak to him?"

"You're joking!" She had had a mushroom on her fork for quite a while. She ate it, then asked, "What would I say? Long time no see—but not long enough?"

She had thought they were joking, he usually smiled about her dislike for Leon Aldridge, but now he said quite seriously, "I know how you feel about him, but he will be around."

If she was going to live here they were bound to meet, but of course she wouldn't antagonise a neighbour. She could never like him, but she would be civil. She began to promise that, when there was a rat-tat on the door on the landing.

Once this building had been a house. Two doors connected the crafts shop and flat with the larger premises of the gallery. One door down in the shop, a second on the landing. They were bolted and barred on both sides, the one downstairs had a big display cabinet in front of it, and this was the first time Fran had ever heard anyone knock from the gallery. She hadn't thought that door was ever used.

She tried to laugh, "Don't tell me he's followed me!" still joking but with an uncomfortable stiffening of all her muscles.

Uncle Ted got up and went out of the living room along the landing. Fran heard bolts being drawn back, then she heard him say, "Hello, Gerald, come on through," and she relaxed.

Gerald would be Gerald Maddox who managed the galleries. She jumped up, very glad to see him because he wasn't Leon Aldridge, and also because when she was last here three years ago he was the nice young man with whom she went round to a pub for a drink one night, and to the cinema on another evening.

When she went home she had promised to come back during her next holiday. He phoned her a couple of times in the following six months, and for about the same length of time they had passed friendly messages through Uncle Ted. It was still occasionally, "Remem-

ber me to Gerald," or Fran, but he was rather a dim
memory to Fran as she was sure she was to him.

All the same, she was pleased to see him. She said,
"How lovely, and don't you look well?"

He was in his late twenties, with a dark moustache
and twinkling eyes behind horn-rimmed spectacles. He
wore a conservative navy blue suit, and looked like the
manager of a high class establishment, but Fran remembered he had had a sense of humour, and been
less stuffy than he looked.

He looked at her now and then grinned at Uncle Ted.
"This should be good for trade."

"I hope so," smiled Uncle Ted. "Cup of tea?"

"Thanks."

"I'll get it," said Fran.

They had almost finished the casserole and there was
none left over, so while she waited for the kettle to boil
she found cheese and biscuits, put them on a tray and
took them into the living room. "Now," she said, putting the tray on the table and speaking to Gerald, "tell
me all your news."

"I'm still next door." Still working next door, he
meant. "And how is it you're not married?" he asked
her.

"I take after my uncle, I'm hard to catch." She
poured tea for Uncle Ted, scooping in the sugar, then
asked Gerald, "Milk? Sugar?"

"Milk, no sugar, please."

As she handed him the cup she said, "Anyhow, look
who's talking. Why aren't you married? Or are you?"
Uncle Ted might have forgotten to pass on the news.

He wouldn't have thought it that important. Nor was it, to Fran. If Gerald was married she wished him happiness and she would like to meet his wife.

"Not yet," he said, with such flirtatious meaning that she burst out laughing.

They sat before the fire, talking. He seemed in no hurry to get home. He had the ground floor of a small terraced house in town, she remembered, the same type she had lived in before her mother married Jim, and he made himself comfortably at home now, drinking tea until the pot ran dry.

He was still fired with enthusiasm for his job. He talked about that at length. Next month they were putting on an exhibition for a new painter. "Leon found her," he said, and Fran muttered,

"A great talent-spotter."

"Yes, indeed," said Gerald.

Uncle Ted shifted in his seat, reaching towards the television. "You won't mind if I listen to the news, will you?"

"Is that the time?" Gerald checked his watch in astonishment. "I never realised. I only looked in to say it will be nice having you here."

He sounded as guilty as though he had outstayed his welcome. He hadn't so far as Fran was concerned, although she suspected that Uncle Ted hadn't wanted her disparaging Leon Aldridge to his manager. She doubted if she would have done. She hadn't gone into details three years ago, if Gerald remembered the only thing she had said about Leon was that he wasn't her type. Nor would she now, but Uncle Ted seemed

more sensitive than he used to be about Leon Aldridge.

"See you tomorrow, maybe?" Gerald said to her.

"I'll be here," she said. "Which way out? Through
the connecting door or through our side door?"

He shrugged. "It doesn't matter. I locked up before I
came through, I don't have to go back into the gallery."

He went down the stairs into the crafts shop and
Fran walked down with him, opening the side door for
him. "Just like old times," he said, and that made her
smile because all they had shared were two very in-
nocuous evenings. They had no old times.

"I think you're thinking of two other folk," she said,
and went upstairs still smiling.

Uncle Ted was listening to the news, which soon
took her smile away. It wasn't often there was much to
smile at in the news. She carried the cups and saucers
to the sink and washed them, and came back and sat on
a hassock by the fire, watching the glow and wondering
what time was bedtime for Uncle Ted. Three years ago
it had been around eleven o'clock on a working day,
but he looked wearier now.

As the news ended he turned down the sound so that
it wasn't much more than a murmuring background.
"About Leon—" he began.

"Oh dear, must we?" Fran didn't want to discuss the
man. He had obtruded quite enough on her first evening here.

"It was a long time ago," said Uncle Ted quietly.
"You shouldn't blame him."

"You know I don't." He *was* looking careworn. He hadn't been too robust at Christmas, but that had been winter, now it was spring, and he still looked as though he was carrying a heavy load. If he was concerned that she might cause trouble she must reassure him. She said, "My father would have cleared off even if he'd never met Leon Aldridge. You know he couldn't paint at home."

Uncle Ted nodded silently.

Although she had long forgotten that herself, Isabel had looked on Peter Reynolds' art as a threat to the monthly pay cheque and the secure life. But Uncle Ted and Fran remembered. They knew that Peter would probably have gone one day, even without Leon Aldridge's advice—to get away and paint.

That was what any expert who disliked seeing talent smothered might have said, and fair enough. Her mother blamed Leon Aldridge. Her mother had blamed everyone but herself. Sometimes in the early days, even Uncle Ted and Fran. She said Edward had lent Peter money—although Uncle Ted had never had any money to lend anyone—and Fran had encouraged her father by liking his work. That was part of the dreadful months. She hadn't said anything like that since Peter died, but she would always blame Leon Aldridge.

Fran didn't blame him. He had been twenty-four when her father left home, but he was already a name in the art world. The Aldridge Galleries, under his grandfather and father, had been dignified emporiums, dealing only with established artists, most of them dead. But Leon began his career as an art dealer, buying the work of young painters and sculptors. When he promoted anyone it was an accolade for the artist because, from the beginning, his judgment had rarely been faulted. Having asked for Leon Aldridge's verdict on his work Peter Reynolds had acted on it.

Fran blamed no one for that. But Aldridge had also stressed that an artist must be ruthless, and Peter Reynolds had made a ruthless break. No letters, no birthday card.

Fran hadn't known Leon Aldridge in those days. He wasn't at these galleries a great deal, his father was alive then and permanently in the home-town galleries. Leon was the jet-man, the cosmopolitan. Fran saw him occasionally, but they had never spoken. The young tycoon probably never even noticed the schoolgirl who came to the crafts shop. If she saw him he made no impact on her. He was Leon Aldridge, so what?

Then her father packed his paints and a small suitcase and walked out of their lives, and the man who had called ruthlessness a virtue came into focus for Fran.

Next time she saw him she looked hard at him. He didn't know she was watching. She saw him through the crafts shop window. She was minding the store while her Uncle Ted was round at their house, going through papers, that her father had always handled, with her mother.

Leon Aldridge came out of the galleries and stood talking with another man. Fran knew his features, now for the first time she saw that he had blue eyes, blue as the heart of an iceberg, that he talked without smiling. He was tall and still, without gestures or any wasted effort, and she shivered because he looked so cold, so self-contained.

He could still make her shiver. Seeing him when she'd turned her car this afternoon had sent ice into her veins. She used to call him the Iceman, to Uncle Ted. She never called him anything to her mother, because in those early days the mention of Leon Aldridge was enough to send Isabel into hysterics. There was one scene when Isabel had stormed into the galleries, and then Uncle Ted had lost his temper with her and she'd shut herself in her bedroom for hours.

"She can't blame Leon Aldridge," Uncle Ted had told the twelve-year-old Fran that day. "If your father's going to do anything worth while he has to get away. He'll be back."

"I know he will." Fran had believed it then.

Now she said, "It's just that I'm not fond of icemen. I've got this funny feeling that if you get too near one you're asking for frostbite."

Uncle Ted protested, "You don't know him," and she agreed.

"No, I don't, I'm just prejudiced, I don't really want to know him." As Uncle Ted still looked worried she asked, "Do I have to?"

"Well," his smile was wintry as though he could offer little comfort, "as I said before, he is around more these days, and he's not a man I want to offend."

"But I'm not going to offend him." She was a peace-loving girl to whom aggro had never appealed, although she did tend to find herself where the sparks were flying. She hoped she was here to make Uncle Ted's life easier and she said gaily, "I can't see him bothering me and I promise you I won't bother him."

Her uncle laughed at that, and they spent the rest of the evening quietly and comfortably. Fran phoned her mother, then she and her uncle settled down for an hour or two with a book each, and Leon Aldridge's name didn't come up again.

She had expected to fall asleep as soon as her head touched the pillow, she usually did. But tonight different surroundings and the prospect of a different tomorrow combined to keep her mind active. After she had tossed and turned for over an hour she realised that her throat was dry and she could use a glass of milk.

There was plenty in the fridge. If she got up and warmed some it might lull her to sleep. She could pull the bedroom curtains across the window at the same time, because moonlight was flooding the room so that it was nearly as bright as day.

She didn't need to switch on the light. The landing was quiet and empty. Upstairs Uncle Ted was almost certainly sleeping the sleep of the just. Fran's bedroom was at the end of the passage so that she stepped out by the connecting door into the gallery. It was still un-bolted, and she went to secure it—automatically, not because she expected anything to be coming through.

She had no excuse for what happened next, except that she was born inquisitive. She had never been inside the Galleries, although they had been next door to the crafts shop long before she was born, and she couldn't resist this opportunity for a quick and private peek. She opened the door and looked through.

The small rooms of the upper floors had been opened up, supported by timbers. The landing was an upper gallery, with a carved balustrade and an imposing staircase. This was the main part of the house, of course. The crafts shop and the flat were very unimpressive compared with this, and she tiptoed a little way in, enjoying herself like a Victorian child peeping down at an adult dinner party.

It was light enough to see pictures, on walls, on easels; and sculpture, ranging from tiny pieces in cabinets to a massive creation down below. She might ask Gerald how much they were asking for that, and who on earth would be likely to buy it.

Suddenly she tensed. She had been gazing aimlessly around when she saw one small canvas on the wall, a little farther along, in the same style as her father's work. She went slowly towards it. If it was it was an old picture, there was no doubt at all that her father had drowned. He had been brought from the sea within minutes and identified with no possibility of error. But this could be something he had painted during those twelve months.

It wasn't. She couldn't quite make out the signature, but she could read last year's date, and when she stood closer the similarity was slight. Another artist did bold brush strokes, that was really all it amounted to.

She walked back, towards the connecting door, looking at the wall and the paintings, and somehow brushing against a pedestal that was beside the gallery rail.

It might have swayed back if she had reacted less violently. But as her shoulder touched she whirled round, trying frantically to counteract her clumsiness and making matters infinitely worse. She didn't catch the vase that was teetering, but she did knock it over the rail, down to the floor below.

She daren't look. She had heard the smash, high and thin and delicate like distant sleigh bells, or the breaking of exquisite expensive china.

She ran down the stairs, gulping dry sobs of panic, and went on to her knees at the point of contact. The vase was in so many pieces there was no chance of repair—if indeed that kind of thing could ever be repaired, and offered at a "knock-down" price.

She clapped her hand to her mouth. "Knock-down price" indeed! This was no laughing matter. Not only was she trespassing but she had just destroyed a very valuable item for which she was morally and legally responsible.

She picked up the largest piece. The design on it looked like the scales of a dragon. Chinese? Ming? One of those fabulous dynasties that were priced in thousands?

However much it was, she owed for it, and she would have to explain to Gerald and find out how much, and then start working out how to get the money together. She would have to phone home. "Hello. Yes, I'm fine, thanks, do you think you could let me have a couple of thousand pounds as soon as possible, I've just dropped a Ming vase."

Please don't let it be too valuable. Let it be something she could pay for, even if she had to sell her little car to do it.

She was gathering up the pieces by the light of the moon. They glimmered pale as eggshells on the dark floor, and if she left them scattered all around whoever opened up the Galleries in the morning would think there had been a break-in and probably phone the police. She would have to get whoever came in first and explain and she prayed it would be Gerald.

Perhaps she would phone him at home. She could do that now. It would be easier to confess over the phone, and if she felt like fainting when he told her the price she wouldn't have far to stagger to bed.

She had her hands full with the pieces—it had been a big vase. She went upstairs and put the pieces down by the pedestal, then went back through the door again into Uncle Ted's cosy little flat, wishing with all her heart that she had never left it.

This was a fine start. Poor Uncle Ted, who was so anxious that she shouldn't get on the wrong side of Leon Aldridge. If he knew what she had been up to these last five minutes he'd be having nightmares up there.

She was so shaken that it took her a while to remember Gerald's surname. She sat in the little office behind the crafts shop, where the telephone was, with a phone directory on her knee, going through the C's because that seemed the right initial. When "Maddox" came to her she started again, but she couldn't find one that had a likely address, and she shut the directory with a sigh.

She would have to wait till morning. She dragged herself up to bed, and when she did fall asleep she dreamt of Chinese dragons. But instead of breathing fire they breathed ice, and her first thought when she woke was—however much do I owe Leon Aldridge?

There was no call to worry Uncle Ted until she had to, so she put on the kettle and laid the table for breakfast. And every few minutes after eight o'clock she ran downstairs, and out through the side door to the front of the building to see if the Galleries were open.

Uncle Ted, in pyjamas and an old maroon-coloured dressing gown, came down at twenty past eight, pleased to see her up and about and pink-cheeked. "Did you sleep well?" he inquired.

"Yes," she fibbed. "Did you?"

"Best night's sleep I've had in months," he said.

Oh dear, she thought, oh *dear*! As he went into the bathroom she rushed down the stairs again, out through the side door of the crafts shop, and this time the door of the gallery opened when she tried it.

She went in and Leon Aldridge came to meet her. He wasn't in a denim shirt today. He was in a slate grey suit, impeccably tailored, grey shirt and grey tie. His features would have been classically regular if his nose had not been broken some time. Not badly, she supposed some women might think it made him look interesting. But he was the last man she wanted to see, especially now.

She said breathlessly, "I was looking for Gerald."

"He should be in shortly."

Fran felt she was cringing, that she would creep out like Uriah Heep, but she couldn't tell Leon Aldridge what had brought her here. Uncle Ted had said he was away next week. If she could settle with Gerald, if she could pay for the vase, perhaps Leon Aldridge need never know that she had broken it.

"Would it be anything to do with the vase?" he asked, and then she saw the pieces she had missed. There were several still lying about. "I noticed the door was unbarred," he said.

Her mind ticked over at panic rate. He'd seen the pieces. He'd gone up and found the rest, obviously placed there, and he'd noticed the door unbarred. There was no way round this except open confession, and how could she word it so that Gerald didn't get part of the blame?

She croaked, trying for time to think, "You know who I am?"

"Of course." She wouldn't have been surprised if he hadn't. In other circumstances she might have said, "If you recognised me yesterday why did you look through me?" But in these circumstances she said meekly,

"I'm terribly sorry. It was me. I looked in, you see." She pointed towards the door upstairs, although there was no need, he knew how she had entered his premises. "And I saw a painting that reminded me of my father's work—I thought it might have been one of his." She paused. When he said nothing she said, "Peter Reynolds."

He could hardly have forgotten, although it was ten years ago. "We did sell his paintings," he said, "but there were very few of them."

"He didn't have much time, did he?"

"Unfortunately no." That sounded more like an official pronouncement than genuine sympathy. "They haven't come on the market again," he said, so they were talking about the paintings, not the man.

But it meant that the buyers must have been happy with their pictures, and she asked, "Were they good? Would he have been a great artist?"

"He had talent but, as you say, not enough time."

"So it was a pity he didn't stay where he was, at home," Fran said impulsively.

"Possibly." What did "possibly" mean? He would have lived if he hadn't gone. Although if she pointed that out Leon Aldridge would probably tell her that her father might have been knocked down by a bus.

"Gerald left the door open?" he said, making it a query. She had asked for Gerald and that had given him away, and someone had left the door open, and Gerald would admit it when the questioning started.

"He—came through into my uncle's flat," she said slowly. "He'd noticed my car and he came to say hello."

"... Nice having you here," Gerald had said, but this could change his mind... She went on jerkily,

"And then he went out by our shop door, but of course he thought I'd bolt the connecting door, I said I would, and I *meant* to. He had no idea that I was—" She found herself wondering wildly how his nose had

got broken. She wondered if anyone had hit him because he had stood listening to something they were
stammering out without any sign that he was hearing a
word. Except that those ice blue eyes never flickered,
and the stare was so intense it shrivelled you. "So darn'
nosey," she finished lamely. "And clumsy. I bumped
against the thing it was standing on and the vase went
over and—how much is it worth?" She held her
breath.

"It isn't genuine," he said. "It's a background ornament."

It would turn the hundreds into single figures. That
meant she wouldn't have to sell the car and mortgage
her future. "Wow!" she said inadequately, "that's a
relief."

"It is," he said grimly, and Fran hastily resumed a
downcast expression.

"How much, please?" she said.

"You'd better see Gerald about that."

"Yes. All right. Again, I'm sorry—good morning."

"Good morning."

She wasn't risking knocking over anything else. She
walked slowly and carefully back to the door. Once outside she ran like a rabbit. He wouldn't be watching her.
He had turned away as he said good morning, but as
she turned the corner she realised that if he had looked
he would have seen her through one of the Gallery
windows, and she had cut an undignified figure.

She had cut an undignified figure all along. Her face
was flaming so that it must be matching her hair, although she hadn't done anything so terrible.

She had been nosey and clumsy, but they weren't crimes, they were just being human. Of course Leon Aldridge didn't tolerate human failings. He was the ruthless one, and goodness, didn't he look it? The next time she came up against him she'd make sure she had nothing to apologise for.

She wondered they needed air-conditioning in the Gallery, when he could just walk around, spread a few subzero waves and cool the atmosphere.

She got back to the kitchen two minutes ahead of Uncle Ted, who thought her flushed face was pretty, and healthy, and that she made an altogether charming picture.

She didn't feel up to confessing about her nocturnal adventure. In an hour or two it might start to be ridiculous, so long as Gerald didn't get into trouble over it. But right now she couldn't have raised a smile.

The morning paper had arrived, together with three letters—two that looked like bills and one that had a typewritten envelope and a business letterhead. Uncle Ted opened them, placed the accounts on one side, and read the letter.

When Fran put a plate of bacon and eggs before him he came out of his preoccupation with a start. "Forgive me, my dear, I'm so used to my own company that I've forgotten it's bad manners to read one's mail at the breakfast table."

"Is it? I've never heard that." In leisured times and leisured households maybe, but what a nonsense. "You read them," she said. "Not that they look much fun. All business, are they?"

"I'm afraid so, and where's your breakfast?"

"I'm having toast."

"But you always have a cooked breakfast at home."

"That's because my mother insists." She collected the toast that had popped up from the toaster and brought it to the table. "Why do you think I left home?" she joked. "So that I can please myself how much I eat for breakfast."

"I got in the bacon especially for you," he said reproachfully.

"And I'll join you sometimes, but you'll be getting the cooked breakfasts from now on. I shall enjoy bullying you to eat, there must be a lot of my mother in me."

"No," he said flatly, and Fran spread her toast and asked,

"Am I more like my father?"

"The hair, of course." She hadn't put on any makeup this morning, and her face had a scrubbed endearing quality. The copper hair looked very bright, and her dark-lashed eyes were very green. "You're one on your own," he said.

"Which some might say was not a bad thing." Gerald might be thinking that at this very minute. Fran could imagine how scathing Leon Aldridge would be to a member of his staff who left the Galleries open. Especially when the girl-next-door had taken advantage and blundered around by moonlight.

While they ate breakfast, and discussed the news headlines, her thoughts were on the Gallery and what was happening there.

Her uncle went down to open the crafts shop and she put on her make-up. Her hand was steadier now that she knew the vase wasn't valuable. She doubted if she could have applied lipstick and mascara before, but she managed it now. She was wearing jeans and sandals, and an emerald green T-shirt. She hoped she looked workmanlike, ready to get down to the job, because the flat, like the shop, needed a spring face-lift.

Uncle Ted had been shifting for himself since before Christmas, when his long-time cleaner-lady went off to help her sister run a boarding house in Brighton. The place was all right, but it lacked sparkle, and Fran was eager to start on it.

She got down as Uncle Ted was dragging the wooden garden table out and took hold of one end, helping him set it in place in the small section of the forecourt that fronted the crafts shop. She hoped Gerald wouldn't come out of the Galleries while she was here with Uncle Ted, but she must go see him as soon as she could, to apologise and try to explain.

While the TR7 that was Leon Aldridge's car was still parked she wasn't going into the Galleries. When that disappeared she must go in, and say she was sorry for causing trouble. In the meantime there was plenty to occupy her. The shop dealt in traditional regional crafts, from corn dollies to silverware. The customers were usually tourists, the season was just starting, and it wouldn't be Fran's fault if it wasn't a record.

Uncle Ted did look tired. The morning light showed that and she resolved to take care of him and lift as much strain from him as possible. She started on unobtrusive tidying—she would do the cleaning and polishing when the shop was closed—and a little rearrangement of some of the wares.

Uncle Ted was all for it. He wanted her involved here, busy and happy. And perhaps she had inherited some of her father's artistic talent, she couldn't paint or draw, but she had a good eye for design. She also had youth and enthusiasm and Edward Reynolds watched her with wonder and amusement. A quicksilver girl with hair of flame.

"How about putting some of these outside?" she suggested, indicating the wood carving section. There was a bowl of "worry" eggs, wooden animals, love spoons. Nothing expensive, and on the garden table they might catch the customer's eye and lure them into the forecourt and the shop.

"Yes, we could try that," said Uncle Ted, and Fran was completing her wooden display when Leon drove out from the arch leading to the car park. He stopped for pavement walkers, and looked across at Fran through his open window. She called,

"It's all right, I'm only putting them on this table. I'm not starting a street market."

"I'm glad to hear it." He didn't sound as though he thought that was funny, and she watched his car go, with its fleeting image of the man at the wheel, the fair straight hair, the greyness of his suit. Much more of you, she thought, and I'll be using a worry egg myself.

And now for Gerald and her apologies for last night. She went into the Galleries, and a youngish man she didn't know looked up hopefully. When she asked for

Mr. Maddox he took her to the door marked Manager, and tapped it for her.

"Come in," Gerald called. He was behind a desk. As Fran walked in he got to his feet.

"Hello," she said, hearing the door close behind her. "I'm sorry."

"Sit down." Gerald was smiling wryly, he had obviously had his interview with Leon Aldridge, and Fran perched on the edge of a Chippendale chair. "He came in early this morning," said Gerald. "He's gone to the airport now."

"I'd no right to go gawping around. I feel dreadful." She twisted her hands together. "Was he very mad?"

"Put it like this," said Gerald. "He wasn't pleased. If I use that door again I come back and lock it from this side."

"As far as I'm concerned," she promised fervently, "it's walled up. Nothing would get me through it again. I shall have nightmares about backing into the vase." She wouldn't even have to be sleeping. She didn't think she would ever see priceless Chinese porcelain with any real pleasure again. "I thought about two thousand pounds," she shuddered, and asked, "How much was it worth?"

"The boss said not to bother."

She didn't want to be beholden. She protested, "I'd much rather pay for it."

"You'd better see him when he gets back."

It was no use arguing, if those were Leon Aldridge's instructions. "All right," she said, and stood up, and Gerald inquired,

"What are you doing this evening?"

"Staying home."

"How about coming out with me?"

Fran looked at him with shining eyes. "You *are* nice." Her grin was quick and infectious. "I thought last night would be the end of our beautiful friendship."

"I hope not," he said warmly. "About tonight?"

"I don't think I should be leaving Uncle Ted the minute I get here, so to speak."

"Can I look in tomorrow?"

"Of course."

On Sunday afternoon they hired a boat, and chugged down river, past weeping willows and cows eyeing them from lush green meadows. The past months' rainfall had been high and the river ran deep, but there was sunshine on Sunday and Fran remembered her father rowing her over this stretch of river on summer days. He had loved the river, he had swum in it, but it had not prepared him for the currents around Sicily.

They passed the island on which the Aldridge house stood, reaching the bank by a bridge on one side, while on the other the river flowed. Gerald let the engine idle, looking at the house as though his connection with the firm gave him a proprietorial interest. "Quite a place, isn't it?" he said proudly.

You couldn't see it too well for the trees, but what you could see was impressive. Fran said lightly, "I'd have thought he'd have a drawbridge. Then he could raise it and no one could get near him."

"He doesn't need a drawbridge," said Gerald. She

agreed, Leon Aldridge's eyes put up their own steel plate, but Gerald admired him, and when she asked,

"What's he like to work for?" Gerald said,

"Fantastic."

She didn't want to be told that. She saw the wake of a water creature, and pointed it out and waited for it to surface. It was a vole, and the river really was an enchanting place.

FRAN'S FIRST WEEK went well. Uncle Ted was looking healthier. He was eating the meals she was cooking for him, and both the shop and the flat were brighter and in better order.

She enjoyed meeting customers, showing off the pretty things and the interesting things, telling them why this was lucky and how that was made. She was a natural salesgirl because she enjoyed selling; and Uncle Ted introduced her to a couple who delivered this week, one a schoolteacher who made lovely little hand-stitched samplers, the other a potter who brought a stack of mugs that Uncle Ted had ordered. They were nice people; she was sure that all the folk who dealt with the crafts shop were nice.

Every day was different, which was more than you could have said for being Arthur Deane's secretary, and every day was fun.

She saw quite a lot of Gerald. Working next door he managed to pop round for coffee most days, and Wednesday and Saturday evenings she went out with him.

Saturday they went to the cinema and then came

back to Fran's home with fish and chips for supper. She had her own key. She opened the side door and they went up the stairs to the flat. Voices reached them on the landing. Her uncle's first, and then another man's, at conversational pitch. She couldn't hear what was being said, but she recognised the voice and turned to Gerald and whispered, "Is that Leon Aldridge?"

"Sounds like him."

"What's he doing here?"

Gerald shrugged. "He's often round here."

"Here?" She was still whispering, so was Gerald. "You mean in this flat?"

"Yes."

Uncle Ted had said nothing about Leon Aldridge being on calling terms. "Why?" she mouthed.

"I don't know," Gerald mouthed back. "Ask him," and as she registered reluctance, "or ask your uncle."

CHAPTER THREE

THE VERY FIRST CHANCE Fran had she would certainly ask her uncle why he hadn't told her that Leon Aldridge was "always round here". If she'd known that before she came she might have thought twice about coming. She would have come, but she hated opening the door and seeing him sitting there.

He looked so cool, so in charge as he stood up. As though she was walking into his house instead of the other way round, and the worried wrinkles were deep round Uncle Ted's eyes. Of course she wasn't going to insult a visitor, although she couldn't pretend she was glad to see him.

She said, "Hello. We heard voices, but this is a surprise."

"Good evening," said Aldridge. He looked at Gerald briefly, then back at Fran, clutching her warm bundle of fish and chips and filling the room with their plebeian odour.

"Have you come about the vase?" she asked.

She had told Uncle Ted that tale and he had agreed she was lucky. She didn't really think it had brought Leon Aldridge round here on a Saturday night, and he said, "No."

"Just—dropped in? How nice." She couldn't smile at him, she *couldn't*. She said, "We weren't planning for you. You're welcome to a small cut off the fish and a few chips, but I shouldn't think fish and chips out of the paper are your dish."

"I was just leaving," he said, as though she had opened the door for him, and metaphorically speaking she had. She wanted him to go. "I'll see you out," she said. She wanted to close the side door after him. If he had come through the Galleries she wanted to bolt that door.

He could have said he knew the way. Instead he said goodnight to the men and went ahead of her along the corridor and down the stairs. Fran caught up with him at the side door and said, "About that vase."

He opened the door and his face was cold and still in the moonlight. "Give whatever you think to a charity," he said.

"Charity?" she echoed. "I shouldn't have thought you'd have gone much for charity."

"How would you know what I go for?" he asked. "Or what I eat."

The door was shut again and she sat down for a moment on the wooden bench in the garden furniture set, because her legs were wobbling. Finding Leon Aldridge in Uncle Ted's flat had seemed a threat, as though his presence was a danger to that secure and happy place. She knew it was unfair to blame him because her father had broken up the first home she had ever known, but her instincts had been to get him out of here and bar the door on him.

Neither Uncle Ted nor Gerald was going to understand. It made no sense to herself, and she went back upstairs to find the two men exactly where she had left them. Uncle Ted was still sitting in his chair, Gerald was still standing by the table, and the fish and chips were still in their paper.

She smiled. "Seems he doesn't like fish and chips," she said. "Do sit down, Gerald, I'll dish up."

It wasn't a chatty supper. Gerald did his best, balancing a tray on his knee, discussing the film they had seen tonight, addressing remarks to Uncle Ted, who didn't answer as often as not. Uncle Ted was always polite, it was just that he wasn't listening, he was thinking.

When Gerald put down his tray, leaving half his supper, Fran wasn't surprised. There was a tense atmosphere here, and she couldn't blame a visitor for leaving.

"I'd better be on my way," said Gerald, and Uncle Ted heard that.

"Goodnight then, my boy," he said.

Fran went downstairs with Gerald. She said, "I don't like your employer."

"I know," said Gerald. It had been quite a little scandal in its day. Some people might still remember it. He reached for her rather clumsily, patting her shoulder. "Losing your father was a rotten thing to happen," he said, "but don't blame Leon. You're too nice a girl to be that unfair."

"I don't blame him for anything," she said. "I just don't like him."

Gerald thought she was being unreasonable, and upstairs Uncle Ted had stopped trying to eat his supper. His plate was by his feet, and he was sitting back in his armchair, looking wearier than he had all week.

Fran sat on the pouffe in front of the fire. She knew there was some talking to be done, so she started it by asking, "Does he come round here often?"

"Yes."

"Are you"—she hesitated—"friends?" and Uncle Ted paused for a moment before he replied.

"Yes."

Fran could imagine her mother's reaction to that. No wonder he had kept it quiet. He wouldn't have been welcome at the farm if Fran's mother had known he was matey with Leon Aldridge, although as the two men had worked next door to each other for more than ten years that was natural enough.

"There's no reason why not, of course," said Fran. "I'm sorry I wasn't more welcoming, but it was a shock—I didn't expect to see him here."

"Friends and business colleagues," Uncle Ted elaborated.

"Yes, of course. With the Galleries next door—"

"Closer than that, my dear," he cut in, and she was puzzled until he explained, "I only have a lease on this place and it doesn't have much longer to run."

So Leon Aldridge owned the whole building. This had always been Uncle Ted's shop, he had bought it. She had never heard it mentioned that it wasn't freehold. She whispered, appalled, "You mean he could take over?"

"No," said Uncle Ted very quickly, "he wouldn't do

that," and Fran felt that he was reassuring himself as much as her. "But business hasn't been too healthy lately and I'm not getting any younger. Only a couple of weeks ago the doctor was telling me I ought to be taking a rest."

She could believe that. She must see that doctor and hear what he had to say.

"Looking to the future," said Uncle Ted, "it would ease my mind if you and Leon got on together. He could keep this shop going."

At what cost? What changes would he make? What kind of a going concern would it be once Leon Aldridge had a say in its future?

Fran said bitterly, "You *do* mean he could take it over," and was sorry as soon as the words were spoken, because Uncle Ted looked as hurt as though she had struck him. She wished she could have taken that back and she bit her lip, prepared to agree that she had spoken hastily if he told her again, "He wouldn't do that."

Instead he said, "I thought if you came down here, you're an adult now, not a child—you're not your mother, your mother will always be a child in many ways—you'd realise how prejudiced you've been."

"I know I'm prejudiced." And she was sorry, prejudice was inexcusable although she tried to excuse herself. "But I can't help it. I don't like him, any more than he likes me."

"He doesn't dislike you."

Why should he? She had never done him any harm, except for the vase, of course, and that wasn't worth much. "Maybe he doesn't dislike me," she said caustically. "He's spoken to me, but I don't think he's ever seen me."

"But he has." Uncle Ted smiled then, and she smiled too, because she was glad to see him smiling again. "He said he could understand Gerald forgetting to lock the connecting door. You were a girl who could make a man forget his own name."

She didn't credit that for a minute. Uncle Ted was conning her; although Leon Aldridge might have said something vaguely complimentary because Fran was Uncle Ted's ewe lamb. But if he was prepared to be polite so was she. You didn't have to like a man to be civil to him.

She said gaily, "I'll behave, honestly, next time we meet."

"Tomorrow night," said Uncle Ted. "He's coming round to have a meal with us."

Her spirits hit rock bottom. She felt her mouth and her shoulders droop. It was like being told, "The dentist tomorrow, and two back stoppings." "Do I have to be here?" she pleaded, but that was why Uncle Ted had invited Leon Aldridge, so that he and Fran could meet socially.

Uncle Ted had business worries. Leon Aldridge was his landlord and perhaps his backer, and if Fran was going to be any use in the crafts shop, much less run it on her own, she must get on better terms with the owner of the Aldridge Galleries. She would have to be here because it meant so much to Uncle Ted, and on her best behaviour.

"What can we talk about?" she asked desperately. She didn't know enough about the business yet to keep up an informed conversation, and what else would interest the Iceman?

Her uncle smiled. "You don't usually find it hard to talk."

Fran talked to anyone, and she could get almost anyone talking to her. "Usually no," she agreed. "To him, yes."

"Because you are prejudiced." They were back again at the root of the trouble. "What about taking him as you find him?" Uncle Ted suggested. "Starting tomorrow."

If she could only brainwash herself that she was meeting a stranger she would have an open mind. Tonight she had made two impertinent assumptions—that Leon Aldridge was a snob and that he lacked charity, and, as he had pointed out, how would she know?

She began to gather up trays and plates—no one had eaten much—wondering, "What shall we have tomorrow night? I can't do any more shopping. It's Sunday. What does he eat?"

"Food," said Uncle Ted, with a twinkle. "He is human, you know."

"Oh, you," she said. "A lot of help you are!"

A business colleague of Uncle Ted's was coming to supper, and she would put on as good a meal as she could at such short notice. Then she would sit quietly by and let them do the talking, keep her ears open and maybe learn what the situation really was.

She had phoned home this morning and told her

mother she was enjoying her work, and she was dating the young man she had gone around with the last time she was here. Her mother had remembered Gerald, and had asked, "He isn't married?" Reassured on that she had said, "That's nice." But Fran wondered now what her mother would say if she had been told, "I'm cooking a meal for Leon Aldridge tomorrow, and I hope it's only a business truce that Uncle Ted has in mind. It would be gruesome if he was matchmaking."

She was sure that such an idea had never crossed Uncle Ted's mind. That was entirely her mother's province, and Leon Aldridge was the last man her mother would consider. Uncle Ted simply wanted an end to Fran's old antagonism, and so did Fran. It didn't matter when she never saw Leon Aldridge, but it would be awkward when he might pop up any minute. Bad for business, according to Uncle Ted; and not much good for Fran's nervous system.

The meal would have been their Sunday dinner, which they would have eaten midday. She cooked the menu she had planned for seven-thirty in the evening instead. Nothing fancy, an ordinary traditional rib of beef with Yorkshire pudding, roast potatoes and spring greens, with gooseberry tart and cream to follow.

Uncle Ted had produced a bottle of wine that was warming to room temperature, and Fran was in the last stages of preparation in the kitchen. She was wearing a long skirt in bright patchwork cotton, and a white cotton blouse, with drawstrings at throat and wrists; and a bibbed white apron covering all.

Uncle Ted was laying the table in the living room,

and with kitchen and living room doors open Fran chatted away, raising her voice so that he could hear her.

Every time she started to feel apprehensive she told herself firmly, "A stranger is coming. I've seen him before, but I know next to nothing about him, and he's a friend of Uncle Ted's so he can't be too bad."

Her uncle passed the kitchen door and went down the stairs into the shop, and Fran stopped what she was doing—carving the meat—to listen in case he'd heard the door bell and she hadn't. But there were no voices and she went on carving.

At twenty-five past seven she had the meal ready for serving and as she took off her apron a bell did ring, the phone bell in the office behind the shop.

She expected the ringing to stop as her uncle answered the phone, but it went on, and she figured that he must have come back up here and gone up the next flight of stairs to his bedroom. If he heard the phone he was leaving it to her, so she called, "Uncle Ted, phone!" and plunged down the stairs, switching on a light and hurrying into the office.

"Hello," she gasped into the receiver.

"Uncle Ted here," said the receiver, and she goggled at it. "I've just popped out to see a friend," he went on blithely, "and I've got caught up. I'll be along later."

"What?"

"Start the meal without me," and she was left babbling at the dialling signal.

"Where are you? What do you mean, you've got caught up?" When she put down the phone she still went on, as though he could hear her, "You can't do this. You can't leave me to deal with him on my own!"

What was he playing at, pitching her into a tête-à-tête with Leon Aldridge? What did he imagine that would achieve? Well, if he was out she was out. She wouldn't answer the door. Uncle Ted had invited the man, she hadn't.

Right on time the doorbell rang and she knew she had to answer it. She was down here with lights on all over the place, but when Uncle Ted did put in an appearance she'd have plenty to say to him. It would serve him right if she took the early light back to Yorkshire in the morning.

Leon Aldridge was wearing a thin black polo-necked sweater and a grey suit. He didn't smile, of course. He looked at Fran with that impassive scrutiny that might have disconcerted her if she hadn't been fuming over Uncle Ted. She said, "I don't know where my uncle's gone, but he isn't here. He vanished while I was in the kitchen, and he's just this minute phoned to say he'll be along later."

"Would you rather I came back later?"

She was blocking his way, but to have agreed to that suggestion would have been like saying she was afraid to be alone with him, which would be ludicrous and insulting. She moved reluctantly, opening the door wider so that he could step past her. "Of course not," she said stiffly.

She told herself again, "He's a businessman whom Uncle Ted knows well, but whom I'm meeting for the first time," and led the way upstairs. "Is it raining

again?'' she asked. She had heard it on the windows
and seen it as a background when he stood in the doorway.

He said it was and they went into the living room,
where the table was laid for three, and the moment he
had finished laying it Uncle Ted had taken himself off.

"Will you have a drink?" Fran offered mechanically.
"A sherry? Do sit down."

"Thank you."

She poured two glasses, very pale and dry—much
too dry for her taste but exactly his, she'd bet—and
handed him one. They sat facing each other in the
matching wicker armchairs, which were comfortable
but hardly smart. She smoothed her skirt and would
have liked to smooth her hair, she knew it was unruly
from all this dashing, and she realised that she was still
wearing her apron.

She took a gulp of her sherry and went on with her
role of hostess. "I went by your home last Sunday,"
she told him brightly. "The island. The river's high,
isn't it, with all this rain?"

"Exceptionally." He didn't drink. He sat there looking at her, then he said abruptly, "I asked your uncle if
he'd let me speak to you alone."

Fran blinked her thick dark lashes. So this was a plot
between Leon Aldridge and Uncle Ted. "Why?"

His eyes seemed darker and the line between them
deeper. His voice, she thought, was huskier. "I know
that you hold me responsible for what your father did,"
he said, "and also, I suppose, for what happened to
him."

She should have said, "Of course not," but she said what first came into her mind: "How do you know?"

"Your mother blamed me. Your uncle told me how you feel, and you haven't tried to hide it."

Fran was struck dumb. This was completely unexpected. She had always known that her feelings were irrational, but she couldn't think what to say. She sat miserably silent and Leon went on, "He brought his work to me several times. He had talent, but he was getting nowhere. He was into his thirties, he had a job that he hated, and I told him to go somewhere where he *could* paint."

He was appealing for her understanding. "The accident was a tragedy," he said, and she couldn't doubt that he meant it.

She said slowly, the admission dragged out of her, "It could have happened here."

"Your mother didn't believe that." Her mother had called him a murderer in the gallery that morning long ago. That had been a terrible scene. He was remembering it now, Fran felt, and she said,

"I know he couldn't paint at home. The advice you gave him was sound."

Now that Leon Aldridge had expressed regret it was easier to see him as a human being, instead of an iceman. He still had an impassive face, but when he said, "Thank you," she could read relief, as though she had taken a weight off his mind, and she began to smile.

He smiled back, and the smile transformed him. Sweet and devilish, it radiated an astounding charm, so that Fran opened her eyes wide.

"I've never seen you smile before," she said.

"I've never seen you smile either."

As she was the one who went around grinning like a
Cheshire cat it seemed impossible that there was someone who had never seen a smile on her face. She
wondered how much her smile changed her. Not drastically, she thought. "Oh dear," she said. "Well, let's
start from here." She put down her glass and walked
across to him holding out her hand. "How do you do,
Mr. Aldridge. My uncle tells me you're a friend of his.
I'm very glad to meet you."

He stood too, tall and elegant. "This is a great pleasure. Do you think you could call me Leon, and may I
call you Fran?"

"Please do. After all, we are neighbours."

He had taken the hand she offered, and they shook
gravely. She could feel the strength in his hand although it was the lightest of pressures, and she was
aware of the taut athletic build of his body. She was
looking at him for the first time without prejudice, and
he was something to look at.

"Shall we eat?" she said. "The meal's ready and
Uncle Ted said we were to start." She added grimly, "It
would serve him right if we ate the lot, and drank all his
wine."

But the plan had worked out well. She was released
from that childhood bitterness, and getting to know
Leon Aldridge promised to be exciting. This really was
a first meeting, and she had the confidence of a girl
whom most men found attractive.

"I'm grateful to him," said Leon. "I think we should leave his share."

"His plate can stay in the oven," she said gaily. "But we're starting ours. I don't know about you, but I'm hungry. Would you see to the wine while I dish up?"

Uncle Ted didn't go in for vegetable dishes, although there were dishes galore down in the shop. Up here he had always served his own meals straight on to the plate, and so did Fran. She had deliberately cut out the frills on this meal for Leon, but now she began to wish that the fare had been less hearty and more unusual. Even that there had been candles on the table, instead of the choice between electric light or firelight, too much or too little.

She carried in the plates and apologised, "This isn't a very ambitious meal, but I didn't have much warning."

"It looks delicious." It was all right. As Dr. Johnson once said, "A good dinner enough... but not a dinner to *ask* a man to."

But Leon seemed to be enjoying it. He asked, "Are you fond of cooking?"

"I don't know. I haven't done much. My mother's a good cook, I'm not a bad one."

The Yorkshire pudding had come out just right, and that was a favourite with Uncle Ted. Fran hoped he would be home before it became indigestible. On the other hand, this twosome could develop more interest than a threesome.

"I've been feeding Uncle Ted up since I came," she said, "I was shocked when I saw him. He didn't look well at all to me. He's been worrying, I think. He says business isn't too good."

She looked inquiringly at Leon, who took a sip of wine. So she asked him outright, "Is it the general recession or is it the crafts shop in particular?"

"These are hard times," he said, which everybody knew, "but Ted does have his problems," and before she could ask, "What problems?" he was asking her, "You haven't worked in a shop before, have you?"

He wasn't going to discuss Uncle Ted's circumstances and she had to let it go, following the new twist in the conversation. "I've always been a secretary. Nothing very thrilling. I ended up at an estate agents."

That sounded aimless, and she hadn't got as much satisfaction from any of her other jobs as she was finding in the crafts shop. "I suppose you always knew what you were going to do." She sounded a little wistful.

"The Galleries were always waiting," he said.

She could imagine the satisfaction that gave him, knowing how he had enlarged their scope and made their name a power in the art world. She supposed that for her the crafts shop had always been waiting, but it was hardly the same thing. She wasn't going to build an empire on that, especially if the lease ran out.

He was watching her and she knew how easy it was to read her face. She didn't want him asking what was making her scowl. The lease was Uncle Ted's business so long as all went well. If there were troubles then Fran would pitch in for all she was worth, but of course there would be no trouble, and she smiled broadly.

"That big statue, on the ground floor." She gestured

vaguely, sketching it in the air. "I saw it from the balcony and it looked very odd. What's it supposed to be, exactly?"

It wasn't a statue so much as a huge rock, carved into a strange fluid shape. "It's called Windrode," he said.

"Does that mean anything?"

"It's a nautical term. It means riding the wind at anchor."

"Oh!" Fran tried out the name against her memory of the work. Her expression made him smile. "Well," she said dubiously, "I only saw it by moonlight, but I couldn't imagine it in my drawing room."

She didn't have a drawing room, and the thing was as high as a bungalow. "Neither did the artist," said Leon. "In a garden, now—"

"Ah yes, a garden." She leaned across the table towards him, her green eyes sparkling. "When you sell it send the customer round to us afterwards. Tell them we've got some gorgeous garden benches in natural elm. They can buy a bench to sit on and look at their statue."

"And if you sell a bench send them to me for the statue."

"It's a deal. How much is the statue?"

"A thousand."

"Reasonable. You could almost say dirt cheap." She pulled a grimace of exaggerated approval. "Oh, I'm sure I can get rid of that for you."

They laughed at each other, and he said, "Your hair is an incredible colour."

"Red."

"Flame." The electric light overhead shone down on her so that her hair was aureoled, and when she moved her head the copper glinted gold.

His hair was so fair it was almost silver, fine and straight, flopping over his forehead. The mouth was strong and clean cut. The toughness was there, like steel, but without that slight thickening of the bridge of the nose he could have modelled for a statue from Ancient Greece.

"How did your—" Fran began, then checked herself. He waited for her to go on, then said,

"How did what?"

She had been going to ask, "How did your nose get broken?" but suppose it wasn't broken and this was its natural shape, then that would be a tactless question. Although if he was sensitive about it he would surely have had it straightened.

"How did I break my nose?" he said.

"Well, yes."

"I fell out of a tree, when I was much younger."

She could imagine him as a boy if she tried, but it was harder to imagine him clambering up trees. She grinned, "I should hope you were younger, it's no way for a distinguished art dealer to go on. What were you doing in a tree?"

"Trying to get to the top," he said solemnly.

"But you didn't?"

"Not that day."

One day, while he was still a boy. He wouldn't give up. She said, "I'd have forgotten about reaching the top if that had happened to me."

"But, looking at your nose, it's obvious you've never fallen out of a tree."

She had a pretty nose, neat and small and straight, and she found herself blushing slightly, as though no one had ever paid her a compliment before.

"When I did I landed on my feet," she quipped. "I've cat's eyes, haven't you noticed?"

He had been looking into her eyes. She had known long ago that his eyes were blue, but tonight she would not have described them as Arctic. "And they see in the dark," he said. "Sometimes."

He was talking about her tour of the Galleries on her first night here. She had wondered if she would ever manage to see the funny side of that and now, suddenly, it was a joke and she laughed. "I was just looking at the pictures, that was why I bumped into the vase."

"The painting that reminded you of your father's work?" She nodded. "Would you like to see it properly?"

"Very much."

"Shall we go round?"

They had eaten as they talked, the first course had almost disappeared. Fran would have let the gooseberry tart wait and gone round to the Galleries now, she always had had this tendency to rush things. Leon, she felt, would expect to finish his meal first, and then go calmly, without fuss. He was not an impulsive man, not one whose arm you could grab and say, "Come on!"

But she brought in the dessert promptly and suggested, "We could have coffee later." When her plate was empty she wrote a note on the back of an envelope. "Gone next door, Fran." in case Uncle Ted returned before they did, and in case he had gone out without his key. She found a drawing pin in the office, and pinned the envelope to the side door.

The rain was a fine drizzle as they hurried from door to door, and once inside the Galleries Leon switched on lights, placed to illuminate the exhibits, so that Fran stood looking around her for a moment, eyes darting.

The central sculpture dominated the ground floor, and she stared up at it, asking, "You were joking about the price?"

"No."

"*No?* Do you mind if I laugh?"

"Not at all."

When you looked hard at it it was certainly impressive, and she said slowly, "In the right setting, I suppose, it would be rather exciting."

"The picture you saw is upstairs?"

"Yes."

They went up the staircase and along the balcony, to stand in front of the painting that had lured her through that connecting door. The similarity was even less by clearer light. Looking at it now she wondered how she could have mistaken it for her father's, and she said, "Not so close, is it?"

"I can see what you meant," he said.

She wished it had been. She wished she could have bought something to show for that lost year. She clasped her hands in a tight little grip, and her voice was tight, too controlled.

"We only have one of his paintings," she said, looking at the painting on the wall but seeing the picture that hung in the living room at the farm.

"It was in my bedroom, my mother didn't like them around in those days. When he went I hid it, I think she thought I might have destroyed it. She didn't ask about it. I brought it out after he died and now it has pride of place at the farm."

She smiled, hiding sadness, "She's proud of it now, she shows it to everybody. She's forgotten it was mine, that he gave it to me. He always gave his pictures away, and of course they were never worth much, were they—not in money, I mean? No one really valued him."

"They would have done," Leon said, and she blinked on a mist of tears.

"If he hadn't gone swimming that day. If the currents had been different. If he hadn't had cramp or whatever it was that happened. If..." She moved away and he said,

"I'm sorry," and that made her turn back.

"I'm not blaming you." She shouldn't have given way to that moment of bleakness. She put her hand on his arm in a spontaneous gesture of reassurance, not sure whether he was tense or if the muscles in his arm were iron-hard.

He said, "If I can get hold of any of his pictures for you I will."

"Thank you."

He took her along the row of paintings, telling her a little about each artist, each painting. He showed her the sculpture—like the paintings there was traditional and modern—and in one of the rooms was some work ready for an exhibition in two weeks' time.

These pictures had an almost Japanese delicacy that made everyday objects strange and beautiful. "They're exquisite," she said.

"I think so."

"Who painted them?"

"A woman who found she could paint when the children grew up."

"They must be proud of her," said Fran. "Thank you for showing me around."

"It's been a pleasure," and he said that as though he meant it.

The note had gone from the side door, and upstairs Uncle Ted was finishing his dinner. "I've been looking round the gallery by invitation this time," Fran told him, and his smile was smug, although he didn't actually say, "I told you so."

"And where have you been?" she asked.

"Up the road to see an old friend," he said nonchalantly.

"That was very sneaky." She smiled at both of them. "Coffee?"

She made it and they sat together around the fire, the men in the wicker armchairs, Fran on the pouffe. She was glad her mother couldn't see them, but so far as Fran herself went it was a very comfortable arrangement.

There was no business talk. She had thought there might be, but there wasn't, and she didn't see how she could drag the future of the crafts shop into the conversation, unless she got some sort of opening. The Sunday papers were there and they talked around the headlines, with Uncle Ted doing most of the talking and in fine form.

He was in such good humour that he went off into rambling anecdotes like the absent-minded professor he might well have been. He had a scholar's wit, and he sat back in his chair, tapping the tips of his fingers together, funny and happy, and Fran felt again that protectiveness that had brought her dashing down here. She wanted to keep him happy, he was such a dear good man.

When Leon got up to go she was sorry the evening had to end, but it was work tomorrow. She went downstairs a couple of steps ahead of him and at the door he said, "Goodnight, and thank you." Not just for the meal, he meant, but for admitting that he was not to blame for the past.

She smiled. "See you," she said.

"Yes." He didn't touch her in passing her, but when she closed the door behind him she realised that her heart was pounding as though she expected him to kiss her. Most men might have done, tonight had got off to a promising start for the future. He found her attractive, she was sure of that, but he hadn't kissed her goodnight. She hadn't expected him to, she told herself. He was a very attractive man, but he was also a very cool customer.

Uncle Ted was whistling softly to himself, clearing away the coffee cups. "You see," he said, "I knew you two would get on all right together."

"Oh, you're smart. But don't start dashing around because the doctor did say you should be taking it easy!" She took the tray from him. "At least, that's what you told me."

"All right." It was getting late, and he looked surprised as though he had suddenly realised he was tired. "I think I will go up," he said. He kissed her cheek. "You won't be long, will you?"

"Five minutes. See you in the morning. Sleep well."

He walked out of the room briskly, but his step was slow on the stairs and she thought again—I must talk to that doctor...

Fran was serving in the shop next morning when the roses came. She was wrapping up a loving spoon, and telling her two customers the way to the nearest café where they could get home-made cakes, when the man came in carrying a cellophane-covered bouquet and asked, "Miss Reynolds?"

"Yes."

"For you." He handed them over as though they were his own idea, and went off whistling.

"Roses!" breathed the woman who had bought the loving spoon. "I just love roses."

They were peach-coloured buds, just opening, and Fran fumbled with the packaging in feverish haste to get at the little white card. It said, "Thank you again, Leon."

She was pleased about that. They might have been from Arthur. He had written to her last week and she hadn't answered the letter yet. Uncle Ted would be tickled pink, he was in the office, and she picked them up to take along and show him.

As she passed the door leading outside Gerald came in, almost bumping into her with her arms full of roses.

"Is it your birthday?" he asked. "I saw the van."

"Er—no."

She had the little white card between her thumb and finger. He leaned closer and read it and said, "Thank you for what?"

"He came round here for a meal last night."

"It must have been some meal."

"Fair to middling." She didn't want trouble with Gerald, she never wanted trouble, but from the way his glasses were gleaming he wasn't thrilled about her roses.

"I thought you didn't like him," he said.

"I think I've changed my mind."

"Have you?" He breathed deeply. "Then I think you ought to know that he's an expert all round, and he collects more than pictures."

"Does he?" she said. He was waiting for her to say something, and nothing brighter came to mind.

Gerald looked at the roses and then at her, speaking quietly, almost as though he was sorry for her. "Just watch out he doesn't add you to his collection."

CHAPTER FOUR

FRAN HADN'T IMAGINED she was the first girl to whom Leon had sent roses. He must be—thirty-four? and eligible in every way, and hardly an iceman after all. "Thanks for the warning," she said. "I'll watch out."

In the office Uncle Ted was typing a letter on an ancient machine. Fran was a better typist and could probably have handled the clerical work more efficiently, but so far he had preferred her to concentrate on dealing with the public. She was a breath of fresh air in the shop, he said.

Now she held out her bouquet of roses and said, "Look what I've got. Aren't they beautiful?"

"Very fragrant." He sniffed one obligingly, and asked, "Who sent you these?"

She showed him the card and he beamed. She was glad he was pleased. Gerald had banged out of the shop as she came into the office, and that was a nuisance. He wasn't likely to complain to Leon, but it looked as though he was considering himself an injured party.

Fran had had trouble with jealous boy-friends before. Perhaps she didn't look the faithful kind but, like Arthur, the men she went around with took too much for granted, and expected exclusive rights to her company.

Sometimes it was crazy. She had once actually found herself in the middle of a fist fight. She was eighteen and a studious young man had taken her to the cricket club dance, and resented her dancing with anyone else. Fran was happily unaware he was smouldering until he erupted, and swung a wild right at his rival, who promptly knocked him flat.

Her mother was very upset about that. Mrs. Boyd, the mother of Fran's escort, was a friend of Isabel's, and Graham was a nice quiet boy who had never been in any trouble at all. "Until he started to go out with Fran," Mrs. Boyd had said, as though that had pitched him straight into a life of crime.

Jim had burst out laughing when he was told. Uncle Ted had thought it was funny too, but it had been a long time before Isabel and Mrs. Boyd spoke to each other again, and from then on Fran had become wary at any sign of possessiveness.

She couldn't imagine Leon being possessive. He was much too civilised, and a cool man around would be a welcome change.

He came into the shop that afternoon. There were several customers browsing around. Fran was with two American girls who were trying on clothes, and looking at themselves in the long mirror on the wall.

There was a miniature boutique of woven garments in a little alcove, and a Victorian screen for changing behind. They were trying on cloaks, and when Fran turned and smiled at Leon they turned to look. "Thank you for the roses," she said.

"I'm glad you liked them. I wondered if you'd care to come to the theatre tonight."

Yes, she thought, I would. He was in a denim shirt again, and the beige trousers. His voice was quiet and cultured, he was in no way obtrusive, but she knew exactly what his impact was on the two girls standing beside her. They didn't know he ran an empire, but Fran heard them gasp. She looked across at Uncle Ted, who was showing a customer a range of pewter tankards, and Uncle Ted said, "Yes, my dear, you go."

"All right," said Fran. "I'd like that."

"I'll see you at seven," said Leon.

"I wouldn't have waited for Dad's O.K. if he'd asked me," laughed one of the girls so that Leon heard her, but he didn't turn and smile, and they went back to looking at themselves in their cloaks while Fran took down a skirt.

It was ankle-length in fine black wool, with a scarlet pattern of geometric flowers, and the girl who was considering a scarlet cloak said, "That matches."

Fran grinned. "I've just treated myself to it, for tonight, but we do have some smashing skirts."

She sold them a cloak and a skirt each, and Uncle Ted said of course she could have the skirt with the scarlet flowers. By the time this shop shut the other shops in town would be closing too, and although she had brought an adequate little wardrobe with her she fancied something new for tonight.

Goodness knows this was an occasion, a date with

Leon Aldridge. Again she baulked from imagining what her mother would have to say if she heard, but by blotting out her childhood memories Fran was finding Leon a man of compelling charm.

She was looking forward to tonight, and the thrill of challenge had something to do with it. Her admirers to date had been uncomplicated, she had provided the excitement in their lives. Leon was different. Fran wasn't going to bowl him over, but it might be amusing to try.

She had a black velvet waistcoat which complemented the skirt, showing bare arms, smooth throat, and the shadow between firm young breasts. She made up skilfully, put on very small single pearl earrings, and thought she looked well enough.

Uncle Ted said she was a picture. He was biased, of course, and delighted that she was dressed up and waiting for Leon. She sat with him, watching the early evening news, and feeling a fluttering of apprehension that was unusual for her.

When the doorbell rang she sat bolt upright, clutching the chair arms with fingers that seemed unwilling to let go, so that she could get up and walk downstairs and open the door to Leon. After a moment Uncle Ted said, "The bell."

She jumped up then. "Yes, I heard it—'bye for now."

"Enjoy yourselves," he said benignly, as though he was saying, "Bless you, my children."

Fran picked up her coat and handbag from the settee and hurried, expecting the bell to start ringing again. Most people ring again after they have waited for a minute. But it didn't ring, and it was Leon who was waiting.

He looked dark. It was a dark night and he was wearing a dark suit. The silver-fair hair, and the light tan of his skin, contrasted sharply. "Ready?" he said.

"Ready and waiting." She was struggling into her coat, and he held it for her to get her arms in, but left her to do the buttoning up herself.

"I'm sorry if I kept you waiting," he said.

He had rung the bell at exactly the time he was expected, and last night too. This time last night Fran had been cooking the dinner, and dreading the moment he would walk into the house. There was a radical change in only twenty-four hours.

She said, "You didn't. Just a cliché." She peered out into the cold air. "Do we walk it?"

It was only about ten minutes' walk to the theatre, but it was dark and damp, and when he said, "I don't think so," she was glad to make for the car park behind the building. Uncle Ted's car had its usual spot, up against the wall, and Fran's Mini stood close to Leon's car.

They were an ill-matched pair and she laughed. "Bit like the Galleries and the crafts shop, aren't they? I hope your car doesn't give mine an inferiority complex." She patted the bonnet of the car. "Never you mind, Poppy."

"Poppy?" Leon echoed.

"She's always been Poppy. It seems to suit her."

"Was it ever red?"

"No. She came in this colour." The colour was green and Leon said,

"I give up."

"I bet you don't," said Fran gaily. "But Poppy's very easily hurt, so how about us taking her along tonight?"

She wouldn't have been surprised if he had preferred his own car. Poppy was rather a scruff, but he said what she was thinking, "It would be easier to park," and she fumbled for her car keys in her handbag.

Leon took the passenger seat beside her, long legs jack-knifed, saying nothing while she pulled out the choke and turned the ignition key to a series of discouraging clicks.

"I haven't used her for a week," she explained defensively, "and you know how damp it's been." She pushed the choke half in, she didn't want to flood the carburettor, tried again and got another click.

"Is Poppy going to take it personally if we use my car?" Leon asked at last, and as he spoke the engine spluttered, coughed and caught, with Fran getting into gear fast before it could stall again.

"Very female," said Leon.

"I suppose males never wait till the last minute before making a move." She felt him laugh silently beside her as she drove out through the archway.

It was a short journey, but she was glad she was driving because that meant she had to keep her mind on the hazards of the road. Just sitting, with him driving, she might have been too conscious of him for comfort in this confined space. She thought—trying to smile at herself—I feel as though I have a panther riding with me. I feel as though there isn't enough air and I have to breathe faster.

She said, "I don't suppose we'll be able to park in front of the theatre, it's usually full there, isn't it? We'll try farther along the road, shall we?"

They were lucky. There was a small space, near and handy, just big enough for a little car like Poppy, and Fran edged in. She opened her door and got out, and Leon came round to meet her.

He took her arm as they went into the foyer, where the crowd of tonight's theatregoers was milling around. They were nearly all tourists; this was one of the things they came to Stratford for, to see one of Shakespeare's plays. Most of them were in holiday mood, chattering, laughing.

Leon took her coat and went off with it towards Cloaks, and Fran watched the audience as though they were part of the play. She always did enjoy the time before the curtain went up.

Some of the men gave her second looks, her bright hair was an eye-catcher, and she was a pretty girl. But she got much less attention than Leon did. He was tall, strikingly distinguished, and he moved with arrogance and grace.

She watched the effect he had, crossing the foyer towards her, although he seemed to neither know nor care. That was true arrogance, not to care how you looked to anyone else. Fran was appreciative of being appreciated. She smiled back when anyone smiled at her, within reason, of course. But Leon's smiles were few, and he reached her without stopping, or speaking, or smiling at anyone. But as an escort she had no complaints against him at all. He was attentive, concentrating entirely on her until the curtain rose. She was almost sorry when they had to settle down and watch the play, because it might have been more fun to have gone on talking.

The play was one of the doleful ones, and as the agony thickened on stage she looked surreptitiously around for a little light relief. Leon, in profile beside her, was interesting to study, out of the corner of her eye. She could hardly turn in her seat and stare at him without him turning too to see what she was up to.

He'd make a good Hamlet, she thought, except that Hamlet was a dreamer, not a doer. Or a Romeo maybe, if Romeo had fallen off that balcony on to his nose.

She swallowed on a giggle, turning it into a cough—there were no giggles in this play. But the cover-up couldn't have been too convincing because in the interval, while they were sitting in the bar, Leon asked her, "What were you laughing at just now?"

She said airily, "I was thinking you look like an actor."

"And?"

"And—the sort of roles your face might fit."

"Such as?"

"Hamlet?"

"The gloomy Dane?"

She laughed at him. "You don't smile that much, do you?"

That made him smile. "No," he said, agreeing with her, and she went cheerfully on,

"Romeo perhaps, if Romeo had fallen off the balcony."

"Instead of out of a tree?" He shook his head. "I don't see myself as Romeo."

"Who died for love?" She made her voice theatrically tremulous, then shook her head too. "On second thoughts, not Romeo."

"Now you'd look the part for Rosalind." That was a compliment, Rosalind was probably the most famed and fascinating of Shakespeare's women, but Fran raised astonishing eyebrows.

"You mean I could pass for a boy?" knowing that the cut of her waistcoat revealed her as all girl, and Leon chuckled,

"Not even from the back of the stalls." They were both laughing when a girl said,

"What's the joke, darling?"

Her softly waved, beautifully cut hair was as fair as Leon's. Her face was pale and perfect, and smooth as though she had never had a care in her life. She stood by Leon, her hand on his shoulder—as expensively dressed as he was, in a silk striped grey-and-blue tabard and skirt—and Fran's first impression was: they look like a picture in a glossy magazine, well bred beautiful people, advertising something very pricey.

That was immediately followed by a reaction of dislike, because the girl was looking daggers at her. Lips curled sardonically, there was nothing friendly in that smile.

"Hello," said Fran, chin tilted.

"This is Judith Waring," said Leon. "Judith, Fran Reynolds."

"The crafts shop girl," said Judith, and Fran wondered how she knew, and come to that who she was.

"Yes," she said.

Judith looked her up and down. "Is that a homespun skirt?"

Fran smiled brilliantly, "Of course." She touched her tiny pearl earrings. "And I dived for these as well."

Judith went on smiling with closed lips. "Aren't you clever?" She looked pointedly at Leon, who was sitting imperturbably sipping his drink. "And you'll need to be," she said.

She went back to a little group at the bar who were waiting for her and Fran said, "Don't tell me what I've done to her, I can guess. I'm here with you."

Leon shrugged, not in the least put out, and she wondered what it would take to embarrass him. More than a jealous girl-friend, and that was what Judith Waring was, of course.

"Who is she?" Fran was about to ask. "What does she do for a living that gives her the right to sneer at the crafts shop as though it was stocked by ham-fisted amateurs?" But that was when the back-to-your-seats bell rang, so she said instead, "Saved by the bell!" and Leon finished his drink and stood up.

Saved by nothing, she thought. You might have told me what Judith Waring does for a living, but you would not have discussed her, or explained or excused.

She looked for Judith again in the crowds leaving the theatre, although she didn't particularly want to see her. But sure enough there she was, in a three-quarter pale mink jacket, belted with casual elegance. Real mink, of course. Fran couldn't claim to recognise real from phoney out of touching distance, but she knew that Judith wore nothing but the best.

A pale gloved hand waved at them and Leon nodded back while Fran grinned graciously from ear to ear, not to be outdone, and nearly slipped off the step. If Leon hadn't had a hand under her elbow she would have measured her length, and Judith would have loved that.

"Thanks," Fran muttered.

They walked along the pavement towards the parked Poppy and she asked, "Will you come back for coffee?"

"Is your uncle expecting you back so soon? I've booked a table."

"Oh, lovely! Yes, that's all right." Perhaps she had better phone Uncle Ted and warn him, he might want to go to bed if she was going to be out till midnight or so. Or she could look in and tell him. Or phone from where they were eating. She asked, "Where are we going?"

He told her. It was about ten miles away and she hadn't been there. There weren't many places around here that she had been, she had left too soon and returned too rarely. Now around the farm she had tried out every good eating house within a twenty-mile radius.

"Shall I drive?" Leon suggested as she opened the passenger door.

"Don't you like being driven?"

"No."

"Male chauvinism?" She hadn't crashed any gears

getting him here, and she had parked neatly, but she was prepared to hear he was against women drivers.

"It's not personal," he said, "You're an excellent driver."

"But you don't really trust anyone else at the controls?" She wasn't only talking about cars, and when he said slowly,

"I suppose I don't," neither was he.

"Well, I don't mind being a passenger." She slid into the passenger seat and reached to open the driver's door. "Up to a point," she said as he got in beside her. She liked to be in charge of her life too. She was used to getting her own way.

She sat back and watched him. She didn't tell him about Poppy's little tricks, let him figure them out for himself. To begin with this wasn't the easiest car to get into reverse. You could be certain the reverse gear had locked and still sail forward, and if he did they'd be up on the pavement. There was no one walking here right now so it wouldn't matter and might take him down a peg.

But he reversed smoothly and competently, and off they went with no more than Poppy's usual bangs and rattles.

"What does Judith do?" Fran asked, surprised to find that uppermost in her mind as there was a quiet moment.

"Do?" Leon echoed.

"I mean what's her job, her profession?" She sounded tart, and why not? Judith had sounded as though Fran's job was a joke.

"She's a designer, wallpapers, textiles."

"And very successful from the looks of her. Does she live around here?"

"Most of the time."

An art expert and a top designer should make a compatible pair, so Judith and Leon had more in common than dazzling good looks, and Fran was consumed with curiosity, although she had never probed into anyone else's affairs before. What she was wondering was, "When did you last make love to her?" She couldn't ask that, but it stayed at the back of her mind.

She said, "I hear you collect more than pictures. I was told to watch out I didn't get pinned down in your collection."

"Who warned you?" He sounded amused. "Gerald?"

"Why pick on him?"

"Because you've got him pinned down already."

"I hope not." She spoke more emphatically than she knew. "I'm no collector," she said.

"No?" He gave her a quick sidewards grin. "According to your uncle you left a job lot of them in Yorkshire, pinned down with needles through their hearts."

"The scandalous old gossip!" She wouldn't have believed it of him. Or would she? Yes, she would. He thought she was irresistible, which was a long way from the truth, and he must have talked about her as though she was Scarlett O'Hara. She said, "Don't believe it. I don't know what he said, but don't believe it."

She didn't want to know. She was sure she would

find it embarrassing, and she wished passionately that Uncle Ted had kept his mouth shut.

"Not even that you came down here to escape the latest who wants to marry you?"

"Uncle Ted," she said solemnly into the night ahead, "when I get home I shall poison your malted milk. And why on earth should you and my uncle be discussing me?"

"You're his favourite subject."

"Well, that must have been terribly boring for you. I do apologise."

"Don't apologise, it wasn't boring at all." It was all very well to joke about it, but it was embarrassing. She said,

"The real reason I came down here was because I was worried about him. I still am." There was no response. He didn't even ask what she meant.

She turned her head, wondering if she should ask him outright about the business. She was used to driving this car and in this unaccustomed seat the side of the road seemed too close so that she frowned and tensed for a moment. Then she adjusted to the situation and looked back at Leon. "I didn't know the crafts shop was leasehold," she was going to say, but he spoke first.

"There's no need for you to worry," he said.

Later she felt that she might have asked some questions, instead of accepting that as the answer to them all, but for the moment she was reassured.

The Plover was a typical Cotswold hotel, set in lonely

lovely countryside. It had once been a manor farm and it was run by three generations of the same family, all plump and well-fed and glowing, who welcomed Leon with broad smiles.

While Fran was phoning Uncle Ted Leon and mine host were chatting over the menu, and Fran wondered who had come with him last time. Judith perhaps? As Uncle Ted had told Leon so much about Fran maybe Uncle Ted could tell Fran rather more about Leon. Such as the story of Judith.

But right now she said, "We're having supper just outside Chipping Campden. Don't wait up for me, I do have my key. Are you all right?"

Uncle Ted said he was just going to bed anyway, and of course he was all right.

She enjoyed herself very much. Articulate, cultivated and worldly, Leon made a superb companion, and she gave herself up to his charm, savouring the company like the food. Although he smiled rarely he could be very funny indeed. He had her gurgling with laughter, alight with it. And chattering nineteen to the dozen herself, so that it was a fairly riotous meal.

When they came out, to drive back home again, Poppy protested a little before she started, but no more than usual and Fran had no qualms. She snuggled down in her seat and said, "Nobody but me has driven this car since I had it. Is that an honour for you?"

"I appreciate it," said Leon. "You can drive my car some time."

"Me at the wheel, you in the passenger seat?"

"I'll try to overcome my prejudices for a short trip."

"You should," she said impulsively. "I've overcome mine."

He knew what she meant, and she thought—I really have. I like you now. I'm not being added to any collection, but if we stop on the way home I wouldn't mind a goodnight kiss. She pushed back her hair with both hands as though she felt other fingers against her temples, and pushed away the thought of Judith in Leon's arms at the same time.

Poppy sighed and stopped. They were going downhill at the time. As the impetus ended Fran realised that the engine was silent, and slowly they came to a halt. "Oh *no!*" she gasped.

"Petrol?" She pointed to the fuel gauge, still registering a couple of gallons. "Does that work?" he asked.

"Of course it does."

"Well, something doesn't. You steer while I get it on to the verge."

The verges and hedgerows were sodden with rain, a heavy vehicle would have sunk in and got bogged down, but Poppy was lightweight and it would be more than risky to stay on the narrow lane on such a dark night. It was late and you couldn't guarantee that a car or a lorry wouldn't come hurtling down that hill.

Fran moved behind the wheel while Leon went to the back and shoved, and Poppy bumped over the rough grass, stopping just short of the ditch as Fran put on the brakes.

They weren't far from the hotel. They'd have to go back there and phone for help. If only it would stop drizzling. If the moon had been out and a few stars, and if it had been dry underfoot, this could have been an amusing end to the evening instead of a wretched nuisance.

She got out, her heels making little sucking sounds in the spongy turf as she walked round to the front of the car, where Leon had the bonnet up. She said, "It makes a change, doesn't it, the girl's car breaking down?"

He grunted. "Got a torch?"

She went to the side compartment and fished around for the flat pocket torch that she was almost sure was there. She hadn't used her own car after dark for ages, she wished she hadn't tonight, and when she did find the torch and switched it on the beam was so pale it was almost invisible.

"This isn't going to be much use," she said. It crawled over the engine like a glowworm, and she ventured, "What are you looking for?"

"Damned if I know," he said. "Do you know anything about engines?"

"I read the book once, it's in the car. But I just take it into the garage, and it's never done this before."

"I notice you've stopped calling it 'she'."

"Poor Poppy. Do you think it's serious?"

"Let's get back," he said, "before they put up the shutters at the Plover."

It seemed to be uphill all the way, and she wouldn't have blamed him if he'd blamed her. If it had been his car she wouldn't have been in the sunniest of moods herself, but as Poppy's owner she was responsible for their plight. She said, "I'm sorry about this," when they were half way up the first hill, and he grinned.

"Cheer up. They'll put another log on the fire for us and we'll get help for Poppy as soon as the first garage opens."

He put an arm around her and they strode on, the thought of the big open fire ahead getting more tempting every minute. There had been some nice deep armchairs. She could curl up comfortably in one of them and wait till morning. Or take a room. It was residential and they had seemed very nice, very pleased to see Leon. Fran was sure they would do their best to find a couple of rooms.

One lorry passed them. When they saw its lights coming they scrambled on to the verge and she found herself huddled against Leon. In spite of the cold and drizzle that was very comforting. She smiled up at him, "This isn't going to do your velvet jacket much good."

"How's the homespun skirt?" he said.

"Shrinking, I think."

He helped her back on to the road; her long skirt wasn't ideal for walking through the rainy night and by the time they reached the hotel she was out of breath. She sat on a white bench near the closed front door, puffing, while Leon went round the back. There were lights still on, upstairs and down, and in a very short time the front door opened and Fran, damp and dishevelled, was ushered in and taken to the fire, with as much fuss as though she had been in a real accident instead of a simple breakdown.

The fire was still burning brightly, and she sat in front of it, sipping a hot drink that was put into her hand, while Leon was talking to the proprietor.

A girl of about Fran's age, the owner's daughter,

came and sat beside her and talked about the weather, "Isn't it foul?" and how the best of cars could sometimes break down. "He's got a TR7, hasn't he?"

"Not tonight," said Fran. "We came in my ancient Mini. All the same, I never had any trouble with her before."

"That is a pretty skirt," said the girl suddenly, "I admired it when you first came in."

Fran delved into her handbag. "I got it from the shop where I work." She found one of the crafts shop cards and Leon, who had been on the phone, came over as she handed it to the girl.

"Touting for trade," said Fran, smiling.

"Ted will be proud of you," said Leon. "There's a taxi coming."

A taxi, of course. How odd that she hadn't thought of such an obvious solution. It was Leon saying that about getting help for Poppy as soon as the first garage opened. She had thought they would be waiting till then and she felt deflated, as though she had missed out on a small treat.

"We could easily have put you up," the girl said, and Fran knew they had suggested that to Leon who had turned down the offer. Getting a taxi to get them home tonight was very sensible, but it would have been pleasant to have sat by the fire here a little longer and then gone up to a pretty bedroom and got out of her wet clothes. She wasn't worried about her morning face. She knew that, for a change, she could look quite fetching shining clean, and she did have a lipstick in her handbag.

The taxi took some time. Fran's skirt steamed and

her eyelids grew heavy. This had been a long day, and if anyone had asked for her opinion she would have preferred to stay overnight and order the taxi for early in the morning.

When the girl left them Fran said, "They were offering us two rooms, of course?"

"Of course."

"Why didn't we take them?" She yawned. "If that taxi's much longer I'll be asleep anyway, not to mention a candidate for pneumonia."

"Give it another ten minutes. I'd rather get you home tonight." He smiled his rare smile. "I imagine that Ted could be rather an old-fashioned guardian."

"I did phone him." Once you start yawning it's hard to stop, she was still yawning as she spoke. "He won't wake till breakfast time." She closed her eyes. "And he's not my guardian. I'm not an old-fashioned girl. I please myself where I spend my nights."

She had a few quiet moments after that. In the dining room they had finished laying the tables for breakfast when she opened her eyes, and Leon was sitting watching her.

She suddenly realised that what she had just said might be misunderstood. She should have thought before she spoke, but she was tired and not feeling over-bright.

There was a knock on the door and she was quite relieved to see the taxi driver. Some men might have interpreted that bit about spending her nights as she pleased as a come-on, and Leon Aldridge was both cynical and sophisticated. It could have been awkward trying to explain to him that Fran, in her heart of hearts, was an old-fashioned girl after all.

CHAPTER FIVE

Poppy was a shadow beneath the hedgerows in the beam of the taxi lights, and Fran said dolefully, "She looks abandoned. I hope no one will think she's been dumped."

"She isn't that decrepit." Leon pulled Fran's head on to his shoulder. "You can close your eyes again," he said. "I'll let you know when we get there."

She did close her eyes. She lay against Leon, his arm around her, and thought about nothing at all because she fell asleep and only woke when the taxi stopped.

"You're home," he said.

"So I am. Heavens! Sorry."

"Sorry for what?"

"Falling asleep. Not very polite, was it?"

"It's been a long night."

The taxi was parked in the road just outside the Galleries. Leon paid the fare, and as the taxi drove away they walked across the flagstoned frontage to the crafts shop door. "A longer night than I expected," said Fran, "with plenty of variety."

She found her key and opened the door and said, "Thank you and goodnight," reaching up and brushing his cheek lightly with her lips. She expected him to take her into his arms and kiss her properly, but instead he said, "Thank you. I'm away until Thursday, may I come round in the evening?"

"Yes, of course. We'll be glad to see you." She stepped inside and he went towards the back of the house and his car. Fran turned on a light and walked quietly and carefully between counters and displays. At the top of the stairs, as she turned off the shop light, she heard the soft powerful purr of his car engine and stood listening until it faded. It was well past midnight. She would have to get up early and phone a garage and wash her hair, but the cat-nap in the taxi had refreshed her and cleared her mind.

She tiptoed into the bathroom, she didn't want to wake Uncle Ted, and got out of her muddy shoes and damp skirt. Then, as she was shivering a little and it would be stupid to risk catching a cold, she risked running the hot water and hoped the cistern wouldn't make too much noise.

It *had* been a long and varied night. She had enjoyed most of it very much. She had enjoyed being with Leon, and when she had brushed his cheek with her lips just now a strange tingle had run up and down her spine. She would have liked him to hold her tighter. She was trying to disturb him a little, so that his self-control was a little at risk. It was like driving the car, a small struggle for power. Fran was used to being the one in charge, and Leon was a challenge like Everest, almost impossible to conquer but very exhilarating to try.

She was washing her hair at the sink, where she

could keep an eye on the breakfast cooking at the same time, when Uncle Ted came down next morning. He blinked at her and she said, "I got my hair soaked last night. The car broke down."

"Oh dear!"

"Could you pour yourself a cup of tea? I've just made it. It was my car. I'll have to start looking up garages in a minute. We came back by taxi."

He poured his tea and she began to towel her hair. After he had taken a few sips he said, "I'm sorry about that. Did you have a good time, until the car broke down?"

"A very good time."

"I knew you would," he said smugly.

"Don't rush it. Think what my mother would say if she heard who took me to the theatre last night."

He winced at that. Although Fran was teasing they both knew there was no way in which Isabel would be reconciled to the idea of Ted, much less Fran, becoming friendly with Leon. If she found out there would be ugly trouble.

Maybe she need never know. She wouldn't come down here, so part of Fran's life would always be a closed book to her. If the relationship ever became serious then Fran would have to confide in Jim, and they'd have to go about breaking the news very gently indeed.

But that was leaping much too far ahead, and Fran was astonished to find herself thinking that way. "We met a Judith Waring at the theatre," she said. "She knew Leon *very* well. He says she's a designer—do you know her?"

"Not really," said Uncle Ted. "Except that she's Sholto Wallpapers."

Wallpapers and furnishing fabrics for the better homes. "She works for a classy firm," said Fran, turning her attention back to the stove and dishing up Uncle Ted's sausage and tomatoes.

He was eating his cooked breakfast without protest these days, he was eating all his meals. He picked up his knife and fork and added, "Her father owns the firm," and Fran gave a derisive chortle.

"Well, that should give her a flying start."

Of course she was being unfair. Judith Waring could be a brilliant designer, but if she was, as well as looking exquisite and being the boss's daughter, then that proved yet again that it was an unfair world.

Uncle Ted said, "Leon's a popular young man—"

"And there are bound to be Judiths around," Fran finished it for him. She sat down, reaching for her own half-cold cup of tea. "And talking about colourful pasts, what *have* you been telling him about me?"

"Not much," said Uncle Ted. He'd talked about Fran, but he wasn't admitting that he'd embroidered on anything.

"Not even about Arthur?" Fran persisted. "Sure you didn't tell Leon I dashed down here because Arthur was going crazy over me?"

"Indeed I did not," said Uncle Ted with dignity. "But you did want to get away because Mr. Deane was becoming pertinacious, didn't you?"

"If that means a nuisance," said Fran, "I suppose so."

"I told him you were a popular young lady," said Uncle Ted, as if that pleased him.

"That makes us a popular pair," said Fran lightly. But however Uncle Ted looked at it Judith Waring obviously had far more in common with Leon than Fran did.

Gerald told her that, bluntly, later in the morning. He came in at eleven o'clock and asked, "Any coffee going?"

"Sure," said Fran. This was the time she made coffee, which they drank in the office with the door open so that they could see if any customers came into the shop. Uncle Ted was showing someone paperweights, and Fran had just walked to the door with a customer who had bought a rag doll dressed as Henry the Eighth.

Now she went into the office and switched on the electric kettle, dropping coffee bags into three yellow mugs. She hoped that Gerald wasn't going to take up where he had left off when the roses came, and as he sat down in Uncle Ted's chair behind the desk she was reminded of Arthur cross-questioning her on evenings she had spent away from him.

The two men didn't look at all alike, except in an expression of suspicious sulkiness, which Gerald was doing his best to hide under a jaunty manner. "Enjoy yourself last night?" he asked.

"Who told you?"

Leon might have done, or one of the customers who was in the shop when Leon came in. Or someone who had seen them at the theatre or in the Plover. Gerald said, "News gets around," and Fran shrugged.

"It was no secret."

"I'm not saying it was. I'm only asking if you enjoyed yourself."

"Yes, thank you." She produced the half bottle of milk and the packet of sugar. "Until the car broke down," she said, and Gerald goggled.

"That doesn't sound like Leon's car. Nor like Leon."

"My car."

"Where did you go in your car?"

"Somewhere to eat?"

"Where?" he snapped, and she snapped back,

"Is that your concern?"

He had to admit that it wasn't, and then he grinned ruefully, "Except that I saw you first!"

Gerald couldn't be serious about her, their dates had been completely casual, but it might be a knock to his pride if she started going around with his boss, and he would have to put an affable face on it because he couldn't afford to rile Leon. That must be frustrating for him.

I wish you didn't work next door, Fran thought. This makes a difficult situation. She also wished she could say, "We're just friends, aren't we, all of us?" But she knew that she would rather go around with Leon than any other man. She didn't want Gerald saying, "When will you come out with me?"

The kettle boiled and she made the coffee and Gerald said, "Well, I'll be around."

"There's always a cup of coffee." She smiled and handed it to him, milked and sugared, and he gulped down a little as though it was bitter aloes.

"Funny," he said, "when you said you didn't like Leon I was pleading his cause. It might have been better if I'd given you a few more reasons for feeling that way."

"What reasons?" she demanded instinctively.

After a second or two he said, "The girl he's going to marry for one. Her name's Judith, and her old man is Sholto Wallpapers."

"I met her last night," said Fran with studied casualness. "But nobody said anything about a wedding."

"Others come and go," Gerald insisted, "but Judith Waring is going to end up as Leon's wife."

"Does he know?"

"Of course he knows."

"I'm sure they'll be very happy," said Fran flippantly. There was no marriage understanding between them yet, or Judith would not have walked away and left Fran and Leon together last night. But they had looked as well matched as though a computer had selected them as the perfect couple. Fran could understand why friends took it for granted that they would eventually pair off permanently.

She perched on the side of the desk and sipped her own coffee, then asked, "Anything else?"

"Er—no," said Gerald, taking his time drawling that out, and she marked his hesitation again. Earlier he had paused over what he should say, and Fran had the feeling that he could have told her about something worse than Judith Waring.

She bit her lip, torn between curiosity and caution, and then decided that she shouldn't be prying like this.

It was underhand, gossiping about a friend. Gerald had become almost as biased as she used to be, anything he said against Leon right now was open to doubt. Anyhow she didn't think she wanted to hear. She said,

"I wonder if Uncle Ted's ready for his coffee," and opened the door to look through into the shop.

He was just completing his sale, counting out change. There were several other people looking around, and she gulped down her cup of coffee as fast as she could. "Excuse me," she said. "Business is booming. It's all go, isn't it?"

"Don't you wish it was?" said Gerald.

"Have a heart," she smiled, "it isn't that bad. We're keeping our heads above water."

"Are you?" He looked as though he doubted it, and she was glad to get away from him. Fran touched her uncle's shoulder and told him,

"There's a cup of coffee in there for you." Then she hovered until she could move in to chat up a customer, pointing out that the samplers were handstitched, copies of Victorian samplers but heirlooms of the future.

She was getting a real kick from her job. Her delight and her enthusiasm were infectious, and nearly always customers went out pleased with their purchases and smiling.

As Gerald left he gave her a wry grin and a wave, and thought what a knock-out she looked. She was wearing jeans and a pink cheesecloth shirt that showed an inch of midriff when she stretched for a high shelf. She was a nice girl, but no match for Leon, any more than poor old Ted was.

It's a damn shame, thought Gerald, going back into the Galleries and shutting himself in the room marked "Manager".

Leon was in London for the next three days or Gerald might not have slipped round next door. He had always had a high regard and a healthy respect for Leon Aldridge. Gerald would not have cared to stand up against his employer, and that wasn't just because of the job either.

He wished he could have warned Fran how things stood, because he liked her and it *was* a damn shame, but as Fran had said, it wasn't his concern. He clenched his hands into impotent fists, because he couldn't do a flaming thing, except grin and bear it and get on with his work...

FRAN was looking forward to Thursday and seeing Leon again. Tuesday and Wednesday evenings she spent happily at home with Uncle Ted. There was plenty to do, both in the flat and the shop. Once she was confident about running the shop on her own she would pack Uncle Ted off for that rest he needed, a week or two by the sea maybe, maybe at the boarding house at Brighton.

She darned a couple of pullovers for him—he had always disliked new clothes—answered a few letters and phoned the farm to reassure her mother that all was well. When Fran said how much she was enjoying being here Isabel asked after Gerald.

The last time Fran had phoned she had talked about

Gerald, and her mother supposed she was still going around with him. An eligible young man would be some consolation prize to her mother, even if it did mean Fran staying in Stratford. "He's very well," Fran had said.

"Have you been out anywhere?" her mother asked, and Fran admitted,

"I've been to the theatre."

Shakespeare wasn't her mother's cup of tea, and if she had asked "Who with?" Fran would probably have fibbed, "Several folk. Nobody special." But her mother wasn't interested in discussing the play and she took it for granted that Fran's escort had been Gerald. Fran came away from the telephone wondering how long she could keep Leon's name out of her phone calls. She'd have to talk to Jim before there was any mention of Leon Aldridge to her mother.

On Thursday Fran woke up feeling excited. She couldn't think why for a moment or two. She just opened her eyes feeling marvellous, and stretched her arms high above her head, yawning luxuriously. The sky was grey, glimpsed through her window, but it was going to be a lovely day, and of *course* she was seeing Leon again this evening.

She got up, singing softly, and as the day wore on she realised that she never counted the hours before. Since she was seventeen or eighteen there had always been a man in her life, and she had looked forward to her dates with varying degrees of pleasurable anticipation. But she had never clock-watched, keeping tags on time and feeling excitement build up inside her until she had difficulty in keeping still. She wanted to dance around, and it didn't really matter if she did.

She had always been quick-moving, a little restless. The customers saw a lithe and lively girl, with a smile that could have sold a lawnmower to someone in a high-rise flat. Business was brisk and Uncle Ted was surprised when six o'clock struck.

"A very good day," he pronounced it, checking the till.

They closed the door and Fran ran upstairs. She had braised steak for the evening meal, and she had no idea what time Leon would be calling, nor what they would do when he did.

It had been an haphazard arrangement... "May I come round on Thursday evening?" "Yes, of course, we'll be glad to see you."

But during the last three days she had had time to appreciate the impression that Leon Aldridge had made on her. She had thought about him constantly, lingering in her mind on the way he had looked and acted, the things he had said, as she had never done with any man before. She was eager to reach the next stage of getting to know each other, learning a little more, coming a little closer.

She cleansed her face of the day's dust and grime as fast as she could, then got into another pair of jeans and a yellow and white checked shirt. She was tempted to wear something prettier, but she didn't want to appear dressed up for an occasion. This was how she would have been for another evening with Uncle Ted, comfortable and casual.

It was bad enough to have her heart palpitating without dressing to match. Leon was calling round, as he had apparently often dropped in on Uncle Ted, and it would be idiotic to show herself more than friendly and neighbourly.

Uncle Ted knew he was coming. As they ate their meal he asked, not for the first time, "Do you suppose Leon will have eaten before he arrives?"

"I have no idea," said Fran, yet again. She hadn't saved any steak, but she could find food if food was needed. They talked about the day's happenings and Uncle Ted was unaware she was on tenterhooks, listening for the doorbell all the time.

She tried to concentrate on what she was eating and what was being said, but the undercurrent of excitement kept her from relaxing. If he doesn't come after all, she thought, I'm going to feel like a wet rag by bedtime.

She tried to laugh at herself; this was silly, but it was quite pleasant too, racing and heady as though her blood was sparkling. She had always had energy, always felt alive, but tonight she was on tiptoe with excitement.

Leon didn't ring the doorbell, he knocked on the communicating door at the end of the passage, and Fran said, "I hope this isn't Gerald."

"Unlikely at this hour," said Uncle Ted. It was nearly eight o'clock.

She got up and walked along the passage very calmly. And all the time she was thinking, I never felt this way before. Some girls always do, every new man they date sends their pulses racing, every one is the right one for a while. But I never before walked towards a door and knew that the person I most wanted to see was standing there, waiting for the door to open.

She fumbled with the bolts because her hands were shaking, although she steadied them before she lifted the latch and smiled a nice natural friendly welcome.

He stood looking at her, then he smiled too and said, "Hello."

"We've been waiting for you."

"I'd like that." Fran wasn't sure what he meant, but it sounded right, and when he stepped through the door they brushed against each other, shoulders, hands, and somehow she was in his arms and he was kissing her gently. Or perhaps it was casually, because almost at once they were walking down the passage and he was asking if Poppy was back on the road.

"It was only a fuel blockage," she said. "The garage told me that if I'd put my foot down on the accelerator and blasted away I might have cleared it."

"We'll remember next time."

"Had a good business trip?" she asked.

"Pretty good. How's business been for you?"

"Pretty good. Especially today."

Uncle Ted beamed on them as they came into the room, and that evening Fran sat curled on the settee and tried to decide how much of Leon's charisma was sex appeal, and how much was intellectual. He had a first-class mind. If she had shut her eyes and listened she would still have been impressed and attracted. But when you looked at him you saw that, even sitting in one of those funny little wickerwork armchairs, he was sensuous as a panther, his lithe body smooth hard muscle.

He sat still, with no wasted movements, and Fran tried to ration her own gestures. But it was against nature for her, and almost impossible for her to talk with an expressionless face and motionless hands.

He was self-contained, an introvert, her opposite, and she knew what they said about opposites always attracting. She had never really believed it before, but now she was hoping it was true because she was very attracted to Leon.

He had to be interested in her because one date followed another in the next few weeks. They weren't exactly inseparable but she couldn't see how he could be dating any other girl, she was sure she was around for most of his free time. Besides, when they came upon friends of his she thought she could read from their faces that she wasn't one of the collection. They looked hard at her, weighing her up, as though she was someone to be reckoned with, and although they might have been comparing her with Judith nobody said anything that might have been embarrassing.

After that first night at the theatre they didn't come across Judith again. Leon had a wide circle of friends, or acquaintances. Women's eyes lit up when they saw him and men came eagerly over, but Fran soon realised that he was a loner. Whether they were with a crowd, or

talking to each other, she felt instinctively that he held
back, keeping secrets.

But he was enormously exciting to be near. Physically she was infatuated, she supposed. She fancied him
more than any other man she had met so far. That
might have been because their lovemaking was still at
the uncommitted stage, but a slight contact like his
fingers closing over hers could make her nerves sing
out in a fierce and delicate pain. When they danced one
evening she felt drugged with pleasure, and kisses were
moments of mindless delight.

She could be heading for a very passionate affair,
something very serious. But in the meantime she reported in her weekly phone calls back to the farm that
she was not going around with Gerald any more. She
was into a group now. That was partly true, she had met
other men and women through Leon, and the artists
who stocked the crafts shop were all friendly.

Her mother wasn't sure about this. Arthur had been
up to the farm to complain that he was getting no re-
plies to his letters and to ask for Fran's phone number.
Arthur had phoned Fran that night and got Uncle Ted
who had told him she was out with friends.

"I've written to Arthur," Fran told her mother now.
"I wished him the best of luck and told him not to keep
the job open." He had mentioned the job in both his
letters, and that the girls who turned up to be inter-
viewed weren't up to Fran's shorthand and typing
speeds.

"But if Gerald isn't asking you out any more," her
mother said plaintively, "perhaps you shouldn't be too

hasty about Arthur. He has a good steady business, you know."

"So have I," said Fran. "And I don't love Arthur."

She heard her mother's sigh. "Love isn't everything," said Isabel tremulously. "You can't live on love."

"True," said Fran. It was no good arguing, no use telling her mother that marriage was no longer considered as a meal ticket for life. Fran wanted love. Any permanent relationship she formed would be based on love, and so far she wasn't in love with anybody. But she was powerfully attracted to Leon, and it wouldn't take much to tip that awareness of him into loving.

If he stopped holding back, showed himself to be vulnerable and less self-sufficient, then she was almost sure that she would find she was beginning to love him.

She didn't see very much of Gerald. He didn't come in for coffee now. When she was out at the front of the crafts shop he sometimes joined her and they exchanged a few words.

"You're getting prettier," he'd said the last time, and she'd laughed.

"The climate must suit me." It was another dull day, but everything around here did suit her. She had taken to this way of life so well that she could hardly believe she was only into her fifth week. At the beginning there had been that idea that she should come down for a month and see how things went, but even her mother had realised by now that this was no holiday.

Business wasn't booming, but customers were com-

ing in a steady stream, and Uncle Ted was leaving her
to do more and more of the selling.

In the Galleries an exhibition was running, the artist
whose work Leon had shown Fran that first Sunday,
and she meant to have a look before it closed. There
was a notice by the front door of the Galleries, "Exhibition of paintings by Florence Pizer", a housewife
who had found she could paint when the children grew
up and left home.

During a slack spell one afternoon, after Fran had
been arranging some of her small wares outside on a
polished elm table, she wandered into the Galleries.

Everything in here was on display, with space around
it. The crafts shop customers rooted among the merchandise, but in the Galleries they stood back to
survey, only rarely handling some of the sculptures.

A young man assistant, who knew Fran of course,
stepped forward and she smiled. "Just looking," she
said. The exhibition was signposted and filled a couple
of adjoining alcoves on the ground floor, and several of
the paintings had a little red "sold" sticker in the
corner. Good for Florence, thought Fran. Leon had
said she was selling fairly well.

Another man and a woman were walking around,
and Fran stood for a while in front of the painting of a
young cat, tiger-eyed in a face as pretty as a pansy. I'd
like that, she thought. I might buy that.

She jumped as Gerald touched her shoulder. "You
startled me. Isn't that pretty?"

"Yes," he said. "Looking for Leon?"

"Looking at the pictures."

"Because he isn't here. He won't be in until tomorrow."

"I know he won't," she said.

She walked on with Gerald, talking about the paintings, and the painter who had waited until half her life was over before she had seriously put brush to canvas. "She joined an art club for a hobby," said Gerald, "and discovered she had talent, as simple as that."

It was a serene and gentle talent. Perhaps that was why it had never upset the tenor of her life. Fran said quietly, "I wish my father had never known he was an artist."

"Do you?"

His talent had surpassed this woman's, Fran was sure, but it had given him no peace. "If he hadn't felt that he had to paint he'd never have gone away and he probably wouldn't have died," she said. "He might have been a genius, but I'd rather he'd been happy."

"You're happy, aren't you?" The question caught her unaware. Gerald's spectacles gave him an owlish expression when he was being earnest. He blinked behind them now and Fran blinked too.

"Yes," she said, honestly, "I am very happy."

"Yes, I thought so." They were in the main centre of the Galleries now, still dominated by the massive rock statue. "Look," said Gerald, "how about you having a coffee with me this morning? I owe you a few cups and I'm about due for one."

"I'd better get back."

"Surely your uncle can manage without you for ten minutes?"

She was going to say he couldn't, but that was nonsense, and it was rather bad manners refusing. "Thanks," she said, "I'll look in and see how he's coping."

Of course he was coping, and she went back and went with Gerald into his office. The last time she had been in here, the only time, was the morning after she broke the vase.

"I see you've got another vase up there," she said. "Is it another fake?"

"Yes."

Leon had said, "Send something to a charity," and she had made a donation to a local village church roof in memory of the vase. She laughed now. "I still get nightmares about that." She didn't of course, she was joking.

A young man brought in a tray with two cups of coffee and grinned at her, and began to say something about the Florence Pizer paintings when Gerald cut in, "Thank you," pointedly dismissing him.

Fran stared. Gerald sounded very unsociable, as though this was going to be a difficult interview rather than a neighbourly cup of coffee. He hadn't smiled when she'd laughed, and he wasn't smiling now.

She took her cup and helped herself to milk and sugar. Then she said, "You look as though something rather unpleasant has turned up. I hope it's not me."

He still didn't smile. He was sitting with his cup before him and he frowned down into it, then he looked up still frowning and said jerkily, "We're friends, aren't we?"

"Yes?" Yes, they were, and why was he asking the question?

"You know what I told you about Judith?"

"Yes?" The same intonation came out.

"Nothing's changed," said Gerald abruptly, and after a few seconds of silence Fran said,

"I'm not following you. Let's take it slowly. You say that Leon and Judith are going to marry?"

Gerald looked hot and bothered. He ran a finger round his collar as though it had become tight. "Some time, yes," he said.

"Then she's very broadminded," said Fran gently, "because he's been spending a fair amount of time with me these last weeks."

"I know that." He gulped and blurted, "And I know why."

"Do tell me." He was going to tell her, so she might as well take it calmly. She wasn't worried, but she wished she hadn't said all right to this cup of coffee.

"He likes you, of course," said Gerald. "You're a real girl, going around with you is no hardship." Fran's lips twitched, and she wondered if she should say, "Thank you." "But it's business really," said Gerald.

"Business?"

Gerald leaned forward, narrowly missing his coffee cup. "He wants to take over the crafts shop. He wants your uncle's signature on a few more papers."

She said quickly, "Why? He owns the whole building. Our bit's leasehold."

"Leases aren't what they used to be," Gerald sounded grim. "There's no chucking the tenants out into the street these days. Besides, there are still a few more years to run, and he wants the place now."

"What for?"

"To enlarge the Galleries, I suppose."

Uncle Ted had talked about Leon helping the crafts shop carry on, not closing it down. Gerald only "supposed" Leon wanted to enlarge the Galleries, so he didn't really know. This could be a storm in a teacup, and Fran asked bluntly, "Why are you telling me this?"

"Because I like you," said Gerald.

"Thanks," she muttered ironically, and he went on as though he hadn't heard her.

"It would be a fair business offer, Leon wouldn't do old Ted down as far as money went, and it's legitimate tactics to get you on his side as well. But you're taking it personally, and Leon isn't."

And how did he know that? She couldn't imagine Leon discussing her with Gerald. Leon was the last man to go into any details about his private life with anyone.

"He's the coolest customer I've ever known," said Gerald. "He's—" He hesitated, and because what he had just said was exactly how Fran had thought of Leon for years she murmured,

"Ice? An iceman?"

"What?" Gerald considered that, then nodded. "Yes. Yes, in some ways you could say that." He went on with complete sincerity, "There's no man alive I've got more respect for. He's a great bloke. If I was in trouble he'd help me out in any way he could. But I wouldn't go to him for sympathy. I wouldn't expect any sympathy from him. I don't think he could shed tears for anybody, not even for himself. In all the years I've known him I've never seen him lose his head or do anything that wasn't calculated. He's cool. He's always cool."

Gerald had worked with Leon for a long time, he should know something about him, and he was telling Fran now that Leon was cold and without pity. When she first came here she would have agreed wholeheartedly, but not now. *No*, she thought.

"Women go for him, Fran," said Gerald mournfully. "I don't need to tell you that." He floundered. "I mean, they would, wouldn't they? He's got what it takes, what they want." Fran had said nothing for some time, and Gerald said in a final burst, "Some of them have made proper Charlies of themselves, but he always knows where he's going, every inch of the way."

That was all he had to say. He looked thoroughly miserable, sitting hunched in his chair, his untouched coffee in front of him.

"Can I ask him about taking over the shop?" asked Fran, and saw Gerald gulp again.

"You can," he said huskily. "I suppose you will, and he isn't going to thank me for telling you." Gerald had acted impulsively and was beginning to regret it. "I suppose you couldn't ask your uncle, could you?" he suggested. "Get round it, and leave me out of it?"

"I could do that," said Fran. Of course she would be asking her uncle, and there was no need to tell anyone about Gerald's indiscretions. She didn't want to cause trouble for him. He could even find himself out of a job and he could hardly claim wrongful dismissal if he had been broadcasting business secrets.

But she didn't have to ask Uncle Ted because, just

before closing time, a man came in who produced some of their best selling pottery lines, and he and Uncle Ted were talking ahead. From the way Uncle Ted was acting he didn't foresee the crafts shop closing down.

The potter had a selection of new designs and when Fran went into the office they were discussing next year's market. She was asked for her opinion and chose some attractive little porringers as a likely winner, and Uncle Ted gave an order for delivery in the autumn.

Later, over their evening meal, she told him about the paintings in the exhibition. "They're not very expensive," she said, "and there's one of a cat I might buy. I'm thinking about it. You might go in and have a look at it and tell me what you think."

Uncle Ted said he would, pleased she was asking his advice.

"It seems awfully big next door," she said, stirring her soup thoughtfully. "They're hardly cramped for space, are they?"

"Hardly," Uncle Ted agreed.

"Perhaps they could spare us a bit more," Fran smiled. "We're the ones with the piled-up merchandise."

He chuckled. "I think they need all they've got. I think Leon considers the present boundary a fair division."

She was reassured then that there was no question of enlarging the Galleries by annexing the crafts shop. If that had ever been mentioned Uncle Ted would not have been joking so cheerfully now. So Gerald was wrong.

She didn't believe he had lied to her deliberately. He thought he was right, and he thought he knew Leon. He did know Leon of course, up to a point, but Fran imagined she was a little beyond that point.

She wished she could have told Gerald, "I know Leon better than anyone else does. He isn't always cool and calculating, and the reasons he spends time with me are not business reasons."

They were the usual man-woman reasons. Because he enjoyed her company and he found her attractive. He didn't want the crafts shop, but she was fairly sure that he wanted her. She knew from the way he looked at her, touched her.

The control was always there, but three weeks wasn't long, and they had never been quite alone, except in a car, since the first meal here in this room. They had always gone out and about.

Tomorrow night, she thought; and Uncle Ted asked, "Why aren't you eating your soup?"

He had finished his, and she began to eat. "Still wondering about that picture," she said.

Tomorrow night they would be at Leon's house. She hadn't been there before, but they were having a meal there and they would be alone. She supposed they would be alone, and she supposed he would want to make love to her.

When that happened she knew that she could keep her head because she always had, and Leon was too sophisticated to force an issue or let a scene get out of hand. She had expected an exciting but civilised evening.

But, after listening to Gerald, she was filled with an almost primitive desire to know that Leon could be shaken out of his self-control if it was only for a moment.

Perhaps it was to prove to herself that she was not one of the crowd, but she wanted him to admit that he wanted her terribly, and to hear him say—as though it meant more than it had ever meant when he'd said it before—"I want *you*...I love *you*..."

CHAPTER SIX

ONCE SHE HAD made up her mind what was going to happen tomorrow evening Fran's spirits became buoyant again. She had been a little depressed since her interview with Gerald. It hadn't shown, but she had been left with a slight uneasiness.

She knew that Leon liked her, that that was why he never left her without fixing their next meeting. She had always said, "Yes, I'll come," because that was what she wanted to say. And so, presumably, had the girls who had made "proper Charlies" of themselves, according to Gerald.

If she began to play hard to get, and changed her mind about tomorrow evening, that might make Leon realise how much he had counted on her company. Or it could simply make him decide that she was inconsiderate. Anyhow, Fran wasn't made for the waiting game, she wasn't a calculator. She would find it much more enjoyable to flirt a little...

Getting ready, she dressed with especial care. She always took pains with her appearance when she went out on a date, but tonight she was making herself look as irresistible as possible.

She had a gauzy dress she had bought and worn

when they went dancing. It had a scooped neckline, a sweeping skirt and sweeping sleeves, and it was in a myriad shades of green, from pastel to deep blue-green, so that when you moved it took on the shifting colours of the sea. It was, she decided, her most romantic dress, and some of the green matched her eyes.

She brushed her hair long and hard, until it fell into deep waves, except for the occasional escaping tendril, and wore the tiny pearl earrings.

Dabbing perfume here and there she smiled at herself in the mirror, because who would have thought it—here she was dressing up to seduce a man, the huntress for the first time in her life. Not that she intended to seduce him all the way, she was a long way from a *femme fatale*. To lure, to entice, that was her aim, just to make him admit that she was special. Because he was. She hadn't told him yet, but tonight she would tell him.

"Very nice, my dear," said Uncle Ted, just as her stepfather always said. Fran had had more than her share of unquestioning male devotion. The only real hurt she had ever known had been her father's silence during those last twelve months of his life.

Uncle Ted would have thought she looked very nice if she had been wearing a sack, but as she twirled around he practically gave her a round of applause. Then he said sharply, "Mind the fire!" as the skirt flared out.

"It's flameproof," she said. "Non-combustible."

"I like that dress," said Leon, when he collected her.

"Me too," she said gaily, "that's why I'm in it."

He laughed as though he was glad to see her, quiet laughter, and she realised all over again how attractive he was.

She knew there had been other girls, of course, there had been no need for Gerald to stress that. She had often wondered these last weeks, meeting women Leon knew—were you and he lovers? Were you ever the one beside him as I am now?

And Judith. They hadn't mentioned Judith again. Suppose she asked now, "By the way, are you going to marry Judith Waring? And if you're not why does Gerald insist that you are?"

But she thought she knew the answer to that. "Because Gerald has no idea. Because Gerald doesn't know."

It was lovely in the car, close together and shut off from the world outside. Leon had been in Rome. Fran had been there once on a package holiday and they talked about Rome for a while. Then about the crafts shop, and she told him about the next-year stock Uncle Ted had just ordered, and he said nothing that could indicate there might not be a next year for the shop.

Of course there would, although she realised that she had been double checking.

She told him she had been into the Galleries to see the exhibition, but not that she had made up her mind to go in tomorrow and buy Florence Pizer's cat if it was still for sale. She wanted it for her bedroom wall, so that she could open her eyes in the morning and see those glowing eyes in that flower face.

The drive to Leon's house was along the bend of the

river that was swollen and dark these days, flooding
fields so that cattle and sheep had been moved on to
higher ground, and creeping ominously near some of
the riverside homes.

His garage, high on the river bank, had once housed
a carriage and stabled horses. There were lights on in
the flat above it, and Fran asked, "Who lives there?"

"A couple who look after the house and garden."

He didn't say their names, and it was beginning to
rain again, which cut short her curiosity. They had to
get down a path and over a bridge, and then through
the trees and across to the house.

"Come on," said Leon, and they ran. The bridge
had iron railings and wooden slats, with the river flowing fast just below. Weeping willows edged the island,
some of them half submerged, and then the path went
through a little fringe of trees that effectively screened
the house.

Once out of the trees the gardens were mainly lawns,
with occasional shrubs and flower beds, very well kept,
and right in the centre was the house.

It was a three-storey Edwardian house, big but not
rambling. It looked more elegant and less fussy than
most prosperous Edwardian homes, but Fran was intent on getting inside rather than inspecting the outside. She kept under the porch as Leon opened the
front door with a key, and turned off a burglar alarm as
he stepped inside.

The staircase wound up to the top floor. There was a
grass green carpet in the hall and on the stairs, white

walls and white paintwork except for bitter-chocolate gloss door frames.

A number of pictures were hanging. It was just coming up to dusk, and when he switched on lights she saw the details of the pictures. All the doors were closed and it was very quiet. She wiped her muddy shoes on a mat and asked, "Anyone else here?"

He took her coat. "I've no living-in staff these days. Do you mind?"

"No," she said. "But it's a big house for one."

"It's a showplace. I sell as many pictures off the walls here as I do from the Gallery." He looked around. "Well, not quite, but that's what it is."

Fran stopped herself saying, "What a shame," but it did seem rather a pity that this wasn't a home. It was certainly beautiful, with a combination of antique and modern.

The drawing room had Hepplewhite mirrors and chairs and a Persian carpet, as well as a modern sofa and easy chairs covered in natural linen, and glass-topped tables. The long window drapes took up the Persian carpet motif, and Fran wondered if they were a Sholto Wallpapers design, even Judith's own.

She could imagine Judith in this room, acting the gracious hostess. She wondered if Judith would mind if someone admired a painting on her walls and Leon promptly sold it to them.

It was warm, just the right temperature, and nowhere was there even a mark on a carpet or the suspicion of dust on the highly polished woodwork. Even the deep cushions on the sofa and chairs were plumped and free of wrinkles, and set smoothly in their place.

It was almost too perfect and she tried to stop thinking about Judith, who must have been here dozens of times. And the others, whoever they were. She sipped a sherry in the drawing room while Leon made a phone call. He came back in about five minutes and said, "Sorry about that. Business."

"That's all right," she said. She accepted it was business, but if it hadn't been she wouldn't have known. It had been a little eerie, sitting here by herself, imagining Judith's laughter, Judith talking to her guests. No doubt about it, this place would be the perfect setting for Judith.

The dining room was intimately small compared with the drawing room. A fire was burning in an Adam fireplace and the table was laid for two, even to unlit candles. The wallpaper looked like Sholto again, and the food was prepared and ready in a heated trolley.

Fran smiled, as Leon lit the candles and did the serving. "It's like one of those palaces in the fairy tales, where the traveller stumbles in from the storm and everything is waiting. All done by unseen hands."

"It's always been a little like that," said Leon.

There was jugged beef with a colourful assortment of vegetables, and red wine. Then fruit and a cheese board. And in the candlelight and the firelight the meal was delicious and a lot of fun.

Fran found that she was doing most of the talking. Leon led her on to talk about her life in Yorkshire, so that she was telling him all sorts of things. Nothing hair-raising, nothing really spectacular had ever happened to her, but it had been happy and there had been things to laugh at, and good friends.

"But you're staying down here now?" he asked, and she thought he sounded a little anxious.

When she said, "I think so," he said,

"Good."

"Is it?" She looked at him with wide green eyes and he smiled, and her heart flipped in that funny way it had begun to act lately, as she waited for him to tell her why he wanted her to stay. But instead he said,

"Shall we take the coffee into the drawing room?"

"That would be nice."

They sat on the sofa with a coffee tray and two brandy glasses on a long glass-topped table in front of them, and went on talking. Softer now because they were very close. When he moved to fill a coffee cup he touched her and her skin sang out. When she breathed she felt that she could smell the smooth texture of his skin, the fair flopping hair, the warmth of his breath.

They were talking about one of the paintings on the wall, but in a desultory way because neither of them was looking at the painting. They were looking at each other, and Fran's throat was so dry that it ached.

"You're very beautiful," said Leon, as she murmured something about perspective.

"So they tell me," she croaked. She knew that she wasn't beautiful, although from time to time some man told her she was. But it had never affected her before so that she hardly knew what she was saying.

"I'm sure they do," he said.

"So are you." She spoke with awe, without laughter, drawing a long shuddering breath as she slipped into his arms.

His eyes were bluer than any sky, closing over her like the sky, darkening with desire. She closed her eyes, and there were lips on her lips, a questing mouth that drained her of strength in a languor of warmth and pleasure.

She felt the trail of his kisses on her throat, burning through the thin chiffon that covered her breasts, and the sparks ran through all the nerves of her body, faster and wilder like a spark on bracken in high summer, so that her whole body was filled with a breathtaking bright urgency.

And then she heard the words from a distance. They were soft, but they grew louder although they were only spoken once, and they began to echo in her head, as though they were being repeated over and over again. Leon asking, "Do you know what you're doing?"

He spoke gently. Amused, maybe? She opened her eyes, and the fire went out, as suddenly as that.

No, she realised, but you do. You know exactly what you are doing. You are calling a halt and it should be me. I always call the halt, and that's how it was going to be tonight, except that tonight something went wrong with my defence mechanism. Something went wrong, and I think I went crazy.

She jerked herself upright and away from him, and her fingers twitched at the neckline of her dress. For no sensible reason, the neckline was where it had always been, but she moved, instinctively as though trying to cover up every inch of herself.

"I rather thought you didn't," he said.

Fran couldn't look at him. She had hardly touched the brandy in that glass, but that's what he thought it was, the wine and the brandy. She wished it had been. But it was him. She had lost her head because it was him.

She was clear-headed enough now. Nearly as cool as he was. She knew now what was happening, every inch of the way as Gerald had said.

Leon wanted her wanting him, but nothing that might mean an emotional entanglement because she was not that special. She was not special at all, and maybe Gerald was right again and Uncle Ted didn't yet know Leon's plans for the crafts shop.

Uncle Ted was an old-fashioned gentleman, who would expect Leon to act the gentleman where Fran was concerned. Uncle Ted would have been proud of him now—surprised at Fran but proud of Leon, who had so much self-control and was such a gentleman.

Now Leon was pouring Fran another cup of coffee, very black, because he was sure the brandy had gone to her head. Did he think she always acted like this after two sips of brandy?

She was cool. She felt as though there was a block of ice inside her where her heart used to be, and she hated him savagely, sitting there, pouring black coffee with a steady hand. "All right?" he said, and he smiled as he gave her the cup.

"Fine. Just fine." She hadn't realised it was scalding

until she'd gulped some. It made her gasp and tears
came to her eyes, and Leon took the cup away again,
putting it down on the table.

"Take it easy," he advised.

That was good advice. In future that was what she
would certainly do. She never wanted to see him again.
She wanted to go home and she never wanted to see
him again. She said, "I think I would like to go home."

He got to his feet the moment the words were
spoken, as though he couldn't see her off fast enough,
as if her pride hadn't had sufficient buffeting for one
night, and she said silkily, "I don't even like you. I'm
only around because Uncle Ted has been so anxious
that we should get on together."

It was that or throw the coffee cup at him, and that
hit. She saw him flinch and it made her feel a little
better, although immediately he was expressionless,
looking down at her with that cold mask of a face.

"You're a dutiful niece," he said.

"Aren't I?"

"I'm sorry you've been put to so much trouble."

"The meal was lovely," she said inanely.

"Then that was some compensation." He went to
fetch her coat and she thought—I shouldn't have said
that. It's almost true, but it was a stupid thing to say.

There was no taking it back, and she didn't really
want to take it back, because it would stop Leon asking
her out again. After that he would keep out of her way,
and as far as she was concerned the Iceman was back in
town. Her earliest impressions had been right. The
warmth was only skin deep.

She held out her hand for her coat, she didn't want him putting it on her; and even when he opened the front door and it was still raining nothing was said. They reached the car and once inside that he turned on the radio, filling the silence with words that meant nothing.

But the silence was still there, and when the car drew up outside the Galleries, it seemed to Fran that it was nearly tangible. She was still angry, sick with herself, sick with Leon, and she couldn't think of anything that she would ever want to say to him again.

He walked round to the side door with her, and then she did say, "Goodnight."

"Are you all right?" he asked.

"But of course." He watched her put her key in the lock and open the door. When she got inside she stood shaking, her hands clenched. She didn't move until she heard his car draw away, and then she went slowly and cautiously without turning on any lights. It wasn't late, but she didn't think she could face any talk about this evening's outing just yet.

It had not been a successful evening. The last half hour of it had been a horrible evening. She had made a "proper Charlie" of herself and then acted like a spoilt child in a tantrum.

There were no lights on. Uncle Ted must have gone to bed, and that was a reprieve. Fran took off her shoes and crept along the passage, she was so anxious not to have him opening his bedroom door and calling down, "That you, Fran? Did you enjoy yourself?"

She wasn't sure she could call back with any conviction, "Yes, it's me. Yes, I did."

She had offended Leon nearly as much as he had offended her, but she couldn't talk about it tonight.

For the first time since she'd arrived here Fran almost wished she could go back to Yorkshire. But she loved her work in the shop, and Uncle Ted did need her, and she could hardly run away because she had miscalculated Leon's feelings for her.

Gerald was right. With Leon every emotion was under tight control. He had no spontaneous feelings, like most human beings. She got out of her romantic dress and tried to smile. "It's flameproof, non-combustible," she had told Uncle Ted. That was Leon, and it was a pity it wasn't her too. Ah well, she knew now that you can't set fire to an iceberg.

It was a long time since she had wanted to cry. Not since her father left them, and in a way Leon had caused those tears too, but why was she weeping now?

For herself. For a loving man she had dreamed up who wasn't there at all. Gerald's Leon was real. Fran's had been a dream and she was too practical to cry for dreams. But the tears still came.

She didn't sob nor make a sound, but even after she was in bed she could feel the tears trickling through her closed eyelids and like a tight strangling hand around her throat....

She was up early. She hadn't slept well and when daylight came it seemed best to get downstairs and do something useful. She dusted the living room and prepared the vegetables for tonight's meal, and when Uncle Ted put in an appearance Fran was dressed and made up, on her second cup of tea and half way through the morning newspaper.

He was surprised. Neither of them usually had time to do more than scan the headlines before evening, but Fran looked as though she was doing some solid reading, and he asked, "How long have you been down?"

"I woke early." She had woken about two hours after she fell asleep, and for all her efforts with eyeshadow and mascara her eyes were less bright than usual. She smiled at him, his breakfast was ready. She poured his tea, and all the time he was watching her with growing concern.

"Everything all right?" he asked.

"Are you all right?" Leon had asked her last night... "But of course," she said, as she had said then, and Uncle Ted said,

"I don't think so."

He was bound to find out there had been a break between her and Leon. She drank a little of her own tea, to show how composed she was about the whole thing, and said brightly, "I won't be seeing much of Leon from now on."

"Why not?" Uncle Ted's early morning face, with the faint stubble of beard, looked grey and tired, as though these weeks of care hadn't helped at all.

She said slowly, "We had a disagreement last night. I don't think we particularly like each other. We just— went around together, and now it's over."

"I see." He sat down and she got up and went to the stove to fetch his breakfast. He seemed to be taking it for granted that Leon had made a rejected pass, because he said, "You must choose your own friends, of course, and perhaps Leon is too much of a man of the world for you."

She nearly said, "I'm not a child," wondering if that was how both Uncle Ted and Leon saw her, as a "crazy mixed-up kid". But it wasn't funny, and if she was a child how was it that she felt a hundred years old this morning?

Compared to Leon perhaps she was immature, but Uncle Ted was an unworldly man, and in plain common sense Fran was a great deal more mature than he was. She had come here because she had sensed that he needed looking after, and now he was sitting there as though all his worries were winging back, weighing him down again.

She sat opposite him and said, "Now you tell me what's wrong. What's going to happen now? You said Leon wasn't a man you wanted to offend, suppose I have offended him?" She made a grimace of a grin. "By the way, he didn't take any man-of-the-world liberties last night or anything like that, but I told him I didn't really like him, and I don't. There are times when truth will out, and last night happened to be one of them."

She had to know how things stood and she went on, "I've heard rumours that Leon has a personal interest in the crafts shop. Is that a fact? Could he really make things awkward for us?"

"He could bankrupt me tomorrow," said Uncle Ted quietly.

That stopped her pretence of flippancy. For a moment she thought he might be joking, although it would have been a peculiar thing to joke about. She scanned his face, hoping against hope for some sign of teasing, a twinkle in the eye or an upturning of the mouth.

After what seemed a long time she asked huskily, "How?"

"I owe him a great deal of money," said Uncle Ted.

She should have looked at the accounts before, instead of staying entirely on the selling side, and playing at housewife and cook up here. Clerical work was what she was trained for, but she had enjoyed getting out of the office. She said, "You ought to have told me."

"I suppose I should have done." He looked at his congealing breakfast as though he had lost his appetite. "But it didn't seem necessary. Things have been improving, with Leon's help."

"Just financial, is it?"

"He doesn't interfere, but—" Uncle Ted made an unhappy little gesture, and then a flicker of a faint smile touched his lips. "He is all the shareholders we've got. He does have a say in how we're running the shop."

She had been told by Gerald that Leon had had papers signed connected with the crafts shop, she had suspected he had a finger in the pie somewhere, but she hadn't realised that Uncle Ted was deeply in his debt.

He said now, "I've always thought of this place as yours, and I thought once you'd met Leon, away from your mother and her prejudice, you'd be able to work with him."

"Or for him?" muttered Fran.

Perhaps he didn't hear her. He said, "Are you going home?"

"Am I what?"

"Do you want to leave here now that you know how things are?"

"How they are? You mean now I know we're in hock to Leon Aldridge?"

Uncle Ted looked like a guilty man, although she was sure he had always acted honourably, believing what he was doing to be for the best. It wasn't his fault the shop had come on hard times and she couldn't bear to see him so depressed.

"He won't bankrupt us," she said with a cheerfulness she was far from feeling, "while I've got breath in my body."

"I'm sure he won't," said Uncle Ted. His thin ascetic face was wistful. "But I do wish you two could have liked each other."

We might have done, thought Fran, if Leon had stayed the friendly business colleague instead of trying to be more than friend and less than lover. "*Please* eat your breakfast," she begged.

He swallowed it to please her and she offered, "I'll go round and make the peace if you like," and as he looked up, hopeful and eager, "I'll apologise for what I said. He thought it was the brandy anyway."

Uncle Ted choked on a piece of bacon, and Fran patted his back with her first genuine smile of the day. "It's all right, I was cold sober, and if I hadn't been I'd still have been safe as houses. Leon is a gentleman. He's a few other things I'm not over-partial to, but his worst enemy couldn't deny that."

"Is it a bad thing to be?" Uncle Ted asked, and she gave him a hug.

"Of course not. It can be super, you're a super gent yourself. But I don't like him. Sorry, I am sorry. I'll work for him, though, if I have to, because this is our little shop and we're not going to let the shareholders down, even if he is the shareholders."

Her reward for that was a smile from Uncle Ted, although she had no idea how she was going to word her apology nor if it would be accepted. It was bound to sound false. Leon would know her uncle had told her how things stood with the crafts shop, and that was why she was eating humble pie. And how was she going to say, "I'm sorry I said I disliked you," when she did dislike him?

"I'm sorry I said it," she could say that all right, but he was no fool, that wasn't going to butter him up.

She was coward enough to think of phoning and apologising, she shrivelled inside at the prospect of confronting him face to face, but he might very easily answer the phone with others around. Although if she strolled into the Galleries and asked to see him that could be fairly public too. Unless she made an appointment.

She waited until his car was parked round the back, and then she went into the office and phoned the Galleries, and asked to speak to Leon. Whoever answered the phone—she didn't think it was Gerald—didn't ask her name. There was a constriction in her throat that made her voice squeaky, so that even if it had been Gerald he might not have recognised her.

"Leon Aldridge speaking," said Leon.

"It's—er—it's Fran." He said nothing, and she went on, "May I see you? Could you spare me a few minutes?"

"Of course." He didn't sound surprised nor interested.

"I'll be right round," she said, and he put down the phone before she could.

He came to meet her as she walked into the Galleries, and took her through one of the doors that had no name on. It was all antique in here, desk, chairs, everything. Dark carved furniture that couldn't have changed since his great-grandfather's day. Or perhaps it was because she was feeling so gloomy herself that she found it oppressive.

He moved a chair a fraction for her, and she sat down meekly, while he stood with his back to the desk, as though he knew this wouldn't take long and he would soon be seeing her out again. He said, "I presume you've been talking to your uncle, and he's told you why he's anxious that we should get on together."

Colour flamed in her cheeks. She didn't have to say yes, of course he understood why she was here. She made herself look straight at him, although she hadn't much hope of reading anything in his face. "He tells me you could bankrupt him," she said.

"He knows that I won't."

"Thank you."

"Don't thank me. I'm not losing anything by backing Ted."

"I'll bet you're not!" Fran hadn't meant to sound

tart. That was her trouble, one of her troubles. Half the time she spoke as she was thinking, instead of slowing down and using a bit of discretion.

"I'm sorry," she said. "I'm sorry about last night too. I shouldn't have said that. I do say things I shouldn't have said."

"Forget it. Ted wants a business partnership between us, and I'm sure that will work out satisfactorily. We don't have to like each other for that."

It was unlikely that Leon realised what a competent business woman she was, he had only seen her playing around, although the playing had been fun. She asked, "Why *did* you take me around?"

He smiled and the charm was there, but his eyes were cold. They must always have been cold, even in desiring. She had imagined the warmth. "Because you're decorative," he said, "and amusing."

She sat with an even stiffer spine at that, jerking up her head, demanding, "You don't like me either, do you?" and he said, quite gently,

"To tell the truth, girl, I've never even thought about it."

She had blurted out the truth, that his cold-blooded nature repelled her although she admitted his surface charm. Now it was his turn to be brutally frank, telling her that when he wasn't with her she ceased to exist for him.

"I can believe that," she said. "Well, good morning." As she walked towards the door he said,

"Don't worry Ted, he isn't in the best of health," and that stopped her. She rounded on him, scared.

"He isn't really ill, is he?"

She felt that Leon would know, and when he said, "He needs a break, he's worn down," she was tremendously relieved that it was something she could do something about.

Why was Leon concerned? she wondered. Because he had money in the business, or because he *did* like Uncle Ted? If it was affection perhaps there were some human feelings in him after all.

She said, "If I could get him to take a holiday I could cope with the shop, I think. Would you give me any business advice I needed?"

"Of course. It would be in my interests."

The phone rang on the dark carved desk and he turned, answering it with his back to her. She knew from his voice that he was speaking to a woman and that this wasn't a business call. He didn't say much, he rarely did, but he spoke of a date tonight, and she was certain it was Judith Waring on the other end.

It was as though she had become extra perceptive, and it was lucky she wasn't interested in him herself any more or this would have hurt.

He put down the phone with a word of goodbye, and said, "Yes, I think you should persuade Ted to take a holiday. Except for those Christmas visits to you and your family he hasn't had a real break in years."

"Mrs. Mizon, who used to clean the flat for him, has a boarding house with her sister in Brighton."

"Excellent."

"You think I can manage, do you?"

"I've no doubt of it."

He opened the door for her and she saw Gerald, and knew that he knew a call from Judith had been put through to Leon's office while Fran was in there. She was so nervily on edge that she seemed sensitive to all sorts of small signs. She could thought-read Gerald, who came over as Leon closed the door after her, and asked, "Everything all right?"

Everybody seemed to be asking her that. "Of course," she said, and dropped her voice to whisper very softly, "You're wrong, he isn't closing down the crafts shop."

Gerald gulped and she relented, "I didn't say you'd said anything."

"Thanks," he muttered.

"Thank you," she said. "That was the only thing you were wrong about."

She gave him a brilliant smile, and went back next door to get things moving about Uncle Ted's holiday. Because it seemed to her then that her only hope lay in filling her life with as much action as she could cram into it, so that she would have no time for thinking about Leon and Judith.

That phone call *had* hurt. She couldn't imagine why. She didn't want Leon, she really did dislike him, but the thought of him with Judith made her ache.

It couldn't be her heart, because her heart wasn't involved. Her head ached, and her stomach ached. She was sick with an ailment she had never known before that was very like jealousy.

CHAPTER SEVEN

UNCLE TED put up all sorts of obstacles against taking that holiday right away. His main argument was that Fran couldn't manage yet. In another month or two maybe, but until then how could he leave her to deal with everything single-handed?

"I've always got Leon to run to," she said drily. She wasn't likely to bother Leon unless she was in real difficulties, but in an emergency she could call on him.

"It's business as usual," she'd told Uncle Ted, when she came back from the Galleries. "And Leon says he thinks you ought to take a holiday. He says you haven't had one for years, and not to worry because he has every confidence that I can cope."

She wanted Uncle Ted to have a rest, and she wanted to be very busy for a while.

She started packing while he was still shaking his head, not sure what had hit him, but she was very persuasive and he finally agreed that he would go down to Brighton. A few days of sea air and rest would be a tonic, and Fran seemed sure she could manage. Besides, there was Leon next door.

She phoned Mrs. Mizon and booked him into the boarding house for a couple of weeks, starting tomorrow. Mrs. Mizon and her sister said that of course they could find room for Mr. Reynolds any time, and it would be ever so nice to see him again.

That night Fran had a crash course on the office work. She went through accounts with Uncle Ted, through piles of correspondence. She wouldn't be doing any buying until he got back, but now she knew who provided what, and she also knew what kind of stake Leon had in this place.

That, as much as anything, made her determined to make the crafts shop a success. The potential was there. What was needed was drive and flair. She had the drive and she'd work on the flair, and some time they would pay Leon back, and that would be a real red letter day for Fran.

Uncle Ted, who had always thought she was the cleverest girl alive, wasn't surprised at the way she took in all these facts and figures. But she was concentrating so fiercely that she could hardly fail to assimilate them. She was glad to have something like this. It kept her mind off Leon and Judith, until she was alone in her room and too weary to hold back any more.

Leon and Judith were close. He would suit Judith and Judith would be an ideal wife for him. Fran believed it now and it couldn't matter to her, unless Judith persuaded him to close down the crafts shop, and that was unlikely.

Leon wouldn't mind getting emotionally involved with Judith, and with closed eyes and darkness all around Fran could see his house again. Judith's home was probably just as splendid, but Leon's Fran knew, and that was where she was seeing them now. Alone in that house.

She was shaken by the details that came into her mind, slow moving like a film being played, Leon making love to Judith, and by her own instinctive cowering reaction. She was hunched down, her arms over her head, as though she was out in the cold and shivering.

She sat up and shook herself, literally, because this was not on. This was lunacy. She was dead beat and she'd organised herself a hectic two weeks ahead, and she had to sleep, not lie here dreaming bad dreams, awake.

She shook up her pillow too, and told herself, "Sleep, you idiot," and not too long afterwards she did.

NEXT MORNING there was sunshine. Fran waved Uncle Ted off beneath a blue sky, reassuring him that everything was going to run like clockwork. But if it didn't she would either call in Leon, or ring Uncle Ted and Uncle Ted would come right back.

Considering how long he had run the shop without assistance, and profitably until recently, Fran, younger and stronger, felt it would be rather shaming if she had to admit that she couldn't. She wouldn't be calling in anyone if she could help it.

Sunshine got her off to a good start. The long-distance weather forecast said more rain, but weather forecasts were often wide of the mark, and today was just the day for a holiday or a fresh start. Fran went back into the crafts shop, and told herself she felt like a new woman.

She had a busy day. The sunshine brought customers, and she was even more delighted than usual to see them. She found time to make a phone call, accepting a standing invitation from the lady who made the samplers. She was going to get out as much as she could, because now that Uncle Ted was away there wasn't much to stay in the flat for.

One browser who didn't buy was Judith Waring. She came in during the afternoon, when Fran was handling two sales at the same time, and had another customer in front of a row of dolls—"characters from Shakespeare"—trying to make up her mind which to buy for her granddaughter.

Judith looked very stylish. Her fair hair gleamed beneath a black slouch hat. She wore white shoes, a white tailored trouser suit and a black silk shirt; and Fran was immediately conscious of the dust motes floating in the sunshine, and the bare boards of the unpolished floor, because Judith looked so immaculate.

Fran herself was warm and rather sticky. Her hair was anyhow, and she had been hauling merchandise about all day, so that her hands could have been cleaner. She hadn't looked at her face in the mirror since morning, so goodness knows what it was like.

She went on serving, giving Judith the smile she gave everyone who walked in, as soon as she caught their eye. Judith didn't smile—that could be something else she had in common with Leon. She raised smooth dark eyebrows a fraction instead.

When Fran got round to her she was still standing well back from the counters. "Can I help you?" Fran offered.

"I shouldn't think so," said Judith.

"Just—looking?"

"That's right." Judith did what she had done at the theatre, eyed Fran slowly up and down, and Fran would have loved to say,

"This is my working uniform. I haven't changed radically since the last time you inspected me." But that wouldn't do, with customers around, although it did seem that Judith was here just to look at her.

"I've a few minutes to kill," said Judith. Before she went in next door to Leon, of course. "And this is such an unusual little shop, isn't it?"

"Why, thank you," said Fran. A crafts shop was hardly a rarity, and there was nothing outstandingly different about this one.

"Quite astonishing," drawled Judith, and smiled then as though she had a good joke that she was keeping to herself. Whatever it was the laugh was on Fran, and she could only conclude it must have been something that Leon had told Judith about her.

She moved away quickly because a blush was burning from her head to her toes, and went to a customer the other side of the shop so that she could stand with her back to Judith.

When she turned round again, a minute or two later, Judith had gone.

Fran closed at the usual time, checked the till and secured the takings; and then went upstairs and took a soaking bath.

Half way through that, of course, the phone rang, downstairs in the office, and she answered swathed in a big towel. It was Uncle Ted. He had arrived safely, and everything seemed very comfortable, and he would have chatted for a while if he hadn't realised that Fran's teeth were chattering.

"Have you caught a chill?" he asked her, and she laughed.

"I could do any minute, I was in the bath."

"Oh, my poor child, that wasn't very good timing, was it? Is everything all right?"

"Yes."

"Goodbye then, I'll phone you tomorrow."

"There's no need—" she began, but he had hung up, without giving her a chance to suggest that a rest meant a real break from business worries, not a day-to-day report on what was happening at the shop.

She was off for an evening with the sampler seamstress and her farmer husband. Before she went she fed herself on a tin of tomato soup and two rounds of toast, and she was washing the soup bowl when there was a knock on the communicating door.

Her fingers stiffened. She stiffened all over, and she had to make herself go and answer it. "Oh, Gerald," she said limply, and he must have thought she was at the end of her tether, because he stepped in as though prepared to catch her as she slithered to the floor.

But she stood quite upright and grinned. "The sun was good for trade," she said. "I've earned my keep today."

Perhaps he was surprised to see her smiling. He blinked a bit, and then he said, "You're not—well, sitting around, are you?"

"What?"

"Sitting around. Thinking about things."

It was nice of him to be concerned, but he had the wrong idea. "I don't do much sitting around," she said. "I'm just going out, as a matter of fact."

"Where?"

She hoped he wasn't going to start questioning her whereabouts again, but she told him, "Visiting Mrs. Aubrey and her family. She makes the samplers."

That seemed to reassure him. "She's a friend of yours, is she?" he asked, and Fran said,

"Yes," although they had only talked when June Aubrey had come to the shop.

"What about Sunday?" said Gerald.

"All right." She was going to accept all the invitations that came her way. She was going to fill in every waking moment.

"What time? If we started early we could get down to the sea."

"I'll need the morning to do the chores. About two o'clock?"

"It's a date." He kissed her cheek, because as he went to kiss her lips Fran turned her head.

"I'd rather you didn't use this door," she said. "It reminds me of that vase."

It reminded her of Leon, and the sound of someone knocking on it jangled her nerves.

Gerald said that in future he would use the outer door, and if she needed anything and didn't want to come into the Galleries she could always phone him. He gave her his home number too, which was in the name of the folks upstairs so she couldn't find it in the book, and hoped she had a nice time tonight and hoped that the break would do Ted good.

"Thanks for everything," said Fran, closing the connecting door and hearing Gerald snapping bolts on the other side.

Her mother would like Gerald. Fran liked Gerald. Fran had liked Arthur and a number of other men before him. They were the safe ones and, as the old saying went, better safe than sorry.

She was sorry about Leon, and she was glad that she had June Aubrey to visit tonight, because Leon would be with Judith again and it was going to take a little time before Fran could think about that as calmly as she would like.

She had a pleasant evening, and arranged for the Aubreys to come and have supper with her next week. She came back lateish and slept soundly. She was coping well with the shop, and the weather stayed warm and sometimes sunny, until Sunday when they were back again with the rain.

It would have been nice to have had sunshine. Grey skies and drizzle were depressing, and Fran turned on the radio while she was cleaning floors and furnishings in the flat and the shop.

But the music didn't brighten her, and when the time came for Gerald's arrival she thought—I hope he's in a cheerful mood, I could do with a laugh.

She wasn't getting one. When she opened the door it would have been hard to imagine a more complete picture of misery. Gerald peered through bleary eyes behind his glasses, his nose was pink and his moustache drooped. He said, with an adenoidal accent, "I've got a shocker of a cold. I feel awful."

"You look awful," she agreed, and added with quick sympathy, "You shouldn't have come out in this. You ought to have gone to bed with a hot drink."

He said lugubriously, as she drew him in, out of the drizzle, "Who's going to bring me a hot drink? I thought I'd be better round here with you for an hour or two. I could do with some cheerful company."

She choked back a hollow laugh at that. If he had looked one degree less seedy, or she had been one degree harder-hearted, she would have said, "Sorry, but I need amusing myself, and I don't need your germs around the place, so you'd better go home again." But she couldn't do that.

"Come upstairs," she said, resigning herself. "I'll stir up the fire and get you a drink and some aspirins. When did this start?"

Yesterday, he told her, with a prickling burning sensation behind the eyes and nose. He described his symptoms vividly, almost lovingly, and Fran began to suspect that Gerald was inclined to hypochondria. He seemed healthy enough, but he was making the most of a cold in the head.

She sat him on the sofa and made him a hot lemon toddy, and it was a grim day outside, so they were probably better off where they were. They watched television, read the papers, and Fran felt quite relaxed with Gerald, who was as comfortable as a pair of old shoes.

"What are you thinking about?" he asked her. He

had looked up from the *Times* colour supplement and caught her watching him. She smiled.

"Oh, that we'd have been worse off if we'd gone to the sea for the day." She couldn't tell him he was almost like having Uncle Ted here, and she asked, "Isn't there really anyone who would boil a kettle for you where you live?"

"They would, I suppose," Gerald admitted. "They're all right. But living alone isn't home life, is it?"

"No." Gerald had relatives all around; his parents were in Australia, to which an elder brother had emigrated. He wants looking after, Fran realised. He wants fussing and caring for. So many people did. Like her mother, like Uncle Ted.

She felt a little tenderness for him, because she was a kind girl. She could almost have gone over to where he was sitting on the sofa and hugged him and said, "Cheer up, you'll find someone who wants to marry you and look after you one of these days." But she didn't want to catch his cold, and if she had hugged him he would certainly have got the wrong idea. Fran was not applying for the post.

So she gave him some soup and sympathy, and tried hard to cheer him up, feeling like a sickbed visitor.

During the evening Uncle Ted rang for his daily report, although she had told him yesterday that she would be out today. "It's raining again," she said, "so Gerald and I are watching television."

He wasn't very interested in Gerald, but he was glad that Fran had company. While she was down in the office she rang the farm, and talked to Jim for a minute or two. She hadn't talked to him since she left, her mother loved answering the phone and always got there first if she could. Fran had always sent her love to Jim, and now she assured him that she was enjoying life and work in the crafts shop.

"I persuaded Uncle Ted to take a holiday," she said, "He's badly needing one, so I'm in charge, but it's all right so far."

Her mother took over, as soon as she reached the phone and was told it was Fran calling, and Fran explained about Ted's holiday again. But her mother's reaction was quite different from Jim's. He'd thought Fran ought to manage, he saw no reason why she shouldn't be left in charge, but her mother screeched, "You're not all on your own?"

"Yes. But I'm coping. The customers are all very nice, and as long as I'm nippy I can deal with them."

"You're alone, though? All by yourself in the flat as well?"

"Yes."

"I don't like it," her mother announced.

"I don't think anyone's likely to break in here," said Fran.

"I don't think Ted should have left you. You've only been there a week or two."

"Five weeks." It seemed much longer. "And if I get any business problems I can always go next door for advice."

"Next door?" Isabel shrilled, as though the highly reputable Aldridge Galleries were a house of ill repute, and Fran said to pacify her,

"Gerald works there, you know."

"Ah yes." Isabel didn't mind Fran going to Gerald for advice. It was Leon she couldn't endure.

"Gerald's here now," said Fran. "We were going out, but it's horrible weather. How's the weather at home?"

Talk about the weather should be safe, but after a brief, "It's raining," Isabel returned to the matter that interested her and demanded grimly, "Where's Ted staying? How can I get in touch with him?"

"I don't want you phoning up and bullying him. He needs this holiday."

"I'm not having you put on," said her mother, and Fran burst out laughing.

"As if Uncle Ted would put on me, or on anyone else, and you know I'm as strong as a horse." As her mother started to protest she raised her voice. "Now you take care of yourself, and Jim, and don't you worry about me. 'Bye now, and I'll ring again soon."

"Anyone I know?" Gerald asked as she came back into the living room.

"Uncle Ted." She sat down on the little hassock in front of the fire. The rain was pattering on the windows and she looked into the fire. "Then I phoned the farm," she said. "I probably shouldn't have told my mother I'm trying to run this place alone. She's a worrier. And then, like a fool, I said I could always go next door for advice on the business."

"What's wrong with that?" Gerald inquired.

"Leon," said Fran, staring into a small glowing cavern. "He's still her black beast. She's always blamed

him for my father's going away. And for everything
else.''

For his death too. In some things the past could always catch up with the present. It was in this room that
Uncle Ted had broken the news to Fran, and her
mother, that Peter Reynolds was dead.

"I had to say I'd be going next door to get your advice," she said. "If I'd mentioned Leon's name she'd
have been down here like a flash."

"You blamed him too, didn't you?" said Gerald quietly.

"Not the way she does." She rested her chin on her
laced fingers, elbows on her knees. "I think he had to
go, he had to get away, but he said that Leon had told
him that an artist must be ruthless. I'm sure Leon did, I
suppose it's true, but I always felt that was why he
never even wrote a letter to us."

Fran had waited, while Isabel became increasingly
bitter and resentful. Any mention of Fran's father in
those days had brought an hysterical outpouring of her
mother's grievances. The money came, but no message and no address.

"You never heard from him at all?" asked Gerald.

"He sent money, but he never got in touch. Not
even with Uncle Ted. I was sure I'd hear from him on
my birthday, even if it was just a card."

She smiled, remembering, her face turned away so
that she didn't see Gerald's shocked expression of
dawning realisation. "He used to paint my birthday
cards," she said. "Scenes, that's what he painted, with
a little figure that was me—skinny with red hair. I often

wish I'd kept them, but I was a child, and I thought they'd be coming for ever." She sighed softly. "But I would have liked one last card. It would have meant that he'd thought about me."

"Fran." Gerald came and put his arms around her, but she didn't want pity. She didn't know why she was talking like this, except that it was a miserable day, and Leon's name had come up somehow, and she had rambled miserably on.

She said, "It was a long time ago, and you're here because you need cheering up, and here am I telling you my ancient troubles. Forget it, will you? Honestly, I thought I had. It's a bit of a laugh really, my mother still carrying a hatchet for Leon who's probably forgotten she ever existed."

"So long as you're not still carrying a torch," said Gerald sombrely, and she could look him straight in the face and laugh at that suggestion.

"Not me. I'm no torch carrier. Judith is very welcome to him."

Gerald stared hard, then his face relaxed and he smiled too. He believed her. But of course he believed her, she was telling the truth, wasn't she?

Fran kept busy, and nothing happened that she couldn't handle for the rest of Uncle Ted's holiday. She saw quite a lot of Gerald, whose head cold passed through the usual stages. She went out most evenings, unless she invited guests to the flat. Perhaps she was doing a little too much, because when she stripped off her make-up last thing at night she looked pale, even drawn, in her bedroom mirror.

She was looking forward to having Uncle Ted home again. She needed someone around the place to talk to. First thing in the morning and last thing at night were dreary times when you were living alone.

She hadn't set eyes on Leon. She knew he wasn't there all the time, but he had been in the Galleries, Gerald had said so. She hadn't expected him to come round. He'd told her she could call on him if she needed any advice, but he wasn't likely to drop in uninvited until Uncle Ted came back. Nor invited, if the invitation came from Fran. They might be business colleagues, but they were no longer seeking each other's company.

Fran was sure Uncle Ted would be pleased with the sales figures. She had kept scrupulous accounts, dealt with the mail—by consulting him in her evening phone calls—and experimented here and there with displays. She had worked like a Trojan, and she felt rather pleased with herself.

It seemed a pity that Leon wouldn't know. Uncle Ted might tell him, but Fran would have liked to show him the books, which were all her own work for this fortnight.

Leon had thought she could manage, he'd said so, but she had done really well and it would have been satisfying to hear him admit it. Because apart from being decorative and amusing, and having enough sense to run a smallish shop for a limited time, he didn't think much of her.

Gerald came round at midday on Wednesday. Uncle Ted had insisted that Fran should shut for a lunch hour, although she spent her time dashing around straightening shelves, eating a sandwich or a biscuit and drinking a cup of tea. Gerald had tried, without success, to get her out to lunch, he ate at a nearby pub with a bunch of cronies. But he often rang the side door bell at midday and asked, "Coming?"

"Not today," she always answered.

Today she asked, "Is Leon in?"

"Yes."

"Would you ask if he'd come round, if he can spare the time? I want him to see the accounts before Uncle Ted gets back tomorrow," and as Gerald hesitated, "He's got a share in this business." Gerald didn't know how big the share was, but Fran had told him that was the situation. "And Uncle Ted wants him informed how things are going on." Which was near enough to what Uncle Ted had said.

"Yes, sure," said Gerald, "or you could catch him yourself. He's having lunch with Judith at—"

"I don't care what he's doing with Judith," Fran snapped, "I can't march in on his lunch dates. All I want to do is give him an account of my fortnight's stewardship here, but I'll ring through to him this afternoon if you're too high and mighty to carry a message."

"All right, I'll tell him," said Gerald, looking hurt as she was about to shut the door in his face, and she was ashamed of herself.

"Sorry," she said contritely, "I didn't mean to snap." She gave him what she hoped was an appeasing smile through the gap of the nearly shut door. "I'll be

glad to get Uncle Ted back," she admitted. "I think it is
too much for me on my own. My health's all right, but
it doesn't seem to be doing my temper any good."

She took it for granted that Gerald *would* tell Leon, if
he saw him that afternoon, but she wasn't so sure that
Leon would spare the time to come round. It didn't
matter. It was simply a courtesy on her part, showing
that she accepted and didn't resent his interest in the
crafts shop.

Uncle Ted had inquired several times if she'd seen
Leon. "No," she'd said. "Everything's all right. I
haven't had to bother him." But when Uncle Ted came
home tomorrow he would be pleased that she had
asked Leon round, and that she had been ready and
willing to discuss the business with him.

It wasn't because she wanted to see Leon in particular. Of course she would have done the same with anyone who was backing the shop.

He didn't come during the afternoon, and that was
sense, because she couldn't have left the customers.
She could have shown him the books, but she couldn't
have stayed to explain anything. If he was coming it
would be when the crafts shop had closed. The Galleries sometimes stayed open later, so it could be any time
at all. If he had an evening date it would be no time at
all, and Fran wouldn't lose any sleep over that. It was
just an idea, a courtesy.

She always took a bath after work, but today she
made do with a wash, applying her make-up quickly,
and not even changing her working clothes of jeans and
pink and blue striped T-shirt, and sandals.

She fried sausages for her evening meal. She wasn't going out this evening, and she caught herself looking at the clock, and was irritated because this would never do, she was *not* waiting.

She had a dozen things to do after she had eaten her tea, which was also her lunch and dinner, and would probably be her supper because she wasn't very hungry.

She ate the sausages, washed up, and then she did some more polishing downstairs, and decided at last that he wasn't coming. She wasn't disappointed, it *didn't* matter. She had the office books and some of the correspondence and accounts on the living room table, and she might as well fetch them down into the office again, and then she would wash her hair.

That would prove to herself that she didn't give a hoot if Leon turned up or not. No girl gets her hair dripping wet if she's caring what she looks like.

But before she put the books away, or washed her hair, she stood on a chair at the kitchen window, because that way she could peer down on the spot where Leon parked his car. It was still there, which meant that he was too, and she realised that she was smiling. Not long after that there was a knock on the connecting door.

She didn't put on the light in the passage, she didn't want him seeing her too clearly in case she did something ridiculous, like blushing. There was enough light from the living room to see your way along, and she left that door wide open.

First sight of him caught her breath. "Hello," she said cheerfully. "You got my message?"

"You wanted me to look over the accounts?"

"Yes." She went ahead of him towards the living room, and in there the central light and a standard lamp were burning, as well as the fire. But she was all right now, and breathing normally. "I thought they might reassure you."

"Reassure me on what?" He looked down at the table and up at her.

"Your investment in the crafts shop," she said. "I've had two good weeks."

"I'm glad to hear it." He sounded polite rather than delighted, and she asked,

"Aren't you surprised?"

He wasn't surprised. "Seasonal trade should be improving," he said, which meant that if the customers weren't coming in increasing numbers now they never would be.

"I suppose so," she had to agree. "We even had sunshine, didn't we, the week before last?" She was getting no praise from him. "Anyhow," she said, "I coped."

"Of course you did."

"And you don't want to see the accounts?"

"Not unless you're having problems with them."

"No problems."

But it hadn't been *that* easy. It had been no picnic. Fran had moved around a lot faster on her own two feet these last two weeks than he had. Leon never finished a day's work with his shirt sticking to him, as she had.

"Ted's back tomorrow, isn't he?" he asked suddenly. She nodded. "Good," he said, "you're looking tired," and she had to laugh at that.

"That's what I like to hear! I thought I'd done a really smart job. You can smell the lavender polish if you go down into the shop. I tell you, there's even a shine on the old floorboards. And every customer got served, and nobody asked to see the manager, and now you tell me sales should have gone up anyway because it's that time of year, and that I look as if I could do with a coat of polish myself."

He was smiling as she was talking. When she drew breath he said, "I'm sure you've done an excellent job, but I knew you would."

"Oh!" Well, perhaps that *was* praise of a sort, and she went on quickly, "If you don't mind, now that you're here, I would be grateful if you'd look through some of the paper work. So that I can tell Uncle Ted tomorrow that everything's checked and passed."

She had no clue to what he was thinking. He didn't move for a few seconds, and he might have been wondering how he could word an excuse, although being Leon he was more likely to simply say, "No." Then he sat down.

"Could you get me a cup of tea?" he asked.

"Of course." She brewed up and brought it, putting it beside him, then she sat down herself. Leon drank tea and went through papers, but he didn't query anything. The checking was brisk. This wasn't going to take him long, and she didn't want him hurrying away.

She liked him being here. He wasn't background company, like Uncle Ted and Gerald, but much more satisfying, as though having Leon in the same room was food and drink. She watched the bowed fair head, the strong hands turning over papers, and she felt stronger and healthier and happier.

Judith was there all right, there was no ignoring Judith, and Leon was only here because Fran had sent that message, but maybe there had been misunderstandings. She had said she didn't like him, and perhaps she didn't, but when he was near she felt complete. And that was odd, because she had never realised before that she might be incomplete.

When he finishes, she thought, I'll get some supper. I'll say I haven't eaten, and hope the fried sausage smell isn't still hanging around. I'll say I hate eating anything on my own—and she did, although until this last fortnight she hadn't realised that either; and I'll ask him what he's been doing lately.

Nothing to do with Judith, of course. Nothing about his social life, just work. He was in America earlier this week. She could always ask, "What did you buy or sell in America?"

But until he finished going through the papers she sat very still and quiet, getting stronger every minute. She could feel security washing over her and her heart beat with delight.

When Leon closed the accounts book and looked across at her he said, "Ted will be proud of you."

"You said that before." Joking, the first night he took her out, when she gave the girl at the Plover a trade card. The girl had come into the shop a day or two ago and bought a skirt very like the one she had admired on Fran. If Leon had remembered Fran could have told him that, but he said,

"Ted is always proud of you."

"I'm proud of— him. I'm lucky to have him."

"Yes indeed." He put a hand in front of his eyes for a moment, and taking it away blinked as though his eyes were troubling him. They looked heavy, and there was a fine-drawn tautness about the skin of his face. Now that Fran looked full at him she could see that he wasn't himself.

"You haven't caught Gerald's cold, have you?" she asked anxiously, and he smiled.

"I should have thought you were more likely to have caught that."

She gave a small shrug. "Not particularly." She had been out with Gerald, but there had been no kisses to mention. Her proximity hadn't been much closer than the customers and colleagues next door.

Leon said, "I've had an exhausting couple of weeks." He grinned. "Delayed jet lag."

"Sounds nasty." She hadn't thought that Leon could ever be tired, with his whipcord physique, but the responsibility for everything that happened in the Galleries was his. He shared it with no one, and he jetted between countries as other men took their cars from town to town. Her account books and pile of correspondence could have been the last straw tonight, after he had finished several hours of overtime in his own office.

She said, "Sorry I bothered you with this."

"That's all right." As he stood up she jumped to her feet.

"Don't dash off. You do look bleary-eyed. Please sit down and I'll get some supper."

"Don't bother about supper," he said. "But I've nothing to dash off for."

No Judith tonight? But if Judith had been waiting he wouldn't have come. He sat in the chair Fran had seen him sitting in before, but this time Uncle Ted wasn't in the other armchair, and Fran took the hassock again, by the fireside. She said, "I thought I was the one who'd had the wearing fortnight."

"It seems we both have." That could have a deep meaning, or only a literal one. She said lightly,

"I feel healthier than you look."

"You look healthier than I feel."

"There are some weird old bugs going around these days." Her eyes danced as he quoted what she had said earlier.

"That's what I like to hear," and she continued,

"But you look like plain old-fashioned 'flu to me."

"Do I?"

"I'll get you my stepfather's cure." She got up and he said,

"For 'flu?"

"For anything. You name it and Jim will mix you up a toddy."

That was stretching the truth, but a hot nightcap was a universal remedy for chills and stress. Leon had been away until yesterday, so it wasn't likely he knew that she was making a habit of dispensing Uncle Ted's whisky medicinally.

She got the bottle out of the sideboard and poured some into a tumbler. Leon took it from her, and poured half the measure back into the bottle, saying, "Steady on, I'm driving."

Gerald had walked here on Sunday and Fran had driven him home. It had been raining then and it was raining now, but Leon had his car and he didn't like anyone else at the controls. He had promised her she could drive his car and she never had, and maybe she would remind him of that promise some time.

In the kitchen she boiled water, squeezed a lemon and added sugar, then carried the steaming glass back again to Leon, who asked, "Am I drinking alone?"

"I don't have 'flu."

"I very much doubt if I have."

"All right." Fran was anxious to keep this tedia covered camaraderie going. "I'll join you, as a preventive measure."

She made herself a weaker drink, and sat down again, and asked, "What happened in America?"

"What happened here?"

"Nothing surprising. Just a seasonal rise in trade."

Leon did look very tired, and she talked softly, about the shop and the people who had come in. Not Judith, she didn't mention Judith. She talked quietly, making him smile, taking him with her where she had been since she saw him last and Uncle Ted went on holiday.

She asked no questions, and neither did he. He never mentioned Judith either, nor Gerald come to

that. He said very little and there were silences when
you could hear the ticking clock, and the rain and the
keening wind, and the soft rustle of coals settling on
the fire.

She made up the fire once, poked it a couple of times
sending sparks up the chimney. It was very peaceful
and it was getting very late. Fran wouldn't have moved.
She would have sat here till morning, keeping the fire
going, letting him rest.

He was resting, and so was she. They had both had
two hard weeks and this was resting time. But he
looked at his watch and said, "I must go."

She hadn't looked at the clock on the mantelpiece,
and she didn't want to. She scowled at it now, as
though it was an intruder. Leon would drive back to the
island, and walk over the bridge and through the little
wood, and across the lawns; and he would be wet
through before he could get inside the house. And if
that was the time it wouldn't be long before he would
have to come back again to the Galleries.

She said, as anyone with any consideration would
surely say, as late as this on a night like this, "It's horrible outside. Why don't you use Uncle Ted's room? I
could fix it in five minutes."

There were no sheets on the bed, but the clean
sheets were up there, waiting to be put on.

He said, "Don't go to any trouble, but I'll take the
sofa if that's all right."

"Of course it is. Why shouldn't it be?" It was an
old-fashioned horsehair sofa, long enough for him to
stretch out. "It isn't exactly the softest bed in the

world," she said, "but if you put your feet up and close your eyes I'll get you a pillow and a rug."

She brought them and he thanked her, and they said goodnight and she went to her own room.

She was tired. She didn't usually set the alarm, because she usually woke at the time she needed to wake, but she set it now. They had talked far into the night, and now she was alone she could hardly keep her eyes open long enough to undress and fall into bed. She felt that she might well sleep until midday unless something roused her, and better the alarm bell than Leon.

Not that she would mind Leon waking her, she thought drowsily, but she would look an absolute freak. She had tried to take off her make-up, but there could well be streaks of it left, and her hair would be like a bird's nest.

He would be asleep now, she was sure of it, he was more exhausted than she was. She saw his face, the tight-drawn skin over the strong bones, eyes closed; and it was as though she felt him breathing deep and slow beside her, and she could slip an arm around him and whisper, "Sleep well, I shall sleep well. Outside it's raining and cold, but it's warm in here, and we are together."

CHAPTER EIGHT

THE ALARM CLOCK woke Fran. If it hadn't rung she would have slept on. As it was she had to resist the temptation to pull the pillow round her ears. She reached out, groping, to turn off the bell, then yawned and stretched and crawled out of bed.

A first glimpse of her face in the mirror was hardly refreshing. She looked a sight, and as soon as she was into her dressing gown she slumped on the stool in front of the dressing table, and brushed her hair.

She thought that Leon would still be asleep. She was almost certain that he would still be stretched out on the sofa, and in five minutes or so she would take a cup of tea along.

She opened her door very quietly and peered out into the passage, and heard movements from either the living room or the kitchen. She hadn't wanted him awake. She had wanted to wake him. And she certainly didn't want him seeing her like this.

She dived into the bathroom and washed her face, splashing cold water in her eyes, coming up clearer-headed, with her eyes quite bright and her eyelashes damp and spiky.

Leon was in the kitchen, standing by the window with a cup in his hand. "Hello," he said. "I was debating about bringing you one."

It was coffee. The jar was on the table. He looked as different as could be from last night, relaxed, refreshed, clear-eyed and calm; and suddenly Fran felt shy, unable to meet his eyes.

She went to the stove, lifting the kettle to check if there was any hot water, spooning coffee essence into a cup for herself. "There's a spare razor of Uncle Ted's in the bathroom if you want it," she told him.

He fingered his chin, the fair stubble was less obvious than darker hair would have been, and said, "I've got one next door."

Do you often get ready for the day ahead next door? she wondered. Do you spend many unexpected nights away from home?

She stirred her coffee and said, "Well, I'd better get dressed, it's nearly opening time." She was backing out of the kitchen, but she caught herself at that and turned to make a more natural exit.

She couldn't get back into her room fast enough. She shut the door, and put down the cup from a shaking hand, and started to get dressed quickly. She was dressed, she was at the lipstick stage of her make-up, when she heard him walking along the passage, and then the closing door.

She was crazy, running off like that. She couldn't think why she had felt embarrassed. She had been perfectly properly dressed, covered by her dressing gown, but she had felt *shy*. That didn't happen often. She couldn't remember that happening since she was little more than a child.

She wouldn't have believed that she wouldn't have been able to drink a cup of coffee with Leon in the kitchen this morning, and talk naturally, without blushing or stammering or carrying on like a twelve-year-old.

She opened her door and grinned at the connecting door. "Good morning," she said brightly, "I'm glad you're feeling better. I'm feeling better myself. I hope I'll see you again soon. Tonight perhaps when Uncle Ted is back? You will come round to see Uncle Ted, won't you?"

Of course he would come round to see Uncle Ted, and she was in high spirits, smiling to herself, as she finished her make-up and her cup of coffee, and went downstairs to open the shop.

The skies were grey again, but who cared? This was going to be a good day, and Uncle Ted was due home this afternoon. She would have a special meal ready for tonight. He'd said he'd been eating well but he was looking forward to coming home, and she'd slip out during the lunch hour and buy steaks, and make a fuss of his homecoming.

There were several customers in the shop when Gerald walked in. Fran had just finished serving, and was looking around to see which of the browsers needed attention, when she saw Gerald.

She smiled, but she got no smile back. He came to the counter and said, "I want a word with you."

"Make it quick."

"Leon stayed here last night, didn't he?"

Gerald had probably been in the Galleries when Leon went back. Fran said, "It was pouring with rain and he slept on the sofa."

"It was pouring with rain on Sunday," said Gerald grimly, "but you got me home."

They were talking quietly, but people were drifting around and even strangers were going to find this conversation enthralling.

"Excuse me," said Fran, coming from behind the counter.

Gerald had followed her along and now confronted her, very close and talking very quietly. "If I tell you something will you give me your word not to say I told you?"

She kept a happy face, and hoped she looked as though it was happy talk, and nothing to interest anyone else. She said, "I don't want any more confidential information. I don't want to be told anything else about Leon. You could write a book—maybe you should."

There was a ballpoint pen on the counter. Gerald picked it up and took a scrap of paper out of his pocket. He wrote "F.F." with an ornate flourish and showed it to Fran. "Does that mean anything to you?"

She went white. "Why?"

"It's on a card in Leon's house." She held the edge of the counter, because her legs were suddenly weak.

"I was going through a bureau drawer there about six months ago," he said, "we do business from the house as well as the Galleries, and I saw this card."

Her eyes were very wide. She had never listened to

him so intently before. She hung on his words now, as though she would drag them from him. "It was a beach scene, rugged country, with a thin girl with red hair sitting on a rock. It was signed F.F. like that." He glanced down at the initials on the scrap of paper beneath Fran's fingertips. "Inside it said, 'For my dearest girl. Happy thirteenth birthday.'"

"I don't understand," she said. But she did. She didn't need Gerald's explanation.

"Obviously he sent it to Leon to get to you and Leon didn't forward it."

If it had come home her mother might well have torn it up and never shown it to Fran. Even Uncle Ted would have thought twice about handing over a birthday card, the way her mother was carrying on in those days. But Leon could have done it. He could have given her her last card from her father. Unless he had thought it might reunite Peter Reynolds with his family again, and that would be to the detriment of his art.

She asked huskily, "Was there a letter with it?"

"I don't remember. I wouldn't have read it anyway. The card caught my eye and I picked it up." She could understand how that could happen. "I didn't know who F.F. was. They weren't your father's initials."

"They were." She smiled faintly. "Fran's father. He always signed my birthday cards like that." It was genuine. "It's mine." The colour was coming back in her cheeks, high and angry. "And I want it."

"You promised not to say I told you about it." Gerald's voice dropped even lower. He looked over his shoulder, as though Leon might have followed him into the shop.

"I didn't."

"*Please*, Fran," he begged desperately.

There was still nobody really near. The customers were all chatting among themselves, and traffic noises drifted in from outside. A car hooter sounded angrily and Fran could have screamed with it.

This time she did smile, stretching her lips until the little muscles in her cheeks hurt. "You stick your neck out, don't you? Then you jerk back under cover. You'll dislocate something, the way you're going on."

Gerald looked wounded. "I'm fond of you, that's why I'm here. But I don't want to lose my job and I don't want Leon turning against me."

She stayed behind her smile. She took her hands off the counter and the tiny piece of paper fluttered to the ground. "I can see that might be very nasty," she said. "All right, I won't say anything. But next time you're in the house you might pinch the card for me. He's not going to miss it and it is mine."

"Oh, I wouldn't like to do that," said Gerald hastily, and she laughed and patted his arm.

"You're the daredevil all right. I've got a knight in shining armour in you!"

She went across to the customers in the pottery section and told them what the good luck charms meant on the lucky mugs, and wondered where her own luck had gone.

Damn Leon, damn him for ever and ever. Having kept the card—why had he kept it?—but having kept it he could have given it to her since she came down here. Although then he would have had to admit, "I not only advised Peter Reynolds to cut and run, I saw to it that, so far as it was in my power, he broke completely with his family. I held back the loving message that his daughter would have cherished all her life.''

She smiled and served and chattered, and she knew that this was the final blow. She daren't let herself think of Leon at all, or anger would have suffocated her. It seethed inside her, held down but burning.

She was almost scared to shut the shop at lunch time, because with nobody watching she could run amok and smash something.

All the time Leon had known that her father had thought of her. Just a week or two before he died that card had come for Fran. Of course there was a letter, if only to Leon, and Leon had known the address.

It wasn't out of the bounds of possibility that Fran could have got in touch and her father might have come to see her, or she might have gone to see him. Something might have happened so that he wasn't in the sea on that beach on the day he died. If Fran had received that card everything might have been changed. At the very least she would not have wondered, during these last eight years, if her father had ever really loved her.

But Uncle Ted would be arriving this afternoon. She was cooking tonight and she had to shop at midday. So she did close and hurried upstairs to fetch her purse and a basket.

As she stepped out of the crafts shop Judith came round the corner from the forecourt, wearing a skirt that swished. It was green and finely pleated, and she wore it with a navy blue jersey blazer. She came straight for Fran, who said, "Sorry, we're shut. Unless you're going this way to the car park."

"I came to see you," said Judith.

"Well, I'm off to the butchers."

"This won't take long." Judith stood squarely in her way. "Just stop pestering Leon."

Fran leaned back against the wall and inquired pleasantly, "Had a little chat with Gerald, have you?"

"I was with Leon yesterday when Gerald gave him that message from you." Judith and Leon had had lunch together, and so far as Fran was concerned they could have gone down with food poisoning together and it would have been all right by her.

"You wanted to see him on a business matter," said Judith, with a curling lip and a scornful voice. "Ha!"

"And?" prompted Fran, after about three seconds.

"You don't fool me," Judith proclaimed.

"So you haven't had a chat with Gerald? Or maybe he's learning discretion at last." Fran swung her empty basket. "Then let me fill you in. Leon may have come round last night to discuss business, but he didn't leave till morning."

She walked past Judith, who had fallen back a step and was croaking, "I don't believe you!"

"Ask him," said Fran, striding out. "If you can believe him."

Judith didn't follow her, so Fran must have given her something to think about. She hoped that Judith would create a blockbuster of a scene when she next saw Leon, but she probably wouldn't. There had been other girls in Leon's life, and almost certainly other men in Judith's, although she seemed to be making heavy weather of Fran, as though there was something about Fran that particularly irritated her.

Anyhow, let them sort it out. She went round to the butchers and bought best grilling steak for two, although the way her luck was running today it could turn out as tough as leather.

When she came back from shopping she made the bed in Uncle Ted's room, and prepared the vegetables for tonight. She laid the table so that everything would be waiting and welcoming when he came.

After she opened the shop she stayed down there, and Uncle Ted arrived about half an hour before closing time. Fran had rarely been so glad to see anyone. She was serving when he came in, but she said, "Excuse me," and ran across and hugged him.

"It's good to see you," she said. "You look marvellous. Did you really have a good holiday?"

He looked fitter, he even had a slight tan, and she grinned, "Where did you get that handsome tan? It's hardly stopped raining here."

"Ah, but I've been out in the sea air," he chuckled, enjoying her teasing and the warmth of her welcome. Until now his homecomings had always been to a closed shop and an empty flat. "I had a very enjoyable time," he said, "but home's best," and she gave him another hug.

"I've missed you," she said. "I must get back to my customer. I've been busy. I'll tell you all about everything tonight."

He took up his case and came right down again. Fran

had coped well in his absence, but it was nice to know he had been missed.

She smiled at him over the head of her customer, and slipped upstairs herself shortly afterwards to turn on the vegetables. She no longer had all the responsibility, she could relax a little now, and the break had done Uncle Ted good.

As the last customer left, with the "Do Come In" notice on the door turned to "Sorry, We're Closed", she said again, "Oh, I'm so *glad* you're back!"

"You haven't been working too hard?"

She shook her head emphatically. "No, it's just good to have you around. I don't like being on my own. I did a bit of rearranging, have you noticed?"

"Very nice," he said. Her displays were attractive and he approved of them all.

"And the window. Did you see the window?"

They went outside to look at the window. She hadn't put out the garden furniture during the last few drizzling days, so the forecourt was bare, but the window glowed scarlet.

She said, "I stuck to one colour. Red this week. Anything with red in it is getting a look-in. I thought green next week. What do you think?"

"Very nice," he said again, as Leon's car came through the archway. "Hello there, my boy," Uncle Ted waved vigorously. The car stopped and he went towards it. Fran froze, watching Leon get out and meet Uncle Ted and shake his hand with every appearance of affability.

"Good to have you back," said Leon. "You look better for it."

"I am." Uncle Ted turned to include Fran. "Fran's managed very commendably, hasn't she?"

Judith had told him what Fran had told her. His face was calm, but Fran knew he was angry. "She's just showing me her window dressing," said Uncle Ted, and Leon walked swiftly over, reaching her several paces ahead of Uncle Ted, and long enough to say quietly and savagely,

"What the hell is it with you, or are you just a natural troublemaker?"

She wanted to ask, "Did you have trouble explaining to Judith?" but she couldn't, and that wasn't because Uncle Ted was with them by then. It was because if she opened her mouth she would spit at him, "Why did you steal my birthday card?"

She kept her lips tight and thin, and Uncle Ted said, "She deserves a holiday herself, doesn't she?"

"She deserves something," said Leon blandly.

He talked for a minute or two longer with Uncle Ted about Brighton, but Fran went inside out of the drizzle, and away from Leon.

She was bashing the steak—to make sure it was tender, and because she felt like bashing something—when Uncle Ted came into the kitchen.

"You didn't see much of Leon while I was away, then?" he said.

"He looked at the books. Did he tell you that?" He hadn't. "Well, he did, last night, and he said trade usually improves around now but the figures are good." She suggested, "Would you like to have a look at the paper stuff while I finish this?"

She couldn't tell Uncle Ted about the birthday card. She had promised Gerald, and Uncle Ted was in Leon's debt so they had to stay on friendly terms.

She would get that card one day, though, if she had to burgle the house on the island herself. No, she wouldn't. Of course she couldn't get inside the house unless she was asked in. She'd never get a chance to turn over Leon's bureau drawers.

It shouldn't matter too much. Just knowing that her father had sent her a birthday card was what mattered. That should make her happy. It did make her happy. Her father had remembered her birthday and sketched her where he was, because that was where he wanted her to be. But she still felt deeply and bitterly betrayed.

She went to call Uncle Ted when the meal was ready; and the steak was tender, and afterwards they sat in the living room by the fire and she asked all about his holiday, and thanked him for the two picture postcards he had sent her which she had stuck up on the kitchen dresser.

He had also sent her mother and Jim a card, and Fran hoped her mother wasn't still indignant about Uncle Ted leaving her in charge. When she told him, she thought it was funny, he looked apprehensive.

"A good job you didn't give her your address," Fran joked. "She was for going down after you, or phoning you up."

"Oh dear! You don't think she'll be coming here?"

"Wild horses wouldn't drag her," said Fran. "And you don't need to answer the phone, or if you do and it's Mother you can always say it's a wrong number."

Uncle Ted hated upsets. He had suffered from Isabel's scenes in the old days before Jim took over. Fran was teasing him, because Jim would always stop Isabel making too much of a fuss.

"Jim said he was glad you were taking a break and he knew I could manage," she said reassuringly. "And I did, didn't I?"

She was sitting in a chair tonight, instead of on the hassock. That made it different from last night, when she had been here telling Leon about the things that had filled the past fortnight for her.

She went over them all again now, for Uncle Ted, where she had been and what she had done, in greater detail than she had reported in her phone calls to him.

After he had listened for a while he said doubtfully, "I think you overdid it, my dear."

"Overdid what? The gay life?" She wrinkled her nose. "I had a very mild time really."

"Not many early nights, though. You look tired."

"So they tell me." So Leon had told her last night, and she was suddenly on the brink of tears, so that she had to duck her head and blink furiously, putting a hand in front of her eyes. Leon had done that too, he had been tired too.

"An early night tonight," said Uncle Ted firmly.

Fran took a book to bed with her, and read until her eyes blurred and smarted, but even then it was hard to sleep.

IF ONLY the sun would shine! It was raining again next morning and Fran put on her brightest lipstick and wore a scarlet shirt with her jeans. But instead of livening her up that only seemed to exaggerate everything that was wan and wistful about her face today.

She worked hard at being cheerful, but more than once she caught Uncle Ted looking anxiously at her. With him back she was less busy in the shop, of course, and during the afternoon there was a slack period when they both waited for customers.

In the silence Fran gave an involuntary sigh and Uncle Ted asked at once, "What's the matter?"

"Nothing." But she *had* sighed. "I just wish the sun would shine. I've got a bit of a headache—it's these heavy black clouds."

"Why don't you take a walk round the market?" he suggested. "I can manage here. Have an hour or two off. Have the rest of the afternoon."

That was a tempting offer. It was raining, but she fancied a walk. Down to the river, perhaps. "Are you sure?" As she spoke he chuckled.

"Don't think you're the only shopkeeper in the family! I ran this place before you were born, and now I'm just back from two weeks in Brighton I'm as good as twenty years younger."

"You mean I'm not indispensable?"

"Not for this afternoon."

She wouldn't take the whole afternoon, just an hour or two, and she put on a mackintosh and tied a scarf round her hair. When she came downstairs the shop had several customers, and she grinned at Uncle Ted. "If you're rushed off your feet," she said, "don't blame me."

He was happy to see her laughing, but he didn't see the laughter fade as she stepped outside. Nor how she hurried past the Galleries with her face averted, looking at the pavement and the traffic. Leon wasn't likely to be standing around, staring out, but she wasn't risking it.

She walked fast, over Clopton Bridge, and along the towpath to the meadows and the weir. The river was high and wide, and the rain still came steadily down. But she felt that it was doing her good, washing away her headache if not her depression.

She watched the swans, riding the swell of the water, magnificently unperturbed, and passed a few determined characters who didn't care about the rain.

Then she went round the market, chatted with a girl with whom she had gone to school, and who was now married, with a lively three-year-old boy in tow; and bought a large bunch of yellow tulips. If she put them in a vase in the flat it would be the next best thing to sunshine.

She had been gone about two hours, which made the time not quite five o'clock, but when she returned the shop was shut.

She thought the Closed notice on the door was a mistake, that somehow it had got turned, but the latch didn't open the door, and when she peered through the old green glass panel she saw no movement, and no lights, and rang the bell, alarmed. Something was certainly wrong.

She kept her finger on the bell and her nose pressed

to the glass panel, so that she saw Uncle Ted before he opened the door and thanked heaven for that.

"What's ha—" she began as the door opened, and he caught her arm and yanked her in.

"Your mother's here," he hissed. His grey hair was standing on end, he must have run his fingers through it at least half a dozen times. He was wild-eyed with agitation and whatever her mother had done to upset him like this was inexcusable.

"It's never about you taking a holiday?" Fran gasped.

"No."

"Is Jim all right?"

Uncle Ted gulped, but his voice still sounded strangled. "She arrived in a taxi about ten minutes after you left, and she went straight in next door to see Leon."

"What?" Fran felt as though someone had hit her over the head with something very large. "Why?" she croaked.

"Someone phoned her this morning, and told her Leon was living here with you while I was away."

The enormity of that rendered Fran speechless. Gerald must have gone out of his mind to do that. He knew how her mother would react. Fran had told him herself that if she'd so much as said that Leon was even giving her business advice her mother would have gone spare.

"Gerald?" she whispered incredulously.

"A woman," said Uncle Ted hoarsely, "who didn't give her name."

There was only Judith. It was quite likely that Judith

knew how pathological Fran's mother was about Leon Aldridge.

"It isn't true," Fran groaned. "But what a horrible *mess!*" She couldn't bear the thought of her mother facing Leon with that fandangle of nonsense. How could her mother do that? How could Jim let her? "What did Leon do?" she asked.

Uncle Ted looked punch-drunk. "She'll tell you," he said, and he went slowly ahead of her up the stairs from the shop to the flat.

Her mother was in the living room, lying on the sofa, and the place reeked of eau-de-cologne. She must have emptied a bottleful. Usually she dabbed a handkerchief with it when she had a headache, but this was more than a headache. She had raised herself on an elbow, and she was waiting for Fran to come through the door.

The moment she did her mother wailed, "Fran, how *could* you?"

"How could I what?" Fran dropped the bright yellow flowers on the table, and clenched her hands in frustration. This was her mother in the mood of unreason that was like beating your head on a brick wall. She hadn't been like this for years and years, but now they were right back to those early days.

"Leon came round here to check the accounts for me." Fran raised her voice. If she shouted some of it might get through. "It was pouring with rain, he was dead beat, and he spent the night on that sofa."

Isabel leapt from the sofa as though it was contaminated. "I am not having an affair with Leon!" Fran was near the end of her own self-control. This had put her into the most humiliating situation of her whole life. "Is that what you said next door?" How could she stay here now? How public had that scene been? What would Leon do about this?

"What did you do, for pity's sake?" she moaned. "Rush in and start screaming, like the last time?"

"How could you?" Isabel demanded again, her voice quivering like a child's who finds the whole world against her.

How could Fran remind her of the last time, she meant, and she began to cry, tears rolling down her cheeks. She had the knack of easy tears, she could weep happily when a TV play piled on the pathos, and although Fran loved her she was in no mood now to comfort her.

She found herself laughing "Judith, me, and now you," she said. "Leon must have had his fill of hysterical women." Her laughter was close to hysteria and she bit hard on her lip to stop it. "What did he say?"

"He's evil." Isabel might be weeping, but she wasn't relenting. She still blamed Leon Aldridge for everything. "He said it was all my fault."

"What was your fault?"

"Your father going away."

"So it was."

It was the first time Fran had ever said that. It was the first time anyone had said it except, apparently, Leon just now.

"Fran!" Her mother was stricken to the heart, and Fran went furiously on.

"And this anonymous phone call, you believed it?

You didn't phone me? You didn't even come in here first and try to see me or Uncle Ted? I don't think I'll ever forgive you for that!"

"Because I knew something like this would happen when you came down here." Her mother turned on Uncle Ted, who was practically wringing his hands in the background. "I knew you'd meet that man and he'd take you away, like he took your father away. And he's evil. He's got no heart. The things he said—"

"Be quiet, you stupid woman!" Uncle Ted bellowed, with a vehemence Fran could never remember in that gentle man before. It left Isabel gasping. She stared at Ted, her mouth working but no sound coming out as he went roaring on, "Leon has been like a son to me. I would have been delighted if he and Fran had fallen in love, and I wouldn't have cared if he had been staying here. I'd have been glad to hear it. He's an honourable man, a fine man. Fran couldn't have found a better man in the length and breadth of this land."

"You're mad!" shrieked Isabel, high and shrill.

"Oh no, I'm not." Uncle Ted's voice dropped to a growl. "But you are, about Peter and Leon. It's because of you that Fran can't forgive Leon, although God knows there's nothing to forgive."

"I won't listen!" Isabel clapped her hands to her ears, and rushed out of the room into the passage, and Uncle Ted shouted after her,

"You ought to thank him. He knows Peter wrote to you and you never answered and you never let Fran know."

Isabel stopped dead, and slowly turned round. "That

is a lie," she said, her voice catching between each word, and Fran knew it was the truth.

"It's no lie," said Uncle Ted. "But Leon never told Fran. Did he?" He looked at Fran, and Fran shook her head jerkily; she couldn't speak. "No," said Uncle Ted. "He said to me, 'The girl's lost her father, we can't do anything that could turn her against her mother now.'"

Isabel came very slowly back, with dragging steps, as though she was being pulled in against her will. "Peter never sent any letters," she whispered.

"Isabel." Uncle Ted's anger had ebbed away. He wasn't shouting at her any more. "I know. Peter phoned me and asked me to give you a letter, because you returned every letter he sent you, but I knew what would happen if I did. You'd have torn it to pieces and thrown it in my face. I wasn't on Peter's side at the time. I felt he'd left me with enough trouble, and I told him he'd better stick to the postal services.

"I've blamed myself since, but what difference would it have made? Except that Fran might have taken her father's side, and how would you have been then? It would have destroyed you."

Isabel picked up a flower, and sat down on the sofa, looking at the yellow tulip as though she was talking to it, because she couldn't face the two pairs of accusing eyes.

"He deserted us," she said in a little-girl voice. "He left us, and just to *paint*. I could have understood if it had been another woman, but just because he wanted to paint pictures.

"What was the use of writing and saying how beauti-

ful it was where he was, and how he could get a cheap
house and we could go out to him? It was primitive out
there. What did he think we were? Gipsies? And there
was Fran's schooling and—"

Fran found her voice suddenly. "He sent a card for
my birthday. To Leon."

"Yes," said Uncle Ted.

"You knew?" She stared at this strange Uncle Ted,
who knew so much. "Why didn't Leon give it to me?
Why didn't you tell me?"

"It went to your home first, didn't it, Isabel?" Isabel
said nothing. "And she returned it," he told Fran.
"Then Peter sent it to Leon, and asked him to try to
give it to you, but by the time it reached Leon Peter
was dead."

Isabel gave a convulsive sob, but Uncle Ted still
looked at Fran. "That's when Leon said 'The girl's lost
her father, we can't do anything that could turn her
against her mother.'"

She should thank Leon for that. To have been torn
by divided loyalties at that time of tragedy would have
been traumatic. "He kept the card," she said. "Why
hasn't he given it to me now?"

"I don't know. But I never told you because it would
have been opening an old wound for Isabel," said Ted
grimly. "Although why I should concern myself with
her feelings when she never considers anyone else's I
do not know."

The tears were running down Isabel's cheeks, and
Fran said, "Oh, Mother, do stop crying. Why ever did
Jim let you come?"

"He'd gone to a sale," Isabel sniffed. "I wasn't expecting him back until about now. I left him a note."

Fran smiled weakly. "What did you write? 'Off to save Fran from a fate worse than death'? Although if I was supposed to have been living with Leon for a fortnight it might have been rather late to come charging to the rescue."

"What are you laughing at?" Isabel glared through her tears.

"If I don't laugh I'm going to burst into tears," said Fran, "and I don't think Uncle Ted could stand the two of us howling. I'm going to try and phone Jim. You make a cup of tea, or put the flowers in water, or something. Don't sit there, dripping all over the tulips."

She took off her headscarf and mac and put a hand on Uncle Ted's arm. "I'm sorry we've made things so grim for you."

He covered her fingers with his own, giving them a comforting little squeeze, and she went down into the office and dialled the farm's number.

She got Jim. She got out, "It's Fran," and he said, "Hello, how are you? Your mother doesn't seem to be around."

"There's a note."

"A what? Oh!" He was obviously spotting it for the first time, by the telephone.

"What does it say?" she asked.

"'Had to go down to Ted's to see Fran. Will phone you,'" he read. "What's up, then?"

"A lady who has a vested interest in Leon Aldridge phoned Mother and told her he was staying in the flat with me while Uncle Ted was away."

"Was he?" Jim sounded interested.

"No. Unfortunately. But she arrived here by taxi and went storming into the Galleries to accuse him of seducing her only child."

Even Jim's stolid nature was shaken. "My God!" he gasped.

"That's right," said Fran. "We haven't heard what Leon said on that point, but he did tell her she was to blame for Father leaving home. She came round here in such a state that Uncle Ted had to shut the shop, and now she's up in the living room getting her breath between hysterics."

"Poor lass," said Jim.

"Poor Uncle Ted," she said. "Leon's got a massive stake in this business, and I shouldn't think Mother's endeared him to the family. I suppose you don't have a lot of money you'd like to invest in case Leon asks for his lot back?"

She knew that Jim's capital was all tied up and that he was far from being a rich man. He couldn't help Uncle Ted no matter how much he wanted to.

"I'm sorry—" he began.

"I didn't mean it. I just can't stop chattering. It's all been so awful."

"You're fond of Leon Aldridge, aren't you?" said Jim quietly.

"What makes you think so?"

"You did say—unfortunately."

"What?" She couldn't follow that, but she said, "Yes, I am. Very."

"Tell your mother I want to talk to her." Jim was his solid, steady, reliable self. "And then I'll come down and fetch her. This nonsense has got to stop."

"She doesn't deserve you," said Fran.

"She suits me," said Jim. He often said that, he meant it too. "And I reckon if you had a word with Aldridge he'd understand. This isn't your fault."

Jim didn't know the whole story, but she tried to be comforted.

Isabel came down to the phone with a mutinous expression, and returned looking like a martyr, suffering but saintly. "I'm going to lie down," she announced, and locked herself in Fran's room.

"Let's hope she stays there until Jim comes," said Uncle Ted, who was putting the tulips in a jug. Fran thought she would.

She went down to the phone again herself, and rang the Galleries. The little time the bell was ringing she prayed, both for courage and that she would somehow find the right words to say.

Mr. Aldridge wasn't at the Galleries, she was told, not by Gerald, perhaps she would care to try his home number.

She said, "Thank you," and wrote it down in funny shaky figures. If he wasn't there, or someone else answered, she couldn't take this any further just yet. She was feeling queasy with apprehension, and she groped her way into the chair behind the desk.

"Leon Aldridge speaking," he said.

She said, "This is Fran, I can't begin to apologise—" and he said crisply,

"Then don't. It wouldn't be a rewarding discussion."

With which he hung up on her.

CHAPTER NINE

FRAN WENT back upstairs to Uncle Ted. The jug of tulips was on the draining board, and he was sitting at the kitchen table waiting for the kettle to boil on the gas ring. He looked as though he needed a cup of tea, and she told him, "I tried to phone Leon, but he doesn't want to talk."

"Can you blame him?" he asked her.

"No." In no way. She could do with a cup of tea too. Her throat was parched as though she had been walking through a desert. "It had to be Judith who phoned Mother," she said. "She knew Leon slept here Wednesday night."

"It sounds as though she was jealous." Uncle Ted got up to reach for the tea caddy, and Fran couldn't think of any other explanation herself.

"There's no reason, but I suppose she must have been." Leon wouldn't be too pleased with Judith either. Judith was as much to blame as anybody for the scene next door, and tomorrow Fran would phone and apologise again.

But tomorrow might be too soon. Perhaps she should give him longer than that to calm down. A few days, even a week. Or she might write him a letter. He would surely read a letter.

They drank their tea, and then she sat down at the living room table, with a writing pad, and tried to explain. But an hour or so later she had written little.

Please let us be friends, her thoughts ran, because I want that so very much that I don't know what I shall do if you won't listen. You *must* listen. I'm frightened. I don't know what to say, but I'm afraid that I'm in love with you, and what shall I do if you won't listen?

It was dark outside now. Her mother hadn't emerged, and was very likely sleeping like a baby. Uncle Ted had been reading the newspaper for a long time—or pretending to read, and Fran knew that she couldn't wait, not even till morning.

If she phoned again Leon could just hang up on her again, but if she went to his house he surely wouldn't refuse to see her. She picked up her mac from the chair on which she had dropped it, as Uncle Ted looked up. "Do you mind being left with Mother?" she asked, and he gave her his lopsided smile.

"I shall barricade the door with furniture to stop her getting out until Jim arrives." She smiled at his little joke. "But where are you going?" He sounded apprehensive. "Not to see Miss Waring?"

"Judith? Not likely. I'm going to try to see Leon."

He wasn't much happier about that. "And I don't know that that's advisable."

"I don't suppose it is," she agreed, and grinned. "But if he loses his temper and really has a go at me he might feel he has something to apologise for when he calms down. That might even things a little." She left the rest unsaid. Besides, she *had* to see Leon, and try to make the peace. She couldn't sleep on it.

"Don't expect him to listen to you," Uncle Ted warned her.

"I don't." Fran dropped a kiss on the top of his head and hurried off.

It was a wretched night. She kept the wipers going all the way, but they hardly cleared the streaming windscreen.

"Rain, rain, go away, come again another day," the childish jingle ran through her head. She was being childish. She was being as impulsive and as silly as her mother, but she kept the car heading down river until she turned off the road and drew up in front of the coachhouse.

As she got out a window opened above, and a woman shouted down, "Can I help you?"

"I want to see Mr. Aldridge."

The woman was probably the housekeeper, now craning her neck for a good look at Fran in the lights from the flat. "He's over at the house," she said, "but the river's very high. You want to be careful crossing the bridge. Have you got a torch?"

"Yes, thank you," Fran called back, and the window closed.

She got the torch out of the side pocket of the car. She still hadn't replaced the batteries, so it was even fainter now than it had been the night Leon used it to look at the engine when Poppy broke down.

It glimmered in front of her on the path down to the river, and the bridge, and when she reached that she stopped. The river was high. The slats of the bridge were under water so that only the handrails marked it.

Walking across would be a risk, although if you held the handrail you could still get over.

She hesitated briefly, then paddled into the water, catching her breath at the chill, and at the surprising deepness because very soon it was knee-high. It was flowing fast, tugging, and she had one wild moment when she put down her foot and a slat was missing. She grabbed frantically for the handrail with both hands, dropping her torch.

The torch hadn't been much use, and although clouds hid stars and moon her eyes were used to the dark so that she wasn't much worse off without it. But after that she moved very carefully. Her instinct was to get across the bridge fast, but she had to test for every step. She had no idea how many of the wooden strips had been swept away.

She reached the other side with very real relief, and squelched her way through the trees and across the lawns to the house.

Leon might feel like shutting the door in her face, but on a night like this he would have to let her in, and although she was apprehensive about facing him she was desperate to get under cover.

She rang the front door bell, and shivered for what seemed ages, getting no answer. There were lights on, the woman had told her he was here. He couldn't know who it was, so why didn't he answer?

Even under the porch the rain reached her. Not that that mattered, she couldn't get much wetter, and she *had* to get inside, she couldn't risk the bridge again. She put her finger back on the bell and held it there, and after another long minute Leon opened the door.

He was barefoot, in slacks and open-necked shirt and a dark green silk dressing gown. He looked as nearly dishevelled as she had ever seen him, hair ruffled, eyes heavy-lidded. She stuttered, "Oh, sorry, were you in bed? I mean are you alone? I mean—"

He looked at her and she felt as though she had been pushed away. "What the hell are you doing here?" he said wearily.

"I came to apologise. You wouldn't listen to me on the phone, would you?"

"Go home."

"I don't think I can."

"What?"

She lifted a foot. Her shoe was thick with mud and her jeans had a high tidemark well above the knee. "It was this high when I came. One slat on the bridge has gone and I suppose the rest are being loosened." Leon moved aside and she walked in. She had only taken a couple of steps when she saw her footprints on the grass green carpet and stood still. He left her there, and came back almost at once wearing wellington boots and a trench mac, and carrying a heavy torch. "Where are you going?" she asked unnecessarily.

"To look at the bridge."

He'd find it as she'd told him. When she was alone she called "Hello". Nobody answered, but that didn't mean no one was here, although there was an empty feel to the house. It was warm but empty, a showplace.

She had marred some of its perfection with her muddy shoes, and before she dared take another step she took them off. Then she made her way to the kitchen, carrying her shoes, and got out of her mac and rubbed her feet and her hands to warm herself up.

When she heard Leon call, "Where are you?" she went quickly to the kitchen door.

"In the kitchen."

There was plenty of mud on his boots too, he must have left an awful mess on the carpet, and why she should be thinking about that she didn't know.

"You're crazy," he said. "Did Ted know you were coming here?"

"Yes." Yes to both. She agreed that she must be crazy.

"You'd better ring him. I presume your mother doesn't know?"

She smiled with unsteady lips. "She's been in my bedroom for ages. Jim's coming down to fetch her. When I left Uncle Ted said he was going to barricade the door to stop her getting out."

There was no answering smile to that weak joke, and she padded barefoot after him to a telephone on a small gold and white ormolu table in the hall.

He stood listening while she told Uncle Ted, "I'm at Leon's, and the river's over the bridge so I probably won't be able to get back till daylight. Is everything all right?"

"If you mean is your mother still sulking," said Uncle Ted grimly, "the answer is probably yes. I can hear her moving around, but I'm expecting Jim any time now, so even if she does emerge I think I shall survive."

"Of course you will," said Fran, and Leon held out a hand for the receiver.

"Ted?" he said. "Why did you let her come here?" Fran could imagine Uncle Ted's indignant, "How could I stop her?" and Leon said, "No, I suppose you couldn't. Well, I'll get her back as soon as I can."

As he put down the phone she said, "I'm not a package for delivery, you know. I'll get myself back."

He sighed, as though she was a wearisome problem. "Why don't you try it now? We might both get lucky."

"All right." But she knew he couldn't let her and he said,

"There's a fire in the drawing room."

He turned, he wasn't going in the direction of the drawing room, and she said, "Won't you even listen to me? It wasn't my fault my mother said whatever she said. Somebody phoned and told her—"

"She told me what they told her," he said curtly. "Are you sure it wasn't you?"

She gasped, "Why would I—" and again he didn't let her finish.

"I don't know," he said heavily. "I simply don't know. Why did you tell Judith I stayed the night?"

"Because she told me to stop pestering you and that shut her up."

"You'd better get dry," he said abruptly, and Fran looked down at her wet and muddy jeans.

"I'm not dressed for the drawing room."

"You're going to catch your death in those." He opened a door to a downstairs cloakroom. "There's a robe in here."

"And then I'll see you in the drawing room?"

"Yes."

The robe was a man's short navy-blue towelling. She had wondered if there might be a female robe around, and although this wasn't much of a fit she preferred it. It reached just above her ankles, and gave her the long swinging arms of a gorilla, so she rolled up the sleeves and gathered it in with the belt at the waist.

They had to be friends. That was all she was asking. This time there would be no misunderstandings. She knew a great deal more now. "I want us to be friends," she would say. "Please let us be friends."

Leon was standing by the drawing room fire. He had taken off his gumboots and his trench coat, and now he was in the open-necked shirt and slacks, barefooted like she was.

Her feet were pink from the hot water she had just washed them in, and she stopped herself saying, "Snap!" She mustn't be flippant and silly, even if she was nervous. "Please," she said, "I am sorry about this afternoon."

"It wasn't your fault." But she was still ashamed of her part in it. "Sit down," he said. She took a chair by the fire and he smiled wryly. "It was in private," he said. "She was shown into my office, so there wasn't an audience."

"There was when she got next door." She gave a small grimace. "Uncle Ted had to shut the shop. I was out. When I came back his hair was standing on end."

Leon laughed, and while he was laughing she asked, "Do you think it was Judith who phoned her?" He nodded, and she said, "You're not going to marry Judith, are you?"

"Why not?" But he didn't say he was, and he didn't say it was none of her business.

"I'm sure she'll make a perfectly splendid wife," she said, "but I don't see her for you." The robe was too large. She felt like something soft and vulnerable encased in a protective covering. "Although Gerald says everyone else does," she continued lightly.

"Does he?" said Leon. "Ah well, I can't blame him."

Why not? Because it was a general opinion, or because he understood why Gerald might try to spoil Fran's friendship with Leon? "Uncle Ted told me about the birthday card, the one my father wanted me to have." She need not bring Gerald into this. "Do you still have it?"

"I'll get it for you."

She sat trembling, fiddling with the knotted belt of the bathrobe, loosening it a little. It was warm, sitting right by the fire like this.

He brought the card, and he brought a painting, a scene that gave an impression of open spaces, far vistas. "Is that my father's?" she whispered, and she knew it was, although it was better than any picture he had painted that she had seen. It belonged to the months he was away, and it justified them. He had been growing as an artist when he created this.

Leon put the canvas on a chair and Fran went to kneel in front of it, drinking in every detail. He said, "It's for you. I got it last week."

She remembered his promise, that first night when he took her round the Gallery, and he had remembered it too, and she was overjoyed. No other gift in the world could have delighted her more. She jumped up, flinging her arms around him, stammering, "Thank you, oh, *thank* you! This is just wonderful. Oh, I just can't tell you how thrilled I am!"

He was smiling, slightly, as though her exuberance amused him. She held him and he looked down at her, and her hands fell from him.

The warmth of her joy faded, and she felt chilled. "Sorry," she said. She looked at her hands as though she didn't quite know what to do with them now, or where to put them.

"You don't really want me to touch you," he said quietly.

But she desperately wanted his arms wrapped around her and she stared. "Why do you say that?"

"Your mother hates my guts, and so do you."

"*No.*"

He spoke unhurriedly, he could have been discussing the value of one of the pictures on the wall. There was no sign of emotion in the almost classical face. "This afternoon she said you might be attracted to me, but you'd never forget that I advised your father to go away. And that's how it is, isn't it? Under your skin I'm always the enemy."

Fran sat down on the sofa, dropping down, weak at the knees. Somehow she had to make him understand that she was crazy about him, and that went for her subconscious too. But what to say? how to start?

Things had gone wrong from the time he made love to her, right here.

She looked down at the sofa, where she sat. "The last time I was here—" she began.

"Oh yes, I can probably make you want me. I'm fairly adept at lovemaking." He spoke as though it was a form of athletics. He had the body of a natural athlete, so perhaps it was to him. "But when I asked if you knew what you were doing you weren't too happy to find yourself in my arms," he said.

It hadn't been like that. It had been nothing like that. She asked, "Why did you ask me?"

"I wanted you to say yes, you knew what you were doing."

She sat up straighter, eyes fixed on him. "Then you should have looked as though you wanted me to say—yes, I knew, instead of chilly as charity."

"Did I?" Now there was uncertainty in his voice.

"You did." There was none in hers. "Of course I knew where I was and what I was doing, and as for hating you—that's a laugh!"

"Is it?"

She knew then that she must give him the reassurance he needed. That it was all in her hands. She looked at him, straight at him, and said, "It's as though you've been my lover ever since that first night when Poppy broke down. I've been wanting and loving you ever since. Even when things got snarled up, no matter who I was with—" She paused. "I missed you," was not enough. "I ached for you," she said. "Day and night."

"Do you mean this?" He touched her cheek, his eyes searching hers, and her face crumpled.

"Do I look as though I mean it? How do I look?"

Her love and her need were there for anyone to see and he sat down beside her, stroking her hair, her face, running his hands down her arms, and beneath the robe holding her close and gently as though to convince himself that she was real. He must have dreamed dreams too.

"I love you," he said at last.

"I'm glad." He was a sophisticated man of the world, but his voice was husky, shaking, and Fran said gently, "Was it that hard to say?"

"Yes."

"Why?"

He spoke haltingly at first. She said nothing. She nestled beside him, listening, close to him while he told her, "Perhaps because I never learned to love. My mother died when I was born, and my father never cared for anyone else. Not for me. I'm closer to Ted than I ever was to him, and fonder of Ted." ... "Like a son to me" Uncle Ted had said ... "I've always been on good terms with Ted, especially these last twelve months when the business started to get too much for him, and where Ted is you are. He's always talked about you."

He smiled at her. "I knew how you felt about me— the Iceman," she smiled too, "but I began to feel that I knew you. Then you told him you were leaving your job because you were having trouble with some man who was jealous, and Ted needed an assistant, and you said you'd come."

She was so glad that she had come. Dear conniving Uncle Ted was going to be over the moon over this.

"I'd always thought I'd marry Judith some time," said Leon. "But I'd never been jealous of Judith, and I suddenly realised that I'd never cared enough about any woman to give a damn if she had a string of lovers."

Fran moved just enough to slip her arms around his neck, and hold him so that he had to look at her and smile at her.

"I saw your car turn in the afternoon you arrived," he told her, "and I came out. I'd have spoken if you'd smiled, but you didn't."

"I couldn't then, I thought you were my bad omen." Instead of the best thing that had ever happened, or could ever happen to her. Her green eyes glinted with tender mischief. "Are you jealous of me?" He was the first man she had ever wanted to be jealous.

He looked at her as though all the warmth he would ever know must come from her. "You've set light to me," he said. "I can't bear the thought of another man touching you."

He was due for loving, for warmth and joy and tenderness, and sweet and soaring passion. She kissed his lips and he kissed and kissed her, and then he said, "Your mother said you'd be leaving with her. I thought you would."

She shook her head, but he still wasn't quite sure of her. "She hates me. Could she stop you marrying me?"

She shook her head again, laughing that away, telling

him, "Uncle Ted turned on her this afternoon because of what she said about you. I never heard Uncle Ted shout at anyone before, and Jim's probably spelling out a few home truths right now. She's never going to admit she was to blame for my father leaving us, but they're not going to leave her with any excuse for hating you."

She was in his arms, her head on one of the big soft cushions, and this house was home because of the man beside her. "If you're asking me to marry you you'll have me around for the rest of your life."

"It isn't living without you," he said. "It's loneliness and hunger."

He pulled her closer, until they were locked together without speaking, arms around each other, faces pressed cheek to cheek.

She hadn't realised she was weeping with joy until she felt that her cheek was wet. "This is me crying, isn't it?" she whispered. "It wouldn't be you?"

He raised his head to look at her. "It could be me. I never knew I could cry before, but then I never knew I could fall in love. Nothing and nobody but you could make me cry."

She blinked her damp lashes. "That's a responsibility."

"Yes. You do know what you're doing, don't you?"

"I know, my love," she said, "I know," and she pulled him down again beside her.